Ellanor
and the Search for
Organoth Blue Amber

Kathryn

Ellanor

and the Search for
Organoth Blue Amber

K. T. Durham

PARTRIDGE

A Penguin Random House Company

To order additional copies of this book, contact
Toll Free 800 101 2657 (Singapore)
Toll Free 1 800 81 7340 (Malaysia)
orders.singapore@partridgepublishing.com

www.partridgepublishing.com/singapore

CONTENTS

To my international family, who are scattered all over the globe: in Australia, New Zealand, the United States, Hong Kong, and Shanghai. Elly will explore these places, and many more.

ACKNOWLEDGEMENTS

WRITING THIS BOOK HAS TRULY been a labour of love. Sometimes it really does take that first small push to get the ball rolling. Once I had finally mustered up the courage and strength to do it, the ball just wouldn't stop. Though it was a tremendous amount of work, I really loved every moment of it. Countless hours and late nights after getting off my day job, pages and pages of scribbled notes and doodles, and almost daily visits to coffee shops and cafes in between lessons gave birth to Ellanor and her story.

I love my family. From the bottom of my heart I want to express my deepest thanks and gratitude to Dad and Mum for your many loving sacrifices for the family, and for having always provided, encouraging me to read and draw, to use my imagination, and for allowing such easy access to crayons, paper, and books from an early age. Hubert and Michael, my two big brothers—thank you for being there for me. My gorgeous nieces Chloe and Mikayla—you give our family such immeasurable joy! Both of you darling girls remind me of the innocence and pure magic of childhood.

My dear husband, Sam, you are my best friend, my rock, and soulmate. I love you. Talking late into the night with you about Elly and her story has been truly precious. Your scrumptious cooking, sense of humour, creativity, and undying support have kept me sane.

I'm grateful to Jennifer Woo and Mari Webb for staunchly supporting and encouraging me. Your faith in me has meant the world. Thank you for reading through my manuscript and for being such gracious critics, because you are first and foremost my friends.

Raquel Diaz, my awesome illustrator, I am grateful to you for contributing your immense artistic talent to this book. One day soon, I hope to visit you in Sweden, where Elly definitely wants to explore.

Much solitude was necessary in writing (and rewriting) this book. Though I was often alone, I never once felt lonely.

*The world of men is dreaming, it has gone mad in its sleep,
and a snake is strangling it, but it can't wake up.*

—D.H. Lawrence

PROLOGUE
The Girl from Nowhere

THE DEAD RAT LOOKED AT her with staring vacant eyes.

She stared back silently as she took out a piece of chalk and drew another tally on the cold concrete wall. This was the fifth one this month. It must have drawn its last breath as it tried crawling back to its putrid home somewhere behind the wall.

She had to get rid of the carcass before the smell became unbearable and its comrades came feasting on it. But she really didn't want to touch it, not yet.

She glanced at the cheap plastic clock on the rickety wooden desk: it was almost six. Her heart sank. Veronika would be bringing down her supper soon. She wondered if she might find mould on the food again.

Quickly, she sifted through the sheets of paper before her and retrieved the geography homework that needed to be done in the next fifteen minutes. She scribbled her name in the top right hand corner. She hated her full name, so she always insisted on going by Goldie.

She could have finished her homework half an hour ago. But she had once again pored over the world atlas at the back of her dog-eared geography textbook, playing the game she had been entertaining herself with for the past year: She would close her eyes and randomly put her finger somewhere on the atlas, and see where it would end up.

This time it was Botswana, in Africa. In her scrapbook, she doodled sketches of herself and imaginary friends encountering strange and fantastic adventures in Botswana, and lamented that she had never been to any place so far and exotic. In fact, she had never been out of Hemlock. She would trade all her pencils for just one plane ride to anywhere in the world, if it meant she could get away from this basement forever.

She could spend hours playing that game. There wasn't any television to watch, and she was sick of rereading the same mouldy books on that old shelf in the corner, over and over again. She didn't want to ask for new books. She hated asking Veronika for anything.

With a frown, she tried to concentrate on the remaining questions on the homework sheet. In class, they were learning about demographics in different regions of the world. She hadn't known that almost one quarter of the world's population lived in China, or that there was a place called the Vatican City in Rome that was actually a country of its own.

As part of the homework exercise, she had to put down her own demographics: her age, where she was born, how many family members she lived with, how many rooms her house had, and so forth.

But she did not have the answers to so many of these questions. As a baby, a custodian had found her on the doorstep of a church in the dead of winter, swaddled in warm blankets inside a basket, with her name written on a piece of paper tucked inside. In fat red letters over the worksheet, she scrawled: "Orphan currently living with yet another foster family." This should shut the teacher up.

Why should I be good and kind? Don't go expecting kindness from one who has been shown none, *she thought bitterly.*

The light flickered, and she glanced up in annoyance. It was a wonder that her eyes had not yet been damaged by the constant pool of weak light cast by the bare electric light bulb in the ceiling.

As she glanced up, she saw her reflection in the little silver Christmas ball that was on her desk. Christmas had just come and gone, but she always kept the ball with her. It was the only keepsake left from whatever family she might've once had, tucked into the blankets of her baby basket on those cold steps of the church. The entwined letters TJ that were engraved on the smooth surface stood out, even in the poor light. It might've once adorned her real parents' Christmas tree.

She blinked and rubbed her eyes. Why was she seeing weird things again? She had short hair, not long hair. And the horrid pink night dress she was wearing certainly wasn't purple.

She looked into the gleaming silver surface again. Nothing was out of the ordinary.

Maybe it was a hallucination. She hadn't been sleeping well, after all. The heater wasn't working properly; the freezing cold and the strange dreams she had been having kept her up most nights.

Then she heard footfalls approaching, and her heart started racing. The door to the basement was yanked open, then slammed shut, and Veronika was walking down the narrow steps in her strappy high heels, holding a plastic tray with Goldie's supper.

Goldie froze and quickly turned her geography worksheet over.

Veronika looked very glamorous tonight. Her blonde hair was pulled up into a stylish knot, her face immaculately made-up, and the shiny red lipstick was almost the same shade as her beautiful cocktail dress. She probably had another dinner party to go to with Henrik and their bratty son, Johann.

Goldie couldn't think of a more beautiful-looking couple. Or more terrible.

Veronika raised one perfectly drawn eyebrow when she spotted the dead rat in the corner. She put the tray down on Goldie's small bed with its threadbare blankets. "I see the rat poison has been doing its job. But why haven't you cleaned up the mess?" she asked coldly.

Goldie felt her palms go clammy. She clenched her fists and plastered a smile on her face. "I was about to. I just wanted to finish my homework."

"Oh?" Veronika's icy blue eyes roamed over the desk, and suddenly they gleamed. Goldie did not realize the red marker she had used was a tad too strong—it showed through the paper.

Veronika reached out a manicured hand and turned over the geography worksheet.

"Ah, I see. So we've been lumped into the other foster families that could not stand to keep you, is that right?" Veronika said softly. "After all we've done for you? You have a roof over your head and three meals a day, and you get to have a proper education at our son's prestigious school. Still, you are dissatisfied?"

Goldie looked at her silently, her face shouting defiance.

Veronika sighed. "I really want us to get along, Goldie. You shouldn't make it so hard for me."

Goldie held her breath and closed her eyes.

The blow came as expected. Veronika slapped her across the face, so hard that she was thrown backwards, and she felt her head slam against hard concrete.

Before she blacked out, Goldie thought she heard someone calling her name.

CHAPTER ONE
On the Strike of Twelve

"NO! GET AWAY FROM ME!" Elly cried out and wrestled her eyes open, gasping for breath. She sat bolt upright, her heart pounding wildly as she squinted into the crisp sunshine.

Sighing, she rolled onto her back and tried to remember the dream. All she could recall was fragmented, and there was an inexplicable sense that two dreams had been rolled into one: petrified screaming, head slamming against concrete, bony hands clawing at her, cruel gleaming eyes . . .

"Ellanor Celendis! Get up right this instant and come downstairs!"

It was Mama calling from the kitchen. She wasn't running late for school, was she? The hourglass on the windowsill indicated it was still early. Arching her back, she yawned and stretched. Despite having fallen asleep earlier the night before, she did not feel fully rested.

Then it came back to her, somewhat hazy: In the middle of the night, she was woken by frantic footsteps amidst the sound of tolling bells. Anxious voices were shouting, "Hurry! They're getting away!" But the clamour seemed to abate in a matter of seconds, and she had fallen back to sleep after Mama hurried into her room and whispered soothingly, "It's all right, darling. Just a false alarm. Go back to sleep."

Elly stared up at the leafy ceiling, wondering what all that had been about. Then the delicious smell of her favourite cinnamon sweet cakes with maple syrup drifted up the stairs, and her frown dissolved into a beaming smile. Her griffin, Marlow, gave a low squawk as he opened one dark eye to peer at her, not too pleased to be disturbed earlier in the morning than usual.

But today was special. It was her twelfth birthday, her coming of age!

She leapt out of her hammock. She'd better get downstairs quickly, before Mama went hollering for her again. "Hello!" she called out to the bees that were buzzing at their hive outside her window. "Be sure to leave me some honey!"

The acorns on her windowsill were being devoured by a couple of squirrels. Looking at the acorns, Elly thought about the bonding ceremony that was to take place under the Grand Canopy later in the evening. She wondered which royal acorn would fall. Which acorn would the Tree choose to be her Royan?

Out of habit, whenever she was thinking, she twirled some strands of hair around her thumb. Her long, thick, unruly black curls stuck out in all directions. Absent-mindedly, she grabbed a ribbon from her cluttered dresser, accidentally knocking an empty goblet onto the floor, which was strewn with piles of books. Then, in the mirror above the dresser, she saw something that made her freeze.

Her face stared back; they were the same rosy cheeks, bright emerald-green eyes, and leaf-shaped ears. But in the reflection, her wild, curly black hair was short, and she was wearing some sort of pink nightdress, which was impossible, because she *hated* wearing pink, and avoided it at all costs. She rubbed her eyes.

Her reflection was back to normal. Nothing was out of the ordinary.

Shrugging, she promptly dismissed the odd trick her eyes had played on her and quickly pulled her hair into a ponytail. She gave Marlow a peck on his forehead before tossing two more acorns to the squirrels. As she leapt downstairs, a yellow butterfly landed on her shoulder for a free ride to the kitchen. On second thought, Marlow decided to follow; cinnamon sweet cakes were one of his favourite foods, too.

Elly skipped past the singing golden harp in the sitting room, its strings being plucked as though by invisible fingers. The green vines that snaked over the oak walls in the house were dotted with the small, star-shaped golden flowers that were her namesake—the ellanors were in full bloom. She took a moment to breathe in their sweet scent before darting into the kitchen, where her mother was fussing about at the counter.

Mama smiled. "There you are!" she said cheerfully, kissing her daughter on both cheeks. "I wanted you to come down earlier today for a special treat. Happy twelfth birthday, my darling girl. Oh, you're just growing up too fast!" She stepped back to take a better look at Elly, then scowled. "Oh, for Freya's sake!" she exclaimed. Today Elly's hair looked even messier than usual. The ribbon was already unravelling from its knot, as though the bouncy curls didn't want to be restrained.

Mama shook her head and sighed, absent-mindedly running a hand through her own hair: long, silky, straight, and black. Elly's astonishingly wild, curly hair was unusual for elves; it was one of her daughter's many . . . unique attributes.

Mama decided not to comment further. Smiling, she gestured at the golden flowers that blanketed the kitchen walls. "Look Elly! This is a good sign!" she said brightly. "The ellanor blooms most prettily on auspicious occasions."

Elly thought Mama was stretching it a bit. What was so auspicious about her birthday? She bet nobody in her class would've known it was her birthday if her mother hadn't sent them dratted party invitations *without* her consent. Elly still felt extremely annoyed about it.

"Zooooom!"

Elly saw the flying cucumber first, followed by her younger brother Luca. He dashed into the kitchen as the cucumber whizzed ahead of him. She scowled and rolled her eyes. Luca had just learned how to make things fly, and he was obviously having far too much fun with it. He leapt up gleefully when he saw his sister. "Happy birthday, Elly-Belly!" he chortled, sending the cucumber whizzing around her head.

"*Aarrgh!* Stop it! It's making me dizzy," she howled. A deep voice thundered down the stairs. "Luca Celendis, cut that out this instant!"

Papa's huge frame loomed up, his shoulder-length black hair gleaming in the sunlight.

Luca skidded to a stop, and the cucumber plopped to the ground. Marlow swiped it with his beak and swallowed it in one gulp.

Papa laughed and patted Marlow fondly, and then he scooped Luca into his powerful arms. "Good morning, my darlings!" he boomed, kissing his wife and two children.

Elly's stomach growled longingly as the enticing aroma of the sweet cakes grew stronger.

"*Hmm*, something sure smells heavenly!" Papa said, rubbing his stomach.

Elves who were not close to their family usually recoiled at the sound of the Celendis name; but when it came to sweets, they conveniently became forgetful. Many travelled from all over Alendria to Nidah's Sweet Secrets in Evergreen City. Who really cared about what one black sheep of the Celendis clan had done so many years ago, if it meant that one could savour the most delicious sweet cakes in the land? After melting the silver coins they earned, her papa—the renowned silversmith, Sereth Celendis—would craft all sorts of fine things in his workshop, from swords, spears, and daggers to armour, rings, and necklaces.

Luca burst out laughing and tried to wriggle free when Papa started tickling him. He tapped Elly on the head with a low murmur, and instantly a circlet of white daisies appeared atop her black curls.

"Oh, Papa!" she cried, touching the daisies and giggling. She hugged him around the neck as he scooped her up and whispered, "Happy birthday, my Elly! You've struck the big twelve at last!"

Suddenly, he flinched in pain. She looked up in surprise and noticed that his wrist was bandaged. She frowned. "Papa, what's the matter?" She stared at the bandage. "Has this got anything to do with what happened last night?" she demanded. "I thought I heard the bells tolling, and there were shouts. Did you get hurt last night?" Her words tumbled out breathlessly.

Papa chuckled and shook his head. "No need to be alarmed, my dear. I just injured myself on the job. Now, let's enjoy your birthday!" He then tapped Elly's palm, and a thick, black, bound book with silver-edged pages appeared: *Strange and Delightful Creatures from Other Realms* by Myradeth Riverina.

She squealed in excitement and clutched the book. "Oh, Papa! Thank you so much! I've wanted this for a long time!" It was true, but she didn't mention that she had actually wished for the first edition of *Roaming the Worlds as a Chameleon*, written by her role model, Larabeth Goldberry, who had long since resigned from her duties as an explorer for the High Council. But she was still really happy with this gift; she grinned and kissed Papa on the cheek. He beamed.

"Hey, Papa, no fair! Where's *my* treat?" demanded Luca, stamping his little feet in protest.

Papa chuckled. "It's not your birthday, my boy! Surely, you wouldn't want daisies! Here, how about this?" He tapped Luca on the head, and a little beanstalk shot up.

Elly laughed while Mama attempted to make it vanish, but Luca darted away and shielded the beanstalk with his hands. "Don't, Mama! I like it! I'm going to school with it!" he bellowed, running and dodging from his mother.

Mama threw Papa a dirty look, which made him laugh even harder. "Don't fret, Nidah! Thanks to Elly, it's a day for harmless fun and plenty of celebration!"

After Mama finally managed to get rid of the plant protruding from her son's head, she marched them into the dining room, with Elly and Luca perched on Papa's broad shoulders. When Elly saw what was sitting on the table, she gasped and almost fell off.

Mama had outdone it this time. She had constructed layer upon layer of sweet cake sprinkled with cinnamon, oozing with golden maple syrup, and edged with white vanilla frosting and clusters of wild berries in cream, topped with an iced figurine of Elly with flaming green eyes. The sweet cake tower was so tall that it almost touched the ceiling.

Elly laughed and clapped merrily. "Oh, thank you, Mama! It looks *incredible*! What a treat!" Mama beamed. Papa looked at his wife proudly.

They all sat around the oak table and scooped chunks from the sweet cake tower while Marlow licked off the crumbs from his massive serving. Mama had given Elly the topmost layer so that she could have the iced figurine. "It won't melt for another few days," she said.

Elly closed her eyes as she savoured the first bite. Oh, it was *sooooo* delicious! Maybe she could just stay home all day, curl up with a book in her hammock, and finish off the sweet cake. Surely, nobody in class would even notice she was absent. Even if they noticed, they wouldn't care.

Mama's voice interrupted her wishful thinking. "Ready for your presentation this morning, Elly?" she asked, swatting at Luca as he attempted to topple the sweet cake tower. Elly groaned and buried her face in her hands.

That morning, she had to deliver a presentation in front of her class. Their teacher, Mr Holle, had assigned them the topic "My Dream", requiring them to give a presentation about what career path they wished to take after graduating from Arvellon Academy in five years. So far, most of her classmates' dream careers fell into the following categories: minstrel, muse, jeweller, healer, teacher, culinary artist (like Mama), weaver, law keeper, beast tamer, mind seeker, silversmith (like Papa), historian, painter, silver miner, guard, protector, researcher at the Institute of Elven Magic, and High Council minister.

Elly suspected she was the only one who wanted to follow in her famous grandfather's footsteps and become an explorer. It was not a popular career, nor was it a lucrative one. "As an explorer, you'll want to learn about other worlds and cultures, and even live among the peoples in those foreign places and adapt to changing environments," Grandpapa had once explained. "There'll be plenty of adventure, and endless surprises. But most elves, by nature, prefer to keep to their kind." Then he grinned. "Perhaps you will be an exception!"

Elly, ever the inquisitive one, had looked at him eagerly. "Do you really think so, Grandpapa? Because I really want to become an explorer like you and Larabeth Goldberry. I want to explore all sorts of amazing realms and make all sorts of discoveries!" She knew that Grandpapa had been good friends with Larabeth, but he had not seen her for many years, not since she got married and retired to live a quiet life far away.

When Elly had asked for her whereabouts, Grandpapa laughed. "If Larabeth Goldberry does not want to be found, nobody will find her." He had not elaborated. "Tell you a secret, my dear; Gaya, the human realm, is still one of my favourites, though it has been out of bounds for over a century. You would have read that Larabeth was very fond of the humans, too."

He smiled nostalgically. "I wish you could have been with me when I met with Napoleon of France. He was quite an intriguing fellow, very clever indeed. In those days, despite the lavish use of perfumed water, there was always an underlying smell of unwashed bodies around me. Humans did not make it a habit of washing themselves regularly in the old days. There were exceptions, of course." He winked. "Queen Isabella of Spain . . . She was a woman of strong convictions, and rather beautiful for a human, I might add. I had some very stimulating conversations with her and her husband Ferdinand—when he wasn't drunk, that is." He chuckled, his face animated. "The Chinese poets and scholars of the Song and Tang dynasties wrote some beautiful, heartrending literature, and to this day I still read them when I have time to spare. And Mahatma Ghandi of India, my, he was a beautiful soul who loved his country. I got to know him in his youth.

I was greatly saddened to hear of his premature passing." He paused. "I became quite fond of my Russian friends. They were honest, hard-working people. Many were gifted in the arts. Rachmaninov and Tchaikovsky will forever stay in my fondest memories." Then he knitted his brow. "But Ivan the Terrible, as his name suggests, was a black sheep. You certainly wouldn't have liked him, my dear."

As Elly sat brooding over her class presentation, Luca poked her shoulder and pointed at the iced figurine on her plate with a sly grin. *Hey, it doesn't look entirely like you. The hair should look much crazier!*

Elly threw him a withering look. *You don't want to irritate me. I am not in the mood for any of your tricks. Do you want me to turn you into a cucumber? I won't be sorry if Marlow gobbles you up!*

Luca guffawed, feigning a look of terror. "Oooh, Elly-Belly's in a foul mood!"

Papa gave Elly's arm an encouraging squeeze. "You'll show them, Elly! I've seen how your presentation looks. They'll be blown away." She smiled at him gratefully.

But then her parents began discussing the details of Elly's birthday party to be held at home that evening. This gave Elly another reason to groan.

Turning twelve years old was an important milestone in elf tradition. It was an elfling's coming of age. On this day, Elly would finally receive her Royan, and it was this she was so excited about, not the awful party that her parents were throwing for her.

At another elfling's twelfth birthday party, years ago, she had witnessed for the first time the bonding ceremony under the Grand Canopy, the topmost part of the Tree. She was very young, but the image had been seared into her memory; the birthday girl, named Eribeth, had stood under the twinkling silver lights and cluster of silver leaves and branches where enormous, golden-brown acorns grew. Like the other onlookers, Elly had to stand a fair distance away as the bonding ceremony took place. She had to crane her neck quite a bit to catch a glimpse of Eribeth and her grandmother. After a while, she looked on with wide eyes (and a tinge of envy) as Eribeth walked towards them with an awed expression, cradling something in both hands. It was glowing and splayed like a blooming flower. It was beautiful.

Papa had noticed Elly's stare and whispered, "Every elfling who comes of age is given a Royan, a very special book flowered from the royal acorns of our beloved Tree. Those royal acorns that grow here at the Grand Canopy are much bigger than the small, ordinary ones the squirrels usually feast on below. You'll see what I mean when your time comes."

"But what does a Royan do, Papa?" she asked with wide-eyed fascination.

Papa smiled at his daughter's curiosity. She never ran out of questions. "The Royan will be your friend and your guide, functioning as a journal and intelligence vessel to help you grow in knowledge and wisdom. When you get your Royan, you'll be declared grown-up enough to serve Alendria!" Elly was so excited she spilt her drink all over the front of her dress; which was just as well, because her mother had sneakily changed the colour to pink when Elly wasn't paying attention.

After swallowing a mouthful of sweet cake, Elly heaved a sigh. "Can't we just keep the birthday party to family and best friends?" she protested feebly.

Mama glowered and crossed her arms indignantly. "Elly, we've already had this discussion. It's your coming of age. We must go ahead with it!" she insisted, pouring some unicorn milk from an ewer into silver goblets. "Besides, it's too late to back out now. We've already sent out the invitations to all two hundred guests. Everyone's coming!" She glared at her husband, who looked very amused. "Sereth! Say something!"

Elly dropped her head into her hands and let out a wail. *Two hundred* guests? She didn't know there would be so many people. This was a nightmare. "But I'm just going to be a wallflower! I'll be the joke of my own birthday party!" she cried. Didn't they already know about the despicable Three Flamingos and the names they called her? What was the point of inviting people who weren't even her friends?

Mama shook her head. "It's not simply a birthday party, Elly. You'll be a debutante. We'll be publicly announcing your coming of age!" she said in exasperation.

"A *day-boo-taunt?* What's that?" Luca demanded, his mouth full of wild berries and sweet cake.

"It's what they call a young lady like your sister when she comes of age and makes her formal entrance into society, pledging to take part in serving Alendria and protecting her people," Mama explained, looking at Elly meaningfully.

Papa shook his head as he popped wild berries into his mouth. "What's all this nonsense about you being a wallflower?" he exclaimed. "What boy in his right mind would overlook a girl as pretty as you at a dance?" Elly rolled her eyes and Luca pretended to gag.

Elly brooded while her parents continued to discuss the party and Luca played with Marlow. What was so great about celebrating one's birthday, anyway? She would've much preferred to throw a party once she became a real explorer. Now, *that* would be something worth bragging about. She heaved a sigh and spooned more sweet cake into her mouth. "Why are so many people from school invited to my birthday party? Only two of them really count," she muttered under her breath as she thought about Aron and Edellina, her two best friends.

Aron had been her next-door neighbour from the day she was born, and they had been best friends ever since. Aron wanted to become a historian. "I'll tag along with you on your future expeditions, and we'll both make history together!" he liked to joke.

Then, several months ago, Edellina turned up at the school library when Elly was studying with Aron. She was a head-turner: lithe and tall, and strikingly pretty, with gorgeous, white-silver hair and slightly unusual, slanted violet eyes. She had moved to Evergreen City from a remote region called Morwen Valley that was renowned for the silk they produced there. Edellina seemed very grown-up and independent, for her parents were often away on trips. "They're your regular merchants, obsessed with the family business," Edellina had said with a cool shrug when Elly asked if she missed them. Elly and Aron were drawn to her. She felt rather flattered that someone as cool as Edellina would want to be her friend.

Mama clapped her hands, pulling Elly out of her reverie. At a snap of her fingers, the remains of the sweet cake vanished (there wasn't much of it), to be replaced by two silver goblets filled with unicorn milk. Papa had already gone to get ready for work. "Children, drink up before you head out to school!" She turned to Elly and winked. "Come straight home after school, okay? Don't linger! We'll get you ready to party."

Elly started feeling queasy, barely able to gulp down her milk. Marlow eyeballed the goblet in her hand. Mama frowned. "You better drink up before Marlow swipes it!" When she saw Elly's pale face, she sighed.

"Darling, you'll be great! I've listened to your presentation, and we were *so* impressed," she said, patting Elly on the back. It was true. Nidah was very proud of her daughter, and hated that she was given such a hard time at school. *Children can be so cruel*, she thought.

Elly untangled herself from her mother's embrace, looking down gloomily at the scroll in her hands. Oh, she just *hated* talking in front of the class!

Papa stuck his head through the kitchen doorway. "Do you need Marlow to give you a ride?" he asked. Mama sighed; Marlow had already gulped down Elly's unicorn milk.

Elly shook her head as she put down the empty goblet and absent-mindedly petted her griffin. "No, it's all right. You can take Marlow today. I want to walk and clear my head a bit . . . before I totally humiliate myself in class." Without waiting for Papa's response, she quickly blew her parents a kiss and hugged Marlow before stepping outside. As she leapt down the rope ladder, she greeted several twittering birds perched on their branches. Luca had already gone ahead without her, which was just as well; she really wanted some peace and quiet.

She waved as she passed several guards standing at the cross points. "Good morning!" she called to them. Some of them smiled back, while others remained stoically expressionless. Were there more guards on duty than usual?

She sniffed and wrinkled her nose. Strangely, the air was less fragrant this morning. *Maybe it's just my imagination.* Then she remembered overhearing snippets of a conversation that Papa and Mama were having in the kitchen before she set off for school . . . something about how the climate underground had been warmer recently.

Mama sounded anxious as she spoke in a low voice. "I know the goblins live thousands of miles below us, but still, it never really feels far enough, does it? We can never really shake off the knowledge that all they really want is to have Alendria all to themselves."

Papa had replied darkly, "Hush, Nidah. Let's not speak of this while the children are still in the house."

Elly knitted her brow as she walked along, jumping over some rain puddles. For as long as she could remember, she had always felt safe from goblins. She knew they are vile subterranean creatures who avoid the sunlight and hate the elves. But she had never actually *seen* one before. The guards and protectors seemed to do their job well, vigilantly ensuring that no goblin ever escaped through one of the cross points, where the roots underground connected with the trunk of the Tree. Goblins had invaded through the cross points in the past. But there hadn't been a goblin invasion for eleven years.

As she approached the towering silver-wrought gates of her school, Elly slowed her steps, and her stomach began to knot up again. The flags of the four houses of Arvellon Academy billowed rather grandly in the breeze, each emblazoned with the emblem of Arvellon: red for Seaul, green for Cephrin, blue for Lorne, and white for Graille. Soon, the new season of archensoar would start, and these four houses would be at loggerheads again. Last year, the Archensoar Cup had been snagged by Cephrin for the third year in a row.

Elly glanced around. At least the headmaster, Sir Baerin Greenleaf, was nowhere in sight today. He often liked to greet the students at the entrance and cracked the unfunniest jokes.

Then she spotted Aron and Edellina sauntering towards her, and her spirits lifted. How she wished they were in her class.

Edellina was looking lovely as always, her white-silver hair tied up in an elaborate braid. As usual, many pairs of eyes followed her in admiration.

Oblivious to the attention, she smiled and winked at Elly. "Good luck with your presentation today. You'll be fantastic!"

Carrying a thick book in one hand, Aron grinned and handed Elly a big red toffee-pop. "Happy birthday, Elly! Here, my Mama made this for you! It's your good luck charm," he joked, draping an arm around her shoulder.

Aron had dark silver hair and grey-blue eyes, and he would be called truly handsome if he had been taller and broader for his age. "You're just a late bloomer," his mother would say firmly whenever her son complained of his awkward lankiness. "Besides, your cleverness more than makes up for anything!" But his bookishness seemed to repel most boys in class, who much preferred practising their archery and playing archensoar to studying.

Aron would shrug and scoff, "Never mind. Exercising one's mind will reap greater rewards than exercising one's muscles. They'll see!" Despite this, Aron wouldn't miss watching a single game. Being in Seaul House with Elly, he would often drag her along to cheer for their team.

Edellina, being in Lorne House, had shown little interest in archensoar. "I have better things to do," she would shrug whenever Aron asked her along to the games.

Elly beamed as she tasted the sweet cherry-flavoured toffee-pop Aron had given her; it melted easily in her mouth. She sighed and looked at her two friends, almost tearfully. "I don't know what I'll do without you two!" They agreed to meet up at the Meridien Meadows after school before Elly's birthday party.

Then she remembered: "Did you hear something last night? I was woken up by some noise."

Aron raised his eyebrows. "Yes! I heard bells, and there seemed to be some sort of scuffle in the distance. I got woken up too, but my papa told me to go back to bed. Apparently, some wild wolfhounds had crossed the border, but the guards quickly chased them back. Anyway, I fell back to sleep straight away. I was zonked after staying up late studying." As if to prove this, he yawned.

Edellina shrugged, fiddling with the bracelet on her wrist. "I didn't hear anything. I'm sure it was nothing. But I sleep like a log, you know. I'd probably sleep through a war," she said airily. Aron and Elly laughed. Edellina had a way of making big things sound small.

As Elly chatted with her two friends, she noticed someone staring at them from the corner of her eye. When she turned, she caught a glimpse of cloudy white hair disappearing behind one of the thick pillars at the assembly hall. Elly shrugged it off and turned back to her friends. She really, really didn't want to go to her classroom.

Finally, the bell rang. Elly groaned with dread as she parted from her two friends. Her feet felt like lead as she walked down the hallway, her stomach lurching with nerves. Then her heart gave a horrible jolt when she saw who were standing at the door of the classroom, giggling and gossiping.

Darrius, as usual, was flanked by Lorelana and Morganai. The trio were nicknamed the Three Flamingos on account of their extraordinarily long, skinny legs and their penchant for anything and everything pink. Their parents were on the High Council and were very wealthy, and because of that the Three Flamingos thought they were better than everyone else, especially Elly. Though the Celendis family was renowned for the brave deeds of warriors past, they were not renowned for material wealth. And on top of that, she was treated as an outcast just because her family name was tarnished by someone in her clan long before Elly was born . . . someone she had never even met.

The Three Flamingos spotted Elly as she tried to flit past, desperately hoping they wouldn't notice her. Elly was smaller than other elflings her age—the Three Flamingos were about a head taller than she was. Elly's mother liked to refer to her slight build as another of her "unique attributes", along with her manic hair and her inability to carry a tune.

Life just wasn't fair.

"Hey, little *Raven* is here!" Lorelana sneered. Morganai giggled nastily. "What do you wanna become when you're all grown up? A smithy like your papa?"

Darrius, her silky auburn hair twisted into a braid past her waist, was considered the most beautiful girl at school. She raised an eyebrow and pointed at Elly's faded, worn-looking boots. Her hazel eyes glinted. "Lovely! Is that the new style?" she said coolly before bursting into laughter. Elly hung her head, her face burning.

Lorelana and Morganai were mean, but Darrius was the ringleader, which meant she was the meanest. From the moment Darrius locked eyes with Elly on the first day at the Academy, it was as if she lived to make Elly's life at school as miserable as possible. It didn't help that their class teacher, Mr Holle, didn't do much to discourage it. Elly didn't like him, and she suspected the feeling was mutual.

Elly kept her eyes fixed to the floor as she quickly moved past the three leggy girls. She fumed with clenched fists, a thousand angry comebacks wanting to tumble out. "Those who are slow to anger and hold their tongues are the true victors, Elly," Papa had once told her. The problem was that she wasn't really slow to anger, and she wasn't really good at holding her tongue; she simply lacked the courage to stick up for herself. The thought made her feel more depressed.

Then Darrius blocked her way, and Elly's insides clenched. "Oh, it's your birthday, isn't it? Don't misunderstand—we're only coming to your party because we *have* to." She clapped her hands, her smile mocking. "Happy birthday, Raven!"

Then a voice cried out shrilly, "I *beg* your pardon, young ladies?" The Three Flamingos froze in unison. Elly wheeled around.

Before them stood a small, moon-faced lady with rosy cheeks and white hair piled into a bun high on her head, held together by a peacock-feathered quill. Her startling blue eyes were fierce as she glowered at Darrius and her two friends. Unconsciously, they stepped back.

"Did I hear what I thought I heard? What offensive name did you call this young lady?" she demanded, gesturing towards Elly who wanted to sink right through the floor. The lady clapped her hands, and the Three Flamingos suddenly shrieked and clutched at their heads.

Elly gawped at them. Above each of the Three Flamingos floated the words *Thou shalt not be a nasty name-caller* in bright, fiery red letters. Some classmates pointed and sniggered. Red-faced, the Three Flamingos stalked to their seats clutching their heads, flashing furious looks at Elly. She sank down in her seat in shock. Nobody in class had ever come to her defence before.

The lady glared at the Three Flamingos. "As long as I am here today, nobody will be calling anyone nasty names, nor get away with it!" Then she marched over to the front of the room and turned to face the class, her chin up and hands behind her back, looking formidable for a small person.

She narrowed her eyes as she studied them. "Mr Holle has taken ill, I'm sorry to say," she announced brusquely, not sounding very sorry at all. "So I am here to substitute for him today." With a grand wave of her arm, sparkling white letters appeared in the air: *Mrs L. Silverwinkle.*

The Three Flamingos, still clutching their heads, tried frantically to cast different enchantments to make the fiery letters disappear, but to no avail. Elly looked at Mrs Silverwinkle with a grin, mentally saluting her as she marvelled about this strange and extraordinary start to the day.

Maybe Mama was right. Perhaps there was something auspicious about her birthday after all!

CHAPTER TWO
The Collage

THREE STUDENTS HAD ALREADY DELIVERED their presentations.

Mrs Silverwinkle smiled. "Last but not least—Ellanor Celendis, it's your turn!"

Elly broke out in a cold sweat.

Lucian wanted to become a silver miner; Rainer, a researcher at the Institute for the Advancement of Magic; and Meredyth, a healer. They had all given their presentations competently with Quill-Point, a standard tool designated by the Evergreen Board of Academics for school presentations.

The Quill-Point came in different colours and styles. Storing as many images as it touched, the student simply had to give the Quill-Point spoken commands so that it would know exactly what to project on the presentation board. The students first had to conduct their research, organize how they wanted the information to be presented, write up their presentation, and have the Quill-Point on hand to do the rest. It was all rather straightforward, really. A student couldn't go wrong with the Quill-Point except by failing to prepare sufficiently, which would become obvious during the presentation.

At the beginning of the academic year, Papa had given Elly a Quill-Point with a black handle and purple feather, and she had used it several times. But for this particular presentation, she had wanted to do something different. After all, it wasn't stated that the student absolutely *must* use Quill-Point. *The student delivered the presentation in an appropriate and organized manner*—that was part of the grading criteria. Elly thought she could put a spin on it, which seemed fitting for the subject of her presentation.

Now, she wasn't so sure that she had made the right choice. The Three Flamingos and the rest of the class would probably just ridicule her for sticking out like a sore thumb. Maybe she should have just followed along and used Quill-Point like everyone else.

But it was too late for regrets now. She had to get on with it.

Mrs Silverwinkle smiled encouragingly as Elly stood there looking pale, clutching onto a rolled-up scroll before the class. She tried returning the smile, but she was so nervous that what came out looked more like a grimace.

At least Mr Holle isn't here, she thought, having always hated speaking in front of him. He had an unsettling way of peering down his crooked nose at her whenever she spoke, as though she were a nuisance he had to put up with. She had a habit of stammering and shaking like a leaf during these dreadful class presentations. Once it got so unbearable that she ran out of the room sobbing, followed by much sniggering and laughter (instigated mostly by the Three Flamingos).

Mr Holle gave her a fail grade for that presentation, even though she had prepared a thoroughly researched and well-written paper on the topic. He hadn't even bothered to talk to her about it; he had simply written "Failed: Incomplete" in big red letters on her paper, and below was a scrawled comment: "Perhaps you need to consult a mind seeker about your stage fright."

Elly had felt so humiliated. For days after that, in class she could not look at anyone in the eye.

But Mrs Silverwinkle looked as if she actually *wanted* to hear what Elly had to say.

The class looked on in silence as Elly fumbled with the enormous scroll in her arms. Carefully, she unfurled it and held it up with trembling hands. Everyone stared, their attention piqued. Mrs Silverwinkle leaned forward with a dimpled smile.

Elly took a shuddering breath and licked her dry lips nervously. "Okay . . . umm . . . Good—good morning, everyone. I decided to do something a little different with my presentation. My dream is to become an explorer. Like my Grandpapa Galdor. Maybe some of you have heard of him." Elly's voice broke, and she cleared her throat. Her mouth felt like sandpaper. She couldn't bear to look at her classmates, so she alternated between looking at Mrs Silverwinkle and the back of the room.

"Qualified explorers work for the High Council. A major part of the job is to compile and analyse information they've gathered on other realms, in part to help safeguard Alendria, and to contribute to the intelligence repository of the Tree. Explorers must become accustomed to not using magic, as it may not be appropriate to do so when they are abroad exploring a realm that is . . . non-magical. So, good explorers need to adjust to their surroundings and try their best to . . . blend in. That's why I included the chameleon here . . . to show that explorers need to find ways to camouflage themselves in different environments." Elly paused as she pointed at the picture of her grandpapa.

She cleared her throat and continued. "When my Grandpapa Galdor first visited the dwarves in Nazadum, he adjusted his appearance to resemble the dwarves, so that they wouldn't feel threatened by him. The dwarves knew he was an elf, but by looking more like them, Grandpapa made it easier for them to accept him. By and by, physically he revealed himself as an elf, and by that time he had already won the dwarves over with his sincerity to forge a friendship. And, umm, I thought it would be fitting to prepare for this presentation without using magic, to make a point. As an explorer, it's important to be . . . experimental and willing to adopt the practices of other realms to properly learn about them. That's why I have made this—a collage."

Elly shyly gestured to the work which had taken her two weeks to complete, with bits and pieces she had collected and salvaged from discarded clippings from the *Evergreen Times* and hand-drawn pictures that had taken her countless hours to get right. This is what her collage looked like:

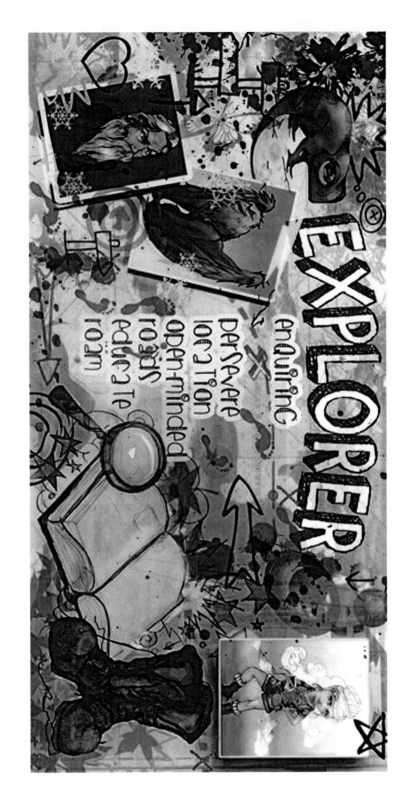

EXPLORER

enquiring
persevere
location
open-minded
roads
educate
roam

There was a great deal of murmuring. Some leaned forward to take a closer look. The collage definitely looked handmade. The Three Flamingos rolled their eyes and crossed their arms, pretending to look bored. Mrs Silverwinkle was beaming and nodding with approval.

"Did you do all this yourself? What is a collage, exactly?"

Elly blinked and looked up. The voice belonged to a boy named Kaelan Tuniveer. He had fixed his serious blue eyes on her.

Elly gaped, at a loss for words. Part of her couldn't believe anyone was actually paying attention.

She had never spoken to Kaelan before, and knew next to nothing about him except that he was quiet, and an outstanding archensoar player for Cephrin House (which partly accounted for their snagging the Archensoar Cup for the third year in a row). He was very good-looking, and it was only now that Elly really noticed.

Darrius shot Kaelan a disapproving look. Lorelana and Morganai were sniggering.

Elly braced herself and looked at Kaelan, who was waiting for her to respond. Her voice quavered slightly. "Well . . . a collage is a . . . a creative work made of different materials such as paper, cloth, wood, pictures, and any objects glued to a piece of paper. A collage is supposed to represent many different aspects of an idea you want to express. This method of expression is popular in, umm, the human realm . . ." She trailed off as the Three Flamingos started scoffing. They shut up when Mrs Silverwinkle glowered at them. "Let us be a mature and respectful audience," she said firmly. "We will leave comments and questions to the end." She looked back at Elly and winked.

Elly gave the smallest of nods and smiled at Mrs Silverwinkle gratefully. She straightened her shoulders and tried to look like someone who would grow up to be an explorer and discover great things and accomplish great deeds.

She talked more about her Grandpapa Galdor and some of his most interesting and dangerous expeditions, including his dealings with the reclusive Vierran elves in the cold northern region, and his friendship with the humans in Gaya.

She talked about wanting so much to meet her heroine, Larabeth Goldberry, because she was the most famous female explorer in Alendria, though she had retired a long time ago and had been living a quiet life away from the limelight for many years. Elly didn't feel so alone knowing there was someone like Larabeth Goldberry to look up to. She explained why it was important for an explorer to possess certain qualities, such as a curious and open mind, and the importance of a sturdy and comfortable pair of boots for the long and occasionally perilous journeys. She hoped that her griffin, Marlow, would be her companion on those very journeys. Then she went on to explain that a Royan was essential to an explorer, acting as a guide, advisor, and protector. An explorer would also need to weather through different climates, including the harsh winters and sweltering summers that some places in Gaya and other realms were known for.

As she talked, her face relaxed and became increasingly animated. There was so much she wanted to share! For the first time during a class presentation, she felt like she was able to express herself freely. It was a thrill.

Finally, she lowered the scroll and breathed a sigh of relief. "That's it. That's what I want to become—an explorer."

There was a silence. She couldn't bear to raise her head.

Then someone started clapping. She looked up. "Bravo!" yelled Mrs Silverwinkle with a grin. To her surprise, Mrs Silverwinkle wasn't the only one applauding now. With a hint of a smile, Kaelan had joined in, along with several others. The applause actually sounded *enthusiastic*. Elly felt her face grow hot.

"Class, any comments or questions?" asked Mrs Silverwinkle, standing up.

Several hands shot up. "I like the idea of the collage," said Jessamyn, a tall, golden-haired girl who was friends with the Three Flamingos. "It's refreshing to see something different, instead of just sticking to Quill-Point like we all did. What you did was really creative and unique."

Not used to receiving compliments in class, Elly went even redder in the face as she nodded shyly. "Thank you," she murmured, shifting on her feet awkwardly.

Darrius shot Jessamyn an irritated look. "I have a question," she said silkily, her eyes flashing with malice. Elly's heart sank. "You mentioned your grandfather being the famous explorer and all. I'm a little fuzzy on my historical facts, so it'll be great if you could clarify things for me. Wasn't your grandfather's brother *the* Idril Gailfrin Celendis?"

A hush fell over the room. Mrs Silverwinkle narrowed her eyes.

Elly's heart was hammering against her ribcage as she tried to keep herself from falling apart.

"Yes," she said quietly. "He . . . he was my grand-uncle. But I never got to meet him." She wanted to wipe the smug smile off Darrius' face.

"Oh. So what exactly did he do? I've been told he was a traitor, that he betrayed us to the goblins. Right?"

By this time, Mrs Silverwinkle had stood up. Her face was grim as she looked over at Elly.

Elly clutched the scroll so hard, her knuckles turned white. "But my grand-uncle didn't get a chance to tell his side of the story," she said hoarsely, her eyes burning. "He was the last person to be seen with the goblins, before . . . before . . ." Her voice broke, and she could only think the words: *Before an army of ten thousand goblins was unleashed on the elves, who were in a secret location that the goblins could not have discovered unless someone had tipped them off.*

Darrius raised her eyebrows, feigning surprise. "So, it mustn't be easy to become a qualified explorer, least of all accepted by the High Council, with such an unfavourable family history?"

"I don't see how this pertains to Elly's dream to become an explorer, Darrius," Kaelan interrupted. All eyes swivelled around to him. Darrius looked taken aback, then narrowed her eyes to slits; she wasn't used to being contradicted.

Mrs Silverwinkle smiled and clapped her hands. "Thank you, Kaelan. What a pleasant interruption to such unpleasant talk. Now, if we could just . . ."

But Darrius would not let it go. Tossing her auburn hair, she scoffed. "Just because we dream about becoming something, doesn't mean it will happen. I mean, isn't it best to recognise your limitations? What's the point of having such big dreams when you know they most probably won't come true?"

Darrius had delivered her presentation already, stating that she wanted to become a weaver. She loved creating her own clothes, and was constantly showing them off. Her family was so rich that they always bought the most fashionable and expensive fabrics.

Mrs Silverwinkle fell silent, then slowly walked up to Darrius. At that moment, Elly thought that she had never seen anyone look more intimidating.

"Do not ever interrupt me again," Mrs Silverwinkle said quietly. "I will not tolerate such atrocious behaviour from any of my students, no matter who their parents are." She stared hard at Darrius without blinking. Darrius looked back defiantly; but after several moments, she looked away and sank down in her chair, cowering at last.

Mrs Silverwinkle shook her head and turned to the rest of the class. "If you never dare to dream, then you'll never know what great things you're capable of. When you do what you fear most, then you can do anything." She smiled, and at that moment Elly felt that maybe, just maybe, she really could accomplish anything. "Must we live with the results of other people's opinions of us? Should we not have the courage to follow our hearts, even if it means we take the path less travelled?"

There was a silence as everyone took in her words. Suddenly, several voices started speaking up at once.

"Actually, I really want to become a grand healer, not a minstrel like my mother wants me to be!"

"Maybe I could really become a law-keeper after all, even though my papa tells me I may not be clever enough."

The students were turning to each other, some reconsidering their future careers and wondering aloud if what they had chosen as their "dream" career was something they really wanted to do, or something they would do to please others.

Amidst all the commotion, Mrs Silverwinkle laughed uproariously. She turned to Elly, who had by now sat down looking bewildered. "Ellanor Celendis, don't underestimate yourself! You can be a mover and a shaker!"

Elly smiled uncertainly. "Thank you. But what does that mean, exactly?"

Mrs Silverwinkle chuckled and winked. "Let's just say it means you have an imagination, and you have the courage to be different because it feels right for you."

Elly thought about that for a moment and smiled. It was definitely a compliment.

As the class was filing out to go home, several classmates went up to Elly and congratulated her on a great presentation. The Three Flamingos ignored her as they stalked past, their heads held high.

Elly sighed. She wished she could have said something sharp back to Darrius. Any sort of clever comeback would have been priceless.

Edellina and Aron were waiting outside her classroom. She beamed and gave them a thumbs up.

Aron whooped and gave her a big hug. "Way to go, Elly!"

Edellina smiled and winked. "See, I told you so."

Then Mrs Silverwinkle came out of the classroom. Elly happily introduced her two friends. It was then that she noticed Mrs Silverwinkle looking a little pale; her cheeks had lost some rosiness, and her eyes looked less bright, like the clouds had obscured the sunshine. Elly wondered if the Three Flamingos, especially Darrius, had tired her out somewhat. She *was* quite old, after all.

"Oh yes, I know of Aron," Mrs Silverwinkle said, smiling warmly. She turned to Edellina. "Hello, Miss Rosebane. I am aware that you joined the academy several months ago. Perhaps your parents can come to Elly's party tonight? I was told that even Headmaster Greenleaf hasn't yet had the opportunity to meet them."

Edellina flashed a charming smile. "That is so thoughtful! Thank you for your concern, Mrs Silverwinkle, but my parents are still out of town. They're very busy merchants, and I think they might even be doing business all the way up in the North with the Vierran these days. They won't be back to Evergreen until next month, but my guardian and I have been managing just fine."

Mrs Silverwinkle nodded. "Yes, I understand. What a shame."

Then she turned to Aron. "Well, young man! I heard from your teacher that you wrote an exceptional history paper on goblin infiltrations. You obviously worked very hard on it." She patted Aron on the back, then she looked up at the sky.

"Oh my, it's already so late! Elly, I need to go home and dress grandly for your birthday party, otherwise your dear mother Nidah would be most cross with me. Off you go now!"

Before Elly could ask whether she had ever gone to Nidah's Sweet Secrets, Mrs Silverwinkle shooed them away. Elly laughed and waved goodbye before turning back to her two friends, heading for the Meridien Meadows.

Mrs Silverwinkle's smile dissolved into a frown as she gazed at their retreating backs.

CHAPTER THREE
The Party

THE THREE FRIENDS CHATTERED AS they were stretched out luxuriously on the grass at the sun-dappled Meridien Meadows, where the blue water sparkled, butterflies and dragonflies swooped over the clovers and wild flowers, and birds were twittering a symphony. When the sky started turning crimson, they headed back to their respective homes to get ready for the party.

Before they parted ways, Edellina pulled Elly towards her. "I have a surprise for you tonight!" she said in a conspiratorial whisper. Then she winked and leapt away, her silver mane flying behind her.

Elated, Elly couldn't stop grinning as she hummed and skipped along, wondering what Edellina had planned. A special present? Was she going to perform a song and dance routine? She giggled, imagining Aron stumbling on his feet while Edellina, a head taller, twirled around him gracefully.

She was having the best day *ever*—the presentation had gone well, several classmates had actually complimented her, Mrs Silverwinkle was *so* much nicer than Mr Holle . . . and to top it off, she was going to receive her Royan tonight!

Mama was standing at the door with her arms crossed, looking anxious. "Where have you been?" she demanded. "I thought you were going to come home straight after school!"

Elly was taken aback. "I just went to the Meridien Meadows to catch up with Aron and Edellina. I didn't stay that long. You know I often go there after school." She looked at her mother curiously. Why was she so upset?

Mama shook her head and muttered something under her breath. "When I ask you to come straight home, you should take it seriously," she snapped before stalking into the house. Elly hurried in after her, bewildered. Maybe she was just nervous about the party. No matter— Mama would cheer up once she had given her an update on her extraordinarily good day.

Indeed, once Elly had recounted what had happened at school, Mama's bad mood dissolved. She squealed and gave Elly a big hug. "Oh Elly, I'm so proud of you! See, I knew you would be fantastic!"

Marlow squawked, putting one cheek close to Elly's face. She snuggled up to him and murmured, "Thank goodness I have you, Marlow. You always try to keep me in good cheer!"

Eleven years ago, Papa brought Marlow home after his mother and siblings had been attacked by a band of goblins that had infiltrated deep in the heart of the Celestan Forest. The guard at one cross point had fallen under some spell that put him into a stupor. The youngest baby griffin survived the attack after Papa fought off the goblins, who scurried away and escaped back down the cross point. "You were only a toddler back then," Papa once told Elly, "but the baby griffin took such a shine to you. He snuggled up to you in the hammock while you were napping. You named him Marlow, and since then you've been inseparable!"

As Elly snacked on blueberry sweet cakes and petted Marlow, Mama grinned and whipped out a large silver package. "Happy birthday!" she cried, carefully placing the gift in front of Elly.

"Oh Mama, you didn't!" she exclaimed. It must be the first edition of *Roaming the Worlds as a Chameleon* by Larabeth Goldberry! They must have remembered after all! Mama looked on with anticipation as Elly unwrapped the package excitedly.

Then her heart sank; nestled in the soft white wrappings was a beautiful leather belt with a silver clasp, a pair of sturdy, light brown boots . . . and a *pink* dress.

Elly liked the belt and the boots, but the dress.

She thanked her mother for the gifts and tried to keep a straight face. But then she blurted, "Oh, Mama . . . the style of the dress is pretty, but you *know* I hate pink! I'm not wearing pink for my twelfth birthday party, and definitely not when I'm receiving my Royan!" Why couldn't Mama just accept that she doesn't have to like what many other girls prefer?

Marlow squawked and shook his head at the pink dress in disapproval.

Mama frowned. "Oh, Elly, pink is nice! You should at least *try* wearing something ladylike on your big day!" she protested. But no matter how much she pleaded with her, Elly would not give in. She simply could not stand pink, and she just couldn't explain it. After all, why did one like any particular colour? Why did one prefer strawberries to apples?

Mama glanced at the sky; the guests would be arriving soon. There was no more time to argue. With a resigned look and a sweep of her hand, Mama changed the dress from pink to dark purple.

Marlow squawked again and nodded with approval. Elly broke into a smile. "Thank you so much, Mama! I love it!" She kissed her mother on the cheek and darted upstairs to her bedroom to change.

Papa ducked his head through the kitchen doorway and chuckled at his wife. "I *told* you so!" he said smugly before ducking out again.

In her room, Elly took great care getting dressed. She dabbed some water on her hair in a futile attempt to make it look straighter and silkier. Her long black curls refused to obey, however.

When Elly had just started attending the academy, she asked her parents why people thought her black hair was ugly, and why some people would sneer and call her names like Raven. "Aren't ravens birds of ill omen?" she asked them tearfully. Papa and Mama exchanged looks before he sat down and perched Elly on his knee.

"My darling Elly, there is nothing wrong with your hair. You are a beautiful little girl. As you know, black hair runs through the Celendis family. Those people don't really think that black hair is ugly; they are afraid of what black hair might represent, because of something very bad somebody from the Celendis clan did a very long time ago." He paused, looking pained. "He was your grandpapa's brother, and your grand-uncle."

Elly had grimaced. "Yes. Grandpapa doesn't like to talk about it," she said softly.

Papa had nodded. "Our clan numbered many before the War of Wrath over four hundred years ago. Back then, the Celendis clan was revered and beloved, for we were renowned for our brave warriors. The Celendis clan had for a long time been like the stewards of Alendria."

At this he paused, his eyes staring into the distance, remembering days of glory past. "But your grand-uncle betrayed us to the goblins during the War of Wrath. Because of his treachery, many elves from the Celendis clan were slaughtered in the war. That is why there are so very few of us left, Elly."

He sighed heavily as he recalled the dark days. "Since then, we've been branded as traitors by association, despite all the good we have done for Alendria. You see, those who are quick to judge and listen to gossip and slow to think for themselves tend to be unkind without good reason."

Elly had listened in rapt attention; then she looked up at Papa with heart-wrenching, misty green eyes. "But what if my friends are mean to me and call me names, too?"

Mama grasped her small hand. "People who dislike you just because of your looks or the colour of your hair are not your true friends to begin with," she said firmly.

Elly thought about that for a moment and gave a faint smile. "If that is the case, then Aron is my one and only true friend."

Aron always comforted Elly whenever she complained about the name-calling. "Hey, I think it's kind of cool to be in the minority! It's boring to be the same as everyone else!" He would tug at his own shoulder-length silver hair and pull funny faces.

Thank goodness for Aron. She could always count on him.

After much brushing and tugging, she sighed in resignation. Her unruly curls just kept unravelling from the ribbons. She gave up and let her hair loose down her back. Several squirrels had gathered on the windowsill to admire her. She blew them kisses as she leapt out.

Elly skidded to a stop with a yelp at the foot of the stairs. In the fading light of dusk, the family room was illuminated by the golden ellanors that glowed on the walls like fireflies. Dozens of thick, round candles shaped as stars, griffins, trees, centaurs, and unicorns were aglow, lending the room a dreamy ambience. The ceiling was enchanted to look like the sky outside; it was an inky black dotted with stars. One was shining particularly brightly—the Star of Freya.

There stood many small, tall round tables covered in shimmering gold cloth, on top of which were perched thin vases holding exquisite flower arrangements of daisies, tulips, roses, chrysanthemums, sunflowers, baby's breath, lilies, peonies, and forget-me-nots. Surrounding these vases were overflowing platters of food—a mouth-watering array of ripe, plump-looking fruits, leafy vegetables, nuts, crispy bread of all shapes and sizes, toffee-pops, and mounds of sweet cakes of various flavours. Silver goblets holding refreshing quenchers such as dragon honey ale and bubbling spring water circulated in mid-air, offering themselves up to thirsty guests. Butterflies fluttered about as they prepared to eavesdrop on conversations about to take place.

In front of the large open windows through which a cool night breeze blew were the Serenities, a popular trio of minstrels; one was on the harp, another played the flute, and the golden-haired beauty in the middle, named Laurien, sang in a melancholic, breath-taking voice.

Elly watched around in amazement. It must have cost a fortune to book the Serenities! They were her favourite band. She had always wished she could sing like Laurien. But she just could not carry a tune . . . which was unusual, for all elves seemed to have an affinity for music. All elves, except Elly.

As Mama liked to say, this was part of her uniqueness. But Elly thought it was just another area in which she was lacking.

Papa, Mama, and Luca were all dressed in their best, though her brother was already tugging impatiently at his new shirt. Even Marlow looked exceptionally well-groomed, his coat of feathers sleek and shiny.

Elly ran to her parents and threw her arms around them. "Oh, you've made this look *amazing*! Thank you for doing this!" she cried. Papa chucked her chin affectionately, while Mama stepped back and looked at Elly. "You're right, purple *is* your colour!" she conceded with a smile.

Grandpapa Galdor was the first to arrive, followed closely by Aron who had ridden over on his griffin, Browning. Edellina then arrived by herself, looking gorgeous in a shimmering grey dress. As her two friends chatted easily with her parents, and Luca had become preoccupied with Browning, Elly went up to her grandfather.

Grandpapa Galdor had a stern face that would look startlingly joyous whenever it broke into a smile, which happened frequently around his granddaughter. He was one of the eldest in Alendria; but his bright blue eyes were alert, and his tall and lean body was still strong. His hair, once jet black, had long since turned silver. There was always a calmness about Grandpapa; even when he was rushing, he never seemed in a hurry. Tonight, he looked grand in his sweeping blue robes as he bent down low to kiss Elly on the forehead.

"Happy birthday, my dear sweet girl!" he said in his deep, resonant voice. "Today is your coming of age and a most important milestone! On this day, you have officially been initiated into a life dedicated to Alendria." He paused and leaned forward conspiratorially. She held her breath in anticipation, certain he was about to embark on yet another thrilling tale from one of his adventures.

"Do you think anyone would notice if I took home a dozen of these heavenly raspberry cream sweet cakes?" he whispered. "Your Mama won't let me overindulge, but whose fault is it that they are so irresistible?" His eyes twinkled.

Elly blinked, then she giggled and wagged her finger. "You'll never escape her notice, Grandpapa! I swear she must have eyes on the back of her head!" He laughed uproariously.

Then she started telling him about her day at school, describing her collage in great detail. "Oh, I can't wait to introduce Mrs Silverwinkle to you! She's just the *best*!" she gushed.

Grandpapa raised his eyebrows and chuckled. "The best, eh? I'll see about that!"

One by one, her classmates and teachers started arriving. The Three Flamingos turned up together in identical long pink dresses, looking down their noses at everyone—though that became rather difficult when they had to greet Papa and Grandpapa, two of the tallest in the room.

Luca gawped at the three pink-clad girls. "Now I know why you call them the Three Flamingos!" he hissed under his breath. Luca was five years younger than his sister, and had not yet started at the Arvellon Academy. "Boy, let me teach them a lesson!" Before Elly could say anything, he had darted off, disappearing among the throng of people.

Elly had to admit that the party was turning out to be quite a success. There were games, much dancing and singing, and jovial faces talking and feasting on the scrumptious food. She had to stifle her laughter when she spotted the Three Flamingos screaming and running away from Luca practising enchantments on them. Aron was deep in conversation with Grandpapa, undoubtedly discussing some historical event. Mama and Papa were doing a slow dance, which made her smile.

She looked around for Edellina, and spotted her standing near Mr Holle, whose perpetual scowl marred his otherwise handsome features. His thin, wispy brown hair framed his tired, pale face. Elly raised her eyebrows when she noticed that his arm was in a sling. She supposed that was the reason for his absence from school today. He caught her curious gaze, and narrowed his watery-blue eyes coldly. Edellina turned around and waved at her, before sauntering over to Aron and Grandpapa and joining in their conversation.

Then Elly caught the sight of cloudy white hair. "Mrs Silverwinkle!" she called out happily. The old lady turned and smiled. Even in the dim light, she noticed that Mrs Silverwinkle still looked pale; in fact, paler than she had seen her in the afternoon. She hesitated before asking. "Mrs Silverwinkle, are you feeling all right?"

Mrs Silverwinkle touched a hand to her face. "Yes, yes. Of course. Just a little tired, dear. I haven't been to a party as splendid as this one in a very long time." She paused, as though she wanted to ask Elly something. Then her gaze shifted, and she smiled broadly at someone behind Elly.

To Elly's surprise, Grandpapa strode up to Mrs Silverwinkle, who clasped his big gnarled hands in her own small ones. "Galdor! It's been a long time since we last met on such a splendid occasion. I am ever so glad to see you looking so well!" she cried, beaming.

Grandpapa chuckled. "I've still got many a year left in me, my dear friend!"

Elly stared at them. They actually *knew* each other?

Before she could enquire, someone tapped her on the shoulder. She turned and almost jumped in surprise as she looked into the bright sapphire-blue eyes of Kaelan.

"Hello Kaelan," she said uncertainly, wondering what he wanted with her. Maybe he was so bored he wanted to leave early.

To her amazement, he bowed and offered his hand. "May I have the pleasure of dancing with the birthday girl?" he asked with a smile. Elly was so taken aback that she just gulped foolishly. Kaelan grinned and took her hand. "I'll take that as a yes," he said. The Three Flamingos stared in disbelief as he led Elly to the dance floor.

Kaelan was a year older and quite a bit taller than Elly, with broad shoulders and wiry arms. His light golden hair fell over one of his eyes, tied up at the back in a long braid. Elly was speechless. An air of unreality descended upon her. Before the presentation, Kaelan wouldn't have given her a second look. Why couldn't she think of something clever or interesting to say?

But Kaelan didn't seem to mind the silence as he smiled down at her. Elly noticed that his hands were calloused, rough to the touch. One of her favourite songs was playing.

He started talking first.

"My father is a craftsman, and he's been teaching me his trade. He takes great pride in the buildings he forges, as he should, for he is very gifted. But to be frank, I take after my mother more. She was a painter. I don't believe I'll be half as good as she was, though."

Elly noticed the use of past tense. "Does she not paint anymore?"

Kaelan's face darkened. "She vanished when I was very young, taken by goblins when they infiltrated through one of the cross points. She was in the forest doing her landscape painting. I guess she was in the wrong place at the wrong time."

Elly blushed. "Oh, I—I'm so sorry," she stammered. She bit her lip, feeling terrible.

Then she realized that Kaelan's mother must have vanished around the time her Papa rescued Marlow from the goblins in the Celestan Forest eleven years ago.

He smiled. "It's all right. Don't feel bad. I haven't talked about it with anyone, though everybody knows about it. Ever since I lost my mother, I've mostly kept to myself. I know my father worries about me because I don't really have friends—not anyone I can talk to, anyway." He paused, then looked into her eyes. "Today when you talked about becoming an explorer, it made me think. Perhaps I can accomplish something that I had never really thought possible before."

Elly wondered how someone as handsome and likeable as Kaelan didn't have any real friends. She nodded. "My grandpapa and my parents have always encouraged me to pursue my dream. I mean," she said, warming up, "who says I can't become an explorer like Larabeth Goldberry? I know I shouldn't let anyone put me down. Grandpapa is always telling me to become the scriptwriter of my own life, not let others do it for me." She smiled sheepishly. "But it's easier said than done."

Kaelan nodded. "You're right. We shouldn't give in to what others think is best for us," he said quietly. He shook his head. "It was terrible, what Darrius talked about in class. You shouldn't be judged for what others in your family once did."

Elly smiled. "Thank you for defending me. That was really the first time a classmate has ever done something like that for me."

He shook his head. "I only wish I had come to your defence sooner." He paused. "You never got to meet your grand-uncle, did you?"

Elly grimaced. "No. He died before I was born. My parents— even my grandpapa—they don't talk about him. I suppose that's not surprising, seeing how he must have caused everyone in the family a great deal of grief. Don't all the history books say Idril Gailfrin Celendis vanished straight after the War of Wrath? Presumed dead?"

Kaelan nodded and fell quiet. "I'm sorry to have brought this up, Elly. Let's not talk about this."

He hesitated. "I realized today that I want to become a protector. But my father is against it. I want to do my best to keep Alendria safe from the goblins. If I become a protector, perhaps . . . perhaps I'll find my mother. If she's still alive, that is."

Elly stared up at him, astounded by this admission. "That's really brave. Wow." She paused thoughtfully. "But isn't it terribly difficult to qualify as a protector? I've been told that one needs to go through years of gruelling training, and even then, you might not qualify unless you prove to be exceptional. They only choose the most elite . . ." She stopped short, mortified. "I'm sorry, I don't mean to discourage you," she said apologetically. "I tend to ramble on about facts, it's a bad habit of mine." She could have kicked herself.

Kaelan grinned. "It's nice to get our facts straight, Elly. Thanks for not trying to flatter me." He was about to say something else when someone tapped her on the shoulder. She turned and saw Aron standing there, unsmiling.

"I've been looking for you *everywhere*. Didn't expect to find you here," he said with a frown, giving Kaelan a furtive glance. As if it was an afterthought, he added, "Sorry for interrupting."

Elly thought he didn't sound sorry at all. She pursed her lips in annoyance, wishing Aron could have left her alone. She plastered a smile on her face. "Kaelan, this is my friend Aron."

Aron nodded curtly, half a head shorter than Kaelan. "Her *best* friend."

Kaelan nodded back with a polite smile. Elly scowled. "Listen, Aron, do you think you could . . ."

Suddenly the lights dimmed. Kaelan leaned down and whispered, "Congratulations, Elly," before letting go of her waist and stepping back into the shadows. The music had died down, and a hush fell over the crowd. A spotlight appeared on Elly. She held her breath.

In the darkened room, fireflies appeared like floating lights. Grandpapa Galdor, tall and regal, walked slowly over to Elly and placed a hand gently over her head. "It is time, my dear grandchild."

Before Elly could respond, they were suddenly bathed in a magnificent, warm, golden light, and everything around her began swirling round and round, while she and Grandpapa seemed to stay rooted to the spot.

Then the swirling stopped, the golden light receded, and she found herself standing under a brilliant array of silver branches and thick leaves, from which gleaming, chestnut-brown acorns the size of her head dangled like bells. She gasped. These must be the royal acorns! She was standing under the Grand Canopy of the Tree, and the bonding ceremony was about to begin.

Elly bowed her head in reverence, her heart thumping with anticipation and awe. It was said that the Grand Canopy was the most sacred part of the Tree, because it was closest to the heavens, where the Star of Freya shone like a brilliant diamond, giving the illusion that it was just within reach.

In her peripheral vision, she could see Aron standing with her parents at a distance. Papa gave her a thumbs up. Mama had her hands clasped to her chest, her eyes shiny with happy tears.

Grandpapa grasped her shoulder. "Go and stand right at the centre, Elly. I shall wait for you."

Swallowing nervously, she walked towards the centre, where there was a small circular patch of grass that was much greener than the rest. She stood there and closed her eyes, hands clasped against her chest, head bowed.

There was a silence, followed by a throbbing sound that grew louder and louder.

Then a deep, resounding voice sounded in her ears.

Ellanor Celendis.

Awestruck and somewhat afraid, she bowed deeper.

She had the strange sensation that somebody was looking at her and considering her carefully.

Well, well. Very interesting, indeed.

The voice of the Tree was in her head.

Elly licked her parched lips nervously.

Split in two, yes, split in two. Do you wish to be whole, Ellanor?

She panicked. The Tree was actually asking her a question? She hadn't expected this.

She swallowed. *Umm, I don't know. It depends on what you mean by whole.*

What do you mean by that, Ellanor? She sensed that the Tree already knew what she really meant, though.

Well, a poisonous flower can be whole but unwholesome for one who chances upon it. Another flower that has been battered about by a strong wind may have lost some petals, but still be wholesome for one who seeks its healing powers.

There was a deep vibration, and Elly had to clench her fists to keep her knees from buckling.

Yes, yes. Very good, Ellanor. What looks whole, may not really be wholesome with its layers stripped bare.

There was a silence, as though the Tree was deep in thought.

Then suddenly Elly felt compelled to look up. She did, and found herself staring at a small cluster of golden-brown acorns, glistening and silent, scrutinising her with invisible eyes.

Then her gaze locked onto one particular acorn. It was smaller than the others, its shell somewhat less shiny, a little less symmetrical. But she could not take her eyes off of it.

Ahh, yes. Good, good. That is my dear child Greymore, whom I love. He may be slight and less handsome, but he is twice as sturdy and stout-hearted. Yes, yes.

At that moment, the acorn quivered as if it was taking a shuddering breath; then it fell. Ellanor gasped and caught it with both hands. It was surprisingly heavy.

In her hands, the acorn glowed golden and slowly flowered into a brown leather-bound book with a golden clasp. She stared. It was one of the most beautiful things she had ever seen.

Her Royan.

Then Grandpapa was standing next to her, and he gently lifted the glowing book from her hands. With his back to her, he cradled the Royan and spoke rapidly in Yahana under his breath, blessing it with words that Elly could not quite catch. Then he gave the Royan back to her, and she kneeled ceremoniously, keeping her head bowed as she clutched the book with both hands.

In a strong voice that those standing at a distance could hear, Grandpapa spoke. "Ellanor Celendis, my dear granddaughter, today is your coming of age. I hereby present you the Royan named Greymore, ordained to you by our beloved Tree."

"Thank you, Grandfather. It is an honour," she said softly in Yahana. Then Grandpapa held her face gently between his hands and kissed her on the forehead. He smiled. "Freya looks down upon Alendria and rejoices at this occasion. Do you pledge to do your utmost to love and protect your people and your homeland?"

Elly nodded solemnly and bowed deeply, both arms crossed over her chest. "Yes. I, Ellanor Celendis, pledge to love and protect Alendria to the best of my ability."

She put her hand on the Royan, feeling its smooth, cool surface. To her surprise, it seemed to be vibrating slightly.

Greetings, Ellanor.

Elly blinked at the voice, unfamiliar yet warm, authoritative yet comforting.

Grandpapa Galdor smiled down at her. "Journey well with Greymore, Elly. You are bound to each other now." He squeezed her hand and whispered, "Greymore will take some getting used to, my dear. But trust me, he always has your best interests at heart, even if he might seem harsh at times."

Elly looked at the Royan in her hands and caressed the sleek leather. Then she strapped it to her belt; it fit perfectly. She grinned. Suddenly, she felt very grown up.

Once again, she was bathed in a magnificent golden light, and everything before her swirled. Then they were back in the living room of her house.

She was suddenly surrounded by a crowd extending their congratulations. Kaelan joined the fray, followed by Aron and her parents. Papa lifted her up easily and twirled her around. "My darling girl is no longer so little, pledging to help protect our world! Be good to your Royan, Elly. He'll prove to be invaluable to you, as mine was to me."

Luca was jumping up and down impatiently as he tugged on Papa's robes. "What about me?" he demanded, pouting. "Where's my Royan?"

Papa chuckled and lifted him up with one arm. "Don't worry, your time will come, my boy!"

When Papa went over to speak to Grandpapa Galdor, Mama turned to Kaelan. "So!" she said with a smile. "You're Kaelan. How come I'd never heard Elly speak of you before?"

Elly cringed and went bright red. But Kaelan just smiled and bowed deeply. "I wish I could've gotten to know Elly earlier. She gave a really impressive presentation today."

As he began to talk about her collage, Edellina sidled up and pulled her towards a corner in the room. Mama hadn't even noticed. Obviously, Kaelan had her undivided attention.

"Congratulations, Elly!" Edellina gushed with a wink. "Hey, I saw you dancing with that tall handsome boy. You should've seen Darrius staring at you both—she was so green in the face, she could've passed for a goblin!" Elly giggled; she could not imagine Darrius feeling jealous of her.

Edellina then lowered her voice. "We're going on an adventure tonight! Just us two girls, okay?"

"You don't want Aron to come with us?" Elly asked curiously. The three of them usually went *everywhere* together. She glanced around. Papa had joined Mama, and now both of them were deep in conversation with Kaelan. Aron had gone off to get some food in a huff, annoyed that everyone seemed to be interested in the tall, handsome boy.

At that moment, Kaelan looked up and caught her eye; he grinned and waved. Elly smiled at him shyly before turning back to Edellina. "Why don't you want Aron to join us?"

Edellina shrugged. "We don't have to do *everything* with him, do we? I mean, us girls should have some alone time too, don't you think?" Before Elly could respond, Edellina's gaze fell on the Royan on her belt. Her eyes gleamed.

"So this is your Royan!" she said softly, reaching out. To Elly's surprise, the book seemed to give a shudder.

Edellina quickly retrieved her hand and smiled. "It's so wonderful that you have your own Royan!" she said with a sigh. "I can't wait till I get my hands on one."

Elly grinned. "We can take a look at Greymore together tomorrow, if you'd like," she said proudly, pleased that she finally had something Edellina did not have. Edellina hadn't had her coming of age yet, as she was several months younger.

"By the way, what do you have up your sleeve? Something that would make it worth my while, I hope!" Elly joked.

Edellina smiled coyly. "It will definitely be worth our while. Meet me an hour before midnight by the stone bears in the Celestan Forest." She lowered her voice further. "We're taking a peek at the portal!"

Elly's eyes went wide with shock. "But . . . but we're forbidden to go there!" she cried softly.

The portal was the way through which elves travelled to Gaya, the human realm. Only some members of the High Council had crossed over before the portal was sealed over a hundred years ago, and fewer had even laid eyes on it. Elly had always wondered what it might look like. A gigantic mirror? A towering doorway?

The portal was nestled in the middle of the Celestan Forest, housed within the great white marble dome. Its massive doors could be unlocked only with a key held by Sir Jarome, a wizened protector who guarded the portal. The dome was secured with powerful spells that ensured only elves could pass through.

Edellina rolled her eyes at Elly and crossed her arms. "Oh, come on! Haven't you always wanted to find out more about the humans? You can just look, but not touch, right? There's no harm in just looking. If you want to become an explorer, you'll need to be a little daring and adventurous!" She looked at Elly challengingly. "Go on, promise me you'll not be a scaredy-cat!"

Elly hesitated. Years ago, she'd discovered that elves generally are not fond of humans. "There was a time—long, long ago—when elves used to travel freely to the human realm through the portal, and some elves even befriended humans," Grandpapa had once explained to Elly when she asked him to tell her about the humans as a substitute for a bedtime story. "But over time, the relationship soured, especially when humans began to build machines and cut down trees and pollute the seas, killing countless creatures and plant life. Eventually, the

High Council declared that the humans had become too corrupt and deemed them unworthy of our friendship. 'Animal and tree killers! Selfish, greedy, weak, slave-making creatures—that's what they are!' declared many elves on the High Council." Grandpapa had not agreed with them, but he was in the minority. Soon after that, the portal to the human realm was sealed.

But it wouldn't hurt to just take a peek, right? Edellina said it wouldn't harm anyone. This was her twelfth birthday, after all. She was entitled to do something a little extraordinary . . . right?

Before Elly realized it, she was nodding. "Okay, I promise." She desperately didn't want Edellina to think less of her.

Edellina grinned. "That's more like it!" Then she pressed something cool into Elly's palm. It was a small glass vial holding some clear liquid. Elly looked at her quizzically.

Edellina kept her voice to a whisper. "This is something I've concocted. It's a perfume that makes you invisible. You'll need to put some on before you come meet me in the forest—to pass all those guards and protectors. A lone elfling wandering about so late at night would surely invite suspicion."

Elly's jaw dropped open. "How in the world did you learn to make something like this?" She was terrible at concocting potions of any kind, though it was a compulsory subject at the academy. But they hadn't yet learned how to make the invisibility potion in class.

Edellina laughed softly. "I have my vices, Elly. Now, let's go get some food!"

She linked her arm through Elly's as she steered them towards some sweet cakes. Mama was feverishly refilling the platters of food.

Papa was still talking to Kaelan. Apparently, Kaelan's father had once trained with him; the two were apprentices under the same master. "A fine craftsman he is, your father!" Papa boomed, patting Kaelan on the back.

Elly looked around and finally spotted Mrs Silverwinkle and Grandpapa. They were talking at the back of the room, their heads bent close together, their expressions serious. Elly watched them intently.

Then suddenly they both turned to look in Elly's direction. Feeling a pang of guilt, Elly quickly looked away. Neither of them had been smiling.

CHAPTER FOUR
The Portal

THE PARTY HAD BEEN A blast. Everyone seemed to have a good time except the Three Flamingos, who spent most of the evening running away from Luca. Elly noticed that Mama hadn't really tried to stop him.

Elly blushed and giggled to herself as she recalled her dance with Kaelan. She had not been a wallflower tonight after all. As the guests were trickling out, heavy with food and drink, Kaelan went up to her and whispered, "Goodnight, Elly. See you in class tomorrow." Darrius had given her the most withering look.

Elly smiled. For the first time, she was actually looking forward to going to school. Except . . . as Mrs Silverwinkle was leaving, she asked Elly to see her early the next morning. "Come find me at the fountain as soon as you get to school, dear," she said with a smile, looking pale and tired.

Elly frowned. What did Mrs Silverwinkle want with her? She couldn't be in trouble . . . could she? Mrs Silverwinkle couldn't possibly know what she and Edellina were up to.

Then she looked up anxiously at the moon. It was almost time. *It's just a peek.*

She went into her parents' room, leapt onto their large hammock and hugged them tightly, thanking them for a wonderful party.

Mama grinned mischievously. "Tomorrow morning, you have to tell me all about that nice boy you danced with! Very handsome, too."

Papa cleared his throat. "It's perfectly fine to be friends with Kaelan, Elly. I'll cut him some slack since his father and I once trained under the same master. It's tragic, what happened to Kaelan's mother all those years ago. It must have been a grievous loss to bear."

He sighed, then smiled and wagged a finger at her. "I expect Kaelan to be a perfect gentleman around you. Let me know otherwise." Elly giggled and kissed them both goodnight before bouncing out.

She waited until the light went out in their room and Papa's gentle snores could be heard. Then she tiptoed to her room, took out the vial that Edellina had given her, and looked into the mirror. "Here goes nothing," she muttered. She unscrewed the tiny cork on the vial and sniffed at the perfume. It did smell rather nice—a mixture of lavender and some sort of spice. Then she dabbed some onto her neck, feeling very grown up. Mama wore fragrance like this, and she insisted that Elly was still too young for it.

Marlow was looking at her solemnly. Then he squawked and his eyes flashed.

Elly looked into the mirror and gasped. She could not see her reflection. The perfume had worked! She was invisible!

Excitedly, she blew out the candles in her room and peered out of the window into the quiet night. The stars were nowhere to be seen in the unusually murky sky.

Though she was invisible, Marlow could still follow her scent. He moved closer to her and squawked unhappily.

"I'll be back very soon," she soothed, stroking his neck. 'Promise me you'll keep quiet and wait for me to come back?"

Marlow gazed at her, imploring her to stay. He did not like it that Elly had suddenly become invisible, and now she was going off to meet Edellina so late at night. They were definitely up to no good! Marlow shook his head vigorously.

"Please, Marlow," she pleaded, "I'll be fine, don't worry! Wait here for me."

Without another word, she leapt off the windowsill and made her way down the rope ladder into the darkness. She did a double take when she saw that there were about half a dozen protectors on watch very close to the Celendis House. Elly looked around, perplexed. Why was her home suddenly under such tight security?

But she was too excited and nervous to think about it more. As she walked past the protectors as soundlessly as she could, she thought she heard a couple of them sniffing at the air. She breathed a sigh of relief once she stepped into the Celestan Forest. She had done it!

Elly snapped her fingers. A group of fireflies appeared and flew ahead of her, lighting up the way as she walked. The chirping of cicadas grew louder as she meandered through the dark cluster of rustling trees, venturing deeper and deeper into the heart of the forest. For some reason, a feeling of creeping dread came over her.

Legend told that a long time ago, a pair of black Mohawn bears had been patrolling the forest with protectors when they were ambushed by a group of goblins; the two protectors fought off the goblins, but not before the bears had been turned into stone by the goblins' foul black magic.

Finally, up ahead Elly saw two hulking shapes among the trees. Her heart gave a jolt.

In the darkness, Edellina was perched on one of the Mohawn bears, a basket in her lap as she sat swinging her legs. She was talking in a low voice as though to herself, but stopped abruptly when she spotted Elly.

She gaped at Edellina. Papa had once told her that even though the bears had been turned into stone, their souls were still imprisoned inside, and could not find rest. "You should always treat them with respect, as if they were still alive," he had said.

"Edellina, you shouldn't sit on them like that!" she said reproachfully.

The invisibility enchantment must have worn off, because Edellina looked straight at her and sighed. "Don't be stupid, Elly," she scoffed. "These *things* are just stones, it doesn't make a difference whether we sit on them or break them."

She leapt off and rubbed her hands. "Now, let's go take a peek at the portal!" she said brightly. "I'm sure you can convince Sir Jarome to let down his guard, because it's your twelfth birthday. Besides, he's ever so fond of you."

Elly frowned. Did she ever tell Edellina about Sir Jarome? She couldn't remember.

It was true that Sir Jarome was fond of Elly, and he was old friends with her grandpapa. When she was younger, she would sometimes visit him in the forest so that she could listen to the wonderful tales he told, over and over again. In exchange, she would bring along his favourite wild berries. Though Elly had always been curious about the portal, she had never asked to see it. She understood it was out of bounds, and elves were forbidden to trespass ever since it had been sealed.

I'm not really trespassing, she tried to convince herself. *It's harmless to just take a little peek, right? It's not like I'm going to pass through the portal.*

Only then did she realize that the fireflies had vanished. *Where did they go?* she wondered. In fact, the forest suddenly seemed unnaturally quiet, as though all the creatures nearby had scuttled away. The only light now came from the moon in the inky, starless sky.

"How do you know where to go?" she asked Edellina breathlessly, trying to keep up. Edellina was striding along swiftly. "I didn't realize you know the forest as well as I do."

Edellina gave a low chuckle. "I guess I'm full of surprises, aren't I?"

Finally, they saw a flickering light in the distance. As they approached Sir Jarome's small house near the dome, massive and glistening white in the dark, Elly heard a rustling and a banging. Then a large shadow loomed up, and a pair of fierce blue eyes pierced them like laser beams. She froze.

Then those fiery eyes recognised her and softened. "Elly! My goodness, what are you doing out here in the middle of the night?" Sir Jarome spoke in a deep gravelly voice. His face looked older than she'd remembered.

Edellina jabbed her in the back. Elly winced in pain. "Just tell him what I told you," Edellina hissed, thrusting into Elly's hand the basket she had brought with her. In it were bunches of wild berries and a dozen sweet cakes and walnuts left over from the party.

Elly rearranged her face into a big smile. "I bid you a good evening, Sir Jarome! It's my twelfth birthday, and I thought it would be a real pity not to share some of the delicious food we had at my party! I was so sorry to hear you couldn't attend." The latter was true; she had wanted Sir Jarome to have attended her party. But the food basket was Edellina's idea. "A little bribery should do the trick," she had chuckled as Elly looked at her uncomfortably.

What are you doing, Ellanor? You should stop right now.

But Elly ignored that voice. *It's too late to back down now*, she thought.

Sir Jarome's stern face melted into a smile. "Thank you, dear Elly, how very kind and thoughtful. Happy birthday! Indeed I was very disappointed that I could not attend your party. But nobody with the right qualifications could guard in my place tonight. The protectors are being kept quite busy these days. Oh, look! You haven't forgotten . . . my favourite wild berries . . . and your mother's scrumptious sweet cakes!" He grinned and popped several berries into his mouth. Then his eyes fell on Edellina, who had been standing behind Elly.

"Who do we have here?" Sir Jarome asked with a frown. Edellina gave him a charming smile, but did not reply.

Elly forced a laugh. "Oh, this is my friend Edellina! She is ever so nice to keep me company." She nudged Edellina to bow, as was polite of elflings to do when greeting their elders. But Edellina ignored her as she peered up at the tall elf silently.

Sir Jarome seemed oblivious of Edellina's poor manners. He was blinking rapidly, trying to get rid of his blurry vision. His face suddenly ruddy, he sat down heavily on the ground, both hands clutching the basket as he slumped back against the tree trunk.

"Ahh, I could get used to this!" he slurred sleepily, rubbing his stomach. To Elly's horror, he gave a great yawn; then his head dropped to his chest and he began to snore gently.

Elly gasped and cried out in panic. "Oh, my goodness! He's fallen into some stupor!" She looked at Edellina accusingly, alarm bells sounding in her head. "What did you put in those berries?" she demanded, her head spinning. *What have we done?*

But Edellina laughed as though the funniest thing in the world had just taken place. Elly stared at her.

Edellina scoffed. "Don't worry, you silly girl! It's all harmless, and he'll wake up soon enough! We certainly don't need him breathing down our necks while we do our peeking, now do we?" Then she pointed at the golden key on Sir Jarome's belt, and looked at Elly expectantly.

But Elly shook her head slowly, backing away. "I didn't know you would pull such tricks, Edellina," she said, her voice shaking. "You said I could try to convince him to let us take a look. You never mentioned . . . *drugging* him. We need to put a stop to this before it's too late. Look at what we've done to poor Sir Jarome!" She gazed down at the sleeping protector guiltily.

Edellina's eyes flashed with anger as she clutched Elly's arm, nails digging into her skin. Elly yelped.

"Don't you dare bail on me now! You promised you'll do this with me!" Edellina snarled through gritted teeth.

"All right, all right! Just let go of me!" Elly rubbed the sore spot where Edellina had grabbed her. There were nail marks on her skin. Why was Edellina behaving this way?

Edellina took a deep breath, closed her eyes for a moment, then smiled sweetly at Elly. "Honestly, it's just a peek, Elly. You'll be the first elfling at school to ever lay eyes on the portal! Don't you think Kaelan would be impressed?"

Elly looked at the dome with longing eyes. *Just a peek.* Yes, then she would have something interesting and impressive to tell Kaelan. Bracing herself, she leaned towards Sir Jarome and carefully unhooked the golden key from his thick leather belt.

How was she going to explain her way out of this? She would get into so much trouble. But she'd worry about that later.

The key was cold and heavy in her hand. She had once heard that the key was fashioned to burn off a goblin's hand if one ever tried to seize it. Quivering, she walked towards the dome and stood before the giant white marble doors, with Edellina close behind.

Ellanor, this is dangerous. Don't do it.

Elly inserted the key into the lock, and turned. *Click.*

She pushed open the heavy doors. There was a long, steep flight of narrow stairs that seemed to lead into utter darkness. On either side of the stairway were two high, black stone walls lit by faintly glowing white stones. Gingerly, Elly walked down those stairs, with Edellina close behind.

At the end of the stairway was a brilliantly lit chamber, the white ceiling arching high above. Though it was dark outside, the interior of this chamber was brightly illuminated as though by invisible lights. Then Elly realized that the white marble was actually *glowing,* and there were mirrors lining the walls on either side of the chamber. It was so quiet she could hear her own heavy breathing.

Then she heard something. She stopped, straining her ears. She swore she could hear tiny voices whispering in Yahana. She caught a few words:

Two elves,
Both look fair.
Their eyes shine bright,
But one—what does she hide?

"Can you hear that?" she asked Edellina, who was walking behind her quietly.

Edellina shrugged. "No. There's nobody here but us. You must be imagining things."

On the opposite side of the dazzlingly-bright chamber was a massive black door. Elly walked towards it nervously, clenching and unclenching her hands.

The door was shut tight. It had no keyhole, no handles. Stumped, Elly stepped closer and peered at the ebony surface. Then she gasped.

Etched into the smooth black marble were Yahana runes, the ancient Elvish script that none other than elves could decipher:

Fools fear.
Deaf men hear.
Miser's offering.
Desired by goblins more than the world of the elfling.

"What does it say?" Edellina demanded. Elly was so preoccupied that she did not realize Edellina should have been able to read the ancient runes herself.

Elly narrowed her eyes in concentration. What do fools fear? What do deaf men hear? What do misers offer? What do goblins desire more than Alendria?

In a heartbeat, her eyes widened.

"*Nero,*" she whispered in Yahana. *Nothing.*

Immediately, the sleek door swooshed open. Elly heard Edellina's sharp intake of breath.

"Let's go," Edellina urged, steering Elly forward.

This second chamber was small and almost pitch-black. Elly looked up but could not tell how high the ceiling was; it was too dark. It felt strangely cool. Then she noticed a glowing blue light coming from the far end, about thirty feet away. She stopped in her tracks.

The portal!

It wasn't like anything she had imagined. There stood a massive round slab of a glowing dark blue, about ten times the size of Elly. It seemed to stand upright by itself, and it was made of some sort of gemstone, but none that she had ever seen before. When she got closer, she saw that the surface seemed iridescent, shimmering like water. The edges were lined with a silver glow.

Then she noticed a shaft of light beaming from high above; she looked up and saw the moon through an opening in the ceiling. The portal was literally being bathed in the moonlight.

She put her face close to the shimmering blue surface. It suddenly glowed a golden yellow, startling her. It was humming, emitting a comforting warmth that she welcomed in the cold of the dark chamber.

"Wow," she whispered. This was worth just taking a look. Now, they must turn back.

Ellanor! Behind you!

There was a hissing sound followed by a snarl.

Her heart lurched. "Did you hear that, Edellina?" she cried, swivelling around.

She screamed.

Standing before her was a hollow-cheeked creature with a small pointed face, its scaly skin an ugly mixture of green and grey, looking at her with cruel, lidless, blood-red eyes. Its back was stooped, long sinewy arms hanging low to the ground as it flexed its bony fingers. It let out a screeching laugh, baring jagged yellow teeth as a long, thin, blue tongue darted in and out.

Elly backed away in horror. "Who are you? What did you do with Edellina?" she cried, looking around wildly. This couldn't be happening!

The creature gave a mock sigh of frustration. It spoke in a strange, rattling voice. "Tsk, tsk. Ellanor, I *am Edellina*, you silly girl. Well, to be precise, *my* name is Gutz. You've been a great help to me, haven't you? I wouldn't have been able to come this far without you."

Elly stared at the creature in terror, the truth sinking in. She clutched at her heart. "You're a . . . you're a goblin?" Her face contorted with horror and revulsion.

Gutz threw its head back and laughed. "I suppose the contrast between me and pretty Edellina is quite significant, is it not?"

She staggered backwards. "You . . . you mean all these months . . . you've been masquerading as Edellina? But . . . but *how* . . . ?"

Gutz cackled, saliva oozing from its mouth. Elly shuddered, her skin crawling. "Oh, it did get very tiresome towards the end. You cannot imagine how tedious it is to pretend you like someone when you actually despise them. But I had to follow my orders. And now I've succeeded, have I not?"

"What do you want from me?" she whimpered, her eyes swivelling to the door thirty feet away. But the goblin was blocking her. There was no way out.

"I have much to do, and you are still of use to me," Gutz rasped, taking a step towards her.

"No! Get away from me!" she screamed, swinging her arms out in front of her like a mad person. She had not yet learned any proper defensive magic. Then she felt the warmth of the portal against her back, and she groaned.

The goblin laughed and shook its head, advancing towards her. "Poor, poor Elly. You shouldn't have been so trusting."

Then Gutz stopped in its tracks and swivelled around. Voices and footsteps were approaching. Incensed, Gutz snarled and lunged towards Elly with its long, spindly arm outstretched, bony hands grasping for her belt, its red eyes gleaming with malice and greed. Elly screamed.

Then Gutz let out a blood-curdling shriek that ricocheted through the dome. The Royan had burned its hands. Screaming in pain and rage, the goblin pushed Elly towards the portal, and it was about to follow. But the voices were now upon them, and Elly turned her head just in time to see the writhing goblin being held back by two pairs of hands.

Then a blinding silver light erupted as she plunged head-first into the portal, warmth enveloping her. Elly cried out, shielding her eyes with her arm.

"Elly!" cried a voice.

It was too late. She was taken away from the only home she knew.

CHAPTER FIVE
The Shoemaker and His Wife

SHE WAS THINKING HARD AS she looked down at a piece of paper scribbled with numbers and strange symbols. But they made no sense to her.

She was feeling very sad. But she didn't know why.

Then she was fiddling with something called a pencil case. It was a tattered green thing with loose threads sticking out. She needed to get something called an eraser.

As she opened up the pencil case, a little compact mirror popped up. It was cracked in the middle. She saw her reflection, somewhat blurry: the same rosy cheeks, bright-green eyes, the leaf-shaped ears. The short, curly black hair.

Who are you?

When Elly groggily opened her eyes, her cheek was pressed against hard wood.

Had she been dreaming? Who was that girl?

She got up and groaned, her head throbbing. She blinked and rubbed her bleary eyes. Her vision was spotted with stars. Everything around her looked oddly closed in, stuffy, and dark. How long had she been unconscious? She ached everywhere.

She closed her eyes and waited for the swirling sensation to pass. Then she caught a vague whiff of the invisibility perfume that lingered on her hair, reminding her of the events of the previous night.

The portal. Edellina.

Her pulse quickened as she thought about her friend. No, that creature was not her friend. The goblin infiltrator . . . Gutz. Was this all a bad dream? Tears filled her eyes and spilled over. She wiped them away angrily.

For a while she sat thinking in the dark, shivering, drowning in the blackness of despair and shock.

When she'd first brought Edellina back home to play, her parents were delighted that Elly had made a new friend. Mama in particular was glad that her daughter finally had a girlfriend. "Don't get me wrong, dear—you know I adore Aron. He's practically part of our family. But it's nice seeing you with another girl," Mama said with a smile. Everyone seemed to like Edellina, who was beautiful and charming. All except Marlow.

When Edellina tried to pet him for the first time, Marlow narrowed his eyes and retreated. "He can be a little moody; don't mind him," Elly hurriedly reassured Edellina, who merely shrugged her shoulders and walked away.

Elly felt sorely embarrassed. "You don't have to be so rude, Marlow!" she said crossly as she stalked away from her griffin.

She found Edellina in the hallway looking interestedly at the paintings on the walls. "If you don't mind, I'd like to take a look around. You do have a lovely home," she said sweetly, glancing around. Elly blushed at the compliment. Surely, the Three Flamingos would never say such a thing about her house, which was small and plain compared to their adorned mansions. She thought Edellina was so sweet.

She couldn't have been more wrong. The friendship with Edellina had been a lie.

Elly had never even met Edellina's family. She simply believed everything Edellina told her—all lies, she now realized. In reality, she hadn't really known much about Edellina at all.

But Marlow must have sensed something about Edellina. How could she have been so easily fooled by the goblin all along? Why didn't the other elves sense anything?

She took a deep, shuddering breath to quiet her thudding heart.

At least I've still got Aron, she thought. *As long as Aron is my one true friend, I can bear it.*

She was burning with questions. What did the goblin want with her? Why did it try to take her Royan and push her through the portal?

But there was nobody to answer her.

Then she gasped. The others must be warned about the goblin masquerading as Edellina! Gutz might try to hurt them!

But she slumped back, dropping her head into her hands. She didn't even know where she was right now. If she had indeed fallen through the portal, then she must be in . . .

Gaya. The human realm.

Her heart sank with dread.

It was then she realized that there was a soft pulsating blue light glowing near her. She turned and stared. There was something nestled in a pile of woolly fabrics. She looked closer. It was a slab of stone perched on some sort of stand. Her eyes widened in recognition.

Carved into the strange glowing slab was something that resembled the Tree of Alendria.

Cautiously, she put a palm up close to the surface. It seemed to radiate a gentle warmth. The blue light began growing dimmer, and then went out altogether. As the warmth dissipated, Elly started shivering in the cold. She gazed at the slab. Was this how she had crossed over? Was this the portal? But it looked so small compared to the one in Alendria.

Wrapping her arms around herself, she surveyed the surroundings. She had the odd sensation that she was in some sort of cramped, musty-smelling space. There was a sliver of light in front of her, and it took her a long time to realize it was like some sort of gigantic door that was ajar, as though somebody had tried to close it in a hurry. Slowly, she crawled forward and peeked through the gap.

There was a faint light coming from a strange-looking sun supported by a pillar—or was that the moon? Confused, she blinked, and then it finally registered: It was a huge table lamp near a window, partially covered by drawn curtains. She saw some large, dark shadows that for a moment frightened her. Were they cast by giants? Those dark, hulking shapes turned out to be furniture of sorts, only it was massive: a rocking chair, next to which was a straw basket containing several balls of blue wool; a low table, on top of which was a steaming cup of tea. She sniffed and smelled something like leather mingled with other unfamiliar scents.

Why did everything look so enormous here? Then it finally dawned on Elly that in Gaya, she was a hundredth her usual size. She had read that inter-realm teleporting could do funny things to your size. For all she knew, a human would look like a giant in Alendria. The thought made her shudder.

Then she heard a snarling noise and froze in terror. The goblin flashed across her mind, making her stomach turn.

"What is it, Snowy? Are you hunting down mice again?" a gentle voice chided affectionately.

Then without warning, the doors of the cupboard swung wide open. Gasping, Elly lost her balance and fell backwards. "Ow!" she cried, rubbing the sore spot on her bottom.

Then she looked up, right into the face of an old lady with bleary brown eyes and tousled silver hair tied into a careless bun. Those eyes focused on Elly and widened, by turns in surprise, confusion, then shock. There was a plump black cat at her feet, its round yellow eyes narrowing into slits as it hissed at the strange green-eyed creature in the cupboard.

Elly cried out and jumped to her feet, panic surging through her like electricity. The old lady put a hand over her mouth—and let out a hair-raising scream.

"Horace!" she yelled at the top of her lungs.

Terrified, Elly stumbled as she took flight. Her arm knocked hard against the slab. It lurched out of the woolly fabrics and slid over the smooth wood, teetered on the edge, and dropped onto the cold, hard floor beneath with a resounding crack.

She darted past the old lady's head, brushing against wisps of silver hair. Snowy leapt up and took a swipe at Elly, but luckily she was too swift. Elly flew up and looked around frantically before hurtling towards the chandelier suspended from the high ceiling. Shaking, and oblivious of the old cobwebs spread like a blanket over the dusty brass rungs, she clung on and peered down from a rather great height, swinging lightly back and forth. The old, rickety chandelier groaned from the unfamiliar weight of her, light as she was.

Then heavy footfalls approached. The door to the room creaked open, and there emerged a tall, pot-bellied man with a balding head and snow-white beard. His old suede boots scraped against the worn wooden floor as he trudged towards his wife. He sounded agitated. "What is it now, Miriam?" he grumbled. "I was just working on a new pair of shoes!" Then he noticed her staring open-mouthed at the chandelier, and glowered.

"Oh, for goodness' sake, don't tell me you need me to kill another bloomin' cockroach for you!" he exclaimed. "You know how to use those bug sprays by now, don't you?"

Before he turned away to grab the can of Roach Terminator from the kitchen cupboard, his wife clutched at his arm.

"N-n-not a flying roach this time, Horace!" she stuttered, her eyes wild. She hesitated, then leaned close to him and whispered hoarsely, "I think . . . I think your grandfather was telling the truth about . . . about . . . those creatures." With a shaking finger, she pointed up towards the swinging chandelier.

Horace blinked. "Do you mean," he began slowly, looking up at the chandelier, "there's . . . there's something up there?" Then he caught sight of tiny, pale, slender limbs clutching onto the brass rungs, a purple dress, a shock of long black hair, small pointy ears, and two bright green dots blinking fearfully down at them.

He staggered. "Oh, dear Lord!" he croaked. Was he seeing right? Had he drunk too much brandy? No, that couldn't be it. Miriam and that snooty cat could see the . . . creature, too.

Long ago, when Horace was a young lad, his grandfather, the legendary shoemaker Lawrence Cobble, had recounted some strange events that took place long before Horace was even born. The business was doing so poorly that he and his wife were living on stale bread and were down to their last piece of leather. His rags to riches tale, retold countless times, spread so far and wide that it eventually attracted the interest of two educated German brothers (he couldn't remember whether they were surnamed Green or Grum), who were in the process of compiling a book of folk stories. They paid the famous shoemaker a visit, and shortly afterward, Lawrence Cobble's tale was published in their thick book.

Back then, naive and eager to believe in magic, Horace had listened with undivided attention. But all the grown-ups thought Lawrence Cobble must have been missing a few marbles with all that strange talk about . . . elves.

1930s, London

The first time Horace listened to the tale, he was about to go to bed after a hearty Christmas Eve meal.

"I had to write it all down in my journal, lest my memory fail me!" said Grandfather Cobble as he settled himself comfortably into the rocking chair next to the bed, where young Horace was already nicely tucked up, his eyelids heavy. He had asked for a bedtime story, and had little idea what was in store.

"Your Grandmother Polly and I had fallen on hard times. Our larder was almost empty and business was difficult everywhere, my lad, what with the dismal economy, the flu epidemic, and all the misfortunes that came with the aftermath of the war. By that time, we had sent our little Richard—your father—to relatives in Scotland, for they were doing much better than we were. My sister Elizabeth had taken pity on Richard's welfare, God bless her kind soul. We were down to our very last piece of leather, and most needn't have bothered. Grandmother Polly and I were barely surviving, and we were losing hope. I took it as my final duty to craft a fine pair of shoes with what we had left. I prayed that afterwards we could pass away peacefully in each other's arms as we both died of hunger." He had tears in his eyes as he recalled the dark days. "But that night I was too exhausted to stay up and work, so I retired to bed before midnight.

"The good Lord must have taken pity on us. The next morning, upon my worktable was the most exquisite pair of shoes I had ever seen. The craftsmanship was simply flawless, my dear boy. I was delighted to lay eyes on such a masterpiece; yet I was envious at the same time. *Who could have made such exquisite shoes*, I wondered?"

At this, he paused to take a puff on his pipe. Horace was fighting to keep his eyes open as his grandfather resumed.

"There was something magical about those shoes. Of course they were, because they were made by magical creatures, though we didn't know it at the time.

"There was no way my run-down little shop could've ever attracted the attention of wealthy pedestrians. But those shoes . . . oh my, you should have seen them! Once I put them out in the window display, my whole shop seemed to light up! Suddenly, I was getting wealthy customers coming in asking to try on the shoes. It was like they had been bewitched. They were even willing to pay five times the usual amount! So I sold those shoes to the highest bidder, and earned enough to buy plenty more leather and put some fresh food on the table. That very night, your grandmother and I cried over our first shepherd's pie in two years.

"Day after day, the same thing happened. I would wake up in the morning to more and more pairs of beautifully crafted shoes on the worktable. Over the course of several months, I went from pauper to rich shoemaker. A real rags-to-riches story. Who had ever heard of such a thing—a rich cobbler!" He chuckled and leaned back in his rocking chair.

Horace, his eyes now wide open, sat up in bed. "What happened next, Grandpa?" he asked eagerly. That summer, he had been trying to earn extra pocket money. He wanted to become rich, too.

"We were preparing to have Richard come back to live with us. But before his return, we wanted to find out once and for all who our wonderful benefactors were. We were in their debt, and we wanted to thank them properly. So one night, we decided to stay up and do some spying."

He stretched out his long legs, cringing as his joints cracked.

"In my workshop was a little storage space at the back where I kept old tools. We hid there, behind the curtain. It was dark. The moonlight streamed through the windows. Your grandmother was knitting—oh yes, she could have knitted with her eyes closed—and I was dozing off.

"It must have been long past midnight when Polly shook me by the shoulder. 'Wake up!' she whispered, like she had seen a ghost. 'Tell me I'm not imagining this!' I was still groggy from sleep. I peeked through the gap between the curtains. And I was sure at that moment that my heart had stopped.

"In the moonlight, we saw two little creatures on the worktable. At first it was hard to watch them, because they were moving about so swiftly that their arms and legs at times became a blur. When they stopped for a moment or two, I could see them more clearly. They were about the size of a teaspoon, fair-haired, and very slender, and they seemed to be clad in white summer garments, though it was the middle of January and freezing. I could not tell whether they were male or female. I thought they were both going about things silently, but as I listened more closely, I could make out a soft humming. I realized they were actually singing a rather pretty song, but not in any language I could understand.

"So there we were, both hunched up like thieves in the night, afraid to breathe or move an inch. They appeared to see remarkably well in the dark. By the time they were almost done, dawn was near, and Polly and I still could not take our eyes off them.

"Finally, they stretched like cats and sort of danced about a little, before leaping up onto the cabinet where we kept odds and ends. They literally ran into the blue stone and disappeared.

"The *blue stone*—that's what I called the strange slab of stone that would change from yellow to blue during the day, depending on where it was placed in the sunlight. It was actually rather beautiful, with something like a tree etched into it. We used it as a paperweight from time to time. I was once sorely tempted to sell it. We needed the money, but thankfully, your Grandmother stopped me.

"'You can't sell a family heirloom!' Polly cried. It was something that my grandfather had come into possession of during his business travels in the tea trade, somewhere exotic in the Caribbean. Some old woman at the market had insisted on giving it to him for good luck. So he passed it down to my father, who then passed it on to me. After those two little creatures leapt into that blue stone and vanished, Polly and I realized that the blue stone was magical, must be some sort of portal for them to cross over from their world."

He cleared his throat and took another puff on his pipe.

"We felt such gratitude towards those two creatures. How could we thank them? Polly had a good idea. 'Didn't you see those flimsy things they were wearing? In weather like this, they should be wearing much warmer garments,' she said in a disapproving tone.

"Their tiny size didn't deter her. She was accustomed to making dainty clothes for those elegant dolls that get sold in the fancy little toy shops downtown.

"Anyway, Polly set to work that very morning, despite having barely slept a wink the previous night. She sewed for hours and hours, stopping only to take a few bites for lunch and supper. Your grandmother was the most wonderful seamstress. Even when we were so poor we couldn't afford to buy any meat, she would find a way to make me the warmest sweaters for the bitterly cold months. She had such nimble fingers, my Polly.

"By midnight, she had made three lovely outfits for each, six in total. You should have seen them! Three coats with matching cardigans and scarves, three shirts, three pairs of breeches, and even socks! Such delicate, fine clothes they were, in green, blue, and yellow. We carefully laid out the outfits on the worktable. Like the previous night, we hid in the storage space and waited.

"Once again, I dozed off and fell asleep with one side of my face pressed up against the wall. Polly was knitting again, this time a blue sweater of a complicated pattern for me. By that time, we could have easily afforded to buy new clothes, but she still insisted on making them.

"It was dark, and the moon was out, bright and round like a shiny penny. This time, I got woken up when Polly accidentally stepped on my foot; she was so excited to see the little creatures again! We both peeked through the curtains, and sure enough, the two little angels were there at the worktable. But this time, instead of getting down to work with their tools, they began laughing and clapping their hands. They tried on the new clothes with such glee, you would have thought they had never been given such fine clothes to wear. They sang and danced about for a while, such sweet little voices they had. I cannot describe to you how delightful it was to simply watch them.

"Then suddenly both of them turned in our direction and waved, as though they had known all along we had been watching them! Your Grandmother Polly cried out, 'Wait! Please don't go! We want to thank you. Thank you for everything you have done for us. Who are you?'

"Their sweet voices rang out like little bells. We couldn't quite make out what they were saying, but we did hear one word quite clearly as they pointed to themselves: 'elves'. That was the first time we had ever come across such a word. They bowed in farewell, and then they leapt towards the blue stone and were gone.

"That was the last we saw of the elves. For many days after that, I kept the blue stone beside me on the worktable, hoping they would emerge from it and say hello. Whatever magic they'd left behind, they made sure that we never had to worry about food or money ever again."

Indeed, the burgeoning business made the shoemaker and his wife rich and renowned in London. Thankful for their good fortune, they became philanthropists, donating much of their wealth to the poor and needy. Lawrence Cobble taught his trade to his son Richard, who then taught it to his son Horace.

But Horace, having inherited the house and business from his father, never acquired quite the same love for shoemaking as his predecessors. Elves were never mentioned again after Lawrence Cobble passed away peacefully in his sleep at the ripe old age of ninety-eight. By then, Horace was a disillusioned young man, convinced that his Grandfather had not been quite right in the head.

～

As Horace stared up at the black-haired and green-eyed creature clinging onto his (shamefully dusty) chandelier, he came to the uncomfortable realization that he had wrongfully labelled his Grandfather as a fruit loop.

All along, Grandfather had been telling the truth.

Before he died, Lawrence Cobble bequeathed to Horace the blue stone. "Please take care of this, my boy. The elves used to come through this blue stone from wherever they lived. One day, they might return!"

But by then, Horace had grown tired of his grandfather's crazy tale. The blue stone wasn't encrusted with gold or diamonds; the so-called heirloom looked to be nothing more than a shabby slab of rock. So it got relegated to an old broom cupboard, and for many years Horace forgot all about it. Miriam once asked him to put it away in a safe place. "It is a family heirloom, after all, regardless whether your grandfather was in his right mind or not," she admonished. Horace scoffed and ignored her. "Use it as a paper weight, for all I care!" he snapped.

Horace now swivelled around towards the broom cupboard, and groaned in disbelief at the sight of the blue stone, cracked cleanly in two on the wooden floor. It had turned a dull grey.

Miriam followed his gaze nervously, clutching the front of her floral housecoat. She almost said, "I told you so!" but promptly swallowed back the words. Horace did not like to be corrected.

He gazed at the broken stone regretfully. He would have to deal with it later. Clearing his throat again, he looked up at the chandelier. "H-hello, there? Please don't be afraid, we won't hurt you," he called, trying to adopt a soothing voice that came so easily to his wife whenever she spoke to her snooty cat. Snowy adored Miriam, but treated Horace like he didn't exist.

The chandelier had by now stopped swinging, and Elly wasn't trembling so much. She peered down at the face of the talking man. He looked a little flustered, but otherwise he looked harmless enough. She glanced at the lady, who looked even more frightened than Elly felt. The black cat was glowering up at her with its yellow eyes, unmoving.

His voice shaking slightly, Horace asked, "Excuse me, but are you . . . are you an . . . an elf?" He cringed, hardly able to believe how preposterous he sounded.

Elly was surprised. How did he know about elves? Slowly, she nodded. "Yes, I am an elf from Alendria," she called out. Horace and Miriam both jumped at the sound of her clear voice, not quite expecting her to speak in a way they would understand. Horace swallowed nervously, hoping the elf would not unleash any magic on them. He would have to keep her as calm as possible. It wouldn't bode well for them if she felt threatened.

"My Grandfather had an . . . encounter with two of your kind, long ago. He was a shoemaker, the best in town. But he and his wife fell on hard times, and they would've starved to death if he didn't get help from . . . from your people. We didn't believe him back then. But now that I see you, I wish I had. Please don't be afraid of us. We will not hurt you."

Elly hesitated. Shoemaker? She had read about this in *A History of the Dealings between Elves and Humans*. Apparently, two rogue elves who were particularly gifted in the crafts decided to "interfere" with the affairs of two humans. The two elves, whose identities remained confidential, had been teleporting back and forth between the human realm and Alendria when they chanced upon a poor shoemaker and his wife, and had taken pity on them.

Elly had always secretly admired those two elves, and wondered who they were. If what this man was saying was true, then maybe it would be harmless to reveal herself to them.

She steeled herself. "Excuse me, but what is this place? Where am I?" she asked tentatively. Though she knew she had passed into the human realm, she had no idea where she was exactly.

Horace and Miriam exchanged surprised looks. "You are in London, Great Britain. To be precise, you are presently in the Cobble household on Number Eight, Adelaide Drive, in the suburb of Edgware."

Elly gawped. She was in London? This was on her list of must-see places in the human realm, along with many others.

She was still a little afraid, but the man and the lady really did not look malicious. They were not goblins. Or could they be imposters? Elly just couldn't be sure anymore . . . Edellina had made sure of that.

But she would have to take the plunge. There was no other way.

She took a deep breath and slowly stood up on the chandelier. Horace could see that even at her full height, she was as tiny as a teaspoon. Then she descended slowly, floating in mid-air—then shot down and landed soundlessly on the low table where the cup of tea had long ago grown cold.

Horace looked at Miriam uncertainly. *Men can be so full of it,* she thought disdainfully. *They can get all prideful and controlling, but sometimes they can be so clueless.* She smiled warmly at Elly, who was staring up at them from the coffee table. Slowly, she walked up and squatted, so that her eyes were level with the little green ones. She gasped, pressing her hands together in delight.

"Oh, my!" she said softly, resisting the urge to cradle the small creature in her hands. "You are so beautiful!"

Elly blushed. Then she bowed. "My name is Ellanor Celendis. But everyone calls me Elly. Very pleased to meet you." Her voice reminded Miriam of jingling bells.

"Oh, we are very pleased to meet you, too! Ellanor is such a pretty name. Well, Elly, I am Miriam, and this is Horace." She gestured over to her speechless husband, who suddenly looked like a shy schoolboy. Horace closed his eyes, half wondering if he was actually hallucinating.

Miriam turned to grab something from a table behind her. Gently, she plopped a red grape and a small cup of water next to Elly. "Here, please have something to eat and drink. Don't be afraid—we just want to talk."

It then occurred to Elly that she was famished. Smiling gratefully, she reached out a hand towards the grape when suddenly there was a menacing snarl. Horace cried, "No, you silly cat!"

It all happened too quickly. Snowy had pounced on the table in front of Elly, her fangs bared, ready to strike.

"Don't you dare come between us!" hissed the jealous cat, taking a vicious swipe at Elly. Miriam screamed in horror.

But by then, Elly had already hurtled out of the open window and disappeared.

CHAPTER SIX
Greymore and Hobbes

ELLY CRIED OUT AS SHE plunged into the icy cold. Back home in Evergreen City, weather was always pleasantly warm, a perpetual spring. This sub-zero temperature pricked her like a thousand needles.

She darted upward, her heart hammering madly. She had just narrowly escaped that cat's clutches. If she had reacted a second too late, she would've been badly hurt. She could've died! She wheeled around and around, frantically searching for somewhere to hide.

She was surrounded by a grey landscape of drab-looking buildings, where a thick bank of clouds hung over the horizon. She spotted a patch of green in the distance, and her heart lifted. It was like stumbling upon an oasis in the desert. Trees! She drew a deep breath and flew as fast as she could, hurtled towards the tallest elm tree, darted to the base of the trunk, and ducked behind some tall blades of grass. She couldn't risk being seen by any humans, not looking like this.

Elly could hear voices nearby. Someone cried out, "Mummy, a giant purple butterfly just landed behind that tree! I want to go see!" Her heart almost jumped out as she clutched at the tree trunk in blind fear. Footsteps were approaching. She squeezed her eyes shut. *Please don't, please don't.*

Then an impatient voice rang out. "We don't have time, Jimmy. Let's *go*; otherwise we'll miss the bus!" There were hurried footsteps, then they faded away. The silence that followed was punctuated by low voices murmuring in the distance, and the creaking of a swing nearby.

She wrapped her arms around herself and realized she was shivering uncontrollably. It was *freezing*. "Oh, what should I do now?" she whispered, wringing her hands in desperation. Her breath was turning to steam in the chill air.

Ellanor, what ever will you do?

Startled, she gasped and swivelled around. It was that same voice in her head, the one that had spoken to her when she was in the Celestan Forest.

Then she realized where the voice had come from. How could she have missed it?

"Is . . . is that you, Greymore?" she whispered, touching the book on her belt. She hadn't realized her Royan had been trying to talk to her all along! She had never spoken to a Royan before.

Greymore emitted a low rumble, like a reproach. *So—finally you are ready to listen to me.*

Elly bowed her head in apology. *I'm sorry, Greymore. I didn't realize it was you talking to me back in the Celestan Forest.*

Regardless, you did not want to listen. You knew you were doing something wrong, but you went ahead with it anyway.

Elly's silence was heavy with regret. Greymore was right. She had let curiosity get the better of her. She had let Edellina . . . that wretched goblin . . . goad her on. It was her own fault.

Ellanor, we are now in Gaya, the human realm. Elflings are forbidden here.

She winced. *I know that! I didn't mean for this to happen. Edellina wasn't a friend! She was a goblin! Oh, Greymore . . .*

She began to cry. She had gone behind her parents' backs and snuck out in the middle of the night. She had deceived Sir Jarome, who had let down his guard because he'd trusted her. She had selfishly given in to her curiosity without regard for the consequences. If only she hadn't been so desperate to impress a false friend. If only she hadn't been so weak and foolish.

And now, everyone she cared about could be in danger because of what she had set into motion.

Greymore had fallen silent at Elly's heartrending sobs. From the moment Edellina had tried to touch him at Elly's birthday party, he had sensed there was something *unwholesome* about that girl. The fact that she was a goblin in disguise was beyond disturbing. To his knowledge, this sort of infiltration had never occurred in Alendria before.

But Greymore spared Elly this piece of information. Shame and guilt had already put her in bad enough shape.

Elly was so cold her lips were turning blue, and she could barely feel her fingers. "Please. I just want to go home," she croaked. She had never been away from Alendria, nor Evergreen City for that matter. She had always wanted to see what the human realm was like, but not this way.

Ellanor, the portal through which you came is damaged. For you to return to Alendria, the portal must be repaired.

Elly closed her eyes in disbelief. *No, that cannot be. Isn't the portal supposed to be swathed in protective unbreakable spells if it's something so . . . so important? How could it have broken so easily?*

She placed one hand on her Royan. The leather was warm to the touch, which was comforting in this merciless cold. *Yes, the portal was supposed to be protected. But over the years, it diminished while it was left to collect dust in Horace Cobble's broom cupboard. The portal is not a lifeless slab of stone, Ellanor. The protective magic that it was originally swathed in must have worn off as it slowly diminished. But once the portal realizes how much it is still valued, it will regenerate.*

Elly groaned. As if she wasn't already in enough trouble . . . and now she had to deal with this as well? *Greymore, how can the portal be repaired? What do I need to do?*

The portal is made of an extremely rare substance called blue amber, which is produced in only one place in Gaya. Listen carefully. You must not only find genuine blue amber, but it must be of the purest grade that has been imbued with magic. If it is the right type of blue amber, it will be assimilated into the broken portal, and it shall become whole again.

Elly felt dizzy just from listening. *Blue amber? Purest grade? Magic imbued?* She had no idea what he was talking about.

Greymore continued. *This particular type of blue amber was produced by a special tree that once stood at the peak of a volcanic mountain named Mount Organoth, once the tallest mountain in Gaya. Because it was of the purest grade, the blue amber was used to forge the portals. This was done by one of the Four Guardians many ages ago. He was the most gifted alchemist out of all the guardians, and he was given the task of forging the two portals that connect Alendria and Gaya. He imbued the blue amber with his powers, and forged the portals on Mount Organoth. Shortly afterwards there was an earthquake, and the residual blue amber left over from the forging of the portals was scattered over the land. Those bits of blue amber were then found and taken by the local inhabitants, who called them Organoth blue amber in their own language. They did not know it is at least a hundred times more precious than diamonds.*

Her head was spinning. This was the first time she'd ever heard of the Four Guardians. At that moment, she felt terribly small in this vast world filled with so many things she had yet to see and find out.

Understanding who the Guardians are is not pertinent to our immediate problem, Ellanor. You shall find out about them in due time. For now, focus on your task.

Elly sighed. *All right, so what did those people do with the Organoth blue amber?*

The local inhabitants who once dwelt in the land of Mount Organoth were simple farmers and shepherds who were skilled in the crafts of pottery and jewellery making. They used the Organoth blue amber in the making of these crafts, totally oblivious of the sacred, magical properties of the amber. Bear in mind, Ellanor, much time has passed since then, and many of those crafts are now lost to us. But some have survived to this day. Organoth blue amber can still be found.

Elly shook her head, bewildered. *But how will I know it's Organoth blue amber? I mean, how can I differentiate it from ordinary blue amber?*

Greymore rumbled approvingly. *Good question. You are listening well. Organoth blue amber looks identical to ordinary blue amber. But there is one thing that sets them apart. Organoth blue amber responds to life, Ellanor. Just as it appears golden-yellow when put up against sunlight, Organoth blue amber will glow a golden yellow when you breathe on it.*

She recalled the portal back in Alendria turning a golden yellow when she stood so close to it that she breathed on it.

She frowned and bit her lip. She had a dreadful feeling this was not going to be easy at all. *But where is this Mount Organoth?*

Over thousands of years, the geography of the land has changed. Mount Organoth is no longer found on any map known to humans. The land now goes by another name, one which I do not know. You must do some investigating yourself and find out where Organoth blue amber could have come from, Ellanor. Names of places may change, but deep roots are not easily touched by the tides of time. What used to be Mount Organoth may have survived to some degree.

Elly groaned, fear and anxiety gripping her. *Stop being so cryptic, Greymore! Gaya is enormous, and this is urgent! I don't even know where to begin. Please, surely you can just tell me where to find it? We can't waste any time. I need to get home!*

Greymore emitted such a deep, disapproving rumble that she jumped. *Ellanor, I cannot simply give you all the answers.*

Elly squeezed her eyes shut. *You expect me to find this . . . this Organoth blue amber by myself? Greymore, I'm sure Grandpapa and everyone else wants me to get home as soon as possible. Why don't you just tell me exactly how I can get home?*

Ellanor, I may possess much wisdom as a Royan of Alendria, but I am not a fortune teller, and I am not an instruction manual that lines out every step of the way for you. You have to get out there and do the work, too. I am also limited in what I know about the human realm. I know what the portal is made of, and where it came from, but I do not have information on how it works. The connection that I share with the Tree has been greatly diminished now that we are cut off from Alendria. Also, it appears that much information related to the human realm was removed from the intelligence repository of the Tree when the portal was sealed over a hundred years ago, including information about how the portal works, possibly to prevent elves like you from crossing over. Hence, this is all I can tell you.

Elly sank down to her knees in despair. She sure was in deep, deep trouble.

Then there was a rustling behind her. She froze and slowly turned around.

There in the grass stood a rotund, fat-cheeked hamster with ginger-brown fur. He looked dishevelled and out of breath, as though he had been running. He had fixed his large black eyes on Elly, baffled.

Then the hamster squeaked and scratched behind one ear. "Well! What do we have here?" he exclaimed in a small, high-pitched voice. "You look like a human, but why on earth are you so tiny?"

Elly looked at the hamster warily. She supposed he looked harmless. So she smiled and bowed. "Hello, Mr Hamster," she said politely, as though talking to hamsters was the most normal thing. "My name is Ellanor, but everyone calls me Elly. The reason I'm so tiny is because I'm not a human. I am an elf from Alendria. It is nice to meet you."

You can imagine the hamster's shock when he realized Elly had actually understood what he was saying. Humans never understood him, of course—they just liked feeding and stroking him, and he was more than happy with that arrangement. What was even stranger was that he could understand *every single word* she was saying. Whenever humans talked, he couldn't understand any of their gibberish.

It took the hamster some moments to master himself. Then he straightened and returned the bow clumsily. "It is a pleasure to meet you, Elly the elf! My name is Hobbes, and I am lost."

Hobbes scrambled over to Elly and recounted what had transpired that morning.

Master was the kindest little boy, and Hobbes just adored him. For as long as Hobbes could remember, he had been living in a green-lidded plastic cage, where he enjoyed his days eating his favourite snacks, sleeping in his little pumpkin house, and running on the treadmill whenever he fancied some legwork. Ah, that was the life!

Master loved playing with Hobbes, and every Friday and Saturday he would take Hobbes to the neighbourhood park, where he would read a book on the swing while he petted the hamster on his lap. But that particular Friday morning, Master wasn't home; he had gone off somewhere the previous night. His mother had taken Hobbes to the park instead.

Hobbes belched and rubbed his swollen tummy; he'd had far too much to eat. "We were having such a grand time! She fed me my favourite snacks, took me out of the cage, and petted me for a long time while she sat on the swing, throwing bread pellets to those fat pigeons. She looked a little sad, though. Then she put me back in the food bowl, filled to the brim with yoghurt cookies. I was so happy! The next thing I knew, she had vanished. I was all by my lonesome."

He sniffled and shook his head sorrowfully. "She must've made a mistake . . . must've slipped her mind somehow."

Elly felt very sorry for him. "Don't be too sad, Mr Hobbes. She's probably going to come look for you soon." She smiled sympathetically and patted his back.

She didn't have the heart to tell him that he may very well have been . . . *abandoned.*

Back in Alendria, she had read about such things happening in the human realm. It was not uncommon for animals to be abandoned by their masters. Elly found this shocking. Such things were unheard of back home. In Alendria, elves and animals shared an unspoken bond and lived alongside each other peacefully. She could not imagine abandoning Marlow. No matter how stubborn he got at times, he was fiercely loyal to her, and she trusted him with her life. He was part of their family.

Elly then noticed that Hobbes had fallen quiet. She looked at him, and saw that the hamster was trembling like a leaf and staring past her with bulging eyes. She swivelled around and gulped—about ten feet away stood a large black and brown dog, growling and glaring at them with bared fangs, ready to pounce.

Hobbes was generally afraid of cats and dogs, but most of all hungry German shepherds. His teeth chattered as he stared helplessly.

Elly stretched out her hand to him. "Hurry! We'll hide up the tree!" she urged. Before the panic-stricken hamster could respond, Elly grabbed him by one of his paws and shot up towards the branches. At that moment, the German shepherd leapt forward with a vicious snarl. Hobbes was squealing like a piglet, writhing in abject terror as Elly tried to keep her grip on him.

The dog halted at the base of the tree and barked with frightening ferocity. Thankfully, the branches offered plenty of leafy coverage to conceal two small creatures. The canine's master, a young man with dark dreadlocks and wearing bright orange sneakers, cupped a hand over his mobile phone and glared at his dog, wondering what all the ruckus was about. "Get back here, Borris!" he called. He was trying to convince his girlfriend on the phone that he hadn't partied at the pub last night, but it wasn't going very well.

Borris ignored him and barked incessantly.

Now that they were safely out of reach, Elly breathed a sigh of relief as she settled carefully on a sturdy branch. Hobbes had almost passed out from fright.

The man was calling to his dog again. "You silly chap, stop barking up the wrong tree! The police will come and take you away for causing such a racket! Come, let's get going!" There were stomping footsteps followed by some whimpering; then the barking subsided. Borris had given up and trotted away with his master, whose girlfriend had moments ago angrily hung up on him.

A family of ladybugs on a leaf nearby regarded Elly and Hobbes warily. The terrified hamster clung to the branch as he gazed at Elly in fear and wonder. "Y-you c-can fly!" he stuttered. But then again, she wasn't really human. What did she say she was again? He cocked his head and looked at her quizzically. "But where are your wings?"

Elly blinked, then laughed for the first time since she had crossed over. The hamster had shaken her out of her despondency. She smiled at him. "Back home in my world, *everyone* can fly, except newborn elflings. Elves can fly from the time we start to walk, at two months old. Most of the animals can fly, too. I have a griffin that flies as fast as the wind! I wish you could meet him," she said wistfully. Her heart ached as she thought of Marlow and her family.

Then it suddenly dawned on her that, despite the circumstances, she was actually having a *real* adventure, not the pretend games she often played with Aron back home. She felt a tingling sensation in her fingertips; her heart was beating fast, and though she was still afraid, especially for her family, she also felt something else—a strange, unfamiliar sense of exhilaration.

Greymore rumbled. *What you're feeling, Ellanor—that's one of the true markers of an explorer. Deep down, you are an adventurer. Despite your shyness and your self-doubt, you have the heart of a true explorer. Though right now you are terrified, part of you recognises this as an adventure. Am I right?*

Elly frowned. *Yes, that may be true. But right now, I would give everything to make sure my family . . . and Aron . . . are safe.*

Then she felt a tug on her dress. Hobbes had gingerly put a paw on her skirt. "What should we do now?" he squeaked, praying that birds wouldn't suddenly swoop down and whisk him away.

Ellanor, you must first disguise yourself if you don't want to attract undesired attention. You must blend in and transform into human proportions so that we can make our eventual return home less cumbersome. Remember to keep your hair down so that your ears are concealed.

Elly self-consciously tugged her long hair and ruffled it. She hadn't thought about her leaf-shaped ears . . .

Now, open me up.

Elly did as Greymore said: she opened up her Royan; and there, on a crisp white page, was a red balloon.

Inflate this! Greymore commanded.

"They never told me you would be so bossy," she mumbled. Then she drew in a deep breath, and with a mighty huff she expelled all the air she had from her lungs into the balloon. There was a popping sound.

Hobbes' mouth dropped open. With every expelled breath, Elly grew bigger and bigger and bigger.

After several moments, Elly found herself gazing down at the hamster, who now looked so small he could fit into the palm of her hand! She was now so big that she was straddling the branch, which didn't look so sturdy anymore. She better get off before it broke under her weight.

Hobbes fell back on his bottom in terror and shrank from her. At that size, Elly didn't look so harmless.

But she smiled down at him. "Mr Hobbes, I will not hurt you! I am sorry you are lost, just like me. I would very much like your company. Would you please join me? We shall go on an adventure!" She bent down and cupped her hands.

Hobbes gaped at her. He was not fond of the outdoors, and he disliked anything remotely adventurous. He just wanted things to go back to the way they were, before he had been left behind by Mother. He missed Master so very much.

But he had nowhere to go. He didn't know how to get home by himself. He might as well go off with this strange girl as get eaten by predators that were absolutely *everywhere* . . . snakes, birds, dogs, cats, squirrels . . . He shuddered.

So Hobbes nodded reluctantly. "Alrighty, then!" He scrambled up onto Elly's cupped hands, and she put him carefully inside her right pocket. He was relieved to find that it was deep and rather cosy. He twisted this way and that, and finally nestled into a comfortable position.

Elly was about to fly down the tree when her Royan gave a mighty tremble, startling her.

No flying, Ellanor! You are now supposed to behave like a human. Do what a human would do.

"Oops! Sorry." Smiling sheepishly, Elly swiftly clambered down the tree, agile as a cat. Once she reached the ground, she surveyed her surroundings carefully.

She was in some sort of grassy clearing, surrounded by a white picket fence, where a ghostly white mist hovered. There were swings, a slide, and a couple of wooden tables and benches. Near the swings was a wooden sign shaped like a log, with Berry Grove Park engraved on it in fading gold lettering.

There was nobody around. It was a Friday morning, well past eight o'clock; children had gone off to school, adults to work. Several chubby pigeons were waddling about on the sodden grass looking for food morsels.

She looked around, stumped. She was officially lost.

Where should I go?

You need to decide, Ellanor. After all, you are an aspiring explorer. Trust your instincts.

She grimaced. *My instincts? A whole lot of good that did me. I got completely fooled by the goblin. I don't think I'm qualified to use my instincts.*

You have learned from your experience with Edellina, have you not? With hardship and pain come growth and gain. Life is not about avoiding the storm, Ellanor, but learning how to dance in it. It's the little failures and pitfalls in life that can help you grow. Uses all your senses. You will know what to do.

But she was so afraid. *I don't trust myself, Greymore. Not after what happened with Edellina.*

When you were with Edellina, you were not listening to your instincts. You knew there was something wrong, but you did not quiet your mind and listen to your conscience. Edellina—the goblin—took advantage of your trust, your naivety, your childish curiosity. A part of you didn't want to believe Edellina would deliberately lead you to danger, because true friends would not do that.

Elly fell silent as she thought about what Greymore said. It was true. She had wanted to trust Edellina with all her heart, because she wanted to believe Edellina was her true friend.

She sighed. *All right, I will give this a try.*

Elly closed her eyes and clasped her hands together in prayer. "Freya, please look over me and help me see things with clarity," she whispered. She breathed slowly and deeply. Listened to the sound of the wind. Sniffed the air. Then gradually she could not hear the wind or the rustling of leaves anymore, nor could she smell the grass. All her senses were on full alert, reaching out and seeking.

In her mind's eye, she saw red and gold colours streak by; and a round, golden-brown bread bun emitting an unfamiliar and enticing aroma.

A voice piped up behind her. "Good morning."

Elly nearly jumped out of her skin as she gasped and wheeled around.

There on the bench sat a diminutive, dark-skinned old woman staring up at her.

She looked rather bizarre, with thick, copper-red hair streaked with silver that was tied up into two cone-shaped buns on top of her head, which seemed disproportionately large for her small body. Her eyes were a peculiar shade of brown, almost yellow, and they looked oddly huge behind large glasses. She was wearing layers of clothes underneath some sort of golden-brown fur coat, beneath which a full floral-patterned skirt splayed out on the bench. She was so small that her black boots were dangling several inches from the ground. Her gnarled hands were folded neatly on her lap.

Elly stood there gaping stupidly when the lady's fur coat seemed to shift by itself; her eyes widened as a small golden-brown ferret unfurled from the lady's neck like a scarf. The ferret fixed its round, dark eyes on Elly, as though assessing her.

"H-hello," Elly said uncertainly. Where had this old woman come from? She thought she had been alone in the park.

The old woman smiled, revealing a set of absurdly straight white teeth for someone who looked so old. "Good morning, dear. It's so delightful to meet someone as young as you here at this time of day." Her voice was oddly sing-song. Then she gestured to her ferret. "My friend is also pleased to meet you. You can pet him if you like; I promise you he won't bite."

Elly looked at the ferret warily. Hobbes squirmed, and she placed a hand protectively on her pocket. The old lady chuckled, then peered at her gold pocket watch. "Hmm, it's still early enough for breakfast, little one. Are you hungry?"

Elly shook her head, then went red in the face when her stomach growled. She hadn't eaten anything since her birthday party. She was famished.

The old woman smiled. "Well, my dear, there's no shame in feeling hungry. There's a lovely little bakery down Cornwall Street there." She pointed, and Elly saw the enormous blue-coloured stone on her bony finger. "It's one of my favourites. You should go there and grab a bite. Their pineapple buns are to die for." The ferret seemed to be nodding in agreement.

Elly's mouth watered. "Thank you," she said, turning to look towards the direction she had pointed. "I'll make my way there now. Would you like to come with me?" she asked hopefully, turning back. It would be nice to have some company.

The bench was empty. Elly blinked and turned this way and that. Where did the old woman go?

She didn't have the energy to look around. She had to eat something. And those pineapple buns sounded too tempting.

So she started making her way towards Cornwall Street. There were dreary stone buildings all around, and many looked very old and blotched with dark stains like age spots, with fading colourful shop signs hanging from iron brackets. The sky was a dismal grey, and it was so cold that Elly found it difficult to recall the warmth back home in Evergreen. Noisy vehicles passed by on the roads, which were littered with things from broken bottles, crinkled newspaper, and plastic bags, to cigarette butts. She wrinkled her nose in distaste as she surveyed the waste. People walked past her hurriedly with their heads bowed, their vaporised breath rising like steam. Some stared at her, wondering what a little girl like her was doing out in the frigid cold dressed in a summer frock.

As she walked, Elly realized that nobody in this realm really cared whether she lived or died. The thought made her feel awfully and utterly alone. She bowed her head and crossed her arms with a shiver; a biting wind was whistling down Cornwall Street.

Then she sniffed, catching a whiff of something . . . an unfamiliar, enticing aroma.

Where was it coming from? She let her nose lead her, and eventually she found herself standing in front of a shop that had a couple of fading movie posters taped shabbily on the glass windows. The aroma was so strong now, it made her dizzy.

Hobbes stirred in her pocket. Maybe he was hungry, too.

She peered up at the worn sign etched with red and gold lettering: Aunty Mabel's Bakery.

CHAPTER SEVEN
Of Pineapple Buns and Book Worms

ELLY TRIED TO PEER INTO the shop through the glass windows, but she could not get a very clear view through the fogged-up glass. On either glass door was taped a piece of rectangular-shaped red paper with gold script, which Elly recognised as Chinese characters: "Wishing you good luck, good health, and prosperity!"

She swallowed nervously as she pushed open the jingling glass door.

The shop was small, but warm and cosy. She was now enveloped in that deliciously enticing aroma. Almost immediately, she felt herself thawing out. The pink walls were decorated with sparkling red and gold tinsel, and pretty red and gold paper lanterns hung from the ceiling.

There was a lady behind the counter with dark, almond-shaped eyes and shoulder-length black hair speckled with grey. Elly had read about the dark hair of the Asians in Larabeth Goldberry's *The Beginner's Guide to Human Races*. Apparently, many humans liked to change the colour of their hair, and used some deadly chemical called hair dye to do it. In Alendria, such a thing was unheard of. Elves never sought to alter what they were born with. But Elly wondered if there was something that would straighten her manic hair.

The lady was watching Elly curiously. *What remarkable green eyes*, she thought. Lily would love to have marvellous hair like that—so much volume in all those curls!

Elly shifted on her feet uncertainly as she mustered up the courage to speak up. She had always fancied that her first attempt to communicate with a human would be a dignified, momentous event.

But at that moment, all she could think about was food. Then her stomach growled so loudly that the lady at the counter raised her eyebrows, and Elly's ears turned bright red. Thank goodness her hair covered them.

Mabel Wong knew what real hunger felt like. There was a time back in Hong Kong in the 1960s when her family had so little money that they ate rice with soy sauce every night for many months. Her heart went out to this pretty child, who stood out from the other scrawny and unkempt kids who came in asking for food. The girl's face was pale with exhaustion, and her red-rimmed eyes betrayed that she had been crying. She was shivering like a leaf in that flimsy purple dress. But otherwise, she looked healthy and well-groomed.

Mabel smiled and beckoned to Elly, who stepped forward tentatively. To her surprise, Mabel gently took one of her hands.

"My goodness, you're freezing!" Mabel cried. She fussed behind the counter, then retrieved a steaming bun and plopped it on a plate. "Here, eat this *boh loh bau*, a pineapple bun. It'll warm you up," she commanded.

Stammering her thanks, Elly looked dubiously at the round, golden-brown bun before her. Its top crust had a checkered pattern that resembled the epicarp of a pineapple. This would be her very first taste of human food. At least it didn't contain animal meat. She cringed as her stomach growled again, so she took a small bite. Then another. Elly's eyes shone, and she beamed from ear to ear. The top part was crunchy and sweet, whereas the bread underneath was soft and fragrant. That old woman from the park was right!

Whatever this was, it was *super-duper delicious*!

Mabel smiled smugly as she watched Elly devour the *boh loh bau*, her bakery's trademark. Aunty Mabel's was the only Chinese bakery in the neighbourhood that many London suburbans would flock to, for her freshly baked pineapple buns, egg tarts, and glutinous red bean cakes, all of which sold out by six o'clock every day of the week. Even her wholewheat and barley bread loaves were popular.

After Elly finished off the bun, the colour came back to her cheeks. She smiled at Mabel so radiantly that nobody could have guessed that only moments ago she had felt as though her world was crashing down on her.

Sometimes, one literally needs good food to warm the soul.

Mabel smiled. "I am Mabel Wong; I run this bakery. It is lovely to meet you, dear. What is your name?"

Elly could feel Hobbes stirring again, sniffing for food. She patted her pocket and smiled shyly at Mabel. "My name is Ellanor, but everyone calls me Elly."

Greymore rumbled in a warning tone. *Tread carefully, Ellanor. Don't say a word about Alendria or elves. Tell her you are from the North, and you are traveling with your guardian. Your parents are currently unable to explore London with you as they are not in town, but your guardian takes care of you. This is your first time in London, and you are here for as long as you need.*

"And where are your parents, Elly?" Mabel asked, replacing a pineapple bun in the display cabinet.

Elly gulped, then told Mabel what Greymore had instructed her to say. Alendria was located somewhere to the north of Gaya, the human realm. So it was true that she was from the north, that it was her first time in London, and it was also true that Greymore was like her guardian. Elly realised that Greymore was trying to be as truthful as possible, without revealing the whole unbelievable truth to Mabel—after all, Elly had to be convincing as a human. Mabel would think she was insane if she started ranting on about Alendria and elves and goblins. Mabel listened intently. The girl had a very sweet voice, but Mabel could not quite place her accent. She assumed that Elly must have grown up some place exotic in Europe, judging by the foreign yet articulate way she spoke and the unusual way she dressed.

Mabel secretly loved watching TV soap operas, and speculated whether Elly was one of those "poor rich kids". Perhaps her parents were wealthy foreigners, so busy sealing lucrative business deals that they had little time to be with their daughter. It sounded like there was some sort of au pair who acted as her guardian. She looked at Elly and felt sorry for her.

"You look to be about my daughter's age. She's thirteen. You're too young to be left alone in a big city like London. Where is your guardian?"

Elly swallowed nervously. "I'm quite safe, really. My guardian knows where I am at all times, and he won't let me come to harm." She smiled, a little too enthusiastically.

Mabel raised her eyebrows. The poor girl looked so uncomfortable that she decided to drop the subject for now. *Perhaps they've kept a tracking device on her. Rich people have all sorts of things at their disposal,* she thought wryly.

"Would you like to stay here for a bit, where it's nice and warm? It would be no bother at all, honestly." She thought that Elly was looking much less dejected and pale, but she could do with a warm place to rest.

Elly was so relieved, she wanted to cry. Greymore rumbled his approval. "Oh, *yes.* Yes! I would love that. Thank you so, so much!" She bowed in thanks, not realizing this seemed a little unusual.

Mabel laughed. "You have lovely manners, Elly! My Lily could learn a thing or two from you!"

Mabel then plopped two more steaming pineapple buns on a plate and thrust it at Elly.

"Here, go on inside, we have a little fireplace at the back. You'll get to meet my daughter Lily. She'll be over the moon for an excuse to get away from maths homework. Besides, she's been cooped up in the house for the past two days, recuperating from an ear infection. She's pretty much fully recovered, but I thought it would be best to keep her from school for another day. Don't worry, go on in—she's not contagious!"

She ushered Elly through a doorway behind the counter.

Elly stepped on soft maroon carpet inside a handsome room with dark brown walls covered in framed black and white photographs of sombre-faced people. There were several large scrolls of Chinese landscape paintings in the centre at the back wall.

She had read about the history of the Chinese and found them fascinating. From what she had read, it seems that China boasted quite a glorious history, having been the forerunning innovators of science and technology for many centuries. The Chinese had come up with very clever inventions such as the abacus, printing, paper-making, the compass, the telescope, and many more. Elly had read about immigration, leading many Chinese and other Asian ethnic groups to leave their country to seek their fortune and start families elsewhere, mostly in Western countries such as Britain, America, and Australia.

In Alendria, elves, too, would migrate to different regions out of necessity, but it wasn't common. She remembered thinking it was unusual that Edellina had moved to Evergreen City from Morwen Valley.

Then Elly mentally kicked herself; it still had not fully sunk in that Edellina was an imposter, a wretched goblin.

The room was warm, thanks to the fire at the hearth that had a lovely marble mantelpiece, above which hung a family portrait. Elly guessed that Lily was an only child. There was a pungent smell that she had never come across before, which she later discovered was Chinese herbal medicine. The room was dimly lit; Elly looked up and saw that some of the light bulbs in the chandelier had expired. Several old leather armchairs surrounded a low rosewood table cluttered with empty teacups, old magazines and newspapers, and a chess board with chess pieces strewn all over the place. A couple of tall, disorderly bookshelves lined the left wall. In the far corner was a desk piled with papers and books, and there sat a girl wearing thick glasses with her head bowed in concentration.

When they walked into the room, Lily glanced up with a frazzled look. "Mum, I really need a maths tutor, I just don't understand this gobbledygook!" she wailed, near tears. Then her eyes lit up when she saw Elly. "Hello!" she said with a friendly wave. Elly smiled shyly.

Mabel put a hand on Elly's shoulder and steered her forward. "Lily dear, this is Elly. She's visiting London for the first time, and she can do with some rest and a cup of tea. Make sure she feels at home, all right? Perhaps you can take a break from your homework and spend some time together?"

Lily's eyes grew round, and she beamed. "Sure! If I need to look at any more x's and y's, I'll go insane!"

Mabel laughed. "I knew it! By the way, Elly's parents aren't in town, and she's by her lonesome. I'm sure she'll like to make a new friend."

Then she looked at her watch and clucked her tongue. The bakery was going to get busy soon; it always did at lunch hour. She had to go off and prepare several more batches of pineapple buns and egg tarts. Smiling, Mabel patted Elly on the shoulder. "I'll leave you girls to it! I must get back to work now." She hurried back to the bakery.

Lily stretched and leapt off her chair. "Oh, it's so nice to take a break from this awful homework. Algebra. Yuck!" She patted a pile of books on the desk with a smile. "I much prefer reading novels."

Elly brightened. "Oh, I love stories, too!" She had particularly enjoyed reading *Jane Eyre* and *Oliver Twist,* two famous novels written by humans. The library at Arvellon Academy had only a limited collection of novels from the human realm, but Elly had devoured every one of them. The most recent book was dated one hundred years ago—which was how long ago the elves had sealed the portal. *Before I was foolish enough to trespass and make a mess of things,* she thought unhappily.

Lily beamed. "You're kidding! I just *adore* reading the Brontë sisters and Charles Dickens, but not only the classics—I love contemporary writers, too." She rattled off a list of titles that Elly had never heard of before. Lily sighed. "Oh, you wouldn't believe how hard it is to find a friend who loves books, too."

Then she licked her lips and jumped up. "Boy, I'm parched! Come, let's have some tea. I would offer you soda or juice, but we're out at the moment. Besides, I like having chamomile tea in this freezing weather." Lily poured them some tea into clean mugs. "Here you go. I much prefer this to the strong Pu-erh tea that my folks like to have."

Elly cupped the warm mug with both hands and breathed in the soothing fragrance. She tentatively took a sip. Then another. She beamed; she had never tasted anything like it before! Back home, beverages ranged from bubbling spring water to fresh fruit drinks, unicorn milk, and dragon honey ale, but she had never had tea before. The chamomile warmed her from the inside out!

The two girls sat talking about all sorts of things, from their favourite books to Elly's hair, which Lily claimed was gorgeous. Elly couldn't believe it—back home, she was certain nobody thought her hair looked beautiful. Lily sighed. "I wish my hair had as much *volume* as yours. You seriously could go on one of those hair commercials!" she exclaimed, tugging at her own straight hair with a scowl.

Elly laughed and shook out her own curls. "But I wish my hair were as wonderfully straight as yours!"

Lily giggled. "I guess the other side always looks greener, eh?"

Whenever Lily started talking about something she was unfamiliar with (which happened frequently), she would smile and nod and try her best to appear informed. Lily occasionally asked whether Elly liked some singer or movie star that she had absolutely no clue about. Her default responses ranged from "She's okay", to "He's not bad".

When Lily asked about her school, she shrugged and tried to sound nonchalant. "Oh, it's not anywhere in England, just some boring old school in the north." She attempted to distract Lily by asking her about chess, which was similar to a game called King's Quest back home in Alendria. But Lily persisted. "Oh! You're from somewhere in northern Europe, aren't you? So where exactly are you from?"

Elly gulped. "Oh, you most probably haven't even heard of it, it's such an . . . obscure place . . ." She trailed off.

Help me, Greymore!

Lily laughed. "Wow, you must come from the most out-of-the-way place! OK, let me guess—what letter does it begin with?"

Elly felt doomed. She didn't want to tell an outright lie. "Well, if you must know, it begins with *A*."

Lily thought for a moment, then her eyes widened. "Oh my gosh, you're from the Aland Islands in Finland!" she exclaimed, snapping her fingers.

Elly stared at Lily. The Aland Islands? She had no idea what that was. Taking Elly's look of surprise as confirmation, Lily grinned triumphantly. "Good guess, huh? I first learned about the Aland Islands in geography class several weeks ago. It's not exactly well-known, but I've been told it's *really* beautiful, and has the most hours of sunshine in any part of Scandinavia, right?"

Greymore rumbled. *Perhaps this is for the best, Ellanor. Go with the flow.*

Elly smiled weakly as she thought about Alendria—the rainbow-washed sky that never went grey during the day; the lovely Meridien Meadows where some of the prettiest flowers grew; the bright sun that always seemed reluctant to give way to the moon.

"Yes, my home is a very beautiful place," she said softly, and wished she could tell Lily the truth.

Lily laughed and clapped her hands. "Wow, wait till I tell my folks! I've never known anyone from the Aland Islands. That is *so* cool!"

Then she glanced at the clock and gasped. "Look at the time! It's almost two o'clock, and we haven't even had lunch yet! Let's eat something; I'm starving!" She winked at Elly. "We spent all that time talking about books and stuff. We're a couple of sad bookworms, aren't we?"

They shared the pineapple buns and ate sandwiches that Lily had prepared in record time. She was considerate enough to ask Elly if there was anything she couldn't eat.

"You're a vegetarian?" Lily asked, finding it hard to imagine life without beef and chicken and pork. Elly grinned as she devoured a tomato and avocado sandwich. When Lily wasn't looking, she slipped some bread bits into her pocket for Hobbes, who gobbled them up quickly.

As she waited for Lily to finish her overflowing roast beef and lettuce sandwich, Elly looked around the room thoughtfully. "Has your family always lived in London?"

Lily wiped her mouth with a tissue. "Well, I was born here in London, but my parents immigrated here from Hong Kong. Which used to be a British colony, as you might know—run by the British, that is. My mother's parents came, too. But Gong-Gong—that's my Grandpa—died a few years ago, so now it's just Poh-Poh, my Grandma. She doesn't speak much English, though she's been here for over fifteen years. She spends most of her time with her friends in Chinatown, playing mah-jong and going to yum cha, that sort of thing. My parents learned to speak English pretty well, but they speak Cantonese at home."

Elly nodded as she gulped down the last morsel of her sandwich. "So you can speak fluent Cantonese?"

Lily sighed. "Unfortunately, no. Grandma insists that I speak Cantonese with her, and she complains that I sound like a *gwei-mui;* a Caucasian girl!" She rolled her eyes. Then she glanced up and gulped. "Speak of the devil!" She jumped off the couch and went towards a diminutive old lady who had just shuffled into the room in furry brown slippers. Lily took her by the arm and smiled.

"This is my Grandma," she said, before turning to the elderly lady and speaking in halting Cantonese.

"Grandma, this is my new friend, Elly. She's visiting London for the first time."

Grandma Wong would have looked taller if it wasn't for her stooped back. Her white hair was short and curly, and she was wearing a long-sleeved *cheongsam* of a deep red with gold embroidery. She had on small jade earrings and a matching bangle on her thin, wrinkled wrist.

She smiled and nodded at Elly, then turned to her granddaughter. "She has very beautiful green eyes, the colour of my jade!" she remarked in Cantonese.

Elly smiled at the compliment and bowed deeply. "Hello, Grandma. I am Elly, and I am so pleased to meet you."

She was greeted by silence. Looking up, she saw that Grandma and Lily were both staring at her. Lily's jaw had dropped open. "Oh, my goodness! You can speak *Cantonese?*" she cried, her eyes bulging.

Grandma Wong was beaming from ear to ear. "Finally, someone of Lily's age I can talk to!" she said with an approving smile. Then she looked at her little gold watch. "It's time for my afternoon nap. Do make yourself at home, Elly."

Lily continued to stare at her. "That's amazing! Your Cantonese sounds better than mine!"

Elly panicked. She hadn't realized she had switched to using the Cantonese language. Elves are gifted with the ability to understand and speak any language they came across. This was one elven ability she had not thought of reining in. She had so much to learn, much to adjust if she had to be convincing as a human. She really had to learn to blend in like a chameleon, as Larabeth Goldberry must have done.

Grandma clucked her tongue at Lily. "See, you should practise more!" she admonished her granddaughter in Cantonese. Then she patted Elly fondly on the shoulder before shuffling out of the room.

"How did you learn to speak Cantonese so fluently?" Lily demanded. She was annoyed; now her Grandma would have more reason to pester her about improving her mother tongue.

Greymore rumbled. *Careful, Ellanor.*

Elly swallowed nervously. "Oh, yes . . . I can understand and speak *a lot* of languages . . . it sort of runs in the family, you see . . . We're all multi-lingual."

This seemed reasonable enough. Even some humans are known to be gifted in languages, though not to the extent that elves are.

Lily sighed and flopped onto the couch. "You are *so* lucky!" she groaned. "I'm not very good at learning different languages. I've always preferred using only English, even with Grandma. Cantonese is like a foreign language to me. My parents are forever bugging me to improve. But they just have no idea how difficult it is. Everyone at school and all my friends speak English; how could they expect me to be fluent in Cantonese without ever having taken proper lessons?"

She crossed her arms and scowled. "Grandma likes to joke that I'm like a banana, because I'm yellow on the outside and white on the inside. But I just don't think it's very funny at all!"

Elly was perplexed. Lily had pretty fair skin. "But you don't look yellow to me."

Lily burst out laughing. Then she noticed Elly's confused expression and giggled. "You see, girls like me look Chinese on the outside, but inside I think and feel more like a Westerner."

She propped up her stockinged feet on the couch. "You know what I mean, right? The skin tone of Asian people is generally more . . . yellow or olive, but Westerners have a skin tone that is more pale, more white. That's why girls like me are known as *bananas*." She looked at Elly as though she expected this to be perfectly comprehensible.

Elly imagined Lily as a giant banana, and giggled. "Then, what about a white Caucasian girl who grows up in China and learns to think and feel more like a Chinese person?"

Lily thought for a moment. "White on the outside and yellow on the inside . . . How about an egg?" The two girls doubled up with laughter.

Then Lily sat bolt upright. "Wait, I just remembered something!"

She reached out towards a grey backpack next to the couch, rummaged around, and retrieved a thin book. She was flipping through it when she snapped her fingers.

"Oh Elly, I have a superb idea! Please, please, please come to my school fair on the twenty-eighth of January—that's in over three weeks! My school's just a few blocks away. Please, pretty please, if you're still in town, do come with me! I'm still quite new to St Catherine's, and I don't really have any friends there. I don't want to go to the fair all by myself."

At this, she flopped back onto the couch and turned to Elly imploringly. "I'm auditioning for the part of Cinderella for the school musical that our speech and drama class is putting on for the end of the school year, and it's going to be *huge*. It's a modern, revamped version of the story, so it's going to be really fabulous. Instead of tacky glass slippers, the girl cast as Cinderella will get to wear a pair of gorgeous heels by Manolo Blahnik; they're actually sponsoring us this year! I've never even stepped into their store before!"

Elly had no inkling who Manolo Blahnik was. Oblivious, Lily continued. "You know, I'm not too bad at singing, and I dare say I can act better than Clare Andrews."

She noticed Elly's quizzical expression and sighed. "She's this really horrid girl in my year, and it's gotten worse now that she's recruited a new girl to join her clique."

She jumped up off the couch and started pacing back and forth, speaking a mile a minute.

"Clare thinks Cinderella can't possibly be played by someone like me. To quote her, 'Cinderella is supposed to be pretty. I certainly don't recall Cinderella being Chinese and four-eyed.'"

She sniffed and crossed her arms indignantly. "But I'll show her! I may not have blue eyes and long blonde hair like she does, but I can sing and remember my lines!"

Elly had once read the story of Cinderella in a tattered old volume of *Grimm's Fairy Tales* that was missing about a third of its pages. She didn't think it mattered whether Cinderella had golden, silver, or black hair as long as she was pretty, kind, gentle . . . and had feet small enough to fit into the dainty glass slippers, unlike her wicked stepsisters. For some reason, the Three Flamingos came to mind.

"Maybe Clare Andrews can play one of the wicked stepsisters instead," Elly suggested with a wink.

Lily raised her eyebrows and laughed. "Yes, what a fabulous idea!"

Then Elly heard a low growl. She looked up and saw a handsome, bright-eyed husky with a plush coat of black and white fur trotting into the room, his tail swishing back and forth. *I want some beef jerky!* the dog panted, barking for attention. He tried nudging Lily towards the kitchen with his snout.

Lily laughed and cuddled her dog. "Oh, there you are, you sleepyhead!" she said affectionately, kissing him on the forehead. "Meet my new friend Elly! This is Soybean. He's been with us since I was seven!"

Elly stood very still, trying to look unfazed as the dog sniffed at her suspiciously.

Then her stomach knotted when he barked and demanded to know, *What do you have in your pocket?*

CHAPTER EIGHT
Soybean's New Friend

ELLY GULPED AND PUT HER hand on her pocket, trying to calm Hobbes, who was writhing frantically and clawing at her thigh. Soybean was now barking incessantly, shoving his face close to Elly's dress.

Lily looked mortified as she tugged on Soybean's collar. "Oh dear, he's quite forgotten his manners! He usually doesn't behave like this!"

She put her hands on her hips and glared at her dog. "Soybean, sit!"

But Soybean was on a mission. He could smell something fleshy from that girl's pocket!

Hobbes' squeaks were being drowned out by the barking. Scrambling around in blind fear, he squealed tearfully, "Save me, save me!"

Then Elly had an idea.

She squatted and looked at Soybean squarely in the eye. *Listen and be still, Soybean. I have a hamster in my pocket. Please don't hurt him. His name is Hobbes. Be nice to him, okay?*

If you have never seen a dog look surprised, then Soybean would have been your first.

Soybean froze and fell silent, then yelped. He took several steps back before sitting on his hind legs, his tail wagging furiously. Then he gazed up at Elly with wide, adoring eyes.

Lily stared at her dog, surprised that he had calmed down so abruptly. "Soybean?" she said uncertainly, touching him on the head.

Elly smiled at her. "Soybean is really adorable! Let me give him a cuddle!" She went up to the husky and put her arms around his soft furry neck.

My name is Elly, and I am an elf; that's why I can communicate with you like this. Now, please be a good friend and keep an eye on Hobbes. Promise?

Soybean was so happy that he could hear the voice of this pretty person in his head! Oh, he just *loved* people! He barked happily, eager to please his new friend. *Yes, yes, yes! Whatever you say, Elly!*

Elly grinned and patted him on the head while Lily looked on in amazement. "Wow, what did you *do* to him? All of a sudden, he seems to worship you!"

Elly grinned. "I've always had a way with animals. By the way, I think he wants some beef jerky."

Lily blinked, then picked up a packet of dog snacks that had been stashed underneath a cushion. "Here, you silly boy!" she said, tossing him several strips of his favourite beef jerky. Soybean barked excitedly and started devouring them.

Elly took a deep breath. "Lily, I think . . . I need your help."

Lily looked up, surprised. "Erm, sure. What is it?"

Slowly, Elly retrieved a quivering and dishevelled-looking ball of fur from her pocket. Lily's mouth dropped open.

Elly smiled sheepishly. "Lily, meet my friend Hobbes. I found him this morning." She gently stroked the frightened hamster, and then explained how she had come across Hobbes at the Berry Grove Park.

"I'm sorry, I don't want to impose this on you. But I need to ask. Is it possible for you to take Hobbes? He's all alone, and he really needs a home. Do you think . . . he can stay here?"

Lily's eyes widened further. "So this is why Soybean went berserk! He could probably smell Hobbes a mile away!"

She peered at the quivering hamster and grinned. "I've always wanted one of these cute furballs, but I wasn't sure whether it would be a good idea with Soybean around."

She glanced at her dog, who was now sitting obediently, happy as could be.

Elly gave Soybean a meaningful wink. If you had never seen a dog smile, Soybean would have been the first. "I think Soybean will be good to Hobbes. Right?"

Soybean barked happily in agreement and nodded.

Lily blinked. Did Soybean actually *nod* at Elly? She must not have slept well last night. She was seeing her dog do weird things.

Then she turned and looked down at Hobbes, who was trembling like a leaf, his paws shielding his face. "Aww, he is awfully cute!" she said with a giggle. But Hobbes squealed and shrank from her.

"Let me go ask my mum now!" Lily said, and dashed out of the room. While she was gone, Elly turned to Soybean and wagged her finger. "Remember, you won't harm Hobbes," she said sternly.

Soybean nodded vigorously and barked. *I promise, Elly!*

Hobbes whimpered and curled into a ball. "Elly, I can't stay here! I'm terrified of canines!"

Elly patted him on the head. "Trust me Hobbes, you'll be much safer and more comfortable here than out on the road with me. I need to find a way back home, and it's occurred to me that I might put you in danger. Lily will take care of you, and Soybean has promised to be nice."

But Hobbes cowered from Soybean, who was looking at the hamster with something close to manic zeal.

By the time Lily had bounded back, Hobbes was on the table, hiding behind a teacup. If she hadn't known better, she would've sworn that Elly and Soybean were actually *talking* to each other. She slapped a palm against her forehead. How absurd! What was wrong with her today?

Lily laughed. "Wow, Soybean has really taken a shine to you!"

Then she gently picked up Hobbes as he gave a mighty squeak. She smiled and stroked his quivering head. "Mum gave me the green light! She made me call Dad at work to ask for his permission. Hobbes, welcome to our family!"

Elly beamed and clapped her hands in delight. "Thank you, Lily!" she cried. But Hobbes looked over at her sorrowfully. At that moment, he was the saddest looking hamster you would have ever seen.

With Elly's help, Lily created a makeshift home for Hobbes using a shoebox stuffed with shredded tissue paper as bedding. Then she put a bowl of watermelon seeds in one corner and a little bowl of water in another. Hobbes quickly snatched two watermelon seeds and shoved them into his mouth before darting for cover, burying himself beneath the bedding.

"We'll go to the pet shop tomorrow and get a proper hamster home for him," Lily said, peering at the lump of quivering tissue paper. "He sure is shy, isn't he?"

Then they both jumped when the clock chimed. It was already five o'clock!

"Do you need us to give you a ride home?" Lily asked, glancing out the window. The sky was getting dark. "Mum never lets me go anywhere by myself, even during the day when it's still bright. She says I can't start walking to school by myself until next year, even though everyone in my class already does that. It's *so* embarrassing. I wish they would stop treating me like a baby!"

Elly quickly jumped up from the sofa. She had gotten so comfortable, she lost track of the time! "Oh Lily, please don't worry about me, I don't need you to take me home! I'll be fine. I can, umm, meet my guardian on the way. Trust me, I'll be all right. Where should I meet you on the twenty-eighth?" she asked hurriedly, hoping to distract Lily from asking more questions.

Lily was clearing the lunch plates off the table. "Let's meet at ten o'clock. Wait, you have a *guardian*?" she asked incredulously. "Like a bodyguard or something? That's incredible. What's his name?"

Elly fidgeted. "Erm, his name is Greymore. He keeps an eye on me while my parents are away. Truly, I'll be safe. Greymore will make sure of that. I'll see you on the twenty-eighth, all right?" As much as she wanted to stay with Lily and have her supper with such lovely people, she did not want to overstay her welcome, especially since she had already spent half the day at the Wong household. She did not want them to think she had no home to go back to.

Thankfully, Lily seemed satisfied. She nodded happily as she stacked the plates on top of each other. "All right, then! We'll meet in front of the bakery at ten o'clock sharp that Saturday. It's a date!" Then she put the plates down and threw her arms around Elly. "Oh, I am *so* happy that we're friends!" she cried.

"Me, too!" Elly said sincerely, hugging her back. She thought of Edellina and grimaced. How she wished she had a girlfriend like Lily back home!

Lily wrote down her home phone number and address. "In case you need to contact me," she said, handing Elly the piece of scrap paper. "But how can I get in touch with you?"

Elly started moving towards the door. "Oh, I'll most probably be moving from place to place, so it'll be hard to get hold of me. I'll call you if necessary. I'll see you very soon!"

But Lily was looking at her dress critically. "Gosh, you'll freeze out there with only that flimsy thing on! Did you think it was summer here or something?"

Before Elly could answer, Lily ran upstairs to her room and returned with her arms loaded with garments. She made Elly put on a long thick coat, gloves, and a woolly scarf. "Just return them when you come back properly dressed for the weather next time!" she said cheerfully.

"Thank you so much," Elly said softly, touched by her new friend's thoughtfulness. She liked the feel of the extra layers warming her body.

Then Greymore's reproachful voice made her jump. *Ellanor, aren't you forgetting something important?*

At first, her mind drew a blank. Then she gasped; she had forgotten to ask Lily about blue amber!

She bowed her head sheepishly. *I'm sorry, Greymore. I was having such a lovely time with Lily that it made me almost forget about my predicament.*

Better late than never, Ellanor. Ask her now.

Reluctantly, Elly turned to her friend, who was slipping on her own coat. The temperature had dropped a few degrees. "Lily, I've been meaning to ask you . . . Do you know where I can get blue amber?"

Lily frowned as she zipped up her coat. "Blue amber? I've never heard of it. Amber is some sort of yellow rock, isn't it? But what's *blue* amber?"

Crestfallen, Elly shook her head. "I—I don't really know, actually. I just need to find blue amber. Do you have any idea where I might find some?"

Lily knitted her eyebrows. "I'm sorry, Elly. I have no idea. But maybe I can ask around for you?"

Elly nodded and tried to smile. "Sure, that sounds good. Thanks, Lily." She groaned inwardly. She'd have to go on a proper search for this elusive Organoth blue amber. It sounded like finding ordinary blue amber was already difficult enough.

"Oh, I almost forgot!" Lily took something from the back pocket of her jeans and handed it to Elly. "This is a map of London," she explained, unfolding it. "My dad runs a travel agency in Chinatown, and we have tons of tourist brochures and maps lying around the place. This should come in handy as you explore the city." She pointed to several places on the map, and marked them with a pen. "You should go to the Westminster Abbey tomorrow if you get the chance. It's gorgeous!"

Elly had no idea where she was headed next, let alone tomorrow.

Then she spotted a small, thick, red-bound book in the cluttered bookshelf: *The Pocket Dictionary*. Her eyes lit up.

"Excuse me, Lily, but please may I borrow that little dictionary?" she asked sheepishly. "It would really help me out. I promise I'll return it when I see you next!"

Lily glanced at the little dictionary and laughed. "Oh, of course! That's right, you're from the Aland Islands in Finland. English probably isn't your first language, so this might help! We have several dictionaries lying around. My dad must like collecting them or something!"

Elly went to say goodbye to Mabel in the bakery, who was busily serving customers with the help of her assistant, a tall red-haired young woman named Paige. Mabel asked Paige to take over and quickly excused herself from the counter. She smiled, glad that her daughter had made a new friend. She knew Lily had been having a hard time adjusting to her new school, and she was lonely. Elly seemed like a lovely little girl; besides, she looked like she could do with a friend herself.

She pushed a brown paper bag into Elly's gloved hands, pleased to see her nicely bundled up in Lily's winter clothes. "Are you having supper soon?" she asked, and noticed that Elly had a slightly droopy look, like a wilted flower.

Elly didn't want to think what she could have for supper. "Erm, yes. I'll eat with my guardian," she said softly, wishing she could be at the dining table with her family. She wanted sweet cakes with her favourite leafy greens and Mama's freshly baked bread rolls.

Mabel felt sorry for her and wondered if her parents often leave her alone with her guardian. "All right then, dear. Call us whenever you need to, okay?"

As Mabel waved goodbye to her, a lump formed in Elly's throat, and tears burned her eyes.

"Bye, Elly!" called out Lily, waving furiously. "See you again soon!"

Elly wasn't sure if she would really get to see Lily again. But if she was still stranded here on the twenty-eighth, she would definitely go to the school fair with her.

She started walking away quickly, hoping they wouldn't insist on escorting her. She turned a corner and was out of sight.

Elly pulled the coat tighter around herself as the icy wind whispered down the street. She probably would've eventually frozen to death without these extra layers. She looked up at the dark, murky sky. If only she could get a glimpse of the Star of Freya . . .

Eventually, she found her way back to the Berry Grove Park. She had nowhere else to go to spend the night. It was dark and deserted. People were either heading home for supper, trooping downtown to restaurants, or going for after-work drinks at the pubs. She looked around to make sure that the coast was clear, then leapt up the tree and settled on a high, sturdy branch. Then she retrieved the little dictionary from her pocket and opened up her Royan.

Greymore, please store this dictionary for me. You'll be able to access the words and definitions if I need them, right?

Yes, Ellanor. It was good thinking on your part to obtain a dictionary. You will come across words and situations you may not understand. The dictionary might be able to assist you.

After transforming herself back into elf proportions, she opened up the paper bag Mabel had given her and smiled. Inside were an apple, a pineapple bun, and a bottle of water. How kind of Mabel! She leaned back against the trunk and closed her eyes. It was only then that she realized how utterly exhausted she was.

Within the same day, she had discovered Edellina as a false friend and goblin impersonator; been literally shoved out of her own world into another; almost gotten herself killed by a jealous cat; and finally, she had had to learn to masquerade as a human. *Of course* she was worn out. She had experienced more in one day than she had in all her twelve years put together.

Greymore rumbled. *Ellanor, we have to stay here in Gaya until we repair the portal. You must find Organoth blue amber. Let's begin a proper search tomorrow morning.*

Elly sighed heavily. *I have a feeling it won't be easy. It seems that even ordinary blue amber isn't well known.*

Then she spoke in a low voice, breaking the silence. "Greymore, why hasn't somebody from Alendria come for me? Surely they wouldn't allow an elfling like me to stay stranded all by herself in Gaya? There must be something they could do to save me!"

I am sorry, Ellanor. I do not have the answer to that. We are in this together. I, too, wish to be back in Alendria.

"I miss them a lot," she said softly. "They must be so worried about me. Right?"

You must remember that your family loves you. They would come and save you if they could, Ellanor.

But in that moment, no more words of comfort could have made her feel less wretched and afraid. She tucked herself into a ball to keep herself from falling apart.

She didn't know how much time had gone by. Without an hourglass to tell the time, she could only guess by peeking at the moon, which was often obscured by grey smog. She was very hungry. Eventually, she took out an apple, resisting the urge to devour the pineapple bun. *What a miserable supper*, she thought. Back home, she had never experienced real hunger. Now, it was a different story. She had to ration any food she could get her hands on. She remembered reading about food rationing in Larabeth Goldberry's book, *The Explorer's Guide to Survival Tactics in Other Realms*. Here in Gaya, she didn't have Mama to put food on the table.

She made a face as she bit into the apple; it tasted different from the ones back home, less sweet and juicy. But it was still better than no fruit at all.

On a nearby branch, two squirrels were quarrelling over some acorns. The animals in this realm seemed somewhat different from the ones in Alendria: less fair to look upon, and they even sounded different. Several bugs were looking at Elly curiously, but they kept their distance. It was very quiet except for the occasional hooting of an owl and the rumbling of passing engines.

She watched the squirrels for a little while. Then her eyelids began to feel heavy. She curled up and soon fell into a deep sleep after the tears had dried on her cheeks.

The tears had dried on her cheeks by the time Goldie opened her eyes. She had been having another strange dream. Now that she was awake, she could recall only bits and pieces. She frowned. Who was that girl with the long black hair and green eyes? In the dream, she had felt so forlorn, so lost. Just like me, *Goldie thought.*

The right side of her head throbbed. She touched it gingerly and winced; a huge lump had formed. She had read about people dying from concussions. Maybe I'm better off dead, *she thought.*

She gazed into the darkness as the rickety plastic clock ticked away. The lone light bulb in the ceiling had finally expired. A ray of moonlight offered some solace through the small square window.

Finally, she heaved herself off the cold concrete floor, groped her way to the desk, and fumbled for the clock, being careful not to knock over the silver Christmas ball. Squinting at the two thin hands, she was surprised to see that so many hours had passed. It was now past two o'clock, and the silence was so deep that she could hear the drip, drip of the leaking tap from behind the closed bathroom door from across the room. Veronika and her family would be sound asleep by now. They were all surprisingly heavy sleepers. Goldie marvelled at that. How could they still sleep at night after treating her the way they did?

Her eyes adjusted to the darkness quickly, thanks to the moonlight. The dead rat was nowhere in sight. Veronika must have gotten rid of it. She had left Goldie lying on the floor and bustled off to the party with her husband and son. It was a Friday night, and there was no school tomorrow, so Veronika would come back in the morning and clean off Goldie's wound with cold efficiency, just like the other times. While she was at it, she would probably try to intimidate Goldie into growing out her hair again. "You really ought to cover those ugly ears," Veronika would say maliciously. But no matter how Veronika tried, Goldie would somehow always find a way to keep her hair short, and she didn't care who saw her strangely-shaped ears. "She was probably borne of a witch," the gossipers would whisper.

Everybody in town believed that Veronika and her family were saints for taking in Goldie—the strange, orphaned, ungrateful girl who never smiled. After all, the wealthy Waldorf family who resided at the sixteen-bedroom mansion were respectable in this town—Veronika's great-grandfather, a prominent banker, had been one of the founders of Hemlock.

"*Who would want someone as sullen-faced as her? She brings bad luck. Queer things happen when she's around. Soon, she'll be too old for the foster system,*" they would whisper behind phony smiles. If only they knew what the Waldorfs were like beneath their glittering jewels and expensive tailored clothes.

But those people were right—strange things did happen around her. Like the time when she was a toddler at the orphanage. She had been spanked by the matron for taking a stale cookie without permission. She was so frightened that she screamed at the top of her lungs, and the light bulbs in the room burst. Then there was the time in second grade when a bully irritated her one too many times. She gave him one deadly stare, and suddenly the mirror in the hallway gave a resounding crack.

Maybe she really was a freak, a bringer of bad omen.

She stared out the square window, and it seemed to her that her longing to be free welled up in her and in the basement, until it should surely burst the hateful walls and set her free indeed. Freedom—that word rolled tantalizingly on her tongue. How she longed to get out and never come back. She had always wanted to go see the ocean. The warm sunshine and powdery golden sand were myths to her. Hemlock was a cold, dreary place, and even in the summer the icy drafts seemed to linger.

But the window was too small for her to go through, petite as she was.

Then the uncanniest thing happened. It was so subtle that it took her a little while to notice something had changed.

Her clothes were hanging off her. The sleeves of her ugly pink nightdress were several inches too long, covering her hands. Her sweatpants were now so loose that they had slid down her small hips, and she had to tug them up. She blinked and leapt up. Her right slipper flew off. She stared down at her left slipper and placed a hand at the tip. She wriggled her toes around. It was now several sizes too big.

Over the course of several minutes, she seemed to have shrunk!

What was happening? Her shock and confusion very slowly melted into a smug smile. Maybe it was good to be a freak after all. Whatever devilry this was, it was all to her favour. With a surge of excitement, she looked around the cold basement. Her eyes lit up as they landed on the steel chair at the desk.

She did not have much. Grabbing a large old duffel bag from under the bed, she tossed in her most prized possessions—the Christmas ball, her two favourite dog-eared novels, her scrapbook, crayons and pens, some changes of clothes, and all the money she had in the world—enough to buy herself a one-way train ticket. She was about to throw in the ragged geography textbook when she paused and flipped it open. Taking a deep breath, she closed her eyes and placed a finger somewhere on the atlas. When she opened her eyes, she looked intently at where her finger was pointing: London, the United Kingdom.

Quickly, she pulled on a thick grey sweater over her nightdress, put on the warmest jacket she had (some atrocious thing Veronika had salvaged from the clothing pool), pulled on a pair of loose jeans over her sagging sweatpants for padded warmth, and tightened the belt. She didn't care how awful she must look in these ragged baggy clothes.

As she laced up her boots as tightly as she could, a pain shot up her index finger, and she cried out softly. She peered at the dark drop of blood that was oozing from her broken skin; there must have been a splinter left lurking on her shoelace.

As quietly as she could manage, she knocked the sturdy leg of the steel chair against the glass. Nothing happened. With a scowl, she took in a deep breath, and with greater force, rammed the leg into the glass, and winced when it cracked. She did it again, and this time the glass gave way and broke. She held her breath and waited, her heart pounding madly. Everything was still silent, except for the occasional hooting of an owl and the rustling of the trees in the sighing breeze.

Knocking out the remaining jagged glass, she threw the duffel bag out the window first, took a deep breath, and wriggled out. It worked! She could have laughed out loud if she didn't have to get away like a thief in the night. No—more like a prisoner escaping from a dungeon.

The icy cold made her gasp. Glancing up, Goldie saw the bright full moon. She must get out of Hemlock as quickly as possible. Dropping down onto the grass, she picked up her duffel bag and started running like the wind. She weaved in and out of shadows, having always been an unusually fast runner. As she ran, she barely realized she was slowly reverting to her original size.

In the distance she could hear a sweet birdsong, and it made her smile.

CHAPTER NINE
No Breakfast at Tiffany's

ELLY AWOKE GROGGILY AT THE crack of dawn to a sweet birdsong. Everything was covered in beads of dew that glistened in the twilight. She had been having another dream, but it was all a bit hazy now. Then she winced in pain and stared at her index finger. Why was it hurting? It must be a splinter from the tree.

She had survived her first night away from home. But still, the lump in her throat came back. She thought of the warmth back home, her comfortable hammock, her favourite foods . . . and most of all, her family . . . and Aron.

It was no use feeling sorry for herself. She had to get a move on.

She stretched, breathing in the cold and damp morning air—then coughed. The atmosphere in the human realm was different—less sweet and crisp, perhaps due to all the pollution those machines and vehicles spouted every day. But at least the morning air was fresher, and she welcomed it.

A garbage truck was out doing its rounds. She wrinkled her nose at the stench, pinching it until the truck disappeared around the corner. Then she peered down the tree and listened. There was nobody down at the park, and there were very few vehicles going by at this hour. Quickly, she transformed back into human proportions. Several bugs nearby stopped what they were doing and stared.

The coast was clear. She leapt down the tree and landed lightly. Turning this way and that, she wondered which way she should go. From the coat pocket, she took out the map Lily had given her and peered at it, trying to work out where she was. Then she spotted the red star that Lily had marked on the map for her; she was in a suburb called Edgware. After several minutes of studying the map, she zipped up her coat, took a deep breath, and set off towards the city of London.

She had to find Organoth blue amber.

<hr />

Ding-dong!

Elly jumped in surprise, and turned to see where the tolling sound was coming from. She could see a tall clock tower from where she was standing, on a footbridge near the River Thames. According to the map, it was Big Ben that was tolling at the end of the Houses of Parliament. The sun had finally come out, warming her a little. She stood still on the bridge, bathing in the sunshine, and longed for the warmth back home.

She hadn't been able to resist wolfing down the pineapple bun, and now she had no more food. She groaned. There was only a little water left.

Do not fret, Ellanor. We shall find a way out of this predicament.

Elly sighed. "If only I had your optimism," she muttered.

It was only after she had finished the food in the paper bag that she found a small, folded-up tissue napkin at the bottom. Some money was tucked inside. Though it wasn't much, it was just enough for Elly to pay for some food and public transport. *Mabel must have put it in there,* she thought. *She must have been worried about me.*

Elly had to consult Greymore about the use of the English pound; she had no idea how to handle money. She also had to learn how to cross roads safely. Oblivious of roadside etiquette, she almost got hit by an oncoming car. Shaken, she apologized profusely to the angry driver who blasted her with rude words. A kind, middle-aged man steered her across the road, explaining that she shouldn't jaywalk.

All morning, she had walked miles going to places that were indicated as "tourist attractions" on her map. As she approached the gigantic, sprawling city, the roads became busier and busier. Soaring up majestically was St Paul's Cathedral, once the tallest building in the city before the arrival of skyscrapers. She walked past the Tower of London, a castle of nearly a thousand years old that housed the famous

British Crown Jewels. Farther to the east was the peaceful St James Park, a mirage of green in a city of concrete, where some children and their dogs were running about; the festive and busy Piccadilly Circus with its neon lights and a peculiar-looking statue called Eros; and Covent Garden on Drury Lane, where her mouth watered at the sight of fresh fruits sold at the marketplace.

Like other elves, Elly walked at a swift, tireless pace, allowing her to cover three times the distance that a human could. She wished she could fly, but that would surely attract attention. Even if she were to transform back into elf proportions, it was still too much of a risk to fly in broad daylight. She should have brought along the invisibility perfume that Edellina the goblin had given her.

Everywhere she went, she tried to enquire about blue amber. She received many quizzical looks. One old man she stopped on the street in Piccadilly Circus looked at her suspiciously, as though afraid she was a little pickpocket. Most shops weren't yet open so early in the morning.

After several hours, Elly's stomach was rumbling as loud as ever, and she began to feel her pursuit was pointless and fruitless. Nobody seemed to know what blue amber was.

She began making her way to the west again, this time for Westminster Abbey. According to the map and Lily's recommendation, this was a must-see. Elly thought she might as well see as much of London as she could while she was stranded here.

Elly now understood why the description beneath the map had called London a "cosmopolitan city". It was a historic, vibrant city buzzing as a hive of constant activity, home to a diverse range of people—Anglo-Saxon, Greek, Italian, Chinese, Korean, Japanese, African, Indian, Russian, Arab, Armenian, Jewish, Polish, French, Swiss, and many more. The diversity was fascinating.

Elly thought about Alendria. How would elves cope in a place like London? Elves are insular creatures of habit who would not happily accommodate changes. Though the Vierran elves in the north had in the past helped the elves in the south, they were still treated as a people to be avoided, just because they were quite different in their appearance and traditions, and were known to be proud and fierce. Only explorers like her grandpapa and Larabeth Goldberry had shown interest in the Vierran. Elly wished she could meet them.

On the way to Westminster Abbey, she passed many shops: Marks & Spencer, Topshop, H&M, Pringle, Ashworth, Prada, Chanel, Dior. She had no idea what any of the names meant, nor what those shops sold. Then something in one of the window displays caught her eye: a beautiful sparkling necklace studded with white jewels shaped like flowers. Walking up to take a closer look, she saw the large blue and white sign above the entrance: Tiffany's. Was this the name of the owner? If blue amber was a rare gemstone, then perhaps Tiffany sold it here at her shop? Her heart raced as she pushed one glass door open, warmth rushing to greet her. She stepped on plush grey carpet. It was very quiet, and there was a sweet fragrance in the air.

A brown-haired lady in a smart black suit stood behind the counter, one penciled eyebrow raised questioningly. The small gold nameplate on her blazer read Maud.

"Hello. How may I help you?" Maud asked brusquely, annoyed that the first person to come in was a little girl with wild-looking black hair wearing wet boots and a shabby coat. She plastered a smile on her heavily made-up face, in case the munchkin was the spoiled daughter of filthy rich parents. She had to be careful not to offend these brats. Just last week, a haughty thirteen-year-old had come into the store with her noisy friends, showing off their long, slim legs. That blonde-haired brat had demanded to look at every diamond bracelet available. "It's a birthday present from my parents," she had said with a smirk, speaking to Maud as if she owned the shop. Maud had badly wanted to slap the snotty look off her face. She pursed her lips at the memory.

Elly hesitated. She was on the verge of asking whether Tiffany herself was there, but instinct restrained her; one look at Maud's cardboard expression made her realize it was probably best to get straight to the point. "Hello," she said timidly. "I am sorry to bother you, but . . . umm, do you happen to sell any blue amber?"

Maud stared at her silently. *Great, she's probably one of those hippy sorts looking for those earth stones.* Stifling a sigh, she spoke slowly, as though talking to a much younger child. "No, dear, we sell precious jewels. See?" She pointed to an array of sparkling rings encased in a glass cabinet. "We sell diamonds, not cheap gemstones like topaz or amber. I haven't even *heard* of blue amber."

Elly's heart sank. To make things worse, she was feeling weak in the knees from hunger. Before she could think twice, she blurted out, "I'm sorry, but do you sell any food?" Then she instantly regretted it.

Maud's expression turned even darker. "We're not a shelter or a charity, young lady," she said coldly. "You don't get served breakfast at Tiffany's."

Elly blushed hotly. "I'm sorry for wasting your time, madam. Thank you." She turned on her heel and quickly walked out.

Elly sighed when she was standing out in the cold again.

Better luck next time, Ellanor.

I don't know how many times I'll need to try, Greymore. I didn't like the way she spoke to me. She wasn't very kind.

You need to develop a thick skin, Ellanor. You will come across people like that. The important thing is that you don't become unpleasant like them.

Elly continued walking in the direction of Westminster Abbey, her head filled with thoughts of home and whether she would ever succeed in repairing the portal. She couldn't stop thinking about Mama's sweet cakes and all those plump juicy fruits and leafy green vegetables back home.

She kept on charging ahead, her mind so preoccupied that she did not realize how much time had gone by. Suddenly, she looked up and there it was: Westminster Abbey. She gazed up at the behemoth structure that towered majestically above her. Lily was right; it was beautiful and grand, fit for even the royal elves of the old days.

Once she stepped inside, she marvelled at the hushed, vaulted, glorious space. She stood bathed in the tinted sunlight that streamed through the luxuriantly coloured stained-glass windows and offered up a silent prayer to Freya, wishing with all her heart that she could go home soon.

Walking around, she saw a number of statues that were called "effigies". She halted in front of one that looked especially forlorn: a carved wooden figure of a stern-faced, bearded man. She bent down and started to read the inscription on the plaque.

"That's King Henry VII," said a voice matter-of-factly. Startled, Elly looked up. Standing behind her was a young boy. He was thin, with very fair skin smattered with freckles, and a head of shiny red hair that looked long overdue for a cut. There was something owl-like about him; his large blue eyes blinked at her from behind round tortoiseshell glasses, his head tilted slightly to one side. Elly noticed that he made peculiar movements with his right hand when he talked, as though he were a ventriloquist with an invisible hand puppet. He gripped a bottle of water in his left hand. Elly noticed that the skin on his hands and wrists looked awfully chapped, covered in bright pink scratches.

Elly had read a lot about the history of the English monarchy, especially the infamous King Henry VIII and his six wives (several of whom he beheaded). She wasn't familiar with King Henry VII, though. She smiled at the boy, who continued to stare at the effigy.

"Hello, I'm Elly. What is your name?"

The boy did not answer. Instead, he continued to speak in a flat, matter-of-fact voice. "Henry VII was King of England and Lord of Ireland after he seized the crown on August 22 in 1485, when he defeated Richard III at the Battle of Bosworth Field. He was King of England until his death on April 21 in 1509. He was considered a good king, as he was successful in restoring power and stability of the English monarchy after the civil wars known as the War of the Roses. He was succeeded by his younger son, the notorious Henry VIII, father of Queen Elizabeth I, who was an avid fan of the playwright William Shakespeare." He paused to take a sip from his water bottle.

Elly frowned. Why wasn't he looking at her? It was as though he wasn't really talking to her; more like he was talking *at* her, like he was reciting from a script. She smiled. "You know so much about this place! What else can you tell me?" For some reason, she liked him. There was something inexplicably warm and safe about this boy.

He looked up at the ceiling. "Westminster Abbey is a large Gothic church, the first church in England built in the Norman Romanesque style. To the west is the Palace of Westminster. It is the traditional place of coronation for every King and Queen since William the Conqueror in 1066, and the burial site for those monarchs. It used to be a cathedral, from 1540 to 1550." He paused again to sip from his water bottle.

Then a voice rang out. "Teddy! I told you not to wander off!" Elly turned and saw a tall, slender girl striding towards them. She was very pretty, with long, strawberry blonde hair, light blue eyes, and a very fair complexion, with a sprinkling of freckles on her cheekbones. Her frown melted into a smile the moment she realised her little brother was talking to the girl next to him.

"Oh, hello," she said brightly to Elly. "I'm Maddy, and this is Teddy, my little brother."

Elly smiled shyly. "Hello, Maddy. I'm Elly. Very pleased to meet you."

Then she turned to the boy. "Hello, Teddy," she said.

He started counting on his fingers. "One, two, three, four . . ." he was saying softly, looking around.

Maddy smiled and rolled her eyes. "Please don't mind him, Elly. He loves visiting cathedrals, and he's sort of obsessed with historical facts. He knows how many effigies there are in this place, and he's trying to get to every single one of them."

She glanced at her watch. "We better get going; otherwise we'll be here all day. He just loves spouting facts—our little walking encyclopaedia." She playfully ruffled his hair. He wandered off to some other effigy.

Maddy leaned towards Elly and whispered, "Teddy has autism, you see. But he's harmless. He's really sweet when you get to know him." She winked. "I think he likes you. He wouldn't talk to just anybody."

Elly blushed. "He must be very clever, and he seems very gentle." But what does "autism" mean? She had never come across this word in the books she had read.

Greymore broke into her thoughts. *According to the dictionary, autism is a developmental disorder in humans that is characterized by impaired social interaction and communication, and restricted and repetitive behaviour, all starting before a child is three years old. This means that the child will not be able to communicate or interact normally. Children with autism may like to play by themselves or not talk.*

Elly nodded slowly. Autism isn't something that affects elves. She turned to Maddy and smiled. "Perhaps Teddy can be my tour guide!" she joked.

Maddy laughed. "You're right about that! He could be just as good as any tour guide, minus the tacky sense of humour."

She smiled and looked at Elly more closely. "Would you like to join us as we explore this place? Only if you'd like, of course. Are you with your family here?" She thought that Elly looked rather alone, and there was something a little outlandish about her. Maybe it was her exotic green eyes. She must have grown up abroad, which would explain her strange way of speaking.

Elly shook her head. "No, I am by myself for now. My parents are not in town. But," she added hurriedly, noticing Maddy's look of surprise, "I'm fine, because my guardian takes care of me. I've been exploring the city by myself."

Maddy's eyes widened. "Really! That is so cool. My parents would never let me walk around town alone, especially my mum; she's such a control freak. You're *so* lucky! Whenever my mum goes on one of her business trips, she always gets my grandma to keep an eye on me like a hawk. It drives me crazy!"

Elly smiled, but sighed inwardly. Back home in Evergreen City, she always felt safe, especially with protectors and guards keeping an eye on the cross points. But now things might be different, with the goblin infiltrator on the loose. Home as she knew it might not be so safe anymore. Her parents weren't here to stop her from doing anything dangerous.

But how she wished they were, if it meant she could see them again.

A shout broke into her thoughts. A tall red-haired man with a camera slung over his neck was walking towards them, looking flustered. "There you are!" he exclaimed. "Honestly, Maddy, don't disappear on me like that again. You guys almost gave me a heart attack."

Then he noticed Elly. "And who do we have here?" he asked with a smile. Up close, Elly realized the man must be the father; Teddy was the spitting image of him.

Maddy giggled and encircled her father's arm with her own. "Daddy, this is Teddy's new friend, Elly. I guess he's like any typical boy when it comes to girls: he likes them pretty, too."

Maddy's dad clucked his tongue. "That's my boy!"

He beamed at Elly. "Teddy's found a friend, eh? Well, if you're Teddy's friend, then you're my friend, too!"

Elly smiled. There was something very warm and safe about him, too.

"It is so nice to meet you, Mr . . ."

"I'm Andrew O'Brien, but just call me Andy! None of that formal mister or sir business. I'm still way too youthful for that," he joked with a laugh, draping an arm around his daughter's shoulders.

"We just moved here from Manchester. I've been really busy with work, but I wanted to spend some time with my munchkins this weekend exploring Oxford and more of London. It's a pretty incredible city. But I've had just about enough of museums!" Then he paused and looked at her curiously. "Are you from around here, Elly?"

She shook her head. "No, I'm visiting London for the first time."

"Ahh! And where are you visiting from, if you don't mind my asking?"

Elly swallowed nervously. "I'm, umm, from the Aland Islands in Finland."

His eyes lit up. "How lovely! I went to Finland once as a little boy. Did you know, some linguists and philologists believe that Finnish is one of the most complicated languages to learn?" He grinned. "I guess that must explain why you've mastered English so beautifully."

Elly blushed. Andy laughed. "Well, since we're a bunch of tourists, we better stick together!"

Then he turned to Teddy, who was wandering back over to them. "Teddy loves collecting all sorts of historical facts, and he especially loves going into big old buildings like this one."

He glanced at his watch. "Look at the time! We should go for lunch in about one hour. Let's go explore the rest of this place, kids! Chop-chop!"

Maddy piped up. "Elly's joining us, Daddy. She's going about all by her lonesome. Let's keep her company, okay? Besides, Teddy likes her."

Andy frowned and looked at Elly. "Of course, you're more than welcome to join us, honey. But what about your parents? Are you sure you can just go off with us like that?"

Elly repeated what she'd told Maddy. But Andy did not seem to think there was anything "cool" about her exploring the city by herself. In fact, he looked very worried.

Elly, I have a piece of paper with a number on it. Give it to Mr O'Brien, it will put his mind at ease.

Indeed, Andy felt uneasy knowing that a girl as young as his daughter could be left exploring a big city like London all alone. *Poor dear. I better keep an eye on her and make sure she's safe if her parents are so irresponsible,* he thought.

He watched as Elly opened up a little book strapped to her belt, and was surprised when she handed him a scrap piece of paper. "This is Mr Greymore's number, in case you want to talk to him," she said, trying to look nonchalant.

He took the paper from her, looking slightly relieved. "That's a good idea, I might just give him a call to let him know you're with us," he said, tucking the piece of paper into his jacket pocket.

Suddenly, Teddy was standing next to Elly. He took her hand. "Come," he said. Andy and his daughter exchanged amused looks.

"See, I told you he likes you," Maddy whispered. "He's been a bit moody since our parents got divorced, but you seem to have lifted his spirits."

Divorce? Elly puckered her brow, stumped by yet another word she had not come across in her readings before. Once again, Greymore broke into her thoughts. *A divorce happens after a husband and wife decide not to live together anymore and that they no longer want to be legally married to each other, due to various reasons, one of which is because they believe they no longer love each other.*

Elly was baffled. She could not imagine her parents divorcing. They were soulmates. In fact, a soulmate was destined for every elf. It was only a matter of time before soulmates found each other, and only death could separate them. There was no such thing as divorce back in her world.

Elly often wondered who her soulmate could be. Kaelan flashed across her mind, and she shook her head quickly. Who was she kidding? He probably had his sights set on some pretty girl back home, perhaps someone like Darrius.

As they walked together, Andy took countless photos with his big black camera. They took another flight of stairs down, passing several antiquated wooden chairs on display. One looked rather grand, like a throne of sorts, placed on a raised modern pedestal. Teddy commented, "King Edward's Chair is the throne on which English and British sovereigns were seated when they got crowned. The chair has been used at every coronation since 1308. It is now highly protected."

Maddy sighed. "I'm surprised he hasn't started telling you about all the famous dead people entombed here!"

Andy chuckled and ruffled his son's hair. "That's right! Why don't you tell Elly who some of these people are?"

Teddy didn't miss a beat. "Apart from many of the past monarchs of England, many famous poets, writers, and musicians were also buried here, such as Geoffrey Chaucer. Scientists such as Isaac Newton and Charles Darwin are buried here, too. William Wilberforce, the man who abolished slavery in the United Kingdom, was buried close to his friend, the former prime minister, William Pitt . . ."

He recited a long list of names that Elly soon lost track of.

By the time they walked out of Westminster Abbey, it was almost two o'clock, and the sky was a dreary grey, cold and wet.

"Let's go grab a late lunch near Trafalgar Square, my munchkins! From there we can take a stroll to Leicester Square. I don't know about you, but I'm starving!" Andy announced cheerfully.

Maddy whooped while Teddy walked ahead without waiting for them. Elly hadn't eaten anything since the early morning, and she was close to keeling over.

Elly went on a train for the first time. The London underground railway, also known as the Tube, looked like a very complicated tangle of colourful lines on the map that Lily had given her. She learned from Teddy that London is the world's most visited city; is home to eight million people, where more than three hundred languages are spoken; and has the oldest underground railway network in the world.

"The Great Fire of London in 1666 destroyed many parts of the city. I am scared of fire," Teddy said flatly, looking down at his shoes.

Maddy leaned towards Elly. "When he was younger, he burned his hand on the kitchen stove. It left a scar," she said in a low voice.

Once they arrived at Charing Cross Station, Andy led them up a flight of steps to ground level, where Elly caught the delicious aroma of fruits and vegetables mingled with less appealing smells. She wrinkled her nose as several passing red double-decker buses and black cabs spouted fumes. As they approached Trafalgar Square, they sat down at a bistro tucked inside a massive bookshop.

"Books . . . another of Teddy's great loves," Maddy said. "I'm not so into reading myself, but I don't mind listening to the music CDs over there while Teddy burrows into those books."

Andy ordered a variety of dishes to share: a large pepperoni pizza, a big plate of spaghetti bolognaise, a large garden salad, and fish and chips.

When Andy noticed that Elly was only taking small bites from the salad, he frowned. "Elly, don't you eat meat?"

She blushed and shook her head apologetically. Andy wagged a finger at her in mock reproach. "Honey, you should have told us! You'll starve eating only lettuce and cherry tomatoes!"

He signalled a waiter over and ordered a large fruit salad, half a dozen blueberry muffins, and several thick slices of toast slathered with strawberry jam. Elly's mouth watered when the scrumptious-looking food arrived, and she tried very hard not to wolf it down.

Maddy shook her head at Elly with a smile. "Seriously, you're a vegetarian? Who can resist food like this?" She took a huge bite of her pepperoni pizza slice and grinned. Teddy had picked off the pepperoni from his slice of pizza and was eating them separately from the base. He did the same thing with the salad: He segregated the cherry tomatoes, lettuce, and olives into three neat piles, and ate them separately.

Teddy concentrated on eating his food, occasionally counting on his fingers and muttering to himself. To Elly's relief, father and daughter just let her eat while they chatted comfortably.

"It takes time to fit in at a new school, honey . . ."

"I know, Daddy, but those girls want me to be a part of their group . . ."

Elly tried to pay attention, but she was becoming preoccupied with thoughts about Organoth blue amber again. She fidgeted with her fingers and took a deep breath.

"Um, Andy? May I ask a question?" she blurted, not realizing she had interrupted them midsentence.

But they didn't seem to mind. They smiled at her. "Sure, Elly. What is it?" Andy asked, looking at her closely. She had been quiet throughout lunch so far. Maddy had noticed, too.

Elly's ears had gone quite pink at the tips. It was a good thing that her long hair concealed them. "Do—do you know where I can get blue amber?"

Andy looked at her blankly. "Blue amber? What's that?"

Elly's heart sank. "It's a special type of gemstone, supposed to be very rare. I was told it is found in one place in the world. I want to know if I can possibly find it here in London."

Andy knitted his eyebrows. "I suppose they must have online shops for this blue amber you're talking about?"

Elly frowned. "Online shops?" She turned to Maddy helplessly.

Maddy had a thoughtful look on her face. "Blue amber . . . Something about it sounds familiar. But I can't remember why, for the life of me." She touched Elly's arm reassuringly. "I'll ask around and see what I can find out. But why do you want to look for this blue amber? Is it for a gift?"

"Oh, well," Elly stammered. "Well, it's for something really important. Yes, my parents would be happy if I'm able to find it."

Maddy nodded, assuming that meant her parents probably wanted it as a gift.

Andy watched Elly intently. He could sense her distress. Why would her parents ask her to search for something as obscure as this blue amber? Something was a little odd.

Then he remembered; he had to call her guardian! He jumped up from his chair. "Excuse me, girls. I'll just duck out for a minute." He sauntered out as he took out his mobile phone and the scrap of paper from his pocket.

When Elly mentioned that she had gone into a shop called Tiffany's, Maddy almost choked on her strawberry milkshake. "You went to *Tiffany's*? If they sell that blue amber you're talking about, it must cost a fortune!" She then proceeded to talk about a movie called *Breakfast at Tiffany's*. When Elly looked at her blankly, Maddy's jaw dropped. "It is *such* a classic. One of my favourites. I'll have to watch it with you sometime!"

Elly thought about Maud and cringed. "I sure didn't get any breakfast at Tiffany's," she mumbled.

When Andy returned to the table, he was wearing a bemused expression. "I just called your guardian, Mr Greymore. He sounded so refined, like he was a butler talking to His Lordship! He assured me that he would keep you safe and expressed how grateful he was that we were keeping you company."

He smiled and shook his head slightly, trying to clear his head; he felt a bit muddled. He barely remembered what he had said on the phone. But for some reason, he felt very reassured. "Anyway, we're happy to have you with us, Elly!"

She grinned at him, pressing one hand on her Royan. *Thank you, Greymore.*

I told you I would take care of it, Ellanor.

When it came time to pay the bill, she retrieved some coins from her pocket and blushed in dismay. She barely had enough to pay for a plate of muffins!

Andy immediately waved her away. "Don't be silly! You're our guest, and I won't take money from a little girl! Keep that money for emergencies." Elly smiled with gratitude and thanked him profusely.

After Andy paid for a book on astronomy that Teddy insisted on getting, they all walked back out into the cold. Andy handed Elly a small paper bag; it was filled with blueberry muffins! He grinned at her beaming face. "My treat, in case you get peckish," he said, patting her on the shoulder. She clutched the bag gratefully.

As they walked back to the train station, Elly overheard Andy talking to Teddy in hushed, pleading tones. "We'll go to the Tower of London next weekend, buddy. I need to take you kids home to your mother before supper, so we only have enough time for the London Eye before we call it a day. Otherwise, your mum will never let me hear the end of it. What do you say, eh?"

But Teddy was upset. Lips trembling, he started shaking his head vigorously and made odd clucking sounds with his tongue. His hands were balled into fists, and he began rocking back and forth.

"Uh-oh," Andy muttered, glancing at Maddy. She went up to Teddy and gently put her arms around him. This seemed to have a calming effect. He went limp and quiet.

"Let's go, sweetie," Maddy whispered, taking him by the hand. "We'll go on the London Eye with Elly!" This seemed to cheer him up; Teddy smiled and locked eyes with Elly for a split second before looking away again.

Andy breathed a sigh of relief. "Thank goodness he listens to you, at least," he muttered.

On the way to the gigantic Ferris wheel—which Elly learned was the London Eye—they passed a street performer dressed as a clown, handing out balloons to children. Teddy ran up to him and stuck his hand out.

"I want a balloon, please!" he said loudly. The clown did a little dance and laughed jovially before handing him a red one.

Andy shouted, "Hold on tight, Teddy! It's pretty windy!"

At the London Eye, they joined the long queue. Andy once again refused to take Elly's money. "Honestly, dear, you don't expect a gentleman to let a lady pay, do you?" he joked with a grin.

Once they had all gone inside their capsule, Teddy stood beside Elly and took her hand. Maddy giggled. Elly looked out at the view before her and gasped. Beside her, Maddy smiled and said softly, "Isn't it beautiful? I love coming up here."

Andy was busy clicking away on his camera. "We don't get awesome scenery like this in Manchester city," he murmured.

Elly could only nod, marvelling at the way the River Thames seemed to have turned pink and gold as the sun set over the city, where skyscrapers gleamed and sparkled like precious jewels. Elly could see Westminster Abbey, St Paul's Cathedral, and Big Ben's clock tower.

Teddy pointed towards the direction of a very tall, glassy, cone-shaped building. "Daddy works as a lawyer at the Gherkin now," he announced.

Andy laughed and draped an arm around his son. "I sure do! Anything for you munchkins."

The pink and gold in the sky had given way to the darkness by the time they left the London Eye. Andy checked his watch and frowned. "Elly, we should take you home. It's not safe for a young girl to walk around at this hour. The streets can get pretty rough at night."

Elly feigned a laugh. "Oh, please don't worry! I'm meeting my guardian nearby. I'll be off now. Thank you so much for everything, I had a *wonderful* day!" She gave a little bow, which surprised and delighted Andy.

He laughed. "Maddy, you should pick up some of these lovely manners! I can't recall the last time anyone ever thanked me with such heart!"

Maddy rolled her eyes before turning to Elly. "Give me a ring when you want to hang out, OK? I'll try to ask about blue amber."

To her surprise, Elly's eyes welled up. Maddy frowned and wondered whether there were problems at home with her parents; why else was she wandering the city by herself? She felt sorry for Elly. Although her own parents were divorced, they always tried to spend time with her and Teddy.

Maddy dug out a pen from Teddy's backpack and scribbled their home phone number and address on a crumpled receipt from lunch.

"I've probably said this a million times already, but Teddy has really taken a shine to you. That rarely happens. Needless to say, you've won us over too."

At this, Elly smiled. Maddy grinned and hugged her tightly. "So you must keep in touch, all right?"

Teddy was looking past Elly, his invisible hand puppet in tow. "Goodbye, Elly. See you again soon." He said this matter-of-factly, as though Elly was someone he saw frequently.

She smiled and gave him a hug, and she was reminded of her little brother Luca. "Thank you," she whispered. Though he did not hug her back, he was smiling.

Before they could again insist on escorting her, she started running, turning around once to wave at her new friends. They waved back. "Be careful!" Andy bellowed. "I'll phone Mr Greymore later to check that you got home safely!" Maddy was waving furiously; Teddy was gazing at her.

She wandered around aimlessly for a while, longing for a nice bath in the Shevanie Springs back home. She hadn't washed properly for the past few days, and didn't want to think about the state her hair was in.

Many shops were starting to close, as people rushed home for supper. Elly watched with envy as a little girl raced happily into her house with her mother in tow. It looked so warm and cosy inside.

Then sparkles in a window display caught her eye. She trotted over and peered through the glass. Some necklaces, along with eerie-looking ceramic dolls with large vacant eyes, were on display. The tiny shop was called Zany's.

Elly wandered in, her face frozen from the cold. The middle-aged woman behind the counter was reading a thick, dog-eared romance novel. She looked up and narrowed her eyes warily.

"How may I help you?" Roberta asked with a slight Russian accent that she had not been able to lose even after having lived in London for twenty years. She hoped the girl wasn't a shoplifter. She wouldn't be the first that day.

Elly looked around the small shop. There were pendants and various gemstones on display, such as topaz, crystal, garnet, amethyst. Then her eyes widened when she spotted a yellow-coloured necklace. She swallowed and took the plunge. "Excuse me, do you have any blue amber?"

Roberta raised her thick dark eyebrows in surprise. "Lassie, blue amber is rather hard to come by. We sell plenty of yellow amber, but no blue amber. Here, what about these?" She gestured to a little box filled with yellow amber pieces.

Elly shook her head, dismayed. "I'm sorry, but do you know where I could possibly get, umm, pure grade blue amber?"

Roberta heard the desperation in her small voice. She put her book down and looked at Elly curiously. "Well, perhaps you could look online. But mark my words, you might not even get the real thing when you make online purchases. A lot of fake stuff is on the market these days. Pure grade blue amber can be just as expensive as diamonds, but it is even more rare and unique because you can find it only in one place in the world, all the way in the Dominican Republic. If it is genuine, it is normally very expensive."

Roberta sighed; she still regretted having lost the blue amber ring her husband had given her many years ago.

"You see, the colour of blue amber is best appreciated in natural light or sunlight, which really brings out the beautiful tones . . ." Her voice trailed off. She really could've fetched a pretty sum for that ring.

Elly felt a glimmer of excitement. This was progress: finally, she'd found someone who knew about blue amber! "Excuse me, where did you say blue amber is from?" she asked eagerly, her eyes shining.

Roberta peered at Elly over her gold-rimmed spectacles. "The Dominican Republic, lass. It's an island all the way across the ocean in the Caribbean, very far from here."

Elly's excitement went up another notch. "Do you know if there are any volcanoes there?" she asked hopefully. Mount Organoth may not officially exist anymore, but there could be traces of it left.

Roberta frowned. "Well, I'm no geologist. I would think so, since the Carribean is known to have some volcanoes. But I think I once read that there are no more active volcanoes in the Dominican Republic." Then she looked at Elly sceptically. "Are you prepared to pay hundreds, perhaps even thousands of pounds to purchase pure grade blue amber?"

Elly's face dropped. She bowed her head. "Oh . . . I—I don't have any money," she said softly.

Roberta scoffed. "In that case, you won't be buying *any* sort of amber," she snapped, turning back to her novel with a disgruntled look.

So Elly walked out of the shop, her throat constricted, and she grew tense and anxious.

She hadn't really thought about money. How was she going to get by in the human realm without it? Did she actually have to go all the way to the Dominican Republic to get this Organoth blue amber? If that was the case, wouldn't the long trip require money? How would she get there? Her head pounded with countless questions, and her heart was heavy.

It seemed like an impossible task.

Don't lose heart, Ellanor. You have taken small steps. You have learned something: blue amber is expensive, and it originates from the Dominican Republic. Since it is far across the ocean, it would be impossible to walk there.

Elly stamped her feet in frustration, feeling very cross. *Greymore, I don't need you to rub it in!* She was cold, alone, hungry, and homeless. She was in no mood to listen to Greymore's know-it-all reasoning right now. If he were so superior, he would know how to get her home.

Greymore remained silent for the rest of the night.

Elly was exhausted by the time she reached the Berry Grove Park, which was once again deserted. She had eaten one of the muffins. Though she was still hungry, she had to ration her food.

She felt so tired, so crestfallen, that all she wanted to do was curl up and sleep, and hopefully wake up from what had to be a bad dream.

So she leapt up the tree and transformed back to elf proportions. She flung herself onto her stomach, feeling wretched beyond words, and in anguish she thumped her little fists against the trunk. Then, feeling guilty for taking her anger out on the innocent tree, she stopped and pulled the coat tightly around herself, clutching the bag of muffins close to her stomach. She longed to shut out the world for now.

Once again, it wasn't a dreamless sleep.

CHAPTER TEN
Migration from Tree to House

THE SKY WAS A CLEAR blue, the air fresh and clean. Elly was stretched out luxuriously on the grass under a vast canopy of old oaks, surrounded by mountainous piles of pineapple buns, egg tarts, and strawberry jam on toast. It rained on and off, but the branches above were so thick with leaves they acted as umbrellas.

Elly breathed in the fragrant air, thinking that life could not get any better, when suddenly a gigantic blueberry muffin appeared before her. She gasped.

Then the muffin blurred at the edges, and transformed into a gigantic piece of blue amber shaped like a house!

The door of the house swung wide open, and there stood a girl beckoning her to go inside. She had short, curly black hair, and her bright green eyes stared at Elly. But her face was blurry.

Then the girl turned and started to run.

Wait! Elly leapt up and started running.

Then there was a harsh, ear-piercing squawk. She brightened. It must be Marlow! She looked up into the sky, her heart soaring.

But it wasn't her griffin. Instead, a huge black-winged monster with blood-red eyes was swooping down towards her, its razor-sharp beak open, ready to devour her.

Ellanor! Wake up!

Gasping, Elly wrenched her eyes open. There was something big and black hovering over her. A dreadful *Caw! Caw! Caw!* seemed to make the very air vibrate.

She screamed; it was a crow!

"What do we have here? Something smells tasty!" rasped the foul bird, looking at Elly with cold hungry eyes. Then, in one swift movement, its beak came down, eager for a taste of this sweet little creature.

Luckily, Elly was quick; she darted away just in time, but she cried out in pain when she felt the crow's sharp beak scrape against her leg.

Amid the chaos, she dropped the bag of muffins. It fell down to the ground below, which dozens of sparrows and pigeons would later feast on.

The crow squawked angrily, not expecting his little prey to get away so deftly. It pursued Elly, who flew as fast as she could. She didn't know where she was heading. The sky was still dark, and it was raining; big fat droplets splashed on her. She was soon soaked to the skin, frozen from cold and fear. The crow was close behind, its raucous cries making her hair stand up on end.

Go straight and turn left at the red mailbox, Ellanor! Hide in the bushes!

Elly obeyed silently, too stricken to do anything else. The sound of the crow's flapping wings and the howling wind roared in her ears. There was a distant rumbling of thunder.

Then she saw the red mailbox. She made a sudden left turn, throwing the crow off course. It shrieked and cursed. Elly tumbled into a thicket of rose bushes next to the mailbox, brambles and thorns scratching her skin, tiny branches flipping in her face. Breathing heavily, she lay still as she listened to the crow throw a tantrum.

"Where are you? Where are you?" the crow screamed, poking its sharp beak through the rose bushes. Elly curled into a ball and rolled farther into the thicket of leaves and thorns, squeezing her eyes shut, shaking with terror.

Then a door slammed, followed by sounds of metal scraping against gravel. The deep, grouchy voice of a man shouted, "Get away from my roses, you dirty wretch!"

There was a stomping of footsteps and much clanging. The crow yelped and squawked noisily in protest, and before long Elly heard a fluttering of wings. Then there was silence. She could hear her own ragged breathing.

"Good riddance!" the man's voice called out triumphantly. Elly got on all fours, careful to avoid any spiky branches, and peeked out from the bushes. The crow was gone. She first saw the muddy yellow rubber boots, then she looked up, up, up.

It was the shoemaker!

Horace Cobble belched. "Fancy interrupting my breakfast!" he muttered before trudging back to the house, shutting the door quietly behind him. He did not want to wake his sleeping wife.

Elly stayed as still as a statue near the edge of the bush as she listened carefully. It was very quiet, save for the distant call of a bird. It wasn't a crow. Grimacing, she looked down; there was a long, bleeding gash on her right leg.

She swooned, not used to seeing the sight of blood.

Quickly transform into human proportions, Ellanor!

Elly did as she was told, realizing she was prey to many surrounding predators. She quickly crawled out of the rose bush onto grassy ground and transformed. Back to human size, she found herself wedged between the brick wall of the house and the rose bushes. The branches of a great elm tree shielded her from the rain that was pelting down.

There was only one place she could go to for help now.

Yes, Ellanor. It is time to seek them out. The broken portal is with them, after all.

She bit her lip. *Thank you for warning me about the crow, Greymore. You saved my life. I'm sorry for losing my temper with you last night.*

Greymore gave a low chuckle. *It is quite all right, Ellanor. I knew you would come around. Now, go.*

Smoothing out the wrinkles in the skirt of her torn dress and picking out bits of brambles from her hair, she walked up to the green-painted door and knocked loudly, three times. She licked her parched lips and willed herself to stand straight.

"Who is it?" a voice called out grumpily, displeased with yet another interruption. There was a pause; then the door swung open.

Horace glared at the girl standing at his doorstep. "What do you want?" he demanded. She couldn't possibly have the gall to sell bloomin' school cookies at this ungodly hour, could she?

Then he saw the bleeding wound on her leg, and her ashen face. "What in the world . . . ?" he began, but then he stopped short and stared at her, slowly taking in the shock of sodden black hair, the leaf-shaped ears, those brilliant green eyes, and the tattered purple dress.

Several moments passed before he found his voice again. "Oh, dear Lord," he croaked, clutching the doorknob for support.

Elly felt herself swaying, her vision greying out. Horace bellowed, "Miriam!"

———

When Elly opened her eyes, she found herself sprawled in a tangle of soft, warm blankets. The room was dimly lit by a small bedside lamp. There were muffled voices and footsteps. For a moment, she was so disoriented that she quite forgot where she was.

Then it all flooded back: the crow, the pain, the brambles, and blacking out.

She winced and felt for her right leg. It had been bandaged up. Slowly, she got out of bed. Leaning against the wall for support, she groped her way to the door, opened it a smidgen, and peeked through the gap.

There was a clattering of pans and slamming of cupboard doors as a plump, silver-haired lady bustled about in the kitchen. Elly gave an involuntary shudder when she spotted the black cat perched on a nearby stool like a large ball of wool, eyes closed in half-slumber. Shadows danced on the walls as a cozy fire crackled at the hearth near the kitchen.

Then the cat opened her eyes, looked straight at Elly, and hissed with displeasure. Elly jumped in surprise and accidentally bumped the door wide open.

Miriam turned and gasped, dropping the potato she was peeling.

"You're up!" she cried, rushing over. "Oh, I was so worried when you passed out with that nasty gash on your poor leg! It must have caused quite a shock. You'd been unconscious since Horace found you at our doorstep this morning; and now it's supper time!" She wiped her hands down her apron and looked back at her cat nervously. "Stay there, Snowy!"

"Supper time?" Elly croaked, her throat awfully parched. That meant she hadn't eaten for almost a whole day. Her stomach growled.

Miriam ushered her to a plump floral-patterned armchair in the family room. "Here, come sit down, sit down. Let's have a cup of tea, shall we?" Elly collapsed on the cushioned seat, still feeling a little shaky in the knees.

Before rushing back to the kitchen, Miriam turned to her cat again. "Snowy, you better behave yourself! I don't want to see a single scratch on her!" she said sternly, wagging a finger.

The cat narrowed her yellow eyes and leapt off the stool in a huff. Elly could hear her mutter, "At her current size I'm not likely to gobble her up now, am I?"

Miriam came back with a tray holding a teapot and teacups. Once she sat down next to Elly and poured the tea, she leaned forward and looked at the pale-faced girl closely.

"Your name is Elly, right?"

Elly nodded as she hungrily took a gulp of the lukewarm tea. It wasn't chamomile; it had a slightly woody taste, not at all unpleasant.

Miriam smiled and clasped her hands on her lap nervously. "I'm Miriam, in case you've forgotten. My husband Horace is in his workshop." She glanced around the room. "My cat Snowy has gone off sulking."

She turned back to Elly with anxious eyes. "We are so sorry about what happened last time, Elly. Snowy isn't normally aggressive, I swear. She must've gotten a little jealous; or else she mistook you for a little pet on account of your tiny size. When you flew out the window, we were so worried you'd been badly hurt. Thank goodness you're still in one piece!"

She paused and asked the question that had been bothering her. "That wound on your leg . . . it wasn't from Snowy, was it?"

Elly shook her head vigorously. "Oh, no! Snowy didn't actually leave a scratch on me the other time. No, this morning I was attacked by a crow."

Miriam's eyes went round. "Oh, you poor dear!" she cried. The old lady was looking at her with such concern and tenderness that Elly missed her mother all the more. Tears filled her eyes and slipped down her cheeks.

Miriam patted her on the back. "There, there. We are just so glad you are all right now. I was going mad with worry, wondering if my cat was responsible for injuring you!"

She paused, then looked towards the hallway. "Stop eavesdropping and come introduce yourself properly!" she called out.

There was some muffled muttering. Then Horace sidled out, two hands behind his back like a bashful schoolboy.

Elly was glad to see him; he had practically saved her life from that hideous crow, after all. She smiled so radiantly that for a moment he quite forgot himself and stood there staring at her, speechless. Finally, he cleared his throat. "Well, I'm glad you're better now," he mumbled.

"Thank you both so much for helping me. I didn't know where else to go." Her voice was still hoarse, and it trembled.

Horace shifted awkwardly on his feet before excusing himself, mumbling something about shoes and deadlines. At his retreating back, Miriam grinned and whispered, "Don't worry. He seems like an old grouch, but he's really a softie at heart. You should have seen him fussing over you after you passed out. He carried you into the house like a chivalrous knight!"

Elly imagined an armoured Horace brandishing a sword in one hand, and holding a pair of sparkling shoes in the other. She giggled.

For supper, Miriam had prepared lamb chops with boiled potatoes for Horace and herself, and a delicious broccoli and pumpkin salad with freshly baked bread for Elly, who gratefully finished her meal without leaving a morsel. For dessert, Elly tried home-made apple pie with vanilla ice cream for the first time. Her eyes sparkled as she swallowed her first bite. "Wow, it's scrumptious!" she exclaimed, mentally putting it on her list of favourites alongside pineapple buns, blueberry muffins, and strawberry jam on toast.

By that time, Horace had begun to relax. Mug of root beer in hand, he laughed uproariously at the way Elly marvelled over every vegetarian food item she had not tried before.

"My wife may not be any good as a cobbler, but she sure makes one fine cook!" he said proudly, rubbing his bulging stomach and loosening the top button of his old waistcoat that looked close to bursting at the seams. Snowy sulked under the table at Miriam's feet, disgruntled with all the attention Elly was getting.

After supper, Elly talked late into the night with the Cobbles in front of the crackling fire. Enthralled, they sat perched on the edge of their seats, holding onto her every word. She told them everything that had transpired from her birthday, the goblin's treachery, falling through the portal, her unsuccessful attempts at tracking down Organoth blue amber, masquerading as a human, to the attack of the crow early that morning. They interrupted occasionally to clarify a point here and there.

When they asked Elly to describe her homeland, she sighed wistfully. "Alendria is . . . *luminos.* In your language, the closest word is beautiful. But in my language . . . *luminos* has a meaning beyond that of beautiful. It's difficult to explain."

She looked at the Cobbles and smiled. "The Tree of Life, which we simply call the Tree, is where elves dwell in Alendria. The Tree is our world. It is a tree so massive that its branches function like platforms of land, housing everything from great cities like Evergreen, to small towns like Morwen Valley." She cringed as she thought of Edellina, then took a sip of her warm chamomile tea before resuming.

"The magnificent canopy has leaves that alternate between gold and silver throughout the year. Evergreen is the biggest city in the southern region where it is always warm; up in the north, where the Vierran elves live, it is always cold. The sky there is nothing like what you see here. It is always awash with a splash of different colours of the rainbow. The Star of Freya constantly shines like a beacon, even during the day."

Her face turned dark. "The goblins live underground, beneath the Tree. They hate us. All I know is that their underworld is the antithesis of ours—it is endlessly dark, cold, and putrid. Nothing good ever grows there."

"Who is Freya?" Miriam asked curiously. Elly had mentioned the name several times.

Elly smiled. "Freya is our Maker. She created elves, and our homeland Alendria. Legend tells that Freya transformed into a star to look over us, for she loves us so."

Miriam leaned back in her armchair and sighed. "That sounds so beautiful. Like something from an epic poem."

Horace cleared his throat and scowled. "But what about those nasty goblins? Where did they come from, exactly?"

"Well . . ." Elly's brow furrowed. She had never really thought about that before. The existence of the goblins was a reality that seemed as normal as the unpleasant existence of snakes. "I think the goblins have been dwelling in the underworld for as long as elves have lived in Alendria. I suppose the Maker created everything, but I can't understand why creatures as foul and evil as the goblins were ever created in the first place."

"Well, I suppose even Alendria isn't utopia," Miriam murmured. When Elly looked at her questioningly, she smiled. "Utopia is a perfect world. But such a world holds up only in theory."

Horace took another gulp of root beer. "What about this . . . this Royan of yours? You mean, it's actually . . . alive?" He eyed the book on her belt warily, half expecting it to spout some magic.

Elly smiled. "My Royan, Greymore, is flowered from a royal acorn of the Tree. A Royan stays with an elf for about two hundred years. By that time, a Royan matures and ripens enough in its acorn form to return to the Tree, where it then flowers, and all that it has learned from its keeper will be assimilated into the intelligence repository of the Tree and shared with the elven community."

Miriam and Horace gawked at her wide-eyed. "Two . . . two hundred years?" Miriam asked meekly.

Elly laughed. "Yes. I suppose you now get the idea that elves have a far greater lifespan than that of humans. In general, elves can live for one thousand years."

"One thousand years!" shouted Miriam and Horace in unison.

Elly giggled. "Yes! So we age very slowly, but we can still die prematurely of extreme grief and severe injury, though our physical constitutions are much stronger than those of humans."

At this, Horace snorted. "How did we get the short end of the bargain?" he muttered.

Miriam was shaking her head in wonder. "If I may ask, Elly . . . how old are you?" *Please don't be older than I am*, she prayed. That would be too strange.

Elly smiled. "I just turned twelve years, whereas my grandpapa is nearly eight hundred years old. To elves like him, who have lived in the world so long, I am like a little shoot beside a grand oak tree that has seen many summers."

Miriam cocked her head. "What about this coming of age ceremony you mentioned? Since elves are blessed with long life, why is the meagre age of twelve years old so significant? Shouldn't you, say, come of age at one hundred or something?"

Elly grinned. To her surprise, she was rather enjoying all these questions. Perhaps talking about Alendria made her feel closer to home. "The number twelve bears much significance in our realm. Grandpapa once explained it to me . . ." Her eyes took on a far-away look as she recounted her grandfather's words.

"My dear Elly, once an elf turns twelve years old, they begin to undergo some significant changes—physically, mentally, and emotionally. This transformation, called *pharowyn* in Yahana, takes place over the course of the next twelve years, until an elf turns twenty-four. Then, it's as though time stands still. Physically, you stay unchanged until your six hundredth year, when elves finally begin to show outwards signs of ageing." At this, he had smiled and gestured at his wrinkles and long silver hair. "But even then, compared to humans, we age with grace, free of bodily ailments, for which we should be thankful."

Miriam and Horace gaped at each other. "My, this *pharowyn* sounds awfully like puberty to me," she murmured, recalling her son's turbulent adolescence.

"Followed by an unjustly and ridiculously extended adulthood, and painless old age," Horace grumbled. Then he frowned and turned to Elly. "So, the Royan returns to the Tree and shares what it has learned over two hundred years. In that case, the intelligence repository is sort of like the Internet, right?"

Miriam nudged him. "I don't think she knows what the Internet is, Horace. We're no experts, either." They had never used a computer in their lives.

She turned to Elly and smiled. "Apart from those gruesome goblins, Alendria sounds unfathomably gorgeous, Elly. I can't quite imagine just how beautiful it is. It sounds even more beautiful than Santorini."

Elly looked at her quizzically. "Santorini?"

Horace belched. "It's an island in Greece. Miriam is dead set on going there before we both expire. But I don't know how, since we can't even afford a trip to Wales at the moment!" Miriam glowered at him, then dropped her eyes to the floor and sighed.

After Elly told them about Edellina, Horace frowned and stretched out his legs. "So you're saying . . . to get back to Alendria, you need to fix the portal with something called Organoth blue amber?" He got up and went over to a wooden chest that was tucked at the bottom of a tall bookshelf.

"I should've listened to Miriam and put this thing away safely. My grandfather would not have been proud of me," he lamented. With a grunt, he lugged it out and wrenched the lid open. Then he carefully retrieved a small wooden box with both hands.

He gestured to Elly. "You should open this."

Nodding, she lifted the lid gingerly. Nestled in the black, velvety fabric was the broken portal. She sighed. It was her fault that the portal broke in the first place.

Miriam patted her on the shoulder. "It was an accident, dear. I must have given you quite a fright when I opened that dusty old cupboard."

They insisted that Elly keep the broken portal with her. "You'll need it with you if you want it repaired on the spot or something," Horace said gruffly, secretly resolved to help Elly find Organoth blue amber. But he had never even heard of blue amber.

Elly nodded and smiled gratefully. "Thank you." Horace and Miriam then looked on with amazement as she unstrapped the small book from her belt, opened it, and started talking to it in her language. Then she took out the two pieces of broken portal and placed them on top of the blank white pages. Suddenly, the broken portal vanished into thin air! Miriam and Horace gasped; the pages were no longer blank; instead, there was a picture of the broken portal as though an artist had just expertly drawn it. This was the first magical thing they had seen Elly do.

Elly smiled. "This is how we carry things around with us. We don't carry physical, bulky baggage like humans do. Greymore will keep the broken portal safe for me," she explained.

By the time they all staggered to bed, it was well past one o'clock in the morning. The temperature had plummeted, and Elly was loathe to leave the fireplace.

After washing for the first time in four days, Elly, at Miriam's insistence, changed out of her tattered purple dress. Miriam held up something with blue and white checkers for Elly. The fabric looked a little worn, but it was soft to the touch.

"These pyjamas belonged to our son Charlie when he was a boy," Miriam murmured, fingering the material. "We kept some of his old clothes as keepsakes, as all sentimental parents do. We shall do something about your clothing situation tomorrow," she said firmly.

Miriam looked around the room with wistful eyes when she tucked Elly into bed. "This used to be Charlie's room. He moved out after he graduated from Cambridge. Now, he's a grown man leading a busy life with his work and family in Surrey." From her expression, Elly guessed that she missed her son very much.

Miriam smiled and gave her a hug. "Good night, Elly dear. Sweet dreams."

That night, Elly barely stirred as she slumbered dreamlessly for once, so tired she was. The next morning, they all slept in and missed breakfast. Even Snowy.

CHAPTER ELEVEN
Of Pennies and Piggy Banks

"IT'S BEEN A LONG TIME since we've had the sound of a child's chatter and laughter cheer up this house," Miriam announced as she bustled about in the kitchen while Elly helped set the table for lunch the day after. The wound on her leg was already closing up nicely. "Elves sure heal fast," Horace grunted, rubbing his stiff knees. "I suppose you won't ever get arthritis either!"

Over the next couple of days, Miriam made Elly several new outfits. "I'm nowhere as good as Horace's Grandmother Polly," she said shyly. "But these should do." She held up two dresses: one was lavender lined with silver, and the other was black lined with gold. Thank goodness there was nothing in pink!

Elly jumped with joy and threw her arms around Miriam. "I *love* them!" she cried, and tried them on immediately. Miriam beamed, already thinking of new designs for more outfits.

Elly wanted to call Maddy to ask whether she had found out anything about blue amber. But when she rummaged through her coat pockets, the piece of paper on which Maddy's phone number was scribbled was nowhere to be found. *It must have fallen out when I was flying away from that crow,* she thought, crestfallen.

Elly had reached a conclusion: her best chance of finding Organoth blue amber was to go to the Dominican Republic. But she didn't have any money to pay for the trip, let alone money to pay for the Organoth blue amber if she ever located it. She had learned that a small piece of ordinary blue amber the size of a grape would easily cost over three hundred pounds.

She was at a loss, and consulted Horace and Miriam over breakfast one day.

Horace puckered his brow as he thought hard about Elly's predicament. "Well, there are several ways to get to the Dominican Republic. It's one of the most popular tourist destinations in the Caribbean. I've heard that the golf courses there are incredible. Not that I've ever played golf. Anyway, there aren't many direct flights. Purchasing a flight over there is very expensive. It's a whopping ten-hour flight from here, after all. Besides, I'm afraid we just don't have that kind of money right now, though I wish we did." He sighed and crossed his arms.

Elly wrung her hands in frustration. "But isn't there an affordable way to get there, somehow?"

Horace shook his head. "It would be much simpler if you could get there by train, but the Dominican Republic is over four thousand miles across the sea, so that's out of the question. Anyway, you don't have a passport that would allow you to pass customs at the airport to board flights, not to mention travelling alone as a child. Another option is to transform to elf size and board a flight to the Dominican Republic in secret, as you would be tiny enough to conceal yourself in someone's luggage. But you might get detected during customs check. If you get caught, I can't imagine what they might do to you." At this, he shuddered, and Elly cringed.

Horace cleared his throat and continued. "Going there by ship would take weeks. What about if you . . . if you flew over there?"

Greymore rumbled. *Ellanor, the journey would be perilous, and deplete you of your powers before you arrived. You have not yet developed the stamina to cover such lengthy journeys. Being depleted of your powers in another foreign country, friendless and alone, could put you in grave danger.*

Miriam gave her a sympathetic look. "I'm sorry, Elly. It doesn't sound like an easy situation at all."

Elly was exasperated. It seemed like her options were so limited. Only Freya knew when she would be reunited with her family.

Even if she did eventually locate Organoth blue amber, all her hard work would be futile if she couldn't pay for it. Besides, she might need money for other things. Greymore had lectured her on propriety and good manners, reprimanding her when she had casually suggested letting the Cobbles pay for everything while she was with them.

You should make yourself useful, Ellanor. You are not to sit idly by while the Cobbles live frugally. It is not honourable to take their help and kindness for granted. You should give something back.

One evening after supper, Elly approached Horace as he was watching a game of soccer on their old television set over a slice of Miriam's delicious pumpkin pie. Elly frowned at the screen; some team called Manchester United was playing against another called West Ham. She thought this thing called soccer looked awfully tame and boring compared to the riveting, adrenaline-filled contest of archensoar, where archers mounted on flying griffins vie to pierce the elusive golden apple of Eris. Elly wondered if she would ever get to watch another game of it.

Horace frowned and turned down the volume. "What? You want to learn how to earn money?"

Elly nodded vigorously. "Yes! I need to learn to make money so that I can buy Organoth blue amber when I eventually get my hands on some."

Miriam raised her eyebrows as she started clearing the table. "Dear, you can always come to us if you need money."

Elly nodded, though she knew the Cobbles were barely making ends meet. They had cut down on several expenses to make sure Elly got to eat fresh fruits and vegetables, which were not cheaply bought at the local supermarket. She could tolerate all foods, but she thrived on fresh foods and everything home-made, and disliked anything processed or artificial. She had tried eating potato chips and French fries, but she never asked to try them again. They had left a horrible aftertaste.

Elly felt indebted to these two kind souls. She wanted to do something for them, too. She smiled at Miriam. "I know I can trust you both to help me. But blue amber is expensive, and I need to find a way to pay for it. Greymore says I should take responsibility and earn my own keep. It's wrong to just sit idly by and expect others to give me money when I'm capable of earning it myself."

Horace knitted his brow. "Elly, you are still a child. Nobody in their right mind will hire you. Child labour is illegal in this part of the world, you know."

She grinned. "Yes, I am a child. But I am not a *human* child from this part of the world, am I? So that law doesn't apply to me," she deduced triumphantly.

His eyebrows shot up, and he laughed. "Yes, you are correct! But the people around here don't know that, do they? You can't tell them you're an elf. They'll throw you in the loony bin faster than you could say 'God save the Queen!'"

She giggled and winked. "Well, I have a better idea. Greymore has already given me his blessing. I shall work for *you*." She puffed out her chest proudly. "I will help expand your business!"

Miriam swivelled around from the sink and gaped. Horace choked on his tea. "What do you mean?" he sputtered, not sure he had heard right.

Under the table, Snowy looked at Elly irritably. "Someone thinks rather highly of herself!" the cat scoffed.

Elly ignored her. "Hear me out. We could really give it a go. Over the past week I have observed how things work around here. You are trying to run a business. I have some ideas about how we could attract more customers."

Horace had gone quite red in the face as he continued to sputter. Miriam thumped him on the back, then smiled at Elly. "Yes, please go on, dear."

Elly rubbed her hands together excitedly. "I've thought a lot about this. My mama runs a shop back home selling sweet cakes. They're like the pastries you make, but they're made from ingredients that you can't find here . . . like unicorn milk, silver lilac sap, dragon honey, and so forth."

Miriam raised her eyebrows and shivered at the thought of dragons.

"Anyway, it is without dispute that Mama's sweet cakes are the best in Alendria. But she really makes an effort to make her shop look nice, too. I helped her with a lot of the decorations."

Elly didn't have to spell it out: Horace's shop looked very old and unkempt, with fading and peeling wall paint, torn carpet, dusty countertops, and a grimy window display. How could anyone even properly see the shoes on display through such muck?

Miriam eyed her husband, who was now rubbing his chest. "I believe the term we're looking for is 'good marketing', dear. The shop hasn't exactly had the best image in the past several decades," she said, a little mournfully.

Horace was speechless. Who was this munchkin to suggest that he change his ways?

Elly frowned and folded her hands in front of her dress. "When was the last time you made a sale?"

Miriam screwed up her face in concentration as she wiped down the kitchen counter. "Hmm, if my memory still serves me well, old Mr Jeeves bought those dusty brown loafers three days ago. But Mr Jeeves is almost a century old and knew Horace's father as a young lad. He's awfully loyal."

Horace coughed. "Mind you, we do get new customers wandering in. They just don't really buy anything," he said lamely.

Miriam rolled her eyes. "That's because they were immediately put off by how shabby this place looks," she muttered. Horace glared at her.

"You need to attract a wider customer base," Elly said thoughtfully, twirling strands of her hair.

Miriam nodded. "Elly is right, Horace. You know we could do better. We still have time to make money to enjoy retirement, you know."

She turned to Elly. "It's gotten much harder with age," she admitted with a sigh, rubbing her back as she sat down heavily next to her husband. "He's half given up on this business. These days, we make just enough to feed ourselves. Thank God we own this house and the shop. If we had to pay rent, we would have been out on the streets long ago." She shook her head. "I guess you just can't teach old dogs new tricks."

Horace grew quite purple. "Excuse me, I'm sitting right here!" he snapped. "Speak for yourself!"

Elly glanced at Horace. Grandpapa's voice echoed in her mind: *Sometimes, all it takes to change your life is to change your routine.* Oh, how she missed him! She sighed and looked at Miriam. "Didn't you say that you've always wanted to go to some place called Santorini if you had the money?" she asked. Horace groaned.

Miriam blushed. "Yes, I would love to go to Santorini. But frankly, I'd love to go anywhere as long as we get to have fun together," she confessed in a small voice.

Horace scowled. "We're too old for fun," he grumbled.

Miriam winced. "How about the time we took the train up to Bristol to see my Aunt Evelyn, eh?" he asked, stabbing his fork into the pumpkin pie. "Didn't you like that little bread and breakfast? Charming, you kept calling it."

Miriam stared at him, and her face contorted. "We made that trip for Aunt Evelyn's *funeral*!" she said shrilly.

Surprised, Horace looked up from his pie.

"For your information, no, I don't think we're too old to have some fun! God forbid that we actually get to enjoy life for a change! We're not young anymore, but we're not *dead*! I want to board a plane at the airport and go on a real *vacation*. Yes! That would be first on my bucket list, if I were to have one!"

Horace stared at her. Miriam was usually very mild-tempered and never raised her voice. For once, he felt small in front of his wife. "But we don't have the money for it," he said feebly.

Miriam put her hands on her hips. "Oh, you don't think I've heard that one?" she retorted. "Even when we did have the money, before you wasted this shop away, you never made the effort to take us on a holiday! You could've taken me *anywhere*, even as close as Wales or Scotland, if it meant we could have fun together! I'm destined to grow old and die in this godforsaken shop . . ."

She stopped short, stifled a sob, then hurried out of the kitchen.

There was a ringing silence as Horace gazed down at his unfinished slice of pumpkin pie. His wife had never really been so plain about her feelings. He had never really known how she felt.

Elly shifted on her feet awkwardly. She wasn't a stranger to arguments; back home, Papa and Mama would argue, too, but not quite so noisily.

Then she brightened as she sat down in front of Horace. "If I can help you get more business, then you might be able to save up enough money to take Miriam on her dream vacation!" she said excitedly, her eyes shining.

Horace blinked. Was it really possible? He thought of his wife's sad face. What did he have to lose anyway? Maybe this could be his way of making it up to his grandfather . . . and to Miriam.

"All right then, you win," he said gruffly. "I'll give you an allowance every day for whatever you have up your sleeve, you little munchkin."

Elly beamed and clapped her hands in delight. "Thank you, Horace! You won't be sorry!" Then, as an afterthought, "You used to do some painting, right? Do you have any supplies left?"

He nodded. "Yes, they're all in storage up in the attic. The paints and brushes should still be good to use, though. Why?"

But before he could get an answer, she had already dashed into her room, madly transferring her thoughts into her Royan. When Horace peeked in, he saw her sitting on the bed with her eyes flaming like green fire as she stared down at the book on her lap, its pages glowing.

Before Horace went off to bed, she made him lug out his old painting supplies from the attic. There was a big boxful of them, stuffed with large tubes of paint and brushes. "What are you going to do with these old things, anyway?" he grumbled. Elly just smiled mysteriously.

As Elly was getting ready for bed, Miriam poked her head through the doorway. She was carrying a cardboard box. "I'm sorry for what happened earlier, Elly," she said softly, sitting down on the edge of the bed. "I don't know what came over me. I'd bottled up all those feelings for so long. But with you there, I suddenly felt this surge of courage. The truth just tumbled out." She shook her head in wonder and smiled.

"But you know, it's sort of worked out for the best. Horace apologized to me for the first time in many years. A leopard does change his spots, after all. I guess my outburst was a little earth-shattering for him."

Elly smiled. "I haven't known you both very long, but I know you love each other."

Miriam blushed. "When you talk like this, you don't seem like a child at all!" Then she took Elly's hand and squeezed it. "Anyway, Horace told me he's agreed to your big plans. I went up to the attic and found something for you."

She patted the cardboard box on her lap, opened it, and retrieved a pink ceramic pig. "My, there's a treasure trove of Charlie's childhood stuff in the attic. I almost forgot all about this piggy bank. It used to belong to Charlie. It's yours now," she announced to a beaming Elly. "Deposit your earnings through this slot, and soon you will have a small fortune!"

"Thank you!" Elly cried, hugging the piggy bank. So far, everything was going according to plan.

Elly crept out of bed shortly after midnight. She could hear snores coming from the master bedroom as she darted soundlessly across the hallway.

The house was silent and dark, and the bone-chilling damp seeped through her slippers as she flitted down the stairs. She went to the bathroom and splashed ice-cold water on her face. Then she rolled up her sleeves, put on one of Miriam's old aprons, and set to work. Miriam and Horace wouldn't be up for another eight hours; they slept in late on Sundays.

Snowy had been curled up in Miriam's bed before she woke and wandered into the workshop. The cat watched with narrowed eyes as Elly worked tirelessly and quietly, her movements so quick that they were a blur. She barely noticed when the darkness gave way to sunlight and the birds started calling. Snowy had long ago fallen asleep, sprawled across the rug in front of the crackling fireplace.

When Horace made his way to his workshop that morning, Miriam in tow with his coffee and porridge, they froze in their tracks. "Oh, dear Lord!" he exclaimed. Miriam gasped and almost dropped the breakfast tray.

Cobble & Son was one of several vintage shoe shops left in town that had long lost its former glory. But the dilapidated shop had undergone a complete transformation, literally overnight.

The peeling and greying beige walls had been mended carefully with tape that somehow blended seamlessly with the wall. The torn floral carpet had been mended with thread and needle. Over the entire left wall was painted a marvellous mural of a town with rows and rows of white houses on a sloping cliff facing the sparkling blue sea with the beach sand a golden yellow, the sky a glorious blue dotted with fluffy white clouds. The distinct strokes reminded Miriam of her favourite painter, Claude Monet. It looked flawless, like it had been done by a real artist.

Miriam gawped in awe. "That's Santorini!" she marvelled, staring at the mural.

The sunlight streaming through the windows was much brighter than usual, and Horace realized why—the display windows sparkled spotlessly. The oak counter gleamed, brought back to its original sheen. Tall pink and red roses that Horace recognized as those from his garden filled several vases. When they looked up at the ceiling, they almost passed out; it was a magnificent blue with *moving* clouds, just like the sky outside!

Hanging above the counter was a prettily painted wooden sign with pink and gold lettering: Miriam's Sweet Secrets. Several clean dessert plates were piled atop a small wooden table next to the counter, gleaming silver forks rammed into two shiny glass jars. Miriam gaped at the sight.

Just when Horace thought there couldn't be any more surprises, he stopped in his tracks in front of his worktable. There before him on the gleaming oak was a pair of woman's stilettos with three-inch heels, of red leather edged with black suede, so expertly crafted that he had to use his magnifying glass to inspect the tiny, flawless stitches. "I can't believe it," he muttered, thinking about the elves his grandfather used to yammer on about.

There was a rustling behind them. Horace and Miriam both turned, still open-mouthed, to see Elly holding several bulky garbage bags. Her face was streaked with paint and dirt, and her curly hair stood up in several places. But she had never looked happier.

"Oh, Elly," Horace breathed, thunderstruck. "How in the world . . . ?"

Elly laughed merrily as she set down the garbage bags. "Did you think I've been wasting my time away, doing nothing but sitting around the past week? I've been observing how you make shoes, and you never noticed! I think I've mastered the basics, and this pair is my first without mistakes. I've been practising late at night on those old fabric scraps that I found stored away in the shed."

Elly was talking a mile a minute, and the Cobbles were still too much in shock to fully digest what she was saying.

Elly fluttered about the room as she talked. "Don't you think Miriam ought to try her hand at selling her delicious pastries? Horace, your workshop is connected to the kitchen through that door, so it's awfully convenient for Miriam to go back and forth. Customers attracted to Miriam's pastries might want to take a look at your shoes. And customers looking at your shoes might feel peckish for scrumptious cake or pie! Either way, there's a good chance you'll get *some* business. And the mural of Santorini does rather brighten up the whole place, don't you think? People would be drawn to a shop that looks bright and cheery and makes them think happy thoughts!"

There was a silence as she finally paused to take a breath.

Then Miriam burst out laughing and kissed Elly on both cheeks.

Horace bent down and embraced Elly. "I can't quite believe my eyes. Thank you for breathing life into this place again," he whispered.

So Horace opened shop the following morning sporting a proud grin on his face, and renewed hope in his heart. Miriam nervously set to work in the kitchen, kneading dough for the first blueberry pie she would be selling. Elly darted from kitchen to workshop, helping out at a feverish pace.

Before the first customer set foot in his revamped shop, Horace's voice boomed throughout the house. "Elly! Come out here!"

Elly jumped and almost dropped the packet of flour she was holding. She raced to the workshop. "What is it?" she cried breathlessly.

Horace was beaming as he gazed out the window. He turned and smiled at her. "Look!"

Elly peered out and gasped. Flakes were falling like rain outside, and the ground was covered in a blanket of white. "So this is snow?" she whispered, delighted. She had never seen anything like it back home. It looked so beautiful.

Day after day for the next two weeks, Elly kneaded dough and applied frosting; washed piles of cutlery, plates, and tea cups; and stitched and sewed leather. Miriam and Horace kept on reminding her to slow down and rest, worried that she might burn out. But she just waved them away as she happily dashed about, tirelessly weaving in and out of rooms. She was glad to be kept busy. All the hard work kept her mind off Organoth blue amber when she wasn't desperately looking for it.

She continued having those strange dreams of the girl, which both puzzled and somewhat frightened her, though she kept it to herself. At times, she had the inexplicable sense that the dreams were so lucid that she had trouble distinguishing her own feelings from those of the girl's. But by the time she awoke, the face of the girl had become a hazy memory.

Lo and behold, business grew. Very soon, Horace found himself apologetically turning away disappointed customers who had to leave his shop empty-handed. For the first time, his shoes were getting sold faster than they were being made! He couldn't imagine how he would manage without Elly's help. The little elfling was proving to be a very skilled apprentice, indeed. By the time the shop closed each day, the Cobbles would collapse on the living room sofa, exhausted to the bone but happy and satisfied as they had not been in a very long time.

Word quickly spread over town. Even the newspapers raved about the phenomenon. *Cobble & Son, the vintage shoe shop that pedestrians mistook for an old hardware shop, has been gloriously resurrected! The Cobbles have worked miracles with their remodelling—the magnificent moving ceiling alone must have cost a small fortune to install! Horace Cobble has totally redefined the vintage shoe shop—he has even started up a joint venture with his wife Miriam, an accomplished patissier, whose scrumptious home-made blueberry cheesecakes, and pecan and apple pies have kept insatiable customers going back for more!*

Indeed, Miriam had to put out some tables and chairs in the front yard as well as the garden for a growing customer base that kept returning for her pastries, day after day.

Unbeknownst to Elly, even after receiving her daily allowance, Horace snuck many extra pounds into her piggy bank when she was fast asleep at night. By the end of the fortnight, the pink ceramic pig was stuffed to the max, notes poking out through the slot.

One night, huddled over as she sat on her bed, Elly counted the notes and coins carefully, and squealed in delight: she had saved up a grand total of six hundred and eighty-two pounds! That was much more than she had hoped for! Now she should have enough money to buy some Organoth blue amber! If she could just find a place that sells it.

Horace had been quietly doing his own research on Organoth blue amber. When he went to the local library for the first time since Charlie was a little boy, he was surprised to see how much it had changed, how modern it looked with its bright lights and rows of shiny flat-screen computer monitors. The librarian assistant was a Gothic-looking young lady wearing black lipstick and black nail polish who looked like she had just graduated from high school. But she gave Horace a friendly smile when he approached her tentatively. The badge on her long black lacy dress read: Falcon. Horace had to squint to make sure he had read it correctly.

"Organoth blue amber?" Falcon repeated quizzically. "Hmm, let me search that up for you on the computer. Hang on, please." Her fingers flew over the keyboard as she faced the large flat-screen. After several moments, she frowned and turned back to Horace.

"There's plenty of information on blue amber. It's some sort of rare gemstone found in the mountain ranges of an island called the Dominican Republic in the Caribbean. We have some books on that. But I couldn't find anything on Organoth blue amber."

Horace cleared his throat. "Do—do you know if there might be any volcanoes in the Dominican Republic? I heard that pure-grade blue amber could be found at one of those volcanic mountains, but long ago."

Falcon smiled as her fingers flew over the keys some more. "Hmm, according to what I'm reading, there are currently no active volcanoes in the Dominican Republic, where the capital city is Santo Domingo. But apparently the island rose out of the sea due to volcanic action thousands of years ago. The tallest mountain there, called Pico Duarte, was at one time an active volcano."

Horace's ears pricked up. In that case, Mount Pico Duarte could once have been Mount Organoth.

Falcon continued reading. "How interesting! Some geologists believe that the blue amber found in the Dominican Republic is so special because of the ancient volcanic activity that might have affected the formation of the rocks and trees in that area, which then might have given the blue amber its special properties. Apparently, under direct sunlight it glows an ocean-blue, and when put against sunlight it turns a golden yellow?" She smiled. "Wow, it sounds beautiful! I wish I had something like that!"

Horace thanked Falcon for her help. Before he turned away, he pointed to the computer and smiled sheepishly. "Excuse me, lass, but can you tell me where I could get something like this?"

So half an hour later he walked into an electronics store, and emerged from it holding a slim black bag. Thanks to Elly, he could now pay for things he could not have afforded before.

"You bought a computer?" Miriam asked incredulously as she watched him set it up on the dining table. Elly had gone off for a walk in the neighbourhood.

Horace puffed out his chest importantly. "To be precise, it's a laptop—a portable computer," he said proudly. "I even called our telephone company and got us connected to the thing they call the Internet." He raised his eyebrows at his wife. "Who says old dogs can't learn new tricks?"

The next morning, with Falcon's help, Horace attended a class at the library on how to use the Internet. By the end of the week he had learned to type slowly with two fingers, chopstick-style. He started looking up information on the Internet by himself. "Hmm, Falcon was right, there's a ton of information on ordinary blue amber, but nothing on Organoth blue amber," he muttered as his eyes roamed the screen.

Miriam frowned and stopped kneading the dough. "Falcon? Who on earth would name their child Falcon?" she exclaimed. Then she approached and squinted at the screen.

She pointed. "Look, that's an online shop selling blue amber. It ships directly from the Dominican Republic! I guess it wouldn't hurt to give it a try?"

So one week later, several parcels arrived for Horace. He and his wife ripped them open, and half a dozen blue amber pieces tumbled out onto the dining table. "Elly!" he bellowed.

Elly's jaw dropped when Horace explained what he had been trying to do. "You've been trying to look for Organoth blue amber?" she cried, immensely touched. She had been away from Alendria for over three weeks by now. She had scoured London for shops that sold gemstones, and she had found plenty of yellow amber; but had had no success locating ordinary blue amber, let alone Organoth blue amber. She threw her arms around him. "Oh, thank you!"

Horace looked embarrassed, but was secretly pleased. He cleared his throat. "Well, don't just stand there! See if they're the real thing or not," he grumbled. He had spent a small fortune on purchasing the blue amber from that online shop.

Elly placed the gemstones on the dark wooden table next to an open window to get the best light. Luckily, for once the sky wasn't overcast that day; the sun was shining brightly. The dozen or so pieces before her appeared blue, tinged with yellow. Some were highly polished, whilst some looked very rough. One by one, she held them up against the sunlight, and smiled when they turned almost fully yellow. She closed the curtains, blocking out the sun. The kitchen was plunged into shadow. Then one by one, she gently breathed on the blue amber pieces.

None glowed a golden yellow.

"Well?" Miriam asked anxiously. Horace stared at her with anticipation.

Elly smiled bravely. "They're blue amber, but not Organoth blue amber. I can make you a beautiful necklace out of these blue amber pieces though!" She planted a kiss on Horace's cheek. "Thank you so much for trying, Horace. I'll go make a start on the necklace! Call me when it's time for supper!"

Gathering up the blue amber, she dashed back into her room before they could see her tears.

Horace sighed and shook his head. "There must be another way!" he said resolutely.

Miriam nodded. She knew Elly must be terribly upset.

The next morning, after Elly had counted twenty-seven days away from home, she was helping Miriam put the finishing touches on a blueberry cheesecake when she glanced at the calendar on the wall and yelped, startling Snowy from her nap.

She had been so busy helping out at the shop, and so preoccupied with hunting down Organoth blue amber, that she had almost forgotten . . . Tomorrow's date had been circled in bright red: January the twenty-eighth. She was due to meet Lily tomorrow!

CHAPTER TWELVE
The School Fair

AT TEN O'CLOCK SHARP, ELLY stood in front of Aunty Mabel's Bakery, munching on a pomegranate that Miriam had packed for her along with a lunch-box filled with healthy snacks. "Don't eat too much of the food they sell at those school fairs, my dear. That junk would rot even your resilient elven teeth!" she had warned.

Lily threw open the door and squealed. "Elly! I'm so glad you came!" she cried. "I've been so nervous about my audition! I wondered whether you would turn up, it's been weeks since we first met and I didn't even have any way of contacting you!" She threw her arms around Elly.

Elly laughed and hugged her back. "Oh Lily, you have no idea how much I've wanted to see you again!"

Soybean bounded towards Elly and pounced on her, almost knocking her down onto the pavement. He barked happily. *Elly! Elly! You've come back!*

Elly giggled and looked him in the eye. *Have you kept your promise, Soybean?*

Yes, Elly! I have been good to Hobbes!

Lily shook her head, stunned. "It's amazing how Soybean's so taken with you. He only met you once!"

Elly went into the bakery to greet Mabel, who was serving several customers at the counter. She beamed at Elly. "Good morning, dear! It's so lovely to see you again!" She waved and mouthed, *Sorry, busy— let's talk later!*

Lily took Elly by the hand and closed the door behind them. Their breath rose like steam in the chill air. "Oh, just giving you a heads-up—my mum might ask to talk with your guardian on the phone. You know, to make sure he does exist, that you're not being neglected and stuff." She rolled her eyes, as though it was an absurd notion.

If she only knew the truth, Elly thought glumly. She smiled. "That's understandable. But really, she doesn't have to worry about me."

Greymore, did you hear that? Mabel wants to talk to you!

Do not fret, Ellanor. I will take care of it. I dealt smoothly with Mr O'Brien, did I not?

Lily shrugged. "She's a mum. All mothers worry, even about other children, I guess." Then she grinned. "By the way, she really wants you to come to our reunion dinner on Monday night! Oh, please say you'll come!"

Elly was puzzled. "Reunion dinner?"

"Yeah, for Chinese New Year. It's a really big deal for us." She raised her eyebrows. "Are you telling me you've never heard of Chinese New Year back in the Aland Islands?"

Elly shook her head apologetically.

Lily laughed. "Never mind. I guess I'm clueless about the cultural things that take place where you're from."

Elly smiled in agreement.

Lily continued, "Chinese New Year is something that we celebrate every year. It's the biggest traditional festive season for the Chinese. It's like Christmas or Thanksgiving to the Westerners. The Chinese celebrate the new year based on the lunar calendar, so every year the New Year's Day falls on a different day, but it's usually sometime in January or February. The night before Chinese New Year, families gather for the reunion dinner to sort of . . . usher in the new year together. It's a huge deal. The coming new year is the Year of the Monkey."

Elly blinked. "Monkey?" Back home in Alendria, there were creatures called oolahs that were similar to monkeys, and they were annoying and mischievous. But what did Lily mean about the Year of the Monkey?

Lily giggled. "I know it sounds a little strange, but there's just so much history behind all this stuff that the Chinese believe in. It's tradition, you know? The Chinese, especially the older ones, take their traditions very seriously." She smiled and shrugged. "The Chinese believe that every year is symbolized by a different animal on the zodiac. Anyway, right now we're still in the Year of the Goat. Next year is the Monkey."

Elly was fascinated. "So what are the other animals on the zodiac? Must they come in a particular order?"

"Yep! Legend tells that the heavenly Jade Emperor wanted to hold a swimming contest for the animals on his birthday, and that the first twelve animals to finish the contest would have their names used to record the years." Lily screwed up her face in concentration and started counting on her fingers. "The first one was . . . the rat . . . then it was the ox, followed by the tiger, rabbit, dragon, snake, horse, goat, monkey, rooster, dog, and the pig. Twelve animals. That makes the Chinese zodiac."

Elly smiled. It was always interesting to learn about the things different people believe in.

Greymore, I would love to attend this reunion dinner!

Yes, Ellanor. Lily is a good friend. If you are still here by Monday, by all means go and join them.

Elly snapped her fingers. "The reunion dinner sounds fun! Count me in!"

Lily beamed. "Excellent! I'll tell my mum!"

The two girls huddled close together against the biting cold as they walked to St Catherine's Grammar School. The sky was still a dreary grey, but at least it wasn't raining.

Elly told Lily about all the sights she had seen in London, the nice family she'd met at Westminster Abbey, and the shoemaker and his wife. Lily's eyes grew wide at the mention of the Cobbles.

"Hasn't that been the talk of the town lately? My dad read an article in the paper about how the shop underwent some sort of major revamping, and now it's really popular. A vintage shoe shop cum pastry house! My mum has been dying to go, but she's been so busy." She looked at Elly with envy. "I can't believe you're friends with them! And you get to stay at their house and everything . . . Your life never ceases to be interesting!"

If you only knew half of it, Elly thought grimly. Then she changed the subject and asked about Hobbes. Lily frowned. "He's doing fine,

I guess, but he's a little mopey. Soybean hovers around him a lot, so Hobbes gets a little antsy." Elly giggled.

Lily was impressed that Elly could explore the city with Greymore, her guardian. "My parents are way overprotective. My dad insists on walking me to school every morning, even though it's just around the corner. It's so embarrassing!" she complained.

Elly smiled wryly and wished she could tell Lily how much she wanted to see her own father again, even if it meant having him walk her to school everyday.

But she didn't want Lily to ask her more about her family. It made her sad. So she switched topics. "By the way, why did you change schools?" She really was curious.

Lily sighed. "My parents wanted me to go to a school that has a better English literature curriculum. You see, I happen to be good at English literature . . . you know, writing essays, stories, poetry, that sort of stuff. I'm hopeless with maths and science, which seems a little unusual, since most Asians seem to do well in those areas. I had some really good friends at St Vincent's, and I really miss them. We don't hang out much anymore since we run on different schedules. Drifting apart was inevitable, I guess."

She looked sad. "It's just not easy for me to make friends at a new school, Elly. I don't know why. And it's worse now that I've become the target of bullies like Clare Andrews and her Space Cadets."

Elly nodded sympathetically. "I understand how awful it can be." She told Lily about Darrius and her friends.

Lily giggled. "The Three Flamingos? They sound even worse than the Space Cadets!"

St Catherine's was a handsome Georgian red-bricked building surrounded by an iron fence, having once been a military hospital before it was converted into a school almost a hundred years ago. A massive, ancient-looking cedar tree stood beside the iron gate like a wizened guardian. Elly felt a sudden urge to climb up and nestle into the trunk, but quickly reminded herself where she was.

Draped high above the entrance was a large blue banner with St Catherine's School Fair scrawled in cursive white letters. Blue and white balloons bumped into each other in the breeze. Loud techno music was blasting through several large speakers, making Elly cringe.

She thought about the tranquil music of the Serenities and sighed wistfully.

Elly saw many colourful booths selling candy floss, donuts, toffees, popcorn, French fries, kebabs and curry rice, sushi, fried rice, pizzas, casseroles, burgers, sausage rolls, meat pies, and much more.

The game stalls were already packed with excited customers eager to win some prize or other.

Students milled about in costume. Some dressed as clowns, comic book characters, fairy tale characters, and even as real-life celebrities. Elly recognised only Alice from *Alice in Wonderland* and Sherlock Holmes, whose stories she had pored over back home. Apart from the hair-raising music blaring from the entrance, there was plenty of chatter and laughter buzzing around.

Lily started talking excitedly. "This year's theme is 'Fantasia'—so we can come as whatever we fancy," she explained, as Elly looked around in wonder.

"Then what about you?" she asked, looking pointedly at Lily's casual clothes.

Lily grinned. "Well, I'm auditioning for the part of Cinderella. That's enough fantasy to last me through the day!"

Lily bought them some candy floss. Elly made a face when she tasted the strange fluffy pink stuff. She did, however, like the home-made toffees; they tasted a tad too sweet, but they reminded her of Aron, whose Mama made the best toffee-pops in Evergreen. She missed him terribly, and wondered how he was doing. Had he found out about Edellina? Was he thinking of her?

As they were walking, a high-pitched wispy voice called out, making them jump. "Riddle, riddle on the wall! Who is the cleverest of them all?" The two girls turned to see a very tall, gangly man staring at them from a booth nearby.

He looked strange. His skin seemed to be painted all white, his flame-red hair slicked back, the top part of his face concealed by a glittering black mask. He was wearing a peculiar green and black polka-dotted suit with a matching bow tie, and his large hands were sheathed in white gloves. The booth was decorated with numerous cut-outs of question marks in all sizes and colours. In front of him was a large green box with a hole at the top, just large enough for one to put a hand through.

The man smiled, showing glistening, pearly white teeth. "If you are able to solve five riddles in a row, you'll get two free tickets to a blockbuster movie!" He gestured to the movie poster plastered on the front of the booth.

"I think he's supposed to be the Riddler from the comics," Lily said in a low voice. "But I can't tell who he is behind that mask and all that make-up. He's too tall to be one of the students. Maybe he's a teacher." She turned to Elly with a grin. "Should we give it a try? I really want to see that movie! It's supposed to be really good!"

Elly laughed. "Of course! Solving riddles is something of a hobby of mine."

Lily beamed. "Really? Great! Let's give it a go!"

The Riddler chuckled and clapped his hands. "First things first, ladies. Please pay the fee upfront. I shall do a reading for you. Comes with the package."

A reading? Elly wondered what that was all about. She quickly took out her purse. "I'll pay," she insisted, shoving the notes into his hand. Then to her surprise, he turned to her. "Your right hand please, little Miss." He bowed and waited, his hand poised in mid-air.

Lily nudged her. "He wants to read your palm!" she whispered, wide-eyed. "Go ahead—it's all part of the game."

Reluctantly, Elly put out her hand. The Riddler narrowed his eyes as he bent down, gazing at her palm like a scientist examining a rare specimen.

"Hmm, very interesting . . . yes, indeed . . ." he murmured.

Elly raised an eyebrow and glanced at Lily, who was waiting with bated breath.

After several moments, the Riddler straightened up. He had a strangely satisfied look on his face. "Well, little girl, you are quite the enigma. The lines on your palm cross and branch out at the most peculiar places. It appears you have before you many difficult choices to make, and your future is unclear at this point. Hence, I'm afraid I cannot divulge anything specific, except to say this: beware the sly one, for she will try to take what is yours."

The Riddler had very black eyes, so black and impenetrable that Elly shuddered and quickly pulled her hand back.

Lily was giggling. "Sly one? I have no idea what he's talking about!" She nudged Elly. "Well, come on! Let's get those riddles going!"

The Riddler snapped his fingers, then asked Lily to put her hand in her left pocket. She knitted her brow. "Wait, how in the world . . ." She retrieved a piece of crumpled paper. On it was scribbled five riddles in spidery handwriting.

Lily gaped in wonder. "How did you do that? You haven't been anywhere close enough to slip this into my pocket!"

The Riddler winked. "I am a jack-of-all-trades, little Miss. Now, let's read out the riddles."

Lily obeyed. "What room can no one enter?"

Elly didn't miss a beat. "Mushroom."

Lily laughed and clapped. The Riddle did not react. "Wow! All right, next one!" Lily squinted at the spidery script.

"What is the beginning of eternity, the end of time and space, the beginning of every end and the end of every race?"

Once again, Elly didn't miss a beat. "E".

The Riddler was now grinning from ear to ear, as though he was enjoying himself.

"What grows bigger as you take more away from it?"

"A hole."

"What won't run long without winding?"

"A river."

At the fifth and final riddle, the Riddler raised a hand, then looked at Elly with a twinkle in his eye. "Let me do the honours for the final riddle." He leaned forward, so close that his face was only inches from hers. In a whisper that only Elly could hear, he said:

"Voiceless it cries,
wingless flutters,
toothless bites,
mouthless mutters."

Elly staggered back in shock.

He had uttered the riddle in Yahana.

"What? What is it?" Lily asked excitedly, oblivious of what had just happened.

"The wind," Elly whispered back in Yahana, rooted to the ground. Her heart was thumping madly as she stared into those deep, black eyes.

Who are you?

Then his voice was in her head.

Hello, Ellanor Celendis. It is a pleasure to meet you.

The Riddler laughed and applauded. "Well, well! I've met my match for today."

He turned to Lily with a bow. "You shall find your reward in your bag, little Miss."

Lily turned around and peered at the backpack behind her. Distracted, Elly turned to take a look, too. "What do you mean?" Lily demanded, unzipping her bag. Then she gasped. "How did you put them in here?" She held up the movie tickets and turned back to the Riddler with a broad smile.

He had vanished.

"Hey, where did he go?" Lily cried, looking around. "Golly, he must be some sort of magician!"

Elly frowned. Who was that man? Could he possibly be . . .

He is not a goblin, Ellanor.

She breathed a sigh of relief. *Then who is he, Greymore? He could speak the ancient language!*

The world is vast and mysterious. There are beings other than goblins who are aware of your presence here, and have an interest in you.

She shuddered as she recalled those probing black eyes.

Do not worry for now. I believe you are not in any danger.

If you say so, Greymore.

Lily was chattering happily. "I *love* the actors in this movie! I've been waiting for it to come out! Why don't you come watch it with me, Elly?"

Elly blinked, still thinking about the Riddler. "What?" she asked distractedly.

"This movie!" Lily waved the tickets in front of her face. "Let's go watch it together next week!"

Elly had never been to see a movie. *Why not?* she thought a little gloomily. She might as well go, if she was still going to be stranded here. Well, she *was* actually curious to experience a movie for the first time, and it would be fun to go out with Lily again. So she smiled. "Sure, let's go together!"

After they finished their kebabs (a chicken one for Lily, a vegetarian one for Elly), they came upon a green lawn with several rows of metal chairs lined up in front of a blue and white platform stage. Nearby were several electrical lamp heaters emitting some much-needed warmth. At a long table beside the stage sat three adults with their heads bent together in discussion. Several students in costume were clustered in groups, buzzing with conversation punctuated by occasional peals of laughter.

Lily looked at her watch nervously as she gestured towards the stage. "That's where I'll be auditioning!" She looked around, then clutched Elly's arm. "Oh my gosh, that's Adam Boon, the boy I told you about! It looks like he just got the part of the Prince!" she whispered, sounding slightly hysterical.

Elly turned to see a tall, handsome boy with curly blonde hair and blue eyes talking and laughing with a couple of other boys in a far corner. Then he looked up and smiled, waving in their direction. Elly saw that Lily's cheeks had turned rosy as she waved back.

Lily sighed. "Adam is *so* nice. He's in my class, and he's probably the only boy who's ever talked to me since I started coming to this school. I didn't realize he was really going to try out for this musical. I wish I could have seen his audition, we just missed it!"

"Hey, Four Eyes!" a girl's voice called rudely.

Lily's face darkened. Under her breath she muttered, "Get ready to meet Clare Andrews and the Space Cadets!"

Elly's eyes widened at the four girls sauntering towards them, showing off their long slim legs in black tights underneath short skirts. They looked older than Lily, who was slender but much shorter. The girl in the middle was very pretty, with long wavy blonde hair and large blue eyes. Elly guessed that was Clare Andrews, the ringleader, who was looking at Lily in a condescending fashion, striking a pose with one foot forward, a hand on one hip, and her pointed chin thrust into the air.

Though none of them wore pink, they reminded Elly of the Three Flamingos.

Then her jaw dropped in surprise as she locked eyes with the strawberry blonde girl on the far right.

Maddy!

Maddy's light blue eyes widened as she stared back at Elly.

Elly smiled and was about to say hello when Maddy quickly looked away and stared at the ground with a frown, her face flushed a bright pink.

Taken aback, Elly put a hand to her own face. Didn't Maddy recognize her?

Then realization dawned as Maddy continued to avoid her gaze.

Maddy was pretending she didn't know Elly.

Hurt and confused, Elly looked down at feet. *Why?*

The other three girls had not noticed Maddy's expression. They were all staring at Lily down their noses, occasionally shifting their gaze to Elly, sizing her up.

"At least her little friend is good-looking," said the dark-skinned one with a sneer. She was the tallest, with wide chocolate-brown eyes that would have looked really beautiful if they didn't look so nasty. "Maybe she should audition for the role instead of Miss Ugly Four Eyes."

Lily went red in the face. Elly glanced over at Adam; he was frowning, and looked as though he was ready to walk up and say something.

Then Lily put her hands on her hips and laughed, startling everyone. She looked up at the sky. "Oh, I saw three Space Cadets land just a moment ago! . . . Wait, *there* you are!" she exclaimed in mock surprise, staring at the girls in front of her.

There was snickering nearby. "Honestly, don't you have anything better to do than living up to your reputations as space cadets?" With that, she rolled her eyes and stalked off, her head held high. Bewildered, Elly went to follow her.

Some of the boys laughed and clapped. "Go, Lily!" one of them called out. Adam was smiling. Elly turned to see Clare Andrews and the other girls staring after them, utterly astonished. Maddy looked mortified. For a second, she held Elly's gaze. Then she bit her lip and looked away.

Elly sighed and turned back to Lily. She had no idea why Maddy was behaving this way.

She broke into a jog and caught up with her friend. "Wow, Lily! I'm amazed that you stood up to them like that!" She wished she could do the same thing with the Three Flamingos. If she could only find her way back home, perhaps she would finally seize the opportunity to stand up to them, once and for all.

Lily glanced back. "Phew!" She breathed a sigh of relief. Then she laughed and linked arms with Elly. "That felt *great*! Believe it or not, it was my grandma who encouraged me to stand up to those bullies! I told her about Clare and her mean friends, and she almost boxed my ears. 'When I was your age, we were so poor that we had to walk miles to school because we couldn't even afford the bus fare. At your age, I was fighting off street bullies with my baby brother on my back! Don't you let those silly girls walk all over you!'"

Lily giggled. "She always tells me that the mean things people say usually reflect who *they* are, not who *I* am." She grinned. "She's a tough cookie, my granny. No wonder my parents are scared of her!"

Elly giggled, thinking of her grandfather and how he could always win an argument with Papa.

Then her face turned serious. "What about that girl with the strawberry blonde hair, the quiet one? She didn't seem so bad."

Lily shrugged. "That's Maddy O'Brien. She's a new girl, like me. Actually, she doesn't seem as awful as the others. She just sort of tags along. But still, she's a little questionable to be hanging out with those bullies!"

Elly nodded reluctantly. But Maddy had seemed so sweet, so nice.

Then Lily looked at her watch and yelped. "Blimey, it's almost time! I'll be back soon, wait here for me!" She dashed off to the washroom, backpack slung over her shoulder.

Elly sucked on her last toffee as she waited, her thoughts drifting. She wondered what she might have done to offend Maddy. Why else would she pretend not to know her? Then she thought about Teddy, and that led to thoughts about her brother. She wondered what Luca was doing, and whether he actually missed her.

After a little while, Lily emerged from the washroom. Elly almost choked on her toffee as she gawped at her friend.

Lily looked very different. Without glasses, her almond-shaped eyes looked wide and bright. She was wearing a touch of pink lip gloss, and her long silky black hair was swept up into a high ponytail. She was wearing a little eye liner that gave her an understated, exotic look. In a purple sweater, black leggings and black ballet flats, Lily looked slender and graceful.

Elly clapped her hands. "Wow, Lily, you look beautiful!" she cried. Then she noticed that Lily was squinting. "But can you see all right without the glasses?"

Lily sighed. "Not really, but I'll be okay for the audition. If I get the part, I'll persuade my parents to let me wear contacts for one day. Otherwise, I won't be convincing as Cinderella with glasses," she grumbled, tossing them into her backpack.

Now that Adam Boon had snagged the role of the prince, the other girls who were auditioning for the coveted role of Cinderella had even more incentive to win. The candidates had to act and sing in two scenes: one where Cinderella gets mistreated by her wicked stepsisters and stepmother; and one where Cinderella dances with the prince at the ball. One of the candidates was Clare Andrews, who did a double take when she saw Lily. Maddy was in the audience, biting her nails nervously. Elly sensed that Maddy was trying very hard to avoid her.

Some of the boys were looking at Lily appreciatively. But Lily only had eyes for one. Adam grinned and gave her a thumbs-up. *I hope you get the part*, he mouthed. She blushed and smiled shyly.

Finally, after several lukewarm performances and a particularly terrible one, it was Lily's turn. The space cadets coughed and giggled. "Here comes Four Eyes," they said in low voices, though Lily wasn't even wearing her glasses.

But they were in for a surprise.

Elly was transfixed as she watched Lily transform into another person. She did it with such poise, and never once stumbled or forgot her lines. She moved and spoke in a way that Elly imagined Cinderella would. Then when Lily partnered up with Adam during the dance scene, they actually looked like a couple!

When Lily opened her mouth to sing the theme song, Elly's mouth dropped open, as did many of the others. She sang with perfect pitch, her voice as clear as a bell. Clare Andrews glowered at Lily. Though Clare had looked beautiful on stage, her own off-key singing and clumsy acting had been less than impressive. Lily had had to clamp her hand over her mouth to keep from laughing when Clare forgot some of the lyrics and improvised on the spot.

After Lily's audition, there was thunderous applause and quite a bit of cheering, mostly from Adam's mates. Elly beamed and clapped until her palms stung. Lily blinked in surprise, hardly daring to believe they were clapping for her. Only the sour-faced Space Cadets did not join in.

As the judges convened to finalise their decision, Lily stood next to Elly and bit her nails. Elly gave her arm a squeeze. "You were by far the best. I had no idea you could act and sing so well!" she whispered with a grin. Then she thought about her inability to carry a tune and sighed. "How I wish I could sing like you!"

Lily giggled nervously. "Thanks, but I can't help thinking that Clare Andrews looks much more like Cinderella," she confessed with a sigh.

Finally, one of the judges, a man with bushy brown hair and a red necktie, stood up and cleared his throat. "The verdict is in. Thank you for your patience, ladies and gentleman," he said grandly. "We've come to a decision. The successful candidate has proven to be ideal for the role." He smiled. "The lead female part of Cinderella goes to . . . Lily Wong! Congratulations!" He went on to announce who had been awarded other roles, but his voice was drowned out by the tumultuous applause for Lily.

"I can't believe it! I'm not dreaming, right?" she squealed. "I'll get to wear my first and possibly only pair of Manolo Blahniks!" Elly laughed, and the girls threw their arms around each other and jumped with joy.

Clare Andrews stormed up to the judges, her face livid. Elly heard her say, "How could you cast her as Cinderella and me in that pathetic ugly role? It doesn't make sense! You could have trained me to sing like a diva, at least I look convincing as Cinderella! She's *Chinese!*"

The bushy-haired judge stood up angrily and spoke in a low voice that others could not hear, except Elly. "Young lady, your behaviour is unacceptable. Showing such poor sportsmanship is already bad enough, but your prejudice is even worse. Appalling. This musical is supposed to showcase not only talent, but exemplify our multicultural community, and Lily Wong has certainly shown she has the talent. She has won fair and square. The fact that she doesn't have the stereotypical looks of Cinderella isn't relevant. If you are implying otherwise, I suggest that you give up your role to another student."

Clare narrowed her eyes to slits. "You can't get away with this," she hissed. "Do you know who my father is? You'll be sorry!" Without another word, she turned on her heel and stormed off. The other Space

Cadets followed, muttering rude words at the judge and throwing withering looks at Lily. Only Maddy didn't say a word; she kept her eyes fixed to the ground and hurried away.

The judge looked a little shaken. "Oh my. Young girls these days can be a scary lot," he muttered, mopping his shiny forehead with a handkerchief.

Elly tried to look for Maddy, but she was nowhere to be seen. Disappointed, she went back to Lily, who looked like she had just won the lottery.

Several students from the audience went up to Lily and congratulated her. Adam was beaming as he gave Lily a high five; then he lowered his head and whispered something into her ear. She blushed furiously.

Later on, Lily emerged from the washroom with her glasses back on, sporting a dreamy smile.

"So, was your Prince Charming bowled over by your performance?" Elly teased.

Lily giggled. "Adam told me that I'm pretty and smart, with or without my glasses," she said happily. "We made a deal—he'll help me out with my maths, and I can help him out with English literature. We're going to see way more of each other. My parents can't say no to free tutoring from the best student in the subject!"

Then she flashed Elly a roguish smile. "And guess who's been cast as one of the wicked step-sisters?"

CHAPTER THIRTEEN
Afternoon Tea on Pine Street

AFTER ELLY GOT BACK TO the Cobbles for supper and had had a long hot bath, she sat in front of the dressing table, while Miriam brushed out her long, curly hair. It had been another busy day at the shop.

"Horace has finally agreed to hire a part-time assistant to help me out with the chores around the shop," Miriam announced, looking very pleased. "He's even thinking of training up apprentices to help him meet the huge demand for Cobble Concept shoes—that's what they're branding us in the media." She chuckled.

Elly was surprised. "But don't I help out enough?"

Miriam smiled. "Of course you do! You are the best little helper anyone could have, Elly dear. But I don't expect you to stay with us forever. We adore you, but you have a family to go back to. Thanks to you, business has taken off, so once you're gone, I'll need an extra pair of hands to help me."

She started tying silver ribbons in Elly's hair, which had grown several inches in the past month. Then she glanced at Elly in the oval-shaped mirror. "Oh! What ever is the matter?" she cried as tears slipped down Elly's cheeks.

Elly wiped away the tears with the back of her hand. "Oh, Miriam! What if I never see them again? It's been almost a month, and I miss them all *so* much. Not a single day goes by that I'm not worried. What if the goblin hurt them? I have no way of knowing as long as I'm stranded here. I just couldn't bear it if something's happened to them!" She buried her face in her hands and sobbed.

Miriam held her in a maternal embrace. "There, there," she said soothingly. "I have been praying for you every night, my dear. I believe the good Lord has His timing for everything. Let's not give up hope."

Elly sniffled, glad that she had a shoulder to cry on. There wasn't anything else she could do but to wait and continue her search for Organoth blue amber.

After she had calmed down, they started talking about plans for tomorrow, since the shop would be closed for business on Sunday. Then she clapped a hand to her forehead. "Oh, I almost forgot! Lily invited me to her family's reunion dinner for Chinese New Year on Monday. I need to prepare some gifts for them; it wouldn't be polite to go empty-handed. But I have no idea what to get!"

Miriam thought for a moment. "Why don't we sleep in tomorrow, enjoy a nice brunch with Horace, then go off to the supermarket in the afternoon to pick up ingredients? Let's make some nice pastries for Lily and her family. I'm sure they would appreciate something home-made."

Elly thought that was a superb idea.

The next morning, Horace went down to the kitchen for brunch earlier than usual. Miriam had just started frying the bacon as Elly was setting the table, wrinkling her nose at the smell of meat cooking.

"Good morning!" she said brightly to Horace, who grunted his usual greeting. Then he cleared his throat and nonchalantly placed a long white envelope on the dining table.

"What's that?" Miriam asked with a frown as she retrieved some eggs from the fridge. Elly sat down and started nibbling on her blueberry jam on toast and stroking a purring Snowy. Despite their rather rocky introduction, the two had become firm friends.

"Why don't you take a look yourself? It's addressed to you," he said gruffly, sitting down and opening up the newspaper.

Miriam heaved a sigh. "It's probably just another bill." She wiped her hands down on her apron and squinted at the envelope. Ever since business took off, she had had to learn to put their finances in order. She slit the envelope with a letter-opener and took out several slips of paper. She looked at them blankly for a moment, then she gasped.

"Oh, my goodness!" she cried, her eyes bulging. "Are these . . . are these . . . ?"

Elly looked at her quizzically. Why was Miriam looking so shocked?

"Oh, Horace!" Miriam threw her arms around him and started planting kisses on his balding head.

"Careful! You're choking me to death!" he sputtered, but then he was smiling smugly.

"Wait! What's going on?" Elly demanded, putting down her toast.

Miriam was clutching the front of her apron, trembling all over. She laughed and clapped her hands. "Elly! For the first time in my life, I'll be flying on a plane!"

Elly's eyes widened. "You're going to Santorini!" she cried excitedly.

Miriam chuckled. "Well, actually, we're headed some place else—with you!" She bent down and hugged Elly. "We're taking you to the Dominican Republic!"

Elly yelped and almost fell out of her chair. "What?" she whispered.

Horace put down his newspaper and grinned. "I've been thinking about it for some time, Elly. It seems that the best chance for you to get Organoth blue amber is to search for it in the Dominican Republic. Miriam and I will board the plane together, with you in our hand luggage. So you'll need to shrink yourself back to elf size. I'm sure you can pretend to be a doll or something, right? You'll just need to keep very still when they scan you under X-ray at customs."

Elly gaped at him.

"I've already done all my research." Horace fondly patted the laptop computer on the table. "Once we get to the Dominican Republic, we'll meet with a couple of experts on blue amber at the local museum. I've made the arrangements, all by e-mail. Technology is a truly marvellous thing!"

He chuckled. "Those experts might be able to help us locate some Organoth blue amber. They might drive a hard bargain. But we'll take our chances."

Elly was speechless for several moments. "You've done all this for me?" she said softly. She felt a surge of gratitude welling up inside her as tears pricked at her eyelids.

Miriam laughed. "Elly, you're like family. We love you! Horace and I want to do our best to help you find your way back home." Then she grinned with a twinkle in her eye. "Besides, because of you, I'll finally get to fly on a plane! We'll all get to go together. Santorini can wait!"

Horace cleared his throat. "Well, I've had to renew our passports for both myself and Miriam. The whole process took two weeks with the Immigration Department. Our old passports had expired long ago. I just got the new ones yesterday. The earliest flight I could book is for this coming Wednesday, and we shall be staying there for one week."

He looked at Elly apologetically. "I wish we could have gone to the Dominican Republic sooner, but this was the best I could do, my dear."

Elly shook her head vigorously. "Oh, Horace! Why are you apologising? This is incredible. You don't know how much this means to me. Thank you so much!"

Greymore rumbled with approval. *Some things are priceless, are they not? One cannot buy true friendship and love with money.*

Elly looked at Miriam and Horace, put her arms around them, and smiled. "I love you both, too."

So after a substantial brunch and admiring beautiful pictures of the Dominican Republic on Horace's laptop, Miriam and Elly set off for the supermarket.

Horace wanted to stay home and tend to his rose garden. "Those blasted crows better not come near me today!" he grumbled as he pulled on his old Wellington boots. It was raining lightly.

Instead of walking to the small grocery shop near Berry Grove Park, Miriam drove them to a large supermarket in a nearby neighbourhood. "This one has a much larger range of quality ingredients," Miriam explained as they hopped out of her old light-blue mini-van. Elly walked with a spring in her step, and could not stop smiling. She couldn't believe she'd be going to the Dominican Republic soon. There was hope!

This was Elly's first time in a cavernous, large-scale supermarket, with high ceilings and endless rows of tall shelves and each aisle devoted to a different speciality: cereals, biscuits, chips, pasta, frozen goods, fruits, vegetables, sauces and condiments, confectionery, beverages, and so on. Miriam let Elly ride in the shopping trolley while she moved briskly from aisle to aisle with a list in her hand, ticking off items one by one: flour, butter, eggs, icing, cream, marmalade, strawberry jam, sugar, salt, pumpkins, strawberries, blueberries, peaches . . . Elly soon lost track. By the time Miriam had finished, the trolley was filled to the brim, and Elly was skipping along beside her.

As Miriam was paying at the cashier counter, Elly wandered off to a florist near the exit. She breathed in the fragrance of the flowers—peonies, baby's breath, roses, poinsettias, tulips, daisies, lilies, forget-me-nots, marigolds—and thought about the golden e*llanor* that would be in full bloom back in Alendria.

Then she felt a tug on her arm. She turned, expecting to see Miriam asking her to help with the shopping bags.

Bright blue eyes stared at her behind round tortoiseshell spectacles. She gasped.

"Teddy!" she cried.

Head tilted slightly to the side, his gaze fixed to her left, Teddy raised a hand in greeting. "Hello, Elly," he said monotonously. "Are you coming to my house?" It sounded more like a statement than a question.

"You're not here by yourself, are you?" she asked worriedly, wondering if he had wandered off by himself and gotten lost.

Then a shrill voice rang out. "Theodore James O'Brien! I've *told* you a million times to stay put!" Maddy looked furious as she strode over in tight jeans, sheepskin boots, and a puffy white jacket, her cheeks flushed. Then she stopped in her tracks when she spotted Elly.

"Oh, hi . . . What are you doing here?" she asked, trying to sound nonchalant. She crossed her arms as she tried to smile, not quite looking at Elly in the eye.

Then Elly realized that Maddy looked *embarrassed.*

At that moment, Elly felt a surge of happiness seeing her two friends again. She smiled. "Hi, Maddy! It's so good to see you both here. I was just doing some shopping with my . . . umm . . . my . . ."

"Grandmother!" Miriam piped up as she walked towards them lugging four heavy bags stuffed with merchandise. "Elly's as good as a granddaughter to me. Now, dear, are you going to introduce your friends, or should I stand here until my arms fall off?"

Elly smiled sheepishly as she took two heavy bags. "Miriam, this is Maddy and her brother Teddy."

"Oh, yes! I've heard quite a bit about you from Elly!" said Miriam brightly. Maddy was blushing. "Are you here by yourselves?"

Maddy shook her head. "Umm . . . no, we're with our mother. She's . . ."

"*Madeline Joy O'Brien!* How many times have I told you not to walk off?" cried another shrill voice accompanied by the clickety-clack of heels. Elly turned to see an attractive woman rushing towards them, two bulging tote bags on her shoulders. She was petite and slender, with short wheat-blonde hair and bright blue eyes lined with kohl, dressed rather fashionably in a trench coat and stonewashed skinny jeans. Maddy was the spitting image of her.

Teddy kept his hand on Elly's sleeve, eyes on the ground. Maddy sighed impatiently and rolled her eyes. "Mum, don't make a fuss," she said defensively, crossing her arms. "I was just looking for Teddy. He saw Elly and wanted to say hello."

Maddy's mother then noticed Elly, and Teddy's hand on her sleeve. Her eyes softened. "Hello," she said with a smile. "I'm their mum, but you can call me Victoria." *What amazing green eyes,* Victoria thought. "Are you . . . are you a friend of Teddy's?"

Annoyed, Maddy nudged her mother. "She's *my* friend too," she hissed before giving Elly a sheepish smile.

Relieved and heartened to hear Maddy call her a friend, Elly beamed and then turned to Victoria. "It is so nice to meet you, Victoria. I met Maddy and Teddy over three weeks ago at Westminster Abbey. I learned a lot from Teddy about the history of that place. Andy and Maddy were ever so nice to me . . ." She trailed off, remembering that Maddy's parents were divorced.

"Ah, so you've already met Andy." Victoria smiled a little grimly.

Then she brightened. "Oh, here's an idea! Elly, please join us for afternoon tea at our home. We live on Pine Street; it's only a ten-minute drive from here. I never get to meet any of Maddy's friends, and as for my Teddy . . ." She eyed her son, his hand still clutching Elly's sleeve. "I can tell he's very fond of you!"

Elly hesitated. She wanted to go, but what about all the baking that needed to be done for the reunion dinner? But Miriam smiled and patted her shoulder. "Thank you, what a lovely invitation!" she cried. "Pine Street is only a couple of blocks from our place. Elly, why don't you go off for a bit with your friends and come home by supper? I'll prepare the sweets, don't you worry." Elly glanced furtively at Maddy, who was smiling broadly and nodding.

Elly grinned. "Thanks Miriam, I promise I'll be back by supper time!"

As Miriam and Victoria were exchanging phone numbers and addresses, Maddy sidled up to Elly. By now, Teddy had let go of Elly's sleeve; he was satisfied that she was going home with them after all. Elly overheard Victoria gasp and say, "My, you're *the* Miriam Cobble? I've been wanting to try your famous pastries, but there's always such a long queue! I must come over one day by myself, without the kids breathing down my neck!"

Maddy rolled her eyes at her mother and turned to Elly. "Boy, I'm so glad we bumped into you! I've been thinking about you, and that business with Lily and those awful girls . . ."

Maddy abruptly fell silent when Victoria sauntered over. "Let's go kids!" she said cheerfully, taking her daughter by the arm.

Maddy made a face. *Let's talk later*, she mouthed to Elly.

After waving goodbye to Miriam, Elly hopped into the back of Victoria's yellow vintage car, sandwiched between Maddy and Teddy. Elly then noticed some small twigs in Teddy's hair. Maddy leaned over and plucked them out. "We took Teddy to the local park on the way over here. Teddy still loves going to that park, *in spite* of everything."

At this, she glared at the back of her mother's head. Victoria glanced in the rear-view mirror and sighed. "Darling, if looks could kill, I would be dead right now."

As they drove along, Victoria put on some classical music and hummed along. Elly closed her eyes, reminded of the minstrels back in Alendria. Whatever faults Maddy's mother had, at least she had good taste in music.

Maddy was quiet throughout the ride home, a brooding look on her face. When Elly looked at her questioningly, she smiled and mouthed, *I'm okay; don't worry. Just don't want to talk in front of Mum.*

Teddy was looking through a picture book about astronomy, engrossed in the descriptions of the planets. Elly looked out of the window and noticed that the houses they passed looked very familiar. Miriam was right—the Cobbles lived only a few blocks from Maddy!

The O'Briens lived in an old, two-story Victorian house with a shabby-looking front porch. There were no rose bushes here, only some sad, withered shrubs and overgrown weeds.

Teddy went off to his room to finish his maths homework. "He's pretty rigid with routines," Maddy explained. "He insists on getting things done by a certain time. Boy, he would make a superb office worker in the future. Meeting deadlines isn't really my strong suit."

Maddy reluctantly agreed to join her mother and Elly out in the small backyard, which looked prettier than the front. There was an apple tree smack in the middle of the yard. "Why can't we just stay inside near the fireplace? It's freezing out here," Maddy complained, stuffing her hands into her pockets, her breath coming out in white puffs.

Victoria laughed a little too loudly. "Oh Maddy, do be a good sport! It's nice to get some fresh air. You don't mind, do you Elly?"

Elly shook her head and smiled. Miriam had made sure she was dressed properly for the weather; the cold no longer bothered her.

They sat in faded yellow canvas chairs under the apple tree. Victoria put out some hot chocolate and glazed donuts on the rickety low table. "Just bought these at the supermarket bakery. I'm sure they're nowhere as good as Miriam's wonderful pastries, but they should be nice enough. I can't bake to save my life!"

Maddy snorted. "Yeah, no dispute there." Victoria blushed.

Elly looked at mother and daughter thoughtfully. Why was Maddy so hostile towards her mother? She had been so different with her father.

Victoria crossed her legs and arched her back as she stretched. "Ahhh, it's so nice to relax on a Sunday!" she chirped, giving Maddy a nervous sidelong glance. Her daughter was nibbling on a donut with a stony expression.

Victoria cleared her throat and smiled. "So, Elly . . . tell me a bit about yourself. My Teddy obviously adores you, which is rather unusual, as he doesn't normally connect with people. Even with us, he can be a bit distant."

Maddy sat bolt upright, her donut dropping onto the ground. "Speak for yourself!" she snapped. "If you hadn't been so obsessed with your work, if you had spent more time with him instead of jet-setting all over the world for your dratted business trips, he would be closer to you! Dad would've been happier with you! And you wouldn't have done what you did behind poor Teddy's back when we were away with Dad in Oxford!"

Victoria's face went white. "Darling, please don't get into a huff with me in front of a guest," she pleaded in a low voice.

Maddy went red in the face and stood up. "Look, let's not pretend we're having such a smashing time here. I've had enough."

She looked at Elly, who was shifting in her chair uncomfortably. "I'm sorry about this, Elly. I really want to catch up. I'll be up in my room, just come look for me when Her Highness is done interrogating you."

She stormed away into the house and bounded up the stairs. Elly could hear a door slam.

There was a silence as Victoria tried to compose herself. Elly felt sorry for her. Victoria smiled wanly, her eyes glassy. "I try, I really do. But it's not easy being a mum to a teenage girl these days, not to mention a boy with special needs," she said shakily. She sighed and leaned back in her chair. Elly didn't say anything.

Victoria massaged her temples. She had a splitting headache. "Maddy's been *so* angry with me since her daddy and I separated." She paused, then looked at Elly. "Are your parents together?"

Elly nodded, her curls bouncing around her face. "Yes. I cannot imagine my parents not being together," she said truthfully. She thought about Mama and Papa slow dancing at her birthday party, and a lump formed in her throat. She missed them so much.

Victoria smiled sadly. "Poor Maddy. Poor Teddy. I guess it's true that divorce is always hardest on the kids."

She looked towards the house, then frowned. "Darn, I keep forgetting . . . I should've thrown out that ruddy cage weeks ago. Seeing that thing just sets her off," she muttered.

Elly followed Victoria's gaze. There was a plastic cage with a green lid near the back door of the house. It looked as though it had been outside for some time. It was covered in mud splatters.

Elly stared. Something flickered tantalizingly at the back of her mind. She turned to Victoria. "Excuse me. Do you have a pet in the house?"

Victoria looked at her blankly for a moment before she realized Elly was gesturing at the empty cage. "Oh! We did, but . . . not anymore. Maddy was furious with me when she found out I had let that little hamster go. Teddy loved that furball to pieces . . ."

She trailed off when she noticed Elly staring at her. "Why, what's wrong?"

"What happened to the hamster?" Elly asked, now perched on the edge of her chair. She looked deep into Victoria's eyes. Victoria blinked, and a dreamy look came over her as though she had been hypnotized. Words poured from her.

"The hamster was a gift from Andy. I'd always warned him not to get pets for the kids. Teddy just suffers from *so* many allergies. But Teddy adored that little hamster. He would insist on bringing it around with him everywhere. He even *talked* to it! Fancy that . . . he barely even *looks* at me, let alone talks to me." She sniffled.

"After a couple of months, I became certain that Teddy was having some sort of allergic reaction to the hamster. He started getting these nasty, itchy rashes on his hands and arms, even his face at times. It was a nightmare watching him scratch his skin raw until it bled. Teddy has a low tolerance for physical discomfort of any kind. He'll cry and scream; it's just *so* awful. So I decided the hamster simply had to go." She buried her face in her hands.

"But . . . it turns out the culprit wasn't the hamster after all. I had completely overlooked that I had switched to a new brand of hand soap at around the same time Teddy got the hamster. After Hobbes was gone, poor Teddy was so upset. And to add salt to injury, the allergies continued and got worse. That was when I realized I had made a big, big mistake." She sighed.

Elly had gone quite still. "What . . . what did you say the hamster's name was?" she asked, not sure she had heard right.

Victoria dabbed at her eyes, smudging her mascara. "Teddy named it Hobbes, after the tiger in Calvin and Hobbes, his favourite cartoon. Poor Teddy. A few weeks ago I took Hobbes to the local park while Teddy was in Oxford with Maddy and Andy. He wanted to show the kids where he went for university." She made a face, as though it had been an absurd venture. "I remember it was on a Friday, because the kids didn't have school due to parent-teacher conferences at St. Catherine's. Since we had just moved from Manchester, and the kids had just started attending the school, Andy and I were excused from going. After much heated debate, Maddy and Teddy had gone to stay with Andy for the long weekend. So the park was pretty quiet that morning—all other kids were at school. No pets are allowed in Andy's fancy rental apartment in the city, so Teddy had to leave Hobbes behind." She bit her lip.

"I even played with the hamster for a while before I left him at the park. I really thought it was the best thing to do. We'd just moved from Manchester, so we don't really have friends here. Our neighbours didn't want to take Hobbes either." She blew her nose on a napkin.

"Oh, the minute I got home and saw Teddy's room, I came to my senses and turned right back to the park. But by the time I got there, the cage was empty and the food bowl had spilled over. Hobbes was nowhere in sight. I saw this big black dog, a fierce thing, barking up the tree. I was certain that poor Hobbes had been gobbled up already."

Elly could barely contain herself; she was close to bursting. "Oh, Victoria!" she cried, jumping up. "This will sound a little unbelievable, but please hear me out."

In a flourish, she explained how she had come across Hobbes at the Berry Grove Park that morning, possibly shortly after Victoria had left, and how she'd taken the hamster to her friend's house on Cornwall Street.

Victoria's jaw dropped open as she stared at Elly. "Blimey, you actually kept Hobbes safe?" she cried, tears of relief filling her eyes. "Oh, *bless you*, dear! Please, oh please, could Teddy have him back? Cornwall Street is just a five-minute drive away from us! He'll be ever *so* happy!" She wiped the tears away hastily and laughed. "Oh, I'm a blubbering mess!"

Then she paused with a frown. "But how can you be sure that hamster was Hobbes?"

Elly gulped. She couldn't very well tell Victoria that Hobbes had told her his name. Giggling, she grinned. "Well, not many chubby, ginger-coloured hamsters get stranded at the park, right?"

At this, Victoria sighed with relief and nodded. "Yes, Hobbes was definitely far too fat for his own good."

Elly beamed. "Let me tell Maddy, and I will give my friend a call right away. I am sure she'll be happy to return Hobbes to Teddy. May I be excused?" When Victoria nodded, Elly darted into the house and bounded up the stairs.

Maddy almost fell off her bed when Elly explained the situation. "Crikey! You're *joking*! All this time, Hobbes has been several blocks away from us—with *Lily*?" she exclaimed incredulously.

Then she threw her arms around Elly. "Oh, you're a champ! See, it's fate! We were meant to bump into you at Westminster Abbey! Wait till I tell Teddy!"

She dashed into her brother's room, where Victoria was already filling Teddy in on the good news. Elly could hear him, and it was the first time she detected excitement in his voice. "Hobbes. Hobbes is coming home!"

After Elly found Lily's phone number in her Royan, she asked Maddy for the telephone. Still very much a stranger to such devices, she pressed the numbers slowly and carefully while Maddy looked on with an amused grin. "Does your guardian usually punch in the numbers for you?" she teased. Elly giggled and breathed a sigh of relief when Lily's voice came on the line.

Lily sounded just as incredulous as Maddy. "I don't believe this! What an uncanny coincidence! Does this mean they want Hobbes back?"

Elly nodded into the receiver. "Yes, Maddy's brother really loves Hobbes. Please understand, it would mean so much to him."

Lily laughed. "Oh, I'm more than happy to return Hobbes to Teddy! He's the rightful master. To be honest, Hobbes hasn't been much fun. He mopes about in the cage like he's depressed, doesn't even go on the treadmill much."

By the time Lily had agreed on a time to meet Maddy and return Hobbes, darkness had fallen. Victoria went to grab her car keys. "Elly, it's time to get you home for supper! I just gave Miriam a call; she's expecting you. Give me a second while I freshen up in the powder room. We'll drop you off on the way to Chinatown." She winked. "I'm celebrating with the kids at The Dragon Eye. They love Chinese food, so it's a real treat!"

Maddy was acting slightly more civil towards her mother since Elly told them about Hobbes. "You shouldn't be too hard on her," Elly urged Maddy in a whisper. "She was really upset when you stormed off earlier. She was just trying to be nice."

Maddy nodded reluctantly. "All right, I'll give her a break. I guess I have been a bit hard on her. I just . . . I just wish my parents were back together, you know?" Her eyes were suddenly over-bright.

Elly nodded sympathetically. "I'm sorry. It must be awfully hard."

Maddy shrugged. "It's what it is. Anyway, I'm glad that Hobbes is still alive, and coming back to Teddy."

Then she sat Elly down on the rug in front of the fireplace while they waited for Victoria. "Look, I'm *really* sorry about the way I behaved at the school fair," she said apologetically, shamefaced. "I kind of panicked when I saw you there with Lily, and I was a little embarrassed to be seen with those mean girls. Honestly, I never intended to be mean to Lily. It's nothing personal. Actually, I think she's pretty cool—brilliant in English literature, and *so* talented. Clare didn't stand a chance at winning the lead role." She bit her lip and sniffled.

Elly smiled, thinking that in distress, Maddy looked awfully like her mother. "Anyway, several weeks back both Lily and I were the new girls, and I just wanted to fit in *so* badly. When this popular clique started paying attention to me, it was like a lifeline. I was flattered at first, and joined them because it seemed to make things easier at school. But it wasn't long before I realized they're pretty nasty. Honestly, I can't stand those girls anymore."

Elly nodded thoughtfully. "I understand now. But I think you should apologise to Lily. She thought you were in league with those girls and making fun of her. Perhaps you can be friends?"

Maddy sighed. "Yeah, you're right. I should apologise. But I'm not sure Lily would want to be friends with me now, not after the way I followed the Space Cadets around and let them treat her like that." She looked so forlorn that Elly felt sorry for her. She patted Maddy on the shoulder, and wondered whether she would ever be tempted to follow the Three Flamingos around just to be popular. She shuddered at the horrid thought.

Then she remembered that she had been wanting to ask Maddy about blue amber. Had she found out anything about it? Maddy blushed. "Oh Elly, I'm so sorry! It totally slipped my mind! I've been so preoccupied with school, and Mum's been driving me crazy. There's something about this blue amber that sounds familiar."

"What are you girls talking about?" interrupted Victoria, who had just walked into the living room. She had changed into knee-high boots and a tight black turtle-neck dress. Elly thought she looked elegant.

Maddy shrugged. "Elly's been looking for something called blue amber, it's a really rare gemstone or something."

She turned back to Elly. "I'll see what I can find out, for real this time," she promised. Elly smiled, masking her disappointment. Well, at least she was going to the Dominican Republic with the Cobbles soon.

Maddy turned back to say something to her mother, but Victoria had disappeared. "Mum!" she called out, annoyed. "Where did you go? I thought we were on our way out!"

There were banging sounds as drawers were being opened and closed from the far end of the corridor. "Yes, I'm coming! Just looking for something before we head out!"

Maddy rolled her eyes. "She's *always* forgetting something," she muttered. She took Elly's hand. "Let's go wait for her in the car."

On the way to the Cobbles' house, Elly and Maddy chattered on about the Cinderella musical at St Catherine's. "Lily definitely deserves the lead role," Maddy gushed. "She was fantastic at the audition! The Space Cadets were livid. Clare will make a perfect wicked stepsister." The two girls giggled. Victoria was humming happily to a song about bluebirds flying over the rainbow. Teddy was playing a video game on a small hand-held device that emitted shooting noises incessantly.

In no time, they arrived at Number Eight, Adelaide Drive. Just as Elly started walking up the driveway, Victoria gave a shout. "Wait, Elly!" She fumbled in her handbag and jumped out of the driver's seat. Then she enveloped Elly in a tight hug. "I want to thank you, so, *so* much for being a good friend to my Teddy and Maddy, and for keeping Hobbes safe and returning him back to us! I can't tell you how much it means to me. You are a very special little girl. I want you to have this, as my gift to you."

She smiled and held out a necklace. It was dark, but Elly could see it was an oval-shaped pendant on a long silver chain.

Victoria fingered the pendant fondly. "This is my lucky charm. It's been with me for as long as I can remember. I was younger than you when I went on a trip with my parents to a very exotic place far from here. My father loved to travel and was *such* an adventurer." She smiled nostalgically. Elly frowned, perplexed.

Victoria continued. "When I was wandering the marketplace with my parents, I came across an old lady selling hand-made jewellery. She stopped me as we were walking, and she said something to me in Spanish as she held out this necklace to me, but I couldn't understand. Later, the tour guide told me the old lady said she was enchanted by my bright blue eyes, and said the necklace would keep me safe, and one day would be of great help to somebody. It all sounded so cryptic and exciting, like she was some fortune teller! So I accepted the necklace. It's supposed to be an extremely rare kind of gemstone, very hard to chance upon, even back in the Dominican Republic . . ."

Elly's head snapped up. "What?" she whispered.

Victoria lowered the necklace over Elly's head. "Yes, it's quite peculiar. Blue amber, it's called. I overheard you and Maddy talking about it. It's something that you've been looking for, right?"

Thunderstruck, Elly stared at her. "Yes," she said hoarsely.

"How is it that a little girl like you would know about something as obscure as blue amber, anyway? Diamonds are supposed to be a girl's best friend," Victoria joked.

Elly gazed down at the necklace that she was now wearing. "I was told that a certain type of blue amber is at least a hundred times more priceless than diamonds," she said softly.

Victoria laughed. "Well, if that's true, then I would be a right old fool to give this away!" She smiled, thinking that Elly would one day become grown-up enough to look for diamonds instead.

"Anyway, it's awfully hard to find, because it's the rarest type of blue amber. Pure-grade, that tour guide told me. He probably wanted to snitch it for himself!" She grinned. "Under direct sunlight, it's a gorgeous ocean blue. When you put it up against sunlight, it's a brilliant yellow. Quite extraordinary."

Victoria stepped back and smiled. "It's an old necklace, but it's meant a lot to me. Since blue amber is something you've been looking for, I hope you like it!"

Elly's head was spinning. She gaped at the pendant in her hand. Even in the dark, she could see that it had a highly polished surface. She shook her head wonderingly. Then something dawned on her.

"Wait . . . The old lady who gave you this necklace . . . what did she look like?"

Victoria knitted her brow in concentration. "Hmm, I don't remember much. Only that she was really tiny, and she had this creepy ferret around her neck. I was young, and found her a little scary."

Dumbfounded, Elly thought about the tiny old lady with the ferret back at Berry Grove Park. Who was she?

Her hand shook as she touched the cool surface of the pendant. "You have no idea what this means to me. Thank you," she whispered, her heart pounding hard. Greymore stirred.

You have found it, Ellanor.

Her heart leapt with joy.

You see, Ellanor, some things cannot be bought with money. Some things do not happen in the way we expect. Life does not always go according to plan, does it?

You can say that again, Greymore!

Maddy had jumped out of the car. "Wait, all this time you actually had this blue amber?" she asked her mother incredulously.

She turned to Elly and shook her head in amazement, then slapped a palm against her forehead. "That's right! No wonder I thought it sounded familiar! Years ago, my mum told me about a necklace she got in the Caribbean as a kid. I didn't think much of it, and I had totally forgotten about it after all this time."

She grinned at Elly. "See, it was meant to be! You helped Teddy get Hobbes back, and we got you your blue amber. It's all worked out for the best!"

"You can say that again," Elly said, and Maddy laughed.

After Maddy had made Elly promise to call her, and Victoria had driven off, Elly grasped the pendant and raced like the wind into the house.

"Elly, is that you?" called Miriam from the kitchen. The delicious smell of baking lingered in the air. "It's nearly time for supper!"

But Elly hadn't heard; she'd raced past without a word and dashed into her room, slamming the door behind her.

The room was dark. She gazed into the mirror. The necklace gleamed in the dim light. Trembling, she opened up her Royan and murmured in Elvish. The broken portal rose from the pages. Then she took off the necklace, held the pendant between her fingers, murmured a prayer to Freya, and gently breathed on the dark, shiny surface.

It glowed an unmistakable bright golden yellow.

It was Organoth blue amber.

She laughed, so overjoyed that she didn't realize she was crying. Then she placed the glowing pendant between the two broken pieces of the portal and held her breath.

CHAPTER FOURTEEN
Fly Me to the Moon

ELLY STARED HARD AT THE broken portal and pendant. It seemed to her that every second was a minute and that every minute was an hour.

"Are you sure this is Organoth blue amber, Greymore?" she asked softly, her heart sinking.

Be patient, Ellanor.

Miriam was calling for her again. Tick-tock, tick-tock. The clock on her nightstand seemed to be mocking her.

She buried her face in her hands and started crying quietly. The tears trickled down her hands and splashed onto the pages of her open Royan. "It's not working. I'm never going to see my family again, am I?" she sobbed.

Suddenly, Elly saw an eruption of dazzling light. She gasped.

The broken portal and the pendant were glowing blue.

She watched in awe as the pendant began melting into a little puddle. Like small magnetic fragments, droplets spread out slowly towards the two broken halves of the portal. After every droplet had been absorbed, the broken halves burned a fierce golden yellow, emitting such a blinding light that Elly had to shield her eyes with her arm. Then she was plunged into darkness again. She opened her eyes.

The two broken pieces had come together seamlessly. The Tree of Alendria that was carved into the surface was now glowing a bright blue.

With trembling hands, Elly clasped the repaired portal as she cried out with unbridled joy.

Greymore! It's worked! The portal's been made whole again!

Yes, Ellanor. Everything has its timing. Magic follows rules, too. For magic to work, certain ingredients are needed. You can bake a cake without sugar, but it will not be as sweet. In this case, to repair the portal with the Organoth blue amber, your tears were needed to initiate the repairing process. Remember, the portal is alive. Once it sensed your desperation, your sincerity, it regenerated.

So her tears had acted like glue for the broken portal to repair itself? The thought made her smile even more broadly.

Elly then cast the unbreakable enchantment on the portal, as Greymore had instructed. Her enchantments were not very strong yet, but this would have to do for now.

Suddenly, she was startled by a heavy pounding on the door. She hadn't even realized she had locked it!

"Elly! Are you all right?" Miriam sounded alarmed.

Elly threw the door open. Miriam and Horace were standing there, looking very worried and frightened. Then they saw her sunny smile and the slab of blue stone she was clutching in her hands.

The old couple stood staring at the stone for several moments. "Oh, Elly!" Miriam gasped.

Horace grinned and patted Elly on the back. "Bravo! You managed to repair it!" Snowy purred at their feet.

They went into the living room together. Clutching the portal to her chest, Elly knelt down on the rug and told them how she had finally come upon Organoth blue amber in the most unexpected way.

Miriam and Horace exchanged looks. "Are you going to be leaving right now, Elly?" she asked quietly. She had just spent several hours baking goodies for Elly to take to the reunion dinner at Lily's. She wanted Elly to be reunited with her family, but she wasn't quite ready to say goodbye so soon.

Elly caressed the portal. The blue light was fading. "To be honest, I'm not sure what's going to happen. I don't know when and how the portal will take me back," she admitted, staring down at the blue slab in her hands.

Ellanor, I do not know how the portal will transport you back. But remember what I said. Everything has its timing. Be patient and wait a little longer. As long as the portal is with me, you need not worry. Just do not ever let me out of your sight.

Of course, Greymore! I have always kept you with me, have I not?
Then we have nothing to worry about.

Elly glanced at Miriam and Horace, who both looked more anxious than she did. "I think I need to wait for something to happen with the portal, but I don't know what it is. I'll be staying put for now. Besides," she added, "I'd find it hard to say goodbye if I had to leave so suddenly."

Miriam's eyes teared up, and Horace put an arm around her. Elly went to hug them both, wishing there were sufficient words to express how much they both meant to her.

"I suppose this means you won't be going to the Dominican Republic with us," Miriam said through her tears. She tried to smile. "I'm sad that you might be leaving us soon, but I am so happy that you finally got the portal repaired!"

Horace cleared his throat and nodded in agreement, then got up and hurried into the kitchen, mumbling something about a fish bone being stuck in his throat.

Elly smiled at Miriam, but she still felt uneasy. After all, she had no idea how the portal would teleport her back home. What if she had overlooked something important? What if, for some reason, the portal won't teleport her back?

She could not bear to think that it was a distinct possibility.

As the sun started to set the following day, Elly got ready to walk over to Lily's house. She had wanted to wear a black dress with gold trim, but Miriam objected. "I'm not an expert, but I do remember my Chinese friend once telling me that it's considered unlucky to wear black during Chinese New Year," she said as she put the black dress back into the closet and took out a red one.

Miriam tied shiny red and gold ribbons in Elly's hair to match the red boots with gold trim that Horace had made for her. Elly put on a red coat and wrapped a red scarf snugly around her neck. Miriam stepped back to admire her. Elly's green eyes were offset even more brilliantly by all the red she was wearing.

"Now you're all set!" Miriam declared as she handed Elly two large tote bags bulging with tins of home-made red velvet cupcakes, pavlova, and strawberry jam-filled donuts. Elly grinned; she knew Lily and her parents would love them.

Horace insisted on driving her. "There's no need, it's only a few blocks away! Besides, I want to get some fresh air. I like the smell of fallen snow!" So off she went, looking very much like Little Red Riding Hood as the wind wuthering down the street sent her red coat and scarf billowing. Swallows swooped over a landscape turned pink and gold by the setting sun.

When she reached Aunty Mabel's Bakery, the sky was already fully dark. Lily had made her promise to get there a couple of hours earlier so that they could catch up before the guests arrived. "Elly, you must watch *The Sound of Music* with me! That film really inspired me to try out acting and singing. Without it, I wouldn't have had the courage to audition for Cinderella!"

A queue snaked out from the bakery to the pavement outside. Some pedestrians threw the customers dirty looks as they squeezed past.

Inside, there was a clamour of chattering, as the throng of customers exchanged Chinese New Year greetings and well wishes. Many of them wore something red. Elly overheard one round-faced woman exclaim in Cantonese, "Thank goodness Mabel doesn't close shop on New Year's Eve! I wouldn't know what I'd do without her egg tarts and pineapple buns. My nieces and nephews can't get enough of them; they demanded that I get some for our reunion dinner tonight!"

Elly smiled, pleased to hear that Mabel was so well-liked in the neighbourhood. She wondered whether Mama was doing all right with her business. What were they all doing at this very moment?

"Hey, Elly!" Lily came bounding towards her and did a double-take. "Whoa, look at you! You really took it seriously when I said you ought to wear some red!" she exclaimed, then looked at herself in dismay. Her mother had made her wear a garish red dress with puffy princess sleeves and a frilly skirt. Lily had protested, but that was the only new item of red clothing she had, so she had no choice but to go along with it.

"It's some sort of unspoken rule to wear new clothes for Chinese New Year, preferably red," she had explained to Elly a few days ago. "The colour red and the newness of the clothes are symbols of good luck, like leaving behind all the bad stuff from the previous year."

She sighed as she glowered at her own dress gloomily. "Mum bought this for me when she went shopping by herself last week. As you can see, she doesn't realize that I'm thirteen, not eight. Even my costume for Cinderella looks way cooler than this!"

Elly giggled. "I know what you mean! My mother keeps on wanting me to wear pink, even though she knows I detest it!"

Lily laughed. "I guess all mums can be a little overbearing, huh?"

As they tried to squeeze through the crowd to get to Mabel, Lily frowned. "You know," she whispered to Elly, "Chinese New Year's Eve is a public holiday in China. It would've been perfectly understandable if mum had taken the day off today! But like every year, they all come at this hour to get last-minute gifts for the reunion dinner."

When Elly handed her the tote bags and told her what was in them, Lily gasped and clapped her hands. "Oh, wait till I tell my mum! Finally, we'll get to taste the famous Miriam Cobble pastries!" She hugged the bags to her chest happily. "Wait here, I'll pop them into the fridge by the counter!"

As Elly waited, she looked around the small bakery wonderingly. The delicious aroma of baking hung in the air, mingled with the sweet fragrance of fresh marigolds, lilies, and peonies arranged prettily in colourful Chinese ceramic vases in every corner of the shop. The customers were greeting Mabel with even more enthusiasm than usual, handing her bags bulging with fresh fruit and other boxed goods, as they exclaimed the same things over and over again in Mandarin Chinese and Cantonese: "Happy New Year!" "Wishing you great prosperity, good health, and good business!" "May your children grow up well and excel at school!"

Mabel was saying similar things and smiling broadly at everyone, looking pretty in a red sweater and beige skirt. She was busily putting pineapple buns, egg tarts, and other pastries into pink boxes, which were then hastily shoved into pink plastic bags. In between serving the customers, she handed out red envelopes to children who happily received them with both hands. Even Lily received red envelopes from the customers.

Then some of the customers started looking at Elly curiously. "Who is that pretty girl?" they asked in whispers.

One old lady with permed white hair hobbled over to Elly on a walking stick and squinted at her. Elly smiled uncertainly. Then the old lady turned to her young granddaughter and spoke loudly in Cantonese. "Is she a white girl? Her hair is even blacker than yours, but her eyes are like emeralds! She looks like a very lucky child, indeed."

To Elly's surprise, the old lady handed her a red envelope and smiled kindly. "Here you go! Grow up nicely and study well!"

Elly smiled, and received it with both hands and bowed. "Thank you! Happy Chinese New Year to you, and wishing you a wonderful Year of the Monkey with good health and happiness!" she said cheerfully, repeating what she had heard Lily say whenever she received those red envelopes.

A hush fell over the crowd. The old lady was stunned. "Why, you can speak perfect Cantonese!" she cried. Before Elly could say anything, Lily had grabbed her arm and yanked her away.

"We have to excuse ourselves, thank you! Happy New Year!" Lily called out to the bewildered customers.

Under her breath she muttered, "You can say hi to my mum later. Let's get out of here before they all realize you speak better Cantonese than I do!"

Elly giggled and waved at the astonished old lady before they made their escape. When they had closed the door behind them in the family room, Lily sighed with relief.

As they were walking upstairs to Lily's bedroom, Elly asked, "What are those red envelopes for?"

Lily flicked a piece of lint off her shoulder. "Oh, it's another tradition. Those red envelopes, or *laisee* in Cantonese, symbolise prosperity and good luck, that sort of thing. There's money in the envelopes." Lily chuckled when Elly's eyes widened. "It's usually not a whole lot of money, probably just six or eight pounds if you're lucky. The numbers six and eight are considered lucky because they rhyme with the Cantonese words for 'prosperity' and 'wealth'."

She grinned at Elly. "For me, apart from all the good food and family time, getting all this laisee is one of the best things about Chinese New Year! I've bought quite a few things on my wish list just from saving up my laisee money every year."

Lily's room was decorated with plush cushions and a lovely quilted blue bedspread. One side of the wall was dominated by a huge bookshelf holding rows and rows of books.

"What a pretty room!" Elly exclaimed, fingering the velvety dark blue curtains. They stretched out on the rug at the foot of the bed and chatted easily, looking and giggling through family photo albums and flipping through old picture books and novels as they nibbled on freshly baked pineapple buns. Then they started talking about Lily's day at school.

Lily tried putting hair clips in Elly's curly hair, and scowled when they bounced off.

"Maddy came up to me during lunch to say hi. I was sitting by myself. You should've seen the dirty looks she got from Clare Andrews and her Space Cadets. Afterwards, they refused to let her sit back with them. I almost cheered when Maddy got this disgusted look on her face and told them good riddance. She came back and sat with me, and we chatted for *ages*! Turns out we have tons in common, except that she hates English literature and I love it, and she loves sports and I'm hopeless at it." She sighed happily. "Oh, it was just the *best* day ever!"

Then she smiled at Elly. "Maddy really likes you. I *so* wish you were going to our school! The three of us would be the best of friends. We would be invincible. The Space Cadets wouldn't stand a chance against us!"

Elly giggled, trying to imagine what that would be like. But all that came to mind was Aron's face. Oh, how she missed him!

Then she thought about Teddy. "I've been meaning to ask . . . Have you already returned Hobbes?"

Lily tried the hair clips on herself. "Yep! My dad dropped me off at Maddy's place early this morning before school. You should've seen Hobbes. The moment he saw Teddy, he went berserk! Got up on his hind legs and it almost looked like he was *smiling*! Do hamsters actually smile?"

As the clock struck six, Mabel closed the shop. By then, Lily and Elly were in the living room watching *The Sound of Music*. Lily had sung along on "My Favourite Things" with perfect pitch. She tried to persuade Elly to sing with her. "Come on, it can't be *that* bad!" she urged when Elly steadfastly refused.

Mabel stumbled into the living room and collapsed onto the couch. "Lily's daddy is preparing the food in the kitchen," she said, taking a sip of cold tea and propping up her tired feet. Elly met Mr Wong for the first time when he came home from work in Chinatown over an hour ago. He was a short, soft-spoken man with greying black hair and gentle eyes.

Lily giggled. "Yeah, dad's much better than mum when it comes to Chinese cooking. But he can't bake to save his life!"

Mabel sat up and glanced at her watch. "The relatives will be arriving around seven. I'll go off and freshen up. Elly dear, I'm so glad you're with us tonight, Lily's ecstatic to have your company." Before rushing off, she smiled and winked. "By the way, you've become quite a sensation with my customers, especially old Mrs Chan. Apparently, you are the first green-eyed person they've ever met who speaks perfect Cantonese!"

Sure enough, at seven o'clock on the dot, Lily's relatives started arriving. About a dozen aunts, uncles, and cousins trickled in with much noise and fanfare. Lily rushed over to greet the guests, offering up a red and gold platter laden with dried fruits, watermelon seeds, and various candies in gold wrappers. "I've been greeting them like this every single year since I was five!" she whispered to Elly. "Fancy still seeing me do this when I'm in college!"

The adults ambushed Lily, making various comments about her height ("Oh, you're still quite short, aren't you?"), her skin ("My, you're getting more freckles! You should stay out of the sun!"), and her face ("Your glasses are getting thicker by the year!"). Lily put on a brave smile, but whenever she caught Elly's eye she would make a long-suffering face.

After they were finished with Lily, the relatives turned to Elly curiously. Who was this girl, and what was she doing at this family gathering? But once Mabel had formally introduced Elly and explained that her parents were not in town, they became quite sympathetic and showered her with laisee. They were utterly delighted when they realized Elly could speak fluent Cantonese.

"Lily, you should take some lessons from your friend!" Aunt Helen gushed. Lily's grandmother nodded approvingly at Elly. "You are a very good influence on my granddaughter!" she said in Cantonese. Elly smiled back politely before flashing Lily an apologetic look.

The Wongs were a large family, with some living overseas in Hong Kong and Shanghai. If the entire extended family had been gathered in London, there would have been over forty people squashed into the modest three-bedroom house. The large, round rosewood dining table was overladen with a dozen dishes. Elbows were touching when all sixteen people squeezed in at the table. Elly was sandwiched between Lily and her cousin Carrie.

With a genteel smile, Lily's father stood up and raised his glass. "Welcome to our humble home, everyone!" he said in Cantonese. "This is a toast to a prosperous, healthy, and happy Year of the Monkey! Cheers!" Everyone stood up and cheered boisterously as glasses chimed together.

With a grin, Elly copied what they were doing, even attempting to use chopsticks (at which she proved to be a quick study). She noticed that Carrie and her parents remained seated and stony-faced.

But when Elly saw what had been plopped right at the centre of the table, she froze and went quite pale. Surrounded by plates of Chinese vegetables, tofu, a large pot of soup, a steamed fish covered in some watery brown sauce under a mound of spring onion, suspicious-looking blobs of black stuff with mushrooms, and various sliced and pickled meats, was the highly anticipated suckling pig; a crispy-skinned barbecued piglet with little red light bulbs where the eyes should be!

It looked so grotesque that Elly quickly reminded Lily that she did not eat meat. Lily noticed her friend's stricken expression and giggled. "You know, this really isn't that much different from the huge turkeys that the English and Americans love to eat for Christmas and Thanksgiving! The Chinese just have a different idea about food presentation." She giggled some more as Elly's face went even more pale. "Don't worry! We won't make you eat it. All the adults will make sure you get completely stuffed on rice and all those veggies alone, not to mention the desserts!" With a grin, she plopped a mound of vegetables on Elly's plate with her chopsticks.

Carrie turned to them. "Aren't you too young to be a vegetarian?" she asked pompously, looking at Elly with raised eyebrows. Elly noticed that she was very pretty. Were those actually diamond earrings in her earlobes?

"Well, my whole family is vegetarian. Animal meat has never been a part of our diet," Elly explained with a smile. She tried the stir-fried broccoli and spinach. Though she much preferred raw vegetables, this wasn't too bad at all.

Beside her, Lily groaned softly. "Watch out," she muttered under her breath as she crunched on the crispy skin of the barbequed pork.

Before dinner, she had given Elly the low-down on her relatives, and had tried to give her ample warning about her cousin Carrie, older by six months. "Carrie's mum is my mother's younger sister. Aunt Brenda is a real narcissist, and her daughter takes after her. Aunt Brenda married into a really wealthy family. Her husband's the big boss of a huge law firm in the city. Carrie's an only child, like me, and she's possibly even worse than Clare Andrews. She's spoiled, arrogant, manipulative, and she feels entitled to *everything*. I can't stand her."

She lowered her voice even further. "Aunt Brenda *hates* us because she's certain my mum was always Grandmother's favourite."

Elly had listened in rapt attention. This talk of family discord was strange to her. Though her little brother Luca drove her crazy at times, she knew beyond a shadow of a doubt that he would give his life for her, as she would for him. Her parents never played favourites with her or Luca. Elly was certain that Mama and Papa loved them equally.

"If Aunt Brenda hates your mother so much, why does she bother to come over every year for the reunion dinner?" she had asked curiously.

Lily laughed. "Families can be very strange. You hate them, you love them. For one, my grandmother lives with us, and as the eldest she gets to decide where the reunion dinner takes place. Aunt Brenda comes here not only because of my grandmother, but because she loves to gloat and put us down. To her, we're the poor blue-collar workers. You'll understand when you hear the things they say about us and our house. You'll be able to smell the unmistakable scent of money reeking from them." She rolled her eyes. "If Aunt Brenda had her way, she'd get everyone to gather at her thirteen-bedroom mansion all the way across town, near Buckingham Palace. She loves telling people she's neighbours with the royal family."

At the table, Elly saw that Carrie's parents were sandwiched between Grandmother Wong and Lily's father. Their faces looked sour as they picked at their food and tutted at every opportunity. Elly noticed how Mabel's smile seemed to have become frozen on her face as she valiantly addressed every nasty insinuation her sister and her husband made. ("Oh, so how's your little bakery doing? Don't you ever tire of slaving away at the ovens? Oh, I see that your wallpaper is peeling; do you want me to recommend a renovator to come redo them for you?")

Next to her, Carrie was examining the piece of tofu she had just picked up with her chopsticks. "I think I just found a strand of hair in my food," she announced curtly, and dropped the tofu on the red table cloth. From across the table, her parents tutted loudly and shook their heads.

Elly was not of this realm, and she was not Chinese, but she could spot bad manners from a mile away. She glanced at Grandmother Wong, who looked strangely serene in the face of such blatant rudeness. Carrie and her parents were dressed so nicely and spoke English with posh accents, but all three of them had the same mean look.

After she had played around with her food some more, Carrie sighed with disgust and turned back to Elly. "As I was saying, your parents shouldn't make you go on a vegetarian diet. Young girls like us need the proteins that meat provides. Your growth will be stunted if you live on just veggies." Then she smiled meanly. "But then again, Lily's practically a midget, and she eats tons of meat."

Lily threw her cousin a dirty look. "At least I'm human, unlike some people," she muttered.

Elly's smile froze as she looked at Carrie. "Is that right?" she said politely. "But seeing how well my parents grew up on a vegetarian diet, I suppose I'll get by unscathed." Beside her, Lily snorted as she stifled a laugh.

Carrie scowled. "Well, you should probably do some research and see for yourself," she scoffed. Then, scrambling for something else to lord over her cousin's unflappable friend, her eyes strayed to Elly's dress and narrowed.

"What's that thing on your belt?"

Elly glanced down. "Oh, that's my Roy— . . . I mean, my journal. I keep it with me all the time."

Carrie wrinkled her nose. "Who carries a journal around with them like that? It's really odd, makes you look like a gypsy or something."

Lily gasped. Elly blushed hotly.

"Hey Carrie, why don't you just shut up?" Lily said quietly.

Carrie's dark eyes flashed angrily. "Don't you dare speak to me that way," she hissed under her breath. "I am older than you, and as a rule you should speak to me respectfully."

Lily rolled her eyes. "Oh? So you and your parents' barbaric behaviour is perfectly all right?"

The next thing Elly knew, Carrie had knocked over her glass of soda, splattering Elly's dress and belt. Her Royan was covered in the sticky orange liquid. Elly gasped and leapt to her feet.

"Oh!" said Carrie loudly, jumping out of her chair. "I'm *so* sorry, Elly! Please, let me help you clean it up!"

Lily stood up, seething. "You did that on purpose!" she hissed. Carrie looked back at her, feigning innocence.

Mabel stood up and walked briskly around the table towards them. "Let's not make a scene," she said to Lily in a low voice. Then she plastered a smile on her face. "That's all right, Carrie. I'll help Elly clean up." Without another word, she steered Elly towards the bathroom. Carrie excused herself, murmuring something about washing her hands. Lily looked at her cousin's retreating back suspiciously, and was about to follow when Grandmother Wong spoke up sharply in Cantonese. "Lily, sit down! Let your mother handle it!"

Elly's entire skirt was drenched. She touched her Royan; it was wet and sticky. *Greymore, are you all right?*

Yes, Ellanor. Such things cannot easily damage me. But do keep that wretched girl away.

The small guest bathroom was too cramped for two people. "Let's keep the door open to let some air in," Mabel said as she turned on the tap water. "Here, sweetie. Let's take off that belt for a minute and let me soak off some of the soda." Before Elly could protest, Mabel had unbuckled her belt, wiped down her Royan gently with a hot wet towel, and placed it behind Elly on the bathroom counter next to the sink. Mabel then proceeded to blow-dry her dress. The roar of the hairdryer drowned out every other sound, including Mabel's voice.

After several minutes, Mabel unplugged the hairdryer and smiled. Elly's ears were ringing in the sudden quiet. "See, there you go! Good as new."

Elly breathed a sigh of relief. "Thank you so much, Mabel." Then she turned to retrieve her belt. It was gone.

She gasped, fear clenching her throat. "Where's my belt?" she cried. *Greymore!*

She ran out, and her eyes bulged when she saw Carrie on the living room couch, about to open up her Royan.

With a cry, Elly lunged forward. "What are you doing?" she cried, grabbing Greymore out of Carrie's clutches.

Carrie looked up innocently, but a small smirk played at her lips. "What's the matter? I was just trying to dry it off for you."

Elly was livid. "You're a *liar!* You had no right to look through my Roy— . . . my journal! You should not take what's not yours!"

"What's going on?" Mabel cried as she ran into the living room.

Elly ran out into the backyard, near tears. Lily rushed over and put a hand on her arm. "Are you all right?" she asked in a low voice. "I'm so sorry about Carrie. I didn't expect her to stoop this low. As I said, she feels entitled to everything."

Then she lowered her voice further. "Her parents tried to keep this all hush-hush, especially since her dad is a hot-shot lawyer and all— but we know that Carrie was caught shoplifting a few months ago. She definitely can't keep her hands to herself."

They could hear Carrie protesting loudly in the dining room, her voice indignant. "Honestly, what is wrong with that weird girl? I was just trying to help!"

Mabel said something to her, and Carrie fell silent. Then there were raised voices. Carrie's parents were now throwing insults at Mabel. "How dare you lecture our daughter!"

Suddenly, there was a collective gasp as Grandmother Wong rushed over to Carrie and slapped her on the head. "You ought to be ashamed! You should display better manners to your elders!" the old lady rebuked an open-mouthed Carrie.

Lily clamped a hand over her mouth. "I can't believe Grandma just did that! I wish I'd been there to see it!" she marvelled in a whisper. Elly groaned. She didn't mean to stir up such a commotion.

After a few minutes, Mabel joined them in the backyard looking extremely harassed. Her eyes softened when she saw Elly.

"My dear, are you all right? I understand you're upset. Carrie has no respect for other people's things. I've been telling my sister to do something about that girl; she's an absolute terror."

She stopped and shook her head. "Lily, why don't you stay with Elly for a bit? I'll get back in there before all hell breaks loose." She gave Elly's arm a reassuring squeeze and hurried back into the dining room.

Elly closed her eyes and tried to calm her pounding heart. What if Carrie had somehow damaged her Royan? Her stomach lurched. What if the portal had been compromised? She shuddered at the thought of being stranded in Gaya indefinitely, forever parted from Alendria all because of that ghastly girl.

She drew a deep breath and smiled at Lily, who was watching her with concern. "Don't worry. I just need some fresh air. Can I stay out here in the garden for a bit? I'll come back inside soon, I promise." She added, "I'm sorry, I didn't mean to cause a fuss. This journal is really, really important to me."

Lily nodded sympathetically. She wondered if the book was some sort of family heirloom. Whatever it was, it was certainly precious to Elly.

"Hey, I totally understand. If I were you, I would've pulled out Carrie's hair." They laughed. "Come back in later and have some dessert, okay? My mum's peach buns are to die for."

She hugged Elly quickly, then glanced up at the sky. "Hey, look! There's supposed to be a full moon tonight. Isn't it beautiful? One of my favourite things about Chinese New Year!" Then she grinned and went back inside, sliding the door close behind her.

Before Elly turned away, she saw Carrie peering at her from the far end of the living room, the corners of her mouth turned up in a sly smile.

<hr />

The Wongs had a lovely backyard with rose and hydrangea bushes surrounded by a white picket fence draped with stringy lights. *Like the fireflies back home*, thought Elly wistfully. The yard was shrouded in partial darkness as she stepped into the shadows, relieved to cope with her anguish in privacy.

The reunion dinner continued on in the house. Elly could hear Lily's younger cousins laughing and talking now, playfully fighting over who should get the largest peach buns. The tension seemed to have abated somewhat. Carrie and her parents were sitting in a corner, talking in low voices. Lily had started playing a game of chess with her Uncle Patrick. Then a Hong Kong movie starring a famous Chinese actor started playing on the TV, and everyone but Carrie and her parents clamoured around to watch it.

Being surrounded by Lily's family made Elly miss her own family even more.

She sighed. *Greymore, I'm sorry that horrid girl got her hands on you. I promise it won't happen again.*

Do not fret, Ellanor. All is well. You got her off me just in time.

It had stopped raining. Elly breathed in the cold night air, comforted by the dewy fragrance of wet earth, flowers and grass. When she was sure that nobody was looking, she leapt up onto the roof, sat down and crossed her legs, and gazed up at the canopy of stars twinkling down at her. The moon was bright and round.

Maybe Mama and Papa are looking at the moon right now, she thought sadly.

Elly heard music playing next door. She could catch bits of the song . . . something about flying to the moon? If only she could fly back home . . .

She sighed. "We better go back in before Lily starts worrying," she muttered. Miriam would be picking her up shortly after desserts.

Then there was a low growl behind her. Elly nearly shot out of her skin as she swivelled around.

Perched at the tip of the roof was a white fox. Its fur shone like snow under the moonlight, and its blue eyes glittered as they stared at her.

It looked like any other fox, except that it had nine tails, fanned out like a peacock's.

Elly gasped. "What—what are you?" she cried softly, one hand flying to her Royan.

To her surprise, the fox chuckled. "I've been sent here to make sure you are safe for the imminent journey." It spoke in a soft caressing whisper.

Elly blinked. "What do you mean, you were sent? By whom? And what journey are you talking about?" she demanded, panic rising by the second. Did this fox have anything to do with the goblins?

The nine-tailed fox laughed. "Do not be afraid, Ellanor Celendis," it said smoothly. "As you might have been told, the world is vast and mysterious. There are some of us who sensed your presence the moment you crossed from the other side. Whether we are friend or foe is for you to decide."

"How do you know my name?" she asked in a shocked whisper. "What do you want from me?"

The fox cocked its ear, as though listening for something. Then it smiled. "You may have met my comrade several days ago. Did he not warn you, saying 'she will try to take what is yours'?"

Elly was confused. Then her eyes widened. "The . . . the Riddler from the school fair?"

The fox laughed. "Oh, is that what he calls himself these days?"

"You mean . . . he's your friend?" Elly shook her head in amazement. "He was warning me about Carrie!"

The fox arched its back gracefully. "Let's just say we share common interests, Ellanor. One of which is your safety. Are you ready?"

"Ready? For what?" She was afraid.

The fox raised its head and gazed upward. "Look, Ellanor."

Elly turned her eyes back up to the sky, her breath shallow.

The full moon had eyes, and they were staring down at her.

Elly's heart skipped a beat. She blinked and rubbed her eyes, certain that they were playing tricks on her. She looked again.

The eyes were now accompanied by a nose, a mouth, and a beard. Elly gasped and almost cried out at the sight of the familiar, beloved face.

Grandpapa!

There was a shuffling sound behind her. She wheeled around. The nine-tailed fox had disappeared.

Greymore's voice suddenly boomed commandingly. *Ellanor, take out the portal at once!*

Stunned, Elly did as she was told. The portal was glowing blue, and it felt almost hot in her hands as she clasped it tightly, afraid it might suddenly vanish into thin air. If anyone had spotted her at that moment, they would have seen that her eyes burned like green flames.

They have found us!

Grandpapa's face on the moon was now focused squarely on Elly. He raised his bushy eyebrows and smiled his dear, familiar smile. Elly's heart leapt, and her eyes filled with tears.

The portal had now become a burning slab of silver, warming Elly's hands as she clutched it for dear life. Then the portal started floating, gravitating towards the moon, pulling Elly up, up, and away.

Then from the moon shone a beam of light that enveloped Elly. Higher and higher she rose, until Lily's house was so small that it looked like nothing but a small square on a patchwork quilt.

But wait! Greymore, I have not said my goodbyes! How can I leave Lily like this? She would get so worried! What about Miriam and Horace?

We will deal with that later, Ellanor. Everything will be fine. Trust me.

The wind roared in her ears as she hurtled upward, faster and faster. She screamed and squeezed her eyes shut against the dazzling light. Then she gasped as she plunged into something warm, spinning round and round as though she had been snatched up by a whirlwind. She did not even realize that her hands were now clutching nothing but her own cold fingers.

Then the next thing she knew, her cheek was pressed up against soft grass, the smell of the soil fragrant and familiar. A clamour of footsteps and voices surrounded her. Strong arms lifted her up. A beloved squawk sounded close to her ear, and she smiled weakly.

Before Elly blacked out, she looked into Papa's smiling, tear-stained face.

CHAPTER FIFTEEN
The Comeback

THREE DAYS LATER

SHE WAS STANDING AT A grassy clearing, surrounded by a field strewn with yellow and orange marigolds. The warm breeze caressed her hair, and she could hear a strange humming in the distance. It took her a while to realize it was the chug-chugging of a train, growing louder by the second.

She had the sense that she was waiting for someone, but she did not know who.

Then a twig snapped in the distance, and she wheeled around. Several yards away stood a slender figure silhouetted against the bright sunshine. Elly squinted; she could make out that the person was shouldering some sort of bulky bag.

Then the clouds momentarily covered the sun, and she caught a glimpse of fiery green eyes and short, curly black hair before everything started greying out.

No, wait! Who are you?

"Ellanor Celendis! Get up this instant and come downstairs!"

Elly's eyes flew open, her heart hammering in her chest. She sat bolt upright in her hammock.

Who was that girl? Why did she keep appearing in her dreams? Elly frowned, clutching her heart.

Then a delicious smell wafted upstairs, and the dream was quickly forgotten.

She sniffed; it wasn't anything with cinnamon or maple syrup. What had Mama made this time?

Yawning, she stretched out lazily on the hammock and stroked Marlow on the head. He opened one eye and squawked happily. She was bathed in delicious sunlight, and she could hear the birds twittering, the crickets chirruping. She smiled; it was so good to be back.

Elly got up and threw some acorns to a couple of squirrels on her windowsill, who caught them deftly and started gnawing on them. The delicious aroma wafting upstairs grew stronger. Curious, she leapt down the stairs with Marlow at her heels. The ellanors were in full bloom, covering the walls like a blanket of gold.

In the kitchen, Mama had concocted a new sweet cake for her daughter's homecoming. She had experimented over and over again ever since Elly told her about Aunty Mabel's delicious pineapple buns. She broke into a huge smile when she saw her daughter.

"Ta-da!" she cried, whipping out a large plate laden with crispy sweet cakes slathered with golden pineapple syrup and fresh cream. The kitchen looked a mess. There were at least a dozen cut-open pineapples strewn all over the wooden countertop, several mixing bowls with contents inside that looked either too lumpy or too watery, and half a dozen rolling pins were scattered about.

"Aww, thanks so much Mama!" Elly cried, touched that her mother had put in so much effort.

She took a crunchy bite. "Hmm!" The sweet cake certainly tasted delicious . . . but it wasn't anything like Aunty Mabel's pineapple buns. Elly had discovered that *boh loh bau* were not made from real pineapple; the bun got its name because of the checkered pattern of the top crust.

She didn't want to disappoint Mama, so she smiled and gave a thumbs-up. "It's scrumptious!" she said truthfully, and Mama beamed. Marlow swiped a couple from the plate.

Papa strode into the kitchen with Luca riding on his shoulders. Her little brother bent down and uncharacteristically planted a sloppy kiss on her cheek before he leapt down and started chasing two squirrels that had just filched some sweet cake off the table.

Papa hugged Elly tightly. "Good morning, my dear. How are you?" he asked, concern in his eyes.

After Elly had passed back through the portal and appeared on the grass before the dome in the Celestan Forest, Papa carried her back home while Mama and Luca staggered along, exhausted from lack of sleep. Elly had remained unconscious for one whole day. Mama kept up a bedside vigil until she opened her eyes on the second day, dazed and confused.

But now, Elly had never felt better. It was as though she'd just woken up from a wonderfully adventurous dream, and it made her feel like a new person. She grinned and kissed her father on the nose. "I feel great, Papa! Honestly, you don't need to worry about me. I'll be off to school now. Aron's waiting for me!" She blew her mother a kiss and bounded out of the house.

Nidah looked out the window and watched Elly skip along. Sereth went to stand by her side.

Nidah sighed. "She looks so happy, Sereth. Even happier than before. Do you think she's really all right?"

Her crystal blue eyes were filled with worry. Elly's disappearance had hit her so hard, the pain of it had been almost physical. Every motherly instinct had screamed at her to go after Elly, to defend and protect her in that foreign realm. Sereth had had to stop her from leaping through the portal.

"Do not be rash, Nidah! It's bad enough that Elly crossed over— and you may not even survive it! We must wait and see what we can do."

Nidah had wept, and in the end there was nothing for her to do but endure the anguish of waiting.

She sighed. "I still can't believe our little girl had to go through an ordeal like that. Being deceived by a goblin was bad enough, but to have been stranded in the human realm for a whole month!" She shook her head. "And why can't they just leave her alone to live her life as an ordinary elf? She's only a child."

Sereth put his arm around her. "Elly is much stronger than she looks, my love. Humans are not all bad, Nidah. You know that." Then he looked into his wife's eyes. "And you know as well as I do, that Elly's not just any ordinary elf." He looked out into the distance, the sun reflected in his deep blue eyes. "Big things are destined for our Ellanor," he said softly.

After Elly regained consciousness, she pleaded with Grandpapa to fill her in on all that had transpired in the past month. So that evening, Grandpapa tucked her in and sat at her bedside, goblet of dragon-honey ale in hand, while Marlow started dozing off by the window. With a flick of his finger, Grandpapa dimmed the candle light in the bedroom. Fireflies began to wander in. They reminded Elly of the stringy lights draped over Lily's white picket fence.

In a low voice, Grandpapa began to recount what had happened.

A throng of elves had gathered at the dome since Elly's disappearance, including her family, Aron, Sir Jarome, and a team of protectors, who kept a vigilant lookout for goblins. Even Kaelan insisted on keeping a vigil by the portal. His father had to plead with him to go home. Aron had to be dragged back home for meals, and asked for news of Elly a dozen times everyday.

Grandpapa and Mrs Silverwinkle had teleported to the dome with a team of protectors seconds after Elly had screamed at the goblin, having just realized Gutz had been disguised as Edellina. The moment Elly vanished through the portal, Grandpapa flew like the wind back to his house, frantically trying to locate her whereabouts through the *earlingrand*, the looking glass, one of the four that were entrusted only to a few select elders.

Elly frowned. "Wait, you could track me and see what I was doing in Gaya? But how? Does the earlingrand enable that?"

Grandpapa shook his head. "The earlingrand only allows us glimpses of the past and the present, sometimes even the future. But it does not normally allow us to track someone from afar. No, it was only because I had secretly placed a tracking device—a *secron*, as we call it—on Greymore during your bonding ceremony, my dear." At this, Elly's eyes went round, astonished.

Grandpapa smiled. "Don't worry. I shall explain about all that, later." He took a sip of his dragon-honey ale.

"Even with the secron on Greymore, we could only track you intermittently while you were in Gaya, for you had entered another realm, which diminished the secron's ability to connect with the earlingrand. But at least we could see that you had arrived safely in Gaya, and you were not in any immediate danger. We couldn't communicate with you telepathically and tell you where to find Organoth blue amber, or warn you that the crow had spotted you out as prey. We couldn't tell you that for the portal's powers to work, there had to be a full moon. It was heart-wrenching watching you from afar, and we could do nothing but pray for your safety. Your mother was so distraught we had to stop her from watching you through the earlingrand."

Elly sat up in bed at the mention of the full moon. "So that's why the portal didn't work immediately after it was repaired with the Organoth blue amber," she said in wonder.

Grandpapa nodded. "The portal's teleporting powers are enabled by the full moon, which is when the Moon is on the opposite side of

Gaya from the Sun. It occurs instantaneously, around once a month. The portal remains open for an hour after the full moon. There was a full moon on your birthday, shortly before midnight, and that was when you fell through the portal. So the goblin knew how the portal works." Elly grimaced.

"We knew you would have to endure staying in the human realm until the next full moon, which is when you could teleport back—provided that the portal had been repaired by that time. If you had not found Organoth blue amber four days ago, you would not be here with us now. Goodness knows how long you would've been stranded in Gaya if you hadn't gotten the portal repaired. My one source of comfort was knowing that Greymore was with you. But you cannot imagine how desperate we all were to have you back with us." His face was grim as he recalled the sleepless nights of anxious waiting.

Elly smiled and took his large hand. "But it wasn't so bad, Grandpapa. Truly. It was awful being away from you all. I was so worried that the goblin might have done you harm! But I don't regret my time in the human realm. You see, I met some truly wonderful people there. I learned so much. I learned what it means to work hard and make a living. I met people I'm proud to call my friends. I got to know a lovely married couple who nursed me back to health after the crow hurt me, and treated me like I was family. In exchange, I helped them go on their first real holiday together."

She thought about Lily, and wished she could have said a proper goodbye. Vanishing in the middle of the party must have been alarming. Elly had no idea what had happened to the portal either.

Do not fret, Ellanor. It has all been taken care of.

Elly blinked. *How, Greymore?*

Grandpapa was watching her closely. "It gladdens my heart that you made good out of a difficult situation, Elly. You have grown from your experiences. You are much stronger than you think you are."

She smiled. "Greymore was my rock, truly. My pillar of strength. I don't know what I would've done without him," she confessed. Greymore, nestled next to her, rumbled proudly. She giggled.

Grandpapa patted her Royan with fondness. "Elly, the best teachers are those that tell you where to look, but don't tell you what to see," he said with a smile. "Remember that Greymore is always on your side, no matter what it seems. But it is his duty to test your strength and push you to your limits. It is the only way you will grow strong."

Elly sighed. "Yes, he certainly succeeded in pushing me to my limits. For a while, I seriously thought I wouldn't ever be coming home."

Then she gasped. "Oh, Grandpapa! I am sure you know about the dreadful thing I did to Sir Jarome. How is he now?"

Grandpapa gave Elly a stern look. "He is deathly ashamed, Elly. He was very angry and disappointed by the way you tricked him. You must apologise to him as soon as you can," he said firmly.

Elly bowed her head, shamefaced. Then Grandpapa smiled. "But he is so glad that you returned home safely. He remembers the sweet Elly who used to sing to him and deliver wild berries. He understands you had been led astray by Edellina . . . or Gutz, I should say."

Elly shuddered. "I still can't quite believe Edellina was a goblin in disguise all along."

Grandpapa leaned back in the armchair. "Mrs Silverwinkle was the first to notice there was something amiss about Edellina. Though outwardly she looked beautiful, just like any other elfling, Mrs Silverwinkle could sense something unwholesome in her eyes. It is said that the eyes are the windows to your soul. It is quite true."

He paused to plop some grapes into his mouth. "However, Mrs Silverwinkle could not have guessed that Edellina was a goblin, because goblins have not been known to take on the fair form of elves. They are not known to be shape-shifters. She had speculated Edellina was an elf with a dark soul."

He raised his eyebrows at Elly's look of surprise. "Elves may be stronger than humans in many ways, but even we are not immune to evil, my dear."

Elly stared at him, the hair standing up on the back of her neck. "You mean," she said slowly, "this was the first time—to your knowledge—that a goblin has disguised itself as an elf?"

Grandpapa nodded grimly. "Yes. It was a most disturbing discovery. It turns out there really is an elfling named Edellina Rosebane in Morwen Valley. The protectors who were sent there to investigate found the real Edellina bound and dazed under some strange spell, along with her parents, in a cave deep in the woods near her home. They had been starved, and were close to death. Thankfully, they are now recovering under the dutiful care of the healers."

He paused and stroked his beard thoughtfully. "Goblins are not shape-shifters by nature. They are foul, cunning, and destructive, but they were never endowed with the ability to take on the form of other beings. So for now, this remains a mystery. However . . ." He hesitated.

Elly's ears pricked up. "Please tell me, Grandpapa."

He cleared his throat. "Well, it is not widely known that some elves are born shape-shifters." At this, Elly's eyes widened. "But most tend to conceal their ability, to avoid arousing fear and mistrust in the community. Trust me, if you knew your friend was a shape-shifter, you might find yourself looking at everyone twice."

He smiled and shook his head. "In fact, in the past five centuries, only one elf was known to be a shape-shifter. But even though shape-shifting elves are extremely rare, such a skill can be dangerous if put to evil purposes. How did that goblin—Gutz—manage to remain disguised as Edellina and elude us for so long? If Mrs Silverwinkle had not alerted me, we would probably have remained blissfully ignorant of the goblin's true motives—until things went disastrously, of course."

Elly remained quiet for several moments. Shape-shifting elves? She had had no inkling. "But I thought goblins shun the light . . ."

"Yes, but goblins shun the light out of *choice*. Gutz, disguised as Edellina, was able to move about in broad daylight, though I imagine the goblin must have loathed it." He paused and looked at her solemnly. "At some point, everyone must choose the path of light or darkness, my dear." Elly flashed him a puzzled look. Why must Grandpapa speak in riddles?

Then she frowned. "When did Mrs Silverwinkle become suspicious of Edellina?" she asked softly.

"The first time she saw you standing with Edellina and Aron at the school entrance on the morning of your birthday. That was the first time Mrs Silverwinkle saw her. You see, Mrs Silverwinkle had been away from Evergreen City for many long years, and she returned just over one month ago. She was disturbed by Edellina's . . . aura. Or lack thereof, I should say."

Elly looked at him questioningly. She knew that an elf's aura, or energy field, conveyed the essence of their character. Beyond that, she had little idea. Grandpapa cleared his throat. "You see, Elly, not all elves are sensitive to auras. But Mrs Silverwinkle is one of those who are." He paused. "She could not make out Edellina's aura clearly, and that troubled her. It was only later that we understood why—shape-shifters also have a way of concealing their auras."

Elly was shaking her head in wonder. Grandpapa continued. "The feeling that there was something amiss about Edellina grew stronger the more Mrs Silverwinkle observed her. Then at your birthday party she noticed the covetous way Edellina looked at your Royan."

Grandpapa gripped the goblet in one hand and stretched out his long legs. "Mrs Silverwinkle shared her misgivings with me at the party, and she decided to talk with you at school the following morning to learn more about Edellina. She did not want to alarm you on your birthday. But nobody could have guessed Edellina was a goblin, and that things would turn out the way they did that night."

Elly recalled their unsmiling faces at the party as they looked over at her and Edellina, and it all made sense. "It's an uncanny coincidence there was a full moon on my birthday," she murmured.

Grandpapa regarded her solemnly. "Was it a coincidence?" She looked at him quizzically, but he did not elaborate. He fell silent and gazed into the distance, as though recalling some long-forgotten memory.

Then Elly said, "I heard shouts and footsteps approaching just before the goblin pushed me through the portal."

Grandpapa nodded. "Yes. We were a second too late to stop you from falling through the portal, but we arrived just in time to stop the goblin from going after you. Freya knows what Gutz would have done to you once it had you all to itself in the human realm. Thankfully, the forest creatures must have been repelled by the presence of the goblin, because they had all scurried away and called for help when they heard your screams. Mrs Silverwinkle and I were discussing matters at her house when we heard their cries. We immediately summoned the protectors."

He interlocked his fingers. "The goblin did not expect such a sudden interference. That's probably why it shoved you through the portal. That foul creature had run out of time."

While Grandpapa was in his house consulting the earlingrand, the protectors threw the goblin into a deep, narrow pit riddled with powerful elven magic that made it impossible for Gutz to escape.

"I think . . . I think Gutz wanted Greymore," Elly whispered, fingering her Royan.

He looked at her gravely. "Yes, and Gutz wanted to escape into the human realm with you and your Royan, fully aware that it would be easier to elude capture in a foreign realm."

Elly asked the question that had been on her mind for the past month.

"But why me? Why did Gutz choose me, and why did it want me in the human realm?"

Grandpapa remained silent for so long that Elly had to look and make sure he had not fallen asleep. Then he sighed. A blue butterfly chose that moment to flutter towards him and alight on his shoulder.

"The goblin obviously had great ambitions. But it was taking orders from a higher power." Elly frowned, confounded.

He looked at her. "Elly, on the night of your birthday, during the bonding ceremony, I entrusted something very, very important to Greymore. It was done in secret. I will tell you more once we've clarified some matters. For now, you must keep Greymore with you at all times. You must always trust him. Do you understand?"

Elly felt dizzy with countless questions swirling and bursting to be asked. So Grandpapa put not only a tracking device but something else as well on Greymore? How could she have missed it? She nodded, baffled. "I promise I will do my best," she said softly.

There was a silence as she pondered what Grandpapa had told her. "Where is Edelli— . . . I mean, where is the goblin now?" she asked shakily.

Grandpapa's frown deepened. "I regret to say that we lost the goblin. It escaped, seemingly with help. It seems that Gutz had its own allies. It was very strange. The guards that were keeping watch over Gutz fell into a deep slumber."

Elly thought about the wild berries that Edellina had given Sir Jarome, and shuddered.

"We have quadrupled our security. You will see many more protectors near the cross points, and Mrs Silverwinkle is working on a way to sniff out imposters like Edellina. She's even concocting an antidote to prevent any sleeping potions from affecting the guards and protectors again. We have to be more vigilant than ever. You'll be followed constantly by a team of protectors, Elly—and don't try to use the invisibility perfume again," he said sternly. Elly ducked her head sheepishly. The perfume that Edellina had given her had already been destroyed.

Grandpapa stroked Marlow on the head. "We believe Gutz has returned to the underworld. But how did it pass through without getting caught in the first place?" He paused. "It is possible that Gutz was disguised as one of the guards to get past undetected."

Elly shivered and looked out the window, half expecting to see the red eyes of the goblin lurking in the shadows.

Grandpapa patted her hand. "Do not worry, Elly. For now we are safe. Your papa and I will make sure of that," he reassured.

Then Elly remembered what she had been wanting to tell him. "Grandpapa, do you . . . do you ever have strange dreams?"

He raised his bushy silver eyebrows. "Well, most dreams can seem strange, Elly. What is really on your mind?"

Elly hesitated, then plunged ahead. "In the past month, I've been seeing the same person in my dreams. I don't know who she is, but there seems to be something familiar about her."

Grandpapa knitted his brow. "Oh? Can you describe what this person looks like?"

Elly propped her chin up thoughtfully. "Well, I wonder if she is someone from our clan whom I might have met when I was little? She has green eyes like me, and black hair like mine, but it's really short. She seems to be about my age. But every time I try to focus on her face, things become blurry, and then I wake up."

Grandpapa had gone very still. "Interesting," he murmured, putting down his goblet and sitting up. "When did these dreams start?"

Elly frowned. "I think . . . it started on the morning of my twelfth birthday. Actually . . ." She wavered.

Grandpapa looked up sharply. "What is it?"

"Well, on the morning of my birthday, I think . . . I think I saw her in the mirror. It happened for a split second, and then she was gone." She looked up at her grandfather. "Do you know who she might be? I mean . . . could she be trying to tell me something?"

Grandpapa suddenly gave a hearty laugh, startling her.

"I'm sorry, my dear. I don't really know what to make of these dreams, but I wouldn't think too much of it. You are growing up, and you have a very active imagination, after all. Perhaps, the girl you've been seeing in your dreams is just another version of yourself?"

Elly cocked her head. "What do you mean?"

"Well, our mind can do mysterious things of which we are not aware. Perhaps there is a part of you that wants to break free. Maybe you want to cut your hair short!"

Elly looked at her grandfather dubiously. "Well, I suppose it's possible."

He patted her on the shoulder. "Don't fret, my dear. You've been through more than any other elfling your age." He paused. "I suggest that you keep your dreams between us, Elly. Your parents don't need more cause for worry, especially your poor mother, distraught as she was."

Elly nodded slowly. She hadn't thought about that. It had taken Papa a long while to convince Mama to leave her daughter's bedside to get some rest. She couldn't imagine what she had put her parents through in the past month.

Grandpapa cleared his throat, then glanced up at the moon. "Look here!" he exclaimed. "It is way past your bedtime. You have been through a lot, and you need your rest. Go to school as usual the day after tomorrow. You will face a curious bunch at school. We had to make a public announcement about a goblin shape-shifter that masqueraded as an elf named Edellina, and news of your disappearance spread like wildfire. You have become rather famous, my dear."

"Or infamous," she muttered. Then she sighed. "I suppose I'll have to face Mr Holle tomorrow," she murmured with dread. Not to mention the Three Flamingos.

Grandpapa shook his head. "No, not Mr Holle. He is currently on a long leave of absence."

"Oh!" Elly brightened, not even bothered to ask why. "Does that mean Mrs Silverwinkle will be substituting again?"

Grandpapa laughed. "No, not Mrs Silverwinkle." Elly's face fell. "You will have another substitute teacher. I dare say he will be more . . . lively and pleasant than his predecessor."

Murmuring goodnight, Grandpapa kissed Elly on her forehead, and a heavy drowsiness came over her. She fell into a dreamless sleep with Marlow next to her, ever watchful.

———————

So three days after Elly returned home, she tried to slot back into her former routine. She walked to school with a sullen-faced Aron.

The instant he was notified of Elly's return, he dropped what he was doing (writing an engrossing paper on the Vierran elves) and raced to the Celendis House. Elly had been gone for thirty days. "It felt like months to me," he said solemnly. "I feel terrible about Edellina. How could I not have sensed anything?" He paused and fiddled with his belt. "But in hindsight . . . there were times when I thought she was a little strange. For one, we never got to meet her family. She always came up with excuses. She never invited us over to her home. And she would become really intense whenever I talked about the goblins." He paused. "Besides, she looked like one of us, and she was so . . ."

"Alluringly beautiful?" Elly offered with a grin.

Aron went red in the face. "I know we shouldn't judge a book by its cover," he admitted grudgingly. "History has taught us that time and time again."

"Don't feel so bad," she said, playfully ruffling his hair. "Grandpapa said that we are too young and too trusting to have figured out Edellina was an imposter. Even the elders didn't suspect anything until Mrs Silverwinkle came along, but by then it was almost too late." She shook her head. "It's not like we had had first-hand experience with goblins, right? In our eyes, she was just a friend."

Aron was silent for a moment. "Speaking of friends, Kaelan called in on your parents while you were missing." His voice was gruff.

Elly's cheeks burned. "Oh, really? What did he want?" She tried to sound nonchalant.

He smirked. "Well, you better ask him. He went to your house almost every day asking for news of you. Luca's gotten pretty chummy with him, not to mention your parents. What can't he do?" he muttered under his breath, kicking at some pebbles.

They arrived at school. Students turned to stare at Elly, whispering to each other. Self-consciously, she put a hand on her Royan. She felt as if a hundred pairs of eyes were boring into her.

Aron gave her shoulder a reassuring squeeze. "You'll be the centre of attention for a while. Just try your best to ignore it. Don't let the Three Flamingos bother you too much. I'll see you later, okay?"

She nodded, and promised to meet him after school at the Meridien Meadows. There was so much to talk about.

Just as if nothing had changed in the past month, the Three Flamingos were standing at their usual spot near the doorway of the classroom, whispering about the new headmaster, who had arrived early that morning, but whom no student had yet seen. The former headmaster, Sir Baerin Greenleaf, had recently handed in his resignation.

"I'm too old to deal with goblin spies parading around as students. Time to pass the baton to someone else with more zest," he'd announced matter-of-factly to the High Council. The new headmaster was to be formally introduced at a special assembly later that morning.

Behind the Three Flamingos, Elly spotted Kaelan beaming at her. Her heart skipped a beat.

That was when she made her decision. This time, she did not try to flit past the three girls.

Darrius gasped dramatically as she tossed back her long auburn hair. "Oooh, look who's back! Our little Raven, returned from her adventures!" She towered over Elly and stared down at her. "You reek of human, don't you? Perhaps I should lend you my perfume!" Lorelana and Morganai tittered.

But Elly did not flinch. Darrius frowned, them leaned over and pushed her face right up to Elly's. "Why don't you go get lost in some other realm and try to make friends there? Or are you worried they'll turn up like your little goblin friend?" she hissed.

For the first time, Elly did not bow her head or look away; and because of this, she could see that many of her classmates were not smiling along with the Three Flamingos. In fact, some of them rolled their eyes and squirmed uncomfortably. Kaelan shook his head and locked eyes with her. He started to stand up, as if to intervene. But she shook her head slightly and gave him a rueful smile.

All this time, I thought all of you had been laughing at me. If only I had held my head high, I would have seen it wasn't true.

I never really paid attention. I'm sorry, Elly. I was too self-absorbed to care about anyone else. The one thing I do regret is that I hadn't taken notice before. I wish we had become friends much earlier.

Don't be sorry, Kaelan. What matters is that we're friends now. I think perhaps I can start coming to my own defence.

Elly took a deep breath and looked squarely at Darrius, who was still smirking. Lily's face flashed across her mind, and gave her the last morsel of courage she needed.

She spoke in a steady voice. "I feel so sorry for you, Darrius. You don't know how foolish you appear. I guess you're not clever enough to realize that when you say such repugnant things. I really shouldn't take it personally, because what you say is a reflection of your character. You're the one with the problem."

There was a ringing silence. All eyes were riveted on Elly, shocked to witness this confrontation. Some started murmuring amongst themselves, impressed. Kaelan was grinning at her.

The Three Flamingos were speechless. They had been totally blindsided by this comeback from small, quiet, mousy Elly.

Darrius was glaring at her, livid, her mouth moving soundlessly. But there was also something like shame in her eyes.

Then someone yelled, "Bravo! Well said!" Elly swivelled around.

A silver-haired elf with sparkling grey eyes stood there with a huge grin on his lean handsome face. The first word that came to Elly's mind was whimsical. Unusually tall and lanky, with a pointed, crooked nose and a strange tear-shaped mark on his cheek, he was dressed all in white, his hair worn in a long ponytail down his back. He walked with a spring in his step as he surveyed the faces before him with a mischievous twinkle in his eye.

There was something inexplicably familiar about him, though Elly was certain they had never met before.

"Good morning, my little elflings!" he sang as he swept into the room, his white robes billowing behind him. He had a strong vibrant voice. He beamed at Elly. "I believe you must be Ellanor Celendis. I am the new substitute teacher, Mr Huerin." Then he snapped his fingers; a spray of glimmering stars sprang from his fingers and swirled into a tiara on Elly's head.

"Oh!" Elly gasped and touched the cold silver atop her black curls.

He laughed merrily. "There! How fitting for a star! Welcome home, Elly!" he cried, applauding loudly.

Then the rest of the class joined in, except the sour-faced Three Flamingos who were still standing. Some students pumped their fists in the air and chanted, "Go, Elly!"

Kaelan beamed at her. *That was impressive. Can I catch you for a few minutes after school?*

Her heart singing, she smiled at him and nodded, trying very hard not to look overjoyed.

The Three Flamingos stalked to their chairs and self-consciously touched their heads to check if any fiery letters had sprung up.

Just as the class was settling down, Mr Huerin beckoned to Elly. "Forgive me for singling you out so early in the morning. The headmaster has summoned you," he said with the same mischievous twinkle in his eye. "Go to the Blue Room at once."

Elly was bewildered. The headmaster? What would he want with her? With a pang, she wondered if she was already in trouble for making a scene with Darrius.

The Three Flamingos glowered at Elly as she walked out, especially Darrius, who made a grotesque slitting gesture across her throat. But they had been quelled into silence for the rest of the day.

In trepidation, Elly took off her tiara and lumbered down the long corridor towards the Blue Room, her former good mood in tatters. She knocked on the tall white doors with dread.

"Come in!" barked a stern voice. Elly swallowed nervously and pushed the doors open.

The sunlight streaming through the tall open windows was so dazzling that she had to shield her eyes with her hand. There was a small figure standing behind a desk, silhouetted against the glaring light. On either side of the room were willowy plants bearing pretty pink and purple flowers, so tall that they reached the high ceiling, its vines snaking over the walls.

Then Elly saw the cloud of white hair held together by a peacock feather, and she found herself staring into familiar, piercing blue eyes.

Chapter Sixteen

What Goes on in the Blue Room Stays in the Blue Room

Elly gasped. "Mrs Silverwinkle!" she cried, staggering a little. "You're the new headmaster?"

Mrs Silverwinkle laughed. "Well, more like head*mistress*, dear."

Elly gawped at her, and noticed the yellow budgie perched on her shoulder. The bird had fixed its small dark eyes on Elly. "But Mrs Silverwinkle, I . . . I thought you were a substitute teacher."

Mrs Silverwinkle chuckled. "Dear Elly, do you think that a headmistress-to-be would neglect to make an effort to get to know the students? Your former headmaster, dear Sir Baerin Greenleaf, had long ago expressed a desire to retire. He asked me to come test the waters over a month ago. The Edellina debacle was the last straw that broke the camel's back. Sir Baerin decided to hand over the reins earlier than expected."

She smiled wryly. "I've come into this position at a very interesting time. But you've been thrown right in the middle of things, so I shouldn't complain."

Elly didn't quite know what to say as she stood there, stunned.

Mrs Silverwinkle rubbed her hands together. "Now, let's sit down and have something to drink, shall we?" She snapped her fingers, and immediately a floral teapot appeared in mid-air. As she settled back into her plush armchair, the teapot started pouring its steaming contents into two teacups on the large oak desk.

Elly sank down in one of the armchairs. When she had calmed down a little, she grasped a cup and took a sip. Her eyes widened. "This is . . . this is chamomile tea!"

Mrs Silverwinkle smiled smugly. "Yes, indeed! You are not the only elf who has acquired a taste for human beverages!"

Before Elly could ask where she had obtained the tea, Mrs Silverwinkle cleared her throat. "Elly, I called you to my office to discuss a matter of great importance. I shouldn't keep you long from your morning classes, so for now I shall brief you." She paused, set down her teacup and clasped her hands together. Elly braced herself.

"Elly . . ."

"Am I in trouble?" she blurted out.

Mrs Silverwinkle blinked, then gave a roaring laugh. "No, no! You are definitely not in trouble. The opposite, in fact. You have no idea how much you have accomplished in the past month, Elly. You are now in a position to do a great service to us. But we need to seek your consent, of course."

Elly stared at her. "A great service?" she asked weakly. What in the world was Mrs Silverwinkle talking about?

The headmistress nodded fervently. "Yes, you are the youngest elf to have ever ventured into Gaya, and the *first* elf to do so since the portal was sealed one hundred years ago. You have come through the ordeal relatively unscathed, and certainly stronger and wiser. You have been sorely tested, and you have shown your quality, Elly. Courage and resilience are even more priceless than the most expensive Organoth blue amber, you know."

Taken aback, Elly blushed. *What could I possibly offer, Greymore?*

Ellanor, just listen patiently.

Mrs Silverwinkle took another sip of tea before continuing. "I am about to make you a proposition. You might take it as an opportunity to serve, or as a burden you do not wish to bear. It is your choice to make. Either way, we will support you in your decision and make best with what we have. But before we proceed, I need you to meet with three of my colleagues after school today. What do you say?"

Elly's head was spinning. An opportunity to serve? Courage and resilience? She did not know what to make of it all. "Mrs Silverwinkle, I am greatly honoured. If indeed I can be of service, then I will listen to what you need from me." She paused. "Have . . . have my parents been informed of this?" she asked tentatively. She didn't want to go behind their backs again.

Mrs Silverwinkle chuckled. "I see you have become more cautious, which is wise! Yes, we have already discussed this with your parents, Elly. They have given us permission to speak with you."

Elly nodded slowly. Was that why Mama and Papa had looked so worried this morning? "Then I shall meet with you after school. Though I can't imagine how I can be of service."

Mrs Silverwinkle beamed. "Excellent! I expect to see you at the assembly later this morning. I dare say some of your classmates will be dismayed to see who their new headmaster is!"

Elly giggled, recalling how Mrs Silverwinkle had put the Three Flamingos in their place. "When Mr Huerin told me I was being summoned to the headmaster, I thought I was in trouble for telling off Darrius this morning!"

"Oh?" Mrs Silverwinkle's twinkling eyes fell on Elly's hands clutching the tiara, and her grin broadened. "Pray, do tell me what happened!"

After Elly described to her how she had stood up to the Three Flamingos, Mrs Silverwinkle threw back her head and laughed. "Well done, Elly! See, I wasn't wrong—you are definitely a mover and a shaker!"

Elly smiled ruefully and shook her head. "But I have a feeling Darrius and her friends will continue to use my grand-uncle's name to torment me," she murmured.

To her surprise, Mrs Silverwinkle looked up sharply, and there was a steely note in her voice when she spoke. "Idril Gailfrin Celendis was condemned as guilty before he was ever proven innocent. In some places, those accused of a crime are innocent before proven guilty. It is unfortunate, given all our strengths, that our judicial system is still so utterly flawed." Then she stopped abruptly, as though she had just caught herself saying something she shouldn't have.

Elly frowned. "What are you saying?" she asked, baffled. "Is it possible that my grand-uncle wasn't a traitor after all? That he didn't actually betray the elves' hideout in the north to the goblins during the War of Wrath, which led to most elves from the Celendis House being slaughtered in the ambush?" When Mrs Silverwinkle didn't answer immediately, her eyes widened. "Wait, were you actually friends with my grand-uncle, Mrs Silverwinkle?"

The headmistress faltered, shook her head, and sighed. "Elly, what happened with your grand-uncle happened a long, long time ago. Most of us wish to forget that it ever came to pass. In any case, you shouldn't worry what other people say about you and your family. Those who slander and gossip about you don't truly care for you. Why waste time on them?"

Elly nodded. "That's true," she conceded sheepishly.

It was only much later that Elly realized Mrs Silverwinkle hadn't answered her last question.

The bell rang. It was time for her to return to class. Mr Huerin would have already started the second lesson.

As she turned to leave, she spotted a painting on the wall facing the windows. "Oh, this is a lovely portrait!" Elly exclaimed, inching closer for a better look at her role model. Was Mrs Silverwinkle also an admirer of her favourite explorer?

Then Elly's eyes fell on the yellow budgie in the portrait. It was perched on the subject's shoulder.

Her jaw dropped, and for a few moments she ogled silently at the portrait, realization dawning like a swift sunrise. Then she turned and stared at the yellow budgie on Mrs Silverwinkle's shoulder. It winked at her.

"Wait," Elly said slowly, "Wait . . . you can't possibly be . . ."

Mrs Silverwinkle laughed merrily and put her hands on her hips. "So, I have been discovered at last! I stopped going by my maiden name after I married Mr Silverwinkle and retired from the field. It has been many years since I was just plain Larabeth Goldberry."

By the end of the school day, Elly was a restless bundle of nerves.

Not only was Mrs Silverwinkle the headmistress, she was actually the famous explorer, her heroine, *Larabeth Goldberry*! Elly felt as though she had just opened up a gift to discover it wasn't what she had expected; it was even better. To top it off, seeing the stricken expressions on the Three Flamingos' faces at the sight of Mrs Silverwinkle had been absolutely priceless.

After school, Elly told Aron that their catch-up at Meridien Meadows would have to wait; she promised to tell him *everything* after an important meeting with the headmistress.

Aron gawped at her. "The entire student body was surprised when Mrs Silverwinkle stepped onto the stage at the assembly! Who could've guessed? But now you're telling me there are more surprises? An important secret meeting, *Larabeth Goldberry*? What . . . is . . . going . . . on?" he asked with exasperation, feeling horribly left out.

Then he narrowed his eyes as he stared past Elly. "Well! You're awfully popular today!" he muttered. She turned to see Kaelan walking up to them. Her cheeks burned as she turned back to Aron. "Listen, I'll talk to you soon, okay? I'll meet you at home tonight after supper. I'll just have a quick word with Kaelan." She had to suppress the huge smile that was threatening to break out.

Aron rolled his eyes. "Fine, I'll see you later." Aron started walking away in the opposite direction of Kaelan, who raised a hand in greeting. Aron nodded stiffly and strode away without looking back.

Kaelan smiled, and she felt her heart flutter as she smiled back shyly. "How are you doing?" he asked in a low voice. He put a hand on her back and gently steered her forward. They began to walk together under the purple weeping willows that lined either side of a long, wide pathway blanketed with purple petals. It was quiet, save the twittering of birds; most of the students had gone home.

Kaelan broke the silence. "I wanted to come visit you the moment I got word you had returned. But I figured I had better let you rest and spend time with your family before I intruded."

She relaxed a little and smiled. *You could never be intrusive,* she wanted to say. "Aron told me Luca's quite taken with you."

He laughed. "Yes! He's a little rambunctious, but he's a good boy. He keeps on insisting that I train him up for archensoar, but I'm sure your father would be a much better instructor." Indeed, Sereth Celendis had been touted as an extraordinarily gifted player when he was a student at Arvellon.

Elly nodded and smiled. "Thank you for visiting my family while I was gone." There was so much she wanted to say to him, but she was a little tongue-tied.

Then her heart almost jumped to her throat when Kaelan took her hand. "I was really worried about you. I'm so glad you made it back safely." Then he paused and hesitated. He took out something from his back pocket. "I want to give you something."

He held it out in his palm; a bracelet made of shining lunar stones entwined with sparkling white crystals harvested from the Shevanie River. "It belonged to my mother," he said. "She used to wear it all the time. It was like her talisman. But she wasn't wearing it on the day she went missing."

Elly gazed at the bracelet. "Oh, it's so beautiful," she said in a whisper. "But surely I can't take this. It's too, too precious."

He shook his head and smiled ruefully. "I'd like to think it will protect you. I know it doesn't make sense, but sometimes I wonder if my mother would've been safe if she had been wearing this." He looked at her with his serious eyes. "You're the first real friend I've come to care about. Please—it'll mean a lot to me." He pressed the bracelet into her hand.

Elly hesitated, then nodded slowly. "Thank you, Kaelan. I will keep it with me always." She slipped the bracelet over her wrist and smiled, barely able to believe this was happening. Did Kaelan just give her his mother's keepsake?

He grinned at her. "You know, I'm going to work really hard to become the best protector in Alendria. I don't doubt you'll become an accomplished explorer one day. Do you think . . ." At this, he looked at her hopefully. "Do you think, perhaps, we can be there to cheer on one another—no matter how tough things might get?"

This time, Elly did not hesitate. She took his hand and smiled. "I promise."

Elly made it to the Blue Room just on time, looking flushed and breathless after having raced all the way from the weeping willows. She had stayed talking with Kaelan longer than she had intended. The sky was slowly getting dark.

Mrs Silverwinkle was waiting for her, and she wasn't alone. There were two other elves seated at the table with their backs to Elly, heads bent together in discussion. When they turned around, Elly froze in her tracks.

One of them was Mr Huerin and the other was . . . Grandpapa! She gasped, quite forgetting to greet them properly.

Galdor Celendis winked at his granddaughter. Elly narrowed her eyes. He must have known all along that Mrs Silverwinkle was her heroine Larabeth Goldberry! Why hadn't he ever mentioned this to her before? She glowered, and made a mental note to interrogate him later.

It was then that she noticed there was a fourth elf at the window, even taller than Mr Huerin, with broad shoulders, a narrow waist, and long, muscular limbs. With his regal bearing, he seemed set apart from the others as he stood shrouded in the shadows, watching the darkness slowly dissolve the ribbons of scarlet and gold that stretched across the horizon.

Then he turned around and looked straight at her with his fierce golden eyes. She stared in amazement.

A Vierran!

Elly had never laid eyes on anyone from the reclusive elven race that dwelt in the remote and cold northern region of Aranon, with its harsh, rugged landscape. The Vierran were very tall, with skin the colour of cocoa and fair hair streaked with gold that complemented their golden eyes. They bore markings on their faces and arms that were ancient runes in their northern dialect.

Elly thought the Vierran looked beautiful.

Then she came to her senses and blinked. "I . . . I'm so sorry," she apologized, her ears growing quite red. "I don't mean to be rude. I have only ever read about your people, but I never thought I would ever have the opportunity to meet you." She smiled bashfully.

But the Vierran did not smile back. He gazed at Elly long and hard. He was wearing some sort of sleek black armour that gleamed even in the fading light of dusk. Then he spoke in a deep, magnetic voice that reminded Elly of the Ancient Wells nestled deep in the hills along the Shevanie River.

"So, this is the child of whom we have been speaking?"

Mrs Silverwinkle nodded. "Yes, this is Ellanor, granddaughter of Sir Galdor Celendis."

The Vierran raised one golden eyebrow. "I see." His expression was hard to read.

Mrs Silverwinkle smiled and beckoned for her to come closer. "Elly, I would like to introduce you to our order. Here is Blaine Eisendor, who has travelled far from his homeland to be with us today."

Elly blushed and bowed deeply to the stern-faced Vierran, who gave her the smallest of nods.

Elly looked around at the faces before her warily. This was some sort of secret order? It seemed ludicrous that she was here in the presence of such prominent elders.

Mrs Silverwinkle continued with the introductions. "I believe you've met Mr Jestor Huerin, your new class teacher. And your Grandpapa, of course." Mr Huerin grinned at Elly and gave her a thumbs-up.

Grandpapa chuckled and leaned forward to embrace Elly. "In time I will explain everything," he whispered into her ear. "Then you can decide whether to be cross with me."

Then Mrs Silverwinkle gestured for Elly to sit down in one of the armchairs. "As you know, we have something very important to discuss with you. This will take some time, as we must explain from the beginning. First, we can do with some refreshments."

A tall crystal ewer of bubbling spring water appeared on the table in front of Elly, along with five silver goblets and a plate of something familiar. Her eyes widened.

Boh loh bau! Pineapple buns!

"Oh!" she cried as she stared at the round, golden-brown buns. "But how . . . how . . . ?" Gingerly, she took one with both hands and breathed in the aroma. These were definitely made by Aunty Mabel!

Mrs Silverwinkle laughed. "Elly, dear, we had to do some damage control after you left Gaya so abruptly. There were quite a few loose ends to sort out with Lily and the Cobbles the day after. I decided to pick up some souvenirs in the process of tying up those loose ends."

Elly's jaw dropped. "You went to see Lily and the Cobbles?"

Mrs Silverwinkle winked. "Yes, and I certainly agree with you—Mabel's pineapple buns are *heavenly*. They go very well with chamomile tea, don't you think?"

Elly was bewildered. "But . . . but how did you teleport to Gaya? There hasn't been a full moon yet."

Mr Huerin was heartily chewing on his pineapple bun when he piped up. "Each of us is gifted with talents of some sort, Elly. No matter how seemingly small, one's gift will have an impact upon the course of the future." He smiled. "One alone cannot change the world. But with each of our unique abilities, we can cast a stone across the water to create many ripples. Everyone has a part to play in the scheme of things. Your mama is gifted in making sweet cakes. Your papa is gifted in the art of silversmithing. Mrs Silverwinkle is gifted in something extremely rare—inter-realm teleporting." His eyes twinkled. "That is, she can cross over to Gaya through the portal *without* the full moon."

Elly looked around wide-eyed at Mrs Silverwinkle, who was smiling modestly. Inter-realm teleporting? That partly explained Larabeth Goldberry's insanely prolific career.

Then she looked at the others in the room. What were their gifts? She suddenly felt very small, certain that she had no special talents whatsoever.

Mrs Silverwinkle took a sip of her bubbling spring water. "I teleported to the human realm the morning after you returned. It would have been ideal if I had done so immediately after you returned, but . . ." She paused and shook her head. "I had to deal with things promptly, before any irreparable damage was done. For one, I had to assure Lily and her parents that you were safe. They were desperately worried when they couldn't find you in the garden that night. They thought you had left without a word, or worse, been kidnapped. We also had to retrieve the portal and make sure it was safe. It had fallen into the bushes in Lily's garden after you teleported back to us."

Elly was shaking her head wonderingly. "But, what—what did you tell them about me?"

"Well, I told them I was your grandmother from the north, and you had to leave the party without giving them notice due to a family emergency, and that you were whisked away by your guardian, Mr Greymore, through the gate in the garden fence. I told them you were very sorry that you couldn't say goodbye. Thankfully they were polite enough not to pry. They were just relieved to know you were safe and sound.

"Lily and her family are rather nice people, aren't they? When they realized you had disappeared, Mabel called the Cobbles right away. They would've notified the police if I had arrived any later!"

She paused and fed her budgie a morsel of pineapple bun.

"Lily asked me whether she could have your postal address, or any way of contacting you. I told her you would be traveling too much to stay in touch properly, but that you will go visit her as soon as you can."

At this, Elly almost choked on her drink. Mrs Silverwinkle smiled. "Don't worry, Lily will be going to the movies with Maddy. She misses you, though."

Elly gawped. "I'll get to visit Lily again?" she asked dumbly.

Mrs Silverwinkle smiled. "Yes."

Before Elly could ask her to elaborate, she continued. "On the way out of the bakery I bought two dozens of Mabel's pineapple buns. She was very pleased, and sends you her regards."

Then she raised an eyebrow. "By the way, Lily is under the impression that you come from a place in Finland called the Aland Islands?"

Elly smiled sheepishly. "Yes, well, that's a long story."

Mrs Silverwinkle looked amused. "As for the Cobbles, they were dreadfully afraid for you. Miriam almost passed out when I appeared in their kitchen that early morning. The portal is back with them, but not in the dusty broom cupboard this time—they've stored it in a safe and appropriate place. They miss you very much, and asked me to send you their love."

She grinned. "By the way, at this moment they are on the beach in the Dominican Republic. They are happy you no longer have to worry about tracking down Organoth blue amber. Miriam was over the moon when she took a plane for the first time."

Elly beamed, thinking of Miriam sunbathing on the beach while Horace mopped his forehead with his handkerchief and complained about the heat.

Then she asked the question that had been on her mind. "Mrs Silverwinkle, if you have the gift of teleporting without the full moon, then why . . . why didn't you come and fetch me from the human realm?"

Mrs Silverwinkle's brow furrowed. Grandpapa and Mr Huerin exchanged looks. The Vierran's expression remained inscrutable.

Mrs Silverwinkle walked over to the window and gazed out, standing very still. Then she turned back to face Elly. "I am so sorry, my dear. I could have teleported over and rescued you. But I was . . . indisposed. I was unable to leave Alendria."

There was a noticeable tremor in her voice before she fell silent and glanced at Grandpapa. He nodded and spoke up. "Elly, I'd promised I would tell you more once some matters were clarified."

He stood up, and with a sweep of his hand an image of the Tree of Alendria appeared in mid-air.

He looked at her solemnly. "What we're about to tell you, must stay in this room. Do you understand?"

The others looked at her, equally solemn.

Elly nodded and braced herself with a shuddering breath.

CHAPTER SEVENTEEN
What Lies Beneath

GRANDPAPA PACED SLOWLY AROUND THE room and stopped in front of the Larabeth Goldberry portrait. "Do you remember being woken up on the night before your birthday, perhaps while you were sleeping?"

Elly frowned and nodded; she remembered the tolling of the bells, the shouts, the running footsteps. "But I thought it was just a false alarm. Aron told me some wild wolfhounds had crossed the border."

Grandpapa nodded. "Yes, they did cross the border. But we discovered it was only a decoy. By the time we found out, the breach had already taken place. Nothing like it had ever happened in Alendria. We did not want to alarm our citizens, so we kept it quiet."

She gulped. "So what really happened that night?" she asked nervously. "Did it have something to do with . . . the goblins?"

Mrs Silverwinkle was sitting in her armchair with her eyes closed, as though she was resting. The Vierran remained silent while Mr Huerin twirled a white-feathered quill with his long fingers. Grandpapa sighed heavily. "Yes. As you know, the goblins are subterranean creatures who dwell beneath the Tree. They shun the light, and in the past they made countless attempts to damage the Tree, but to no avail. The goblins hate the elves; they have always wanted to destroy us and take over Alendria. But the roots of the Tree are impenetrable, immune to any sort of goblin assault, thanks to the Maker. However . . ." At this, he gestured to the image of the Tree he had conjured. Four dots of light appeared on different places on the Tree: white, blue, green, and red.

Elly stared. She didn't know what she was supposed to be looking for.

Grandpapa continued. "Alendria was a star that existed long before the Tree was created, Elly. The Tree is sustained by the four orbs of power, or the *luthains* as we call it in Yahana. The orbs are vessels that house the powers responsible for sustaining the Tree: light, water, earth, and life. Or in Yahana: *graille, lorne, cephrin,* and *seaul.*"

Elly looked at him wide-eyed. "The four houses of Arvellon Academy were named for the orbs of power?"

Grandpapa nodded. "Correct. For thousands of years, the orbs were kept in secret locations." He paused. "But those locations have been discovered."

Elly almost dropped her goblet. "Do you mean the orbs were *tampered* with?"

Grandpapa regarded her gravely. "Yes. The orbs were poisoned with powerful black magic. The only salvaging factor is that the orbs were not *fully* poisoned, because we managed to extract the poison just before full damage was done. However, the orbs have been drained much of their powers, and the Tree has become significantly weakened." He paused. "One of the orbs was hidden in a secret vault in your house, Elly. Your father had been assigned to safeguard it. Thankfully, he discovered the breach just in time. He immediately alerted us. Thanks to him, we are still standing here today."

Elly's mind was reeling. Papa had been safeguarding one of the orbs? "Was that how Papa got hurt?" she asked quietly, recalling the bandage on his wrist on the morning of her birthday.

"Yes, he came upon one of the perpetrators and tried to fight them off. That perpetrator escaped, and thankfully your father sustained only a minor injury."

Elly fell silent. Several months ago, Edellina was looking around her house after Marlow had snubbed her. Edellina had complimented Elly on how nice her house was, how much she wanted to take a look around. Edellina . . . the goblin . . . must have been snooping, looking for the secret vault. Elly had been completely oblivious.

She clutched her goblet so hard her knuckles turned white. "But how did the orbs get poisoned?" She couldn't bear to hear it.

Grandpapa gazed out the window. "The goblin named Gutz, disguised as Edellina, went to poison the orbs in the middle of the night before your birthday. Gutz had an accomplice." He paused: "Mr Holle."

Elly cried out from shock. "What! Mr Holle is also a goblin?"

Mrs Silverwinkle shook her head and spoke up. "No, he had been put under a black spell, probably by Gutz. I'm afraid to say that Mr Holle succumbed to the goblin's influence much more easily because he was more vulnerable to that sort of temptation. There was always a certain darkness to his aura."

Elly recalled seeing Edellina standing next to Mr Holle at her birthday party. Suddenly, it all made sense. "So Edellina—Gutz—was actually in control of Mr Holle," she said in wonder.

Mrs Silverwinkle nodded. "Yes. Mr Holle was the goblin's accomplice, and he was following orders. Together, they could have totally destroyed the Tree if we hadn't stopped them in time. The orbs were being poisoned within a certain time frame—a matter of minutes, really. Mr Holle, like other elves, can teleport within Alendria, so he must have been able to teleport between the orb locations. According to your papa's testimony, the perpetrator who breached your house and poisoned the orb there was swift and strong, but not as tall as Mr Holle. Thus, the perpetrator could have been Gutz. Or somebody else."

Elly trembled; she had been asleep in bed when her house got broken into and her father got wounded.

Mrs Silverwinkle continued. "Mr Holle and Edellina were masked, so their identities were concealed when the protectors made chase. We later learned that in the pursuit, Mr Holle was wounded in the arm by one of the arrows shot by the protectors. By the next morning, he was wearing a sling, and he asked to be excused from his teaching duties that day. He told us he had been wounded by a wolfhound while he was out hunting—which was not entirely unbelievable, as Mr Holle was a hunter before he became a teacher. As a hunter, he'd sustained injuries inflicted by those vicious creatures. However, we were suspicious. What was he doing out in the wild by himself late at night? We had no evidence to prove his involvement, but the protectors monitored his movements the following day—your birthday. He knew he was being watched. So he could not meet up with Edellina . . . until your birthday party." She looked up darkly. "The black spell that Mr Holle had been under began to wear off after Gutz escaped back to the underworld. Then he finally started telling the truth. That's how we know what we know."

Elly nodded, trying to digest what she had just heard. "Where is he now?"

"Mr Holle is being taken care of by the healers. He was on the brink of losing his mind, as he had been under the black spell for a long time—around six months, which was how long Edellina the goblin had been with us in Evergreen. Mr Holle needs to be cleansed and purged of the goblin's foul magic, and for that he must undergo lengthy rehabilitation. He should be more or less back to his normal self by the time he resumes his teaching duties."

Upon hearing this news, Elly wrinkled her nose. She didn't want Mr Holle to teach her ever again.

Then Mr Huerin spoke up. "But what we can't figure out is whether or not Mr Holle was the *only* accomplice. How did they manage to discover the secret locations of all four orbs, not to mention get to all four locations within such a short period of time? Gutz, as a goblin, does not have teleporting powers. Based on our analysis, Mr Holle could only have teleported to at most two locations within that short time frame. That leaves us to wonder whether there was a second accomplice. But by the time we got to asking about that, Mr Holle had become quite delirious. We suspect that the goblin's black spell was fashioned to break Mr Holle's mind under intense interrogation. Indeed, Mr Holle has already suffered some memory loss. We had to send him to the healers before the damage was irreparable."

Grandpapa nodded. "Mr Holle has addressed many of our questions, but not all, I'm afraid." Then he fell silent for a long moment, as though deliberating about something. Finally, he turned to face Elly.

"The Tree plays a crucial role in safeguarding Alendria. I will now show you something, Elly. You may become afraid of what you see. Are you ready?"

Elly's heart sank, but she nodded reluctantly.

Grandpapa then looked at the Vierran, who stood up. He was so tall that he had to bend down on one knee before Elly, who went rigid with the Vierran at such close proximity.

He extended a large, graceful hand. Blue flames shot up from his palm, startling Elly.

"Look into the fire," he commanded.

Elly glanced at the others. Mrs Silverwinkle's face was tense. Mr Huerin was nodding encouragingly. Grandpapa smiled when he looked into Elly's small pale face. "It's all right. Go on." He kept his hand on her shoulder.

She drew a deep breath and looked. Through the flickering flames, she could see the Vierran's fierce golden eyes staring at her, unblinking.

Suddenly, his eyes turned fully black.

Then Elly felt as if she were being literally *sucked* forward and pulled through a very small hole. Everything became pitch dark, and in the sudden eerie silence she could hear her own ragged breathing. She wheeled around, but could not see anyone. Where were they? With rising panic, her heart pounded faster. Why was it getting so hot? She wasn't used to the heat, nor was she used to this darkness that was so black and impenetrable that she could not even see her own hands. The air smelled stale, as though no breeze or sunshine ever reached it.

She jumped when she heard scuttling noises and echoing cries in the distance. *Drip, drip, drip.* Where was that coming from? Blinking hard, she stared into the darkness. Her eyes slowly adjusted. What was that—did something just move?

Greymore! Where am I?

But there was no answer. Her stomach lurched. Why wasn't Greymore responding?

She cried out when she felt something slither on her arm. She looked down, terrified, and saw some sort of gigantic earthworm sliding away from her feet. When she looked up, what she saw almost took her breath away.

High above was an elaborate network of something that looked like a tangle of roots tinged with green that glowed in the darkness. The roots were gargantuan, at least ten times the width of Elly. There were things crawling on them. She could not tell where the roots started and where they ended. They spread out like an umbrella from somewhere far, far above. She looked down, and saw that she was actually standing on one of the thick, winding roots that extended further down from where she stood. Her eyes widened. She wasn't even standing at the bottom of wherever she was; it went much, much deeper than her eyes could see.

That was when it dawned on her: She was underneath the Tree.

Then without warning, she was being sucked downward, hurtling at a terrifying speed. She opened her mouth to scream, but no sound came out.

Down, down, down she went. It went on for so long that for a mind-numbing moment she feared the descent wouldn't stop. But then it did.

She felt sickeningly dizzy as she clutched her head, her legs splayed out in front of her. She started shivering, her breath rising like steam in the sudden chill air. It was so cold that her heart seemed to freeze over.

First she smelled it.

It was a stench so foul that it stung her eyes, and they began to water. She clamped both hands over her mouth and nose as she retched.

Then she saw it.

Tangled up in the dense cluster of gigantic roots slept a monstrous, legless creature, the high sheen on its moist, scaly skin moving to the rhythm of its slow, rattling breath.

Elly kept her hands clamped over her mouth, not to block out the stench now, but to suppress the scream that was threatening to rip out of her.

Grandpapa! Grandpapa! Where are you?

Turn away, Ellanor!

Then the monstrous thing reared its spear-shaped head and hissed, its breath putrid, its thin red tongue darting out like a flaming pitchfork. The creature turned and looked right down at Elly with cold, lidless, blood-red eyes.

She screamed.

Elly was still screaming when Grandpapa put his arms around her. "Shhh, shhh, it's all right," he murmured. He shot the Vierran a thunderous look. The Vierran gazed back calmly.

Mrs Silverwinkle was clutching the arms of her chair, alarm stamped on her face. Even Mr Huerin looked concerned as he gazed at Elly.

She was crying quietly now, shaking from head to toe. Grandpapa whispered reassuringly into her ear. "You're safe, Elly. Do not be afraid. The Vierran used his powers to transport only your mind to that place; you would not have been physically harmed. You were never in any danger." But his face was stony when he eyed the silent Vierran.

She buried her face into Grandpapa's warm shoulder. Her skin was cold and clammy, her forehead drenched in sweat.

"But that thing . . . that thing *saw* me. It looked straight at me," she said hoarsely. "How could it have seen me if I wasn't really there physically?"

The Vierran raised his eyebrows and murmured something Elly couldn't quite catch. Mrs Silverwinkle turned to him and said in a low voice, "It must have sensed her somehow. She didn't need to be that close. You didn't need to take her that far."

The Vierran looked unfazed. "She may be young, but she needs to know what we are facing. Sugar-coating the situation will not do."

Grandpapa shook his head. "But that was not your call to make," he said quietly. The Vierran fell silent.

Elly's shaking eventually subsided. She looked up at her grandfather. "What was that thing?" she asked in a whisper. Even with her eyes squeezed shut, she could still see the terrible blood-red eyes, the slits of black pupils staring at her.

Grandpapa gently took her hands. "That is the Beast that lies beneath the Tree of Alendria, Elly."

"The Beast?" Elly had no idea what he was talking about.

Then slowly she began to understand. "Was the Tree created to keep that . . . *thing* . . . caged?"

Grandpapa nodded gravely. "Yes."

Her mind was reeling. "So now that the Tree has been weakened of its powers . . ."—she looked at them in horror—"will the Beast break free?"

The Vierran spoke up. "That would be our worst nightmare. Yes, it is possible."

"But there is hope," Mr Huerin's piping voice declared. "We need someone to get the orbs restored to their full powers." He paused and looked at the others, then fixed his grey eyes on Elly. "We have found the candidate."

A heavy silence ensued. Then Elly's knees buckled as a cry escaped from her. She stumbled and fell backwards in her chair. "You can't possibly mean that . . . that *I* can get the orbs restored?"

They all looked back at her solemnly. Elly shook her head in disbelief as she sat staring back at them. "No. I don't understand. Why me? Surely, there are many more . . . qualified individuals?" she asked, her voice strangled. "I'm just an elfling. No. I *can't* do it." She shook her head fervently.

The Vierran spoke up. "It has to be you, Ellanor. It is your destiny."

Elly stared at him, her eyes bulging. "What do you *mean*?" she cried. "I'm . . . I'm just an elfling! I could've died when I was stuck in Gaya by myself! Surely, you cannot expect me to—to go on some ridiculously dangerous mission after that ordeal!"

Mrs Silverwinkle gently took her hand. Elly was shaking with indignation and terror.

"My dear, let us explain. You are gifted with the ability to dwell in the human realm without succumbing to the debilitating effects of contamination."

Elly looked at her, flabbergasted.

"You see, elves normally start to show symptoms of contamination after staying in the human realm for several days—extreme tiredness, inability to use magic, loss of appetite, breathing difficulties. We literally fall ill. In extreme cases, elves could die from contamination. To combat this, elves must replenish themselves with *manna* to survive in Gaya. But manna really only treats the symptoms of contamination, not the root of the illness. Even with manna, elves must return to Alendria every full moon, to recharge their powers, so to speak."

She sighed. "It was not always like this. As explorers, your grandpapa and I were once able to dwell in Gaya without any difficulty. But about three hundred years ago, when the humans began to create machines and technology that polluted the air and the seas, we began to fall ill. From then on, to survive on Gaya we had to replenish ourselves with manna every few days." She shook her head ruefully. "Sadly, we could no longer stay there for months at a time."

"Yes," Grandpapa spoke up. "If what I have gathered is true, then it would have been perilous for us when the humans unleashed those horrific nuclear bombs during their Second World War. The radiation that spread like poison might have killed us if we had continued teleporting to Gaya at that time." He gave a sorrowful shake of his head.

Mrs Silverwinkle nodded solemnly. "Gaya is significantly more polluted now. But you dwelled there for a month, and you never showed symptoms of contamination. Even without manna." She looked at Elly. "We had to be absolutely sure that you were truly all right. While you were unconscious in bed, the healers examined you meticulously. You received a clean bill of health."

Elly gulped, astonished. "You mean, other elves wouldn't have been able to tolerate dwelling in Gaya like I did?"

Mrs Silverwinkle nodded. "Manna is produced from a specific sap extracted from the Tree. However, now that the Tree's powers are greatly diminished, the sap that it normally produces has been depleted. As a result, we have not been able to replenish manna for the past month. This has put an enormous strain on the healers, as they use manna for various medical purposes, such as in the case of healing Mr Holle. They're dangerously low on manna, so they have been rationing it as carefully as possible."

"Which means they can't afford to distribute manna for other uses, such as giving a substantial amount to an elf in Gaya," Elly deduced.

Mr Huerin was impressed. "Yes, you are astute. This is one of the major reasons we need someone with your immunity to help us restore the orbs in Gaya. It could be a lengthy, drawn-out process. The fact that you're able to dwell in Gaya without manna, probably for an indefinite period of time, is a godsend to us."

Elly was thunderstruck. So, *this* was her gift.

"So, I could have died from contamination if it weren't for my immunity," she said in a whisper. They regarded her silently. She tried to keep her voice steady. "So, either I stay here and watch the Tree be destroyed along with Alendria; or I choose to go to Gaya and try to have the orbs restored, even though the very thought of it terrifies me beyond measure." She was talking more to herself now. Then she glanced up. They were all looking at her. "Isn't there anyone else? Someone more . . . experienced?" she asked desperately.

Mrs Silverwinkle sighed and shook her head. "Not one that could survive on Gaya without manna, no."

But something nagged at Elly. She scowled. "Wait. I don't understand. Why must we go to the human realm to have the orbs restored? Why can't we get them restored here in Alendria?"

The Vierran spoke up. "The orbs were forged in the human realm. They were created by the Four Guardians of Gaya."

Elly's mind swirled. The Four Guardians? Didn't Greymore mention them once? But she had thought they were the Guardians of *Alendria*. She shook her head, bewildered. "The orbs were made on Gaya, not Alendria? But . . . *why*?"

Mrs Silverwinkle looked at Grandpapa. She snapped her fingers, and an oval-shaped looking glass appeared; it levitated several inches above the desk like a shiny silver coin. Elly's eyes widened: it was an *earlingrand!*

Then suddenly Mrs Silverwinkle stumbled, her face ashen. Elly gasped and stood up; but Mrs Silverwinkle raised a hand to stop her. "I'm all right," she said softly, grasping onto the edge of the desk.

Grandpapa put both hands on her shoulders to steady her. "You need to rest, Larabeth," he said in a low voice. "Let me tell Elly."

Nodding, Mrs Silverwinkle sat down heavily in her chair and closed her eyes. Elly looked at her worriedly, wondering what was wrong with her.

The Vierran stood back in the shadows and continued to watch silently. Mr Huerin was perched cross-legged on the edge of the desk, his face serious.

Grandpapa went to stand behind the desk. "Elly, for you to understand everything, I'm going to tell you a story. Look into the glass and hold onto both my hands. Do not let go." He sat across from her so that they were facing each other, with the earlingrand between them.

Elly nodded and nervously wiped her damp palms on her skirt. Then she took Grandpapa's outstretched hands and looked into the glass. She saw her own reflection staring back, her cheeks flushed and eyes bright.

Then her reflection dissolved, and she was looking into Grandpapa's grim face.

After several moments, his face also dissolved, and the earlingrand showed nothing but an expanse of spotless white. Then two slender figures materialised, silhouetted against the bright light.

Grandpapa began to speak.

"In the beginning, there were two Makers who loved creating things of great beauty. They were twin sisters, and they were also best friends. Their father loved them dearly and equally. Both Freya and Marah were beautiful to behold, and in outlook they seemed so similar that many who did not know them had difficulty telling them apart. But in character, the two sisters were as different as night and day. Freya displayed great humility, and loved to create and nurture; Marah was proud, and loved to create and dominate. But despite their differences, the two sisters loved each other and were inseparable.

"One day, Freya created an exquisite jewel, which she named Gaya. She poured a great deal of her love and powers into making it, and it was a masterpiece, a brilliant mosaic of so many colours that it outshone every other thing the sisters had ever created. Father was very proud of Freya, and gave her his blessing to nurture Gaya. Freya loved her creation dearly, and decided that it would be a shame if she were the only one to enjoy it. So she assigned Four Guardians to safeguard Gaya, and created beings that would inhabit Gaya and make it thrive and grow ever more beautiful.

"And for a time, that was how it went. The rivers and seas were as clear and blue as sapphires, the trees and grass were as bright and green as emeralds, the air was as clean and pure as the most perfect diamond. The beings lived on Gaya happily, and they sang songs of love and celebration in tribute to Freya, their beloved Maker.

"Though she concealed it well, Marah became very jealous of Freya, and she came to desire Gaya all for herself. So she went to Freya and asked, 'My dear sister, I would be so grateful if you could let me dwell in Gaya for a time. Its beauty would inspire me so.' Freya loved her sister, and she wanted to share everything with Marah, so she happily agreed.

"But Marah transformed into a great black snake in secret, and burrowed into the depths of Gaya, coiling herself around and around the core until she finally felt that Gaya was hers and hers alone!

"At first, Freya was not aware of Marah's deception. But changes gradually began to take place. A rift formed among the beings because they began to have very different ideas about how they wanted to live. The humans wanted to explore the vastness of Gaya, conquer their own lands and enslave animals, while the elves longed to dwell quietly in the forests and protect the land, living alongside the creatures of the wild in harmony and friendship.

"Eventually, many humans stopped singing for Freya. Instead, they began burning foul sacrifices for Marah, their snake goddess, who had been luring them with thoughts of power and dominion. Even some of the lesser elves were beginning to fall under Marah's spell.

"Then Freya discovered her sister's treachery, and became enraged. She was grieved by her sister's evil plans to dominate Gaya, and for pitting the humans and elves against each other. All that Marah had done was at odds with everything Freya loved. So she turned to her Father for counsel. They implored Marah to turn from her evil ways. But Marah laughed in their faces. 'Fools! There is no such thing as good and evil; there is only power and victory. Why waste your energy on loving and nurturing beings so that one day they might bite your hand and conquer you?'

"Freya and her father were devastated. To save Gaya and all the beings that inhabited it, they came to the painful decision that Marah must be banished. To the north of Gaya was a star called Alendria, which was created long ago to give light to the vast universe. Upon Alendria, Freya planted a seedling that grew into a massive Tree. Marah would languish far beneath that Tree for the rest of eternity.

"And so it came to be that with their combined powers Freya and their father wrestled Marah from the depths of Gaya and banished her to the Northern Star. The impenetrable roots of the Tree imprisoned Marah as she writhed in agony, having quite lost her mind from rage and bitterness.

"The roots of the Tree were immune to any venom or physical blow. Marah hated her Father, and hated Freya more so. By then, Marah could no longer transform back into her fair bodily form, for her soul had become too closely entwined with the foul, monstrous form she had taken. She had truly become the Beast.

"At Freya's request, the Four Guardians on Gaya created the orbs of power that would sustain the Tree. The first three orbs encompassed the powers of water, earth, and light. Then the fourth Guardian, the most powerful out of the four, breathed life into the fourth orb. The orbs were then concealed in secret locations on the Tree.

"Despite everything, Freya still loved her sister and did not wish to abandon her to solitude forever. In her grief and sorrow, she pledged to stay close to her sister, transforming into a bright star that shone upon Alendria. Freya harboured hope that she would one day reconcile with Marah. She bade her father farewell, and asked the Four Guardians to guard over Gaya in her stead.

"The elves on Gaya did not wish to be parted from Freya, so they made their plea to dwell in Alendria and become stewards of the Tree, to protect and nurture all that would grow there in honour of Freya, whom they loved. Their wish was granted. Only a small circle of high elves were entrusted with the knowledge of the orbs' whereabouts. Even when the goblins came and dwelt in the very depths of Alendria, the beast continued to seethe and plot its revenge.

"To this day we still gaze longingly at Freya in the night sky, our most beloved star."

CHAPTER EIGHTEEN
The Beginning of Things to Come

GRANDPAPA STOPPED TALKING. IT SEEMED as though a shadow had suddenly seeped into the room.

A long silence ensued. Elly sat quite still, transfixed by what she had heard. Dumbfounded.

In the earlingrand, Elly had seen everything that Grandpapa spoke of. Now she could see only her own reflection, her eyes filled with fear.

Finally, she found her voice. "I thought it was just a legend," she said in a whisper. Throughout her childhood she had listened to countless stories about Freya, the Maker of Alendria. But she did not know about Alendria's connection to Gaya, and nothing about the Beast that lay beneath. She did not know that elves once lived alongside humans on Gaya . . . Not to mention that they were created by the same Maker.

The Vierran emerged from the shadows and stood beside Grandpapa, who remained seated and deep in thought. "All legends contain an element of truth, Ellanor. Sometimes, people are not prepared to hear the whole truth. It can be accepted more easily if it is told in the guise of folklore."

Leaning forward, Grandpapa spoke in a low voice. "Yes, elves and humans once coexisted on Gaya, Elly. Despite our many differences, did you never wonder why we also share so many similarities?" He smiled wryly. "Elves and humans love and hate many of the same things. We are moved by music and poetry. We rejoice in happiness, we struggle with tragedy, we blossom or crumble in the face of hardship."

He paused. "Despite being blessed with long life, approximately ten times that of a human life, elves also come of age at twelve years old, very similar to humans."

"And like humans, we have a strong penchant for sweets, though our teeth are markedly more resilient by comparison," Mr Huerin said with a chuckle as he polished off a second pineapple bun.

Elly nodded slowly, then took a deep, shuddering breath. "Tell me what I have to do," she said quietly.

The Vierran spread out his arms in a wide arc, and a silver-lined map of Gaya appeared in front of him. "You must find the Four Guardians and have them restore the orbs. Unfortunately, we have only clues as to where they now reside on Gaya." He shook his head. "It seems that the Guardians have moved to other locations in the past one hundred years, which is not surprising, seeing how much time has passed since they were last consulted by any of us, and how much change the land has undergone from the effects of pollution and industrialization. In the past month, we have raced against time to find out as much as we could. We have compiled this map, which gives us approximations of where the Guardians might be."

Four glowing dots appeared on the map. Elly gazed at them quizzically, lacking the geographical knowledge of Gaya to understand what she was looking at. The dots—blue, green, red, and white—were spread out across the world map. The Four Guardians.

Mr Huerin chuckled. "Don't worry, Elly. We will help you decipher the locations. We do have two famous explorers with us, after all."

"I have a question," she said. "How is it that even without the orbs of power, the Tree is still able to stand like nothing is wrong?"

Mrs Silverwinkle took a sip from her goblet. "All that is gold does not glitter, you see. Looks can deceive. The Tree looks unchanged, but inwardly it suffers grievously."

She sighed. "The Tree is still standing because the elders of the High Council have been channelling their powers to keep it alive, Elly. Alive, but only a shadow of what it once was. I will not go into specifics, but the effort involved in sustaining the Tree is beyond exhausting. It has taken every ounce of our strength. The Beast has long been dormant, but recently the temperature beneath has grown warmer. This could mean that the Beast is coming out of hibernation, though it could take months or years for the Beast to fully wake. It is only a matter of time before it unleashes its devastating strength upon us."

She paused. "Without the orbs of power, Alendria will eventually fall. We can't keep up the channelling process indefinitely. The enormous amount of energy that we expend will be the death of us, sooner or later."

Elly understood. "Is that why you couldn't leave Alendria and teleport to Gaya to fetch me?"

Mrs Silverwinkle nodded. "Partly. Along with the other elders, I have been channelling my powers to help sustain the Tree. The effort is beyond exhausting, but still manageable. Your Grandpapa and Mr Huerin have also been involved in the channelling process. As you can see, they are doing much better than I am.

"But the main reason I could not come rescue you right after you fell through the portal was because I simply couldn't." She paused. "I was poisoned."

Elly gasped. "No!"

Mrs Silverwinkle nodded grimly. "I was the first to touch one of the contaminated orbs. That was my folly. I was far too hasty. The orbs were riddled with powerful black poison, possibly from the venom of the Beast itself." She closed her eyes, looking more fatigued than ever. "The poison very nearly killed me. I was already depleted after the channelling process, but then to be poisoned . . . As you can see, I have not made a full recovery."

Grandpapa spoke up. "The poison did not take effect immediately. It must have been concocted to elicit a latent reaction. Remember, on your birthday Mrs Silverwinkle was still able to function quite normally—though she was starting to feel the effects of the poison."

Elly nodded as she recalled Mrs Silverwinkle looking quite pale throughout the day.

Mrs Silverwinkle put a hand to her forehead. "After you fell through the portal, your Grandpapa, Mr Huerin, and Blaine had to stay put to safeguard Alendria. We had no idea how deep the infiltration had gone, you see. The High Council demanded their presence, for the greater good. After you crossed over to Gaya, the full effects of the poison finally struck me down, and I could not teleport and bring you back to Alendria. Besides, since I had to bow out of the channeling process, the Tree needed your Grandpapa and these two gentleman here more than ever." She flashed a faint, sardonic smile. "As the humans would say—we were in a pickle."

Nodding, Grandpapa sighed. "Yes, Larabeth's condition deteriorated rapidly after you fell through the portal. If the healers and the Vierran had not come to her aid so quickly, she would have died."

Elly swallowed, clutching the goblet in her hands. She glanced at the Vierran. He had helped to save Larabeth Goldberry.

Mrs Silverwinkle's lower lip trembled at the memory. "I was bedridden for almost a whole month. I only began to regain my old strength several days before the full moon. After you returned, I had just recovered enough to teleport to Gaya so I could sort out the loose ends with Lily and so forth. But even that short visit left me depleted once again. I'm afraid the black poison may have stained me forever. It has certainly weakened my powers."

Elly stared down at her hands. "I am so sorry," she whispered. "It's all my fault. If I hadn't been so foolish . . . If I hadn't been so easily lured by that goblin . . ." Tears burned her eyes and spilled over.

Mrs Silverwinkle stood up and put her arms around Elly. "Oh, my dear! You are young, and mistakes are always there to be made. What child has done nothing of which they are ashamed? The most important thing is that you always learn from your mistakes. The goblin was determined to do what it set out to do—if not you, Gutz might well have targeted another innocent elfling."

Elly's sobbing began to subside as she thought about what Mrs Silverwinkle was saying. "I suppose this . . . *quest* . . . will have its share of dangers?" she asked with a wry smile.

The Vierran nodded. "Yes, it will be dangerous, at times greatly so. We do not deny that. But we shall try our utmost to protect you with our powers from afar."

Mr Huerin nodded vigorously. "Hear, hear!"

Then Elly's heart suddenly lurched. "Wait. Grandpapa, you entrusted something very important to Greymore on my birthday. Was it . . . ?"

Grandpapa nodded. "Yes. The orbs of power. I had to hide them after we extracted the poison. If the goblins discover that the orbs had not been destroyed—and they will find out, eventually—then they'll try to return and finish off what they started. We agreed that one of the safest places to conceal the orbs is a Royan, something portable and inconspicuous that we can move from place to place for safekeeping. Concealing them in Greymore during your bonding ceremony was opportune, as it wouldn't have provoked suspicion. A goblin can never touch a Royan without getting its hands burned off. And a Royan will always stay loyal to their keeper."

He smiled. "You and Greymore share an unusually strong bond. You certainly have a very fine Royan; one that you can trust with your life." Elly felt Greymore rumble with pride.

"And that is why I put a secron on Greymore to keep track of the orbs, to make sure they were safe. Little did I know you would end up in Gaya! I'm sorry that I did not tell you about it, dear. It was supposed to be a temporary measure until I figured out a permanent solution." He chuckled wryly. "Anyhow, it worked out for the best. Otherwise we wouldn't have been able to track you while you were stranded in Gaya."

Elly licked her parched lips as she placed a hand on her Royan. It seemed unreal that all this time she had had the orbs in her possession.

Suddenly, her Royan seemed to weigh much more heavily on her belt. Then she scowled. "Could Gutz have known that you concealed the orbs in my Royan? Is that why it tried to take Greymore?"

Grandpapa shook his head. "No, I do not believe Gutz actually knew the orbs were hidden in Greymore. Otherwise, Gutz would have tried much harder to take the Royan from you—or else to destroy it."

He smiled grimly. "I believe Gutz wanted to possess your Royan out of vanity. The goblin may have craved a trophy to take back to the underworld, to offer it as a gift to its beast master, or gloat of its exploits and achievements to its peers. You would be surprised how far some will go to prove their superiority."

Elly pulled a face. "But why me? Out of all the elflings in Alendria, why did Gutz choose to latch onto me and masquerade as my friend?"

Grandpapa sighed. "I believe I am partly to be blamed for that. I speculate Gutz was ordered to single you out and get close to you because you are my granddaughter, and you are sweet-natured and trusting, and a little lonely for some female companionship. The goblin was clever to masquerade as someone like Edellina, wandering around the land with you, watching and observing. Who would be suspicious of a little elfling girl, especially one so fair of face who kept such innocent company, like you and Aron?" He shook his head. "Gutz must have known about my position on the High Council and the likelihood that I knew where the orbs were hidden."

The Vierran nodded. "Your grandfather—in fact, the House of Celendis—was descended from one of the high elves, chosen by Freya herself, who were entrusted with the secret locations of the orbs."

Mrs Silverwinkle spoke up. "Servants of the Beast may look fair, but feel foul." She looked at Elly thoughtfully. "We believe Gutz wanted to use you to get into the dome and teleport to Gaya through the portal. By the time it was your twelfth birthday, Gutz must have finally discovered the locations of all four orbs. But as a goblin, it could not have passed the anti-goblin enchantments at the dome. The key alone would have burned off its hands. So you see, Gutz needed you to reach the portal. I suspect it was given orders to destroy every way that the orbs could be replenished, thus ensuring our doom. It was probably sent to Gaya to cause havoc, perhaps even masquerading as *you*, Elly— and somehow make the guardians believe the elves had waged war on them. Such a move would have severed all ties with the guardians. Perhaps Gutz even wanted to destroy the portals to stop elves from entering Gaya."

There was a ringing silence as Elly tried to process everything. Then she smiled wanly. "I suppose this gives me a head start to becoming a full-blown explorer."

Mrs Silverwinkle laughed. Some colour had returned to her face, and her eyes had a nostalgic gleam.

"When I was a student at Arvellon Academy, I was sent to Gaya as part of my training. Like you, I discovered many wonderful things, and made wonderful friends. Then the humans got caught up in war after war against each other, and finally, just before their First World War, many elves came to conclude it was best that Alendria cut off contact. Your grandpapa and I were against this, but we were overruled by the majority on the High Council." She shook her head sorrowfully. "I can't help but think that decision ultimately did us much more harm than good, especially in light of the fact that we now need the Four Guardians of Gaya to help us save Alendria."

Elly glanced at the Vierran, who had fixed his golden eyes on her. She took a deep breath. "I understand there is a lot that is wrong with the human realm. But there's so, so much in their world that is good, too, and it's worth fighting for. Who are we to judge and say humans are worthless? Even elves aren't perfect. We aren't blameless for the mistakes we've made. If we were created by the same Maker, doesn't that sort of make us family? Shouldn't . . . Shouldn't we look out for each other?"

A look of surprise crossed the Vierran's face for a split second; then the shades snapped shut again. Grandpapa and Mrs Silverwinkle raised their eyebrows. Mr Huerin clapped. "Well said!" he cried, beaming.

Grandpapa was nodding, looking very proud. Mrs Silverwinkle smiled. "Very true, Elly. I just wish the High Council would've come to this conclusion all those years ago," she murmured.

Elly steeled herself. "How much time do I have to restore the orbs of power before . . . before it's too late?"

Grandpapa cleared his throat. "In its dormant state, the Beast can still communicate with its servants—the goblins—and get them to do its bidding. And even when dormant, the Beast can still exercise powers to torture—which is something the goblins only know too well."

At this, he sighed deeply. "But the Beast is slowly coming out of hibernation. We believe it is not a coincidence—the Beast must have ordered the goblins to destroy the orbs, after all. It must be able to sense that the Tree has been compromised, and it will strive to regain strength to overcome the Tree in its diminished state."

Elly gripped the arms of her chair to keep herself from shaking.

Grandpapa leaned back and continued. "However, the long imprisonment of the Beast has weakened it significantly. The Beast has resorted to other ways to feed and regenerate over such a long period of time. We don't know how long we could withstand the Beast once it awakes. There is much urgency, but you'll need time to carry out your mission." He paused, frowning. "Obviously, we will remove the orbs from Greymore. It is far too dangerous for you to carry them around. If the goblins somehow discover that they were hidden in your Royan, they might try to pursue you on the assumption that the orbs are still with you. We will try our utmost to keep you protected, both here and in Gaya."

Then he looked at her solemnly. "We must count on your discretion, Elly. Your mission in Gaya needs to be kept secret for as long as possible, to buy you time."

Elly tried to keep her voice from trembling. "Yes, I will be discreet."

Mr Huerin grinned. "The goblins would not be expecting an elfling like you to be sent to Gaya, Elly. They will likely monitor the comings and goings of the High Council members, including myself and the others in this room. But an elfling like you may well escape their scrutiny. For some time, at least. Hopefully, by the time they discover what we're up to, it will be too late for them to pursue you in Gaya."

Elly looked at them curiously. "But what will you tell the others? I mean, people might start noticing I'm not at school and all that."

Mrs Silverwinkle spoke up as she refilled everyone's goblets. "Don't worry about that, Elly. We'll take care of it." Before Elly could enquire further, she continued. "There will be much trial and error, and you may face obstacles along the way that would delay the process. But it is crucial that you return to Alendria every time you've restored an orb. Reinstating them one by one will help the Tree regenerate."

Elly shifted on her feet, her heart heavy as she asked the next question. "Does this mean . . . I will be away from home for a long time?"

The Vierran nodded. "Yes. Perhaps months or even years at a time, depending on how long it'll take you to restore the orbs. As we have mentioned, each time you've restored an orb, you must return so that we can reinstate it and help the Tree regenerate. Whenever you return at those times, you'll get to see your family. For a limited time."

Grandpapa and Mrs Silverwinkle were nodding slightly, confirming what the Vierran had just said. Elly's stomach twisted as she thought about leaving her family again.

"I have another question."

Grandpapa smiled. "Good. You need to learn as much as you can, Elly."

"Well, if the Beast does wake up and tries to destroy Alendria . . . won't Freya try to save us?"

The Vierran raised his golden eyebrows. "The elves promised to be the Stewards of Alendria, Ellanor. Our ancestors pledged to protect this realm and make sure that the Beast remains imprisoned. Remember, Freya was grieving for the loss of her sister when she forsook her bodily form and transformed into a star. Freya cannot simply come down and intervene for us."

Mrs Silverwinkle nodded. "Even if Freya does intervene, it will be a bitter battle beyond our reckoning. The Beast is powerful, fuelled with hate and rage, and Alendria may perish in the midst of such a colossal battle."

"Also," Mr Huerin chimed in, "it is possible that once the goblins discover that the elders have been channelling their powers to keep the Tree alive, they will wage war on us, knowing that our collective powers have been compromised."

Elly was silent as she pondered this terrifying prospect.

Then she remembered what she had been burning to tell them. She had been drowning in information, and had just now regained some footing. "Umm, I came across several peculiar . . . *entities* . . . while I was in Gaya. I'm not sure who they were."

She divulged about the strange old woman she had encountered at the park, and her hunch that she was the one who had given the Organoth blue amber necklace to Maddy's mother over thirty years ago. She also told them about the Riddler at Lily's school fair, and how he had spoken in Elvish. And finally, she told them about the nine-tailed fox on the roof of Lily's house.

Everyone in the room listened in rapt attention. As they had only been able to track Elly intermittently through the earlingrand, they had not been able to observe all her comings and goings in Gaya. After she finished, Grandpapa leaned back in his arm chair and gave a roaring laugh. "Ah, I see you've already become acquainted with some of the Guardians! They must have been so intrigued by you that they sought you out!"

Mrs Silverwinkle was shaking her head in astonishment. "Well, well. Who would have expected that?" she murmured.

Elly's jaw had dropped. "They . . . they were the Guardians?"

The Vierran was frowning. "Possibly. Keep in mind, they sought you out. But they will not be found easily."

Mr Huerin looked thoughtful. "It sounds like they wanted to check you out, to see who had crossed over from Alendria, the first time in a hundred years."

Elly found this mind-boggling. It was possible that she had actually met some of the Guardians? "I don't understand. If the old woman was the one who gave Victoria the Organoth blue amber necklace over thirty years ago, how could she have known that Victoria would one day meet me in the future? How could she have known that I would need it to repair the portal?"

Grandpapa smiled. "Elly, the Guardians are ancient beings that have existed for far longer than we could fathom. They do not abide by the same rules of time and space that constrain us. It is entirely possible that they can travel through time, and are aware of everything that could come to pass. In my understanding, however, even Guardians are not supposed to intervene in the course of the future. So they merely observe. But if the old woman did pass the Organoth blue amber to Maddy's mother, knowing that she will give it to you, then that suggests intervention to some degree—and that is an enigma."

Elly fell silent. Now that she came to think of it, everything was set into motion the moment she encountered the old woman at the park, who led her to Aunty Mabel's Bakery. There she met Mabel's daughter Lily, who suggested that Elly visit Westminster Abbey. When she did, she met Maddy and Teddy. They got Hobbes back because of her. And that prompted Victoria to give Elly the Organoth blue amber.

Elly frowned. "Do you think the girl in my dreams has anything to do with the Guardians?"

The Vierran looked up sharply. "What girl?"

Elly was about to tell him when Grandpapa stood up. "I'll tell you about it later, Blaine," he said cheerfully. "It is getting late, Elly. We have some other pressing matters to attend to. You should go home for supper. We fully understand this is a very difficult decision. It would change your life forever. But whether we like it or not, Alendria will be plunged into war, sooner or later."

Mrs Silverwinkle took Elly's hands and squeezed them. "You can inform us of your decision tomorrow. We shall count on your discretion. We are so sorry to place this burden on you, but we are in a rather desperate situation. If I were able, I would pledge to go to Gaya in your stead." She sighed and looked down at Elly's hands. Then she froze.

"What is it?" Elly asked nervously. Mrs Silverwinkle was staring at her wrist. Then she mastered herself and smiled. "Nothing, dear. What a lovely bracelet. I have one just like it."

"Oh!" Elly blushed and self-consciously touched the bracelet. "Yes, it is rather pretty, isn't it?"

Before Elly left, Mrs Silverwinkle embraced her. "No matter what happens, I have no doubt you will make an outstanding explorer. Don't ever lose sight of your dream. I hope this will serve as a reminder." With a meaningful wink, she slipped something thick and heavy into Elly's hands.

Elly gazed down at the first edition of *Roaming the Worlds as a Chameleon*, by Larabeth Goldberry.

———⁓⁓⁓———

"I wish I could tell Aron everything," she lamented to Grandpapa as they walked home, flanked by several protectors. "Aron is my best friend, and I trust him with my life. Why can't I tell him?"

Grandpapa put his arm around her. "He is your best friend, and it is fitting that he should not be left completely in the dark. I know Aron is honourable, my dear. But like you, he is young and trusting, and we don't wish to risk another elfling knowing the truth in case the information falls into the wrong hands. When Aron is older and more mature, I believe it will be appropriate to tell him. For now, discretion is crucial." He paused, and his face was grim. "I wouldn't have chosen you, my dear granddaughter, to shoulder this burden. You are still so young. I don't want to put you in any danger. But it seems you are the best chance we have, Elly."

She nodded silently, still steeped in shock. It all seemed too surreal. Then she looked at him and pouted. "Why didn't you tell me Mrs Silverwinkle is Larabeth Goldberry?" she demanded. "You know how much I've always wanted to meet her!"

He chuckled. "Other people's secrets are not ours to tell, Elly. Mrs Silverwinkle wanted to keep a low profile when she returned. It was not an amicable departure when she left Evergreen all those years ago . . ." He stopped short, then smiled faintly. "Maybe one day, she will tell you all about it."

She cocked her head, curious. Not an amicable departure? She couldn't imagine Mrs Silverwinkle parting on bad terms with anyone. Except the Three Flamingos, that is.

Though her heart felt heavy with all that she had learned, a load had been lifted off her the instant Grandpapa retrieved the orbs from Greymore back in the Blue Room. She had watched in awe as he placed one hand on her Royan, murmured some words in Yahana she could not quite catch, and suddenly four glowing orbs of light the size of apples materialised in the air: green, blue, red, white. Then the orbs spiralled and flew straight into a large, silver tear-shaped vessel on the oak table. She watched in surprise as Grandpapa handed the vessel to the Vierran. "We will keep them somewhere else now," he told her. "I don't want you to continue carrying the fate of Alendria around with you, any longer." He paused, and his face was grave. "Not more than you already have to, anyway."

Supper with her family that evening was a solemn affair. She could barely keep any food down. Afterwards, she spoke with her parents as Luca went out playing in the garden.

Papa and Mama had known about the High Council's request of Elly for several days.

"What do you think I should do?" she asked them, wishing they could just decide for her. But Papa shook his head. "Elly, you have already come of age to do your part in protecting Alendria. Remember the pledge you made on your birthday during the bonding ceremony? Though your mother and I wish we could protect you forever, we realize you are now in a position to make your own decisions. No matter what happens, you will always have our love and support."

Mama had tears in her eyes as she embraced Elly. "Our darling girl. I'm so sorry you have to shoulder such a heavy burden. It's just not fair."

She gazed out the window, where Luca was laughing and chasing several twittering red jays around. She sighed. "Your brother is young, but he understands more than he lets on. He was dispirited when you were gone. Thank goodness Aron and Kaelan kept him company. He wouldn't be happy to see his big sister going away again."

As promised, after supper Elly met Aron in front of her house and told him as much as she could about what had transpired since being summoned to the Blue Room that morning. They were perched on one of the lower branches of the Celendis House, close to the Shevanie River, which rippled into the heart of the valley. The night sky was grainy with stars. The Star of Freya twinkled down at her, and she smiled. The cicadas chirruped noisily as they conversed with one another. A family of deer had settled nearby at the riverbank, feeding on the berries they gathered. Elly and Aron nibbled on the pineapple buns that Mrs Silverwinkle had urged her to take home.

They had never had to keep secrets from each other. It pained her that she couldn't tell him everything, including the truth about the Beast, the poisoning of the orbs, and the fact that the Tree had been compromised. Aron knew only that she had to go to Gaya to recover four important relics, and she was chosen because of her immunity to contamination. When he asked for specifics, she told him she wasn't at liberty to tell. He begrudged this secrecy, but he did not press her. He knew his best friend too well; if she had to keep something from him, there had to be a good reason.

"You must not breathe a word of this to anyone, ever," she said quietly. He nodded as he threw a pebble towards the Shevanie River, watched it skip across the surface, and gazed at the water gloomily. "So this means you'll be gone for a long time?"

Elly fiddled with her bracelet. She assured him, "I'll be back every time I've recovered an or— . . . I mean a *relic*," as if it would be the easiest thing to track down the elusive Four Guardians in Gaya.

Aron threw another pebble, but this time it just sank into the water. "But you'll be gone having all those grand adventures while I'll be stuck here," he mumbled. Elly looked at him, and realized what he was really saying: *I'll miss you.*

"Hey," she said softly. "You're my best friend, and nobody can replace you. Not Lily, not Maddy, or anyone else."

Aron gave her a small smile. "Yeah? What about . . . what about Kaelan?" He wasn't looking at her. He knew the bracelet was from Kaelan. Elly almost choked on her pineapple bun.

She coughed and cleared her throat. "Kaelan and I are just *friends*, silly. Pretty new friends, actually. But you and I . . . we've known each other since we were born! We're practically family. You're irreplaceable."

Aron stared at the river for a moment. "Family, huh?" he said quietly. Then he cleared his throat. "I've decided to try out for archensoar next season."

Elly gaped at him. "Seriously?" she cried. "Since when? I thought you hated it! Didn't you always tell me it's more important to exercise our mind than our muscles?"

Aron shrugged. "Well, I guess things change, don't they? Look at how much you've been through."

Elly fell silent. *But I don't want things to change like this! I didn't ask for this!* Oh, how she wished things were different. She wanted to watch Aron play at the try-outs, as well as all the tournaments. So much seemed to be hurtling out of her control, and she couldn't put a stop to any of it.

Greymore rumbled. *It is inevitable, Ellanor. Life is a series of changes.*

Aron glanced at her as she gazed at the sky. "I'm petrified," she said in a small voice. "I can't help but think they've chosen the wrong person. But I'm also thrilled that I've been chosen to do this honour. I guess I'm feeling a little mixed up right now. I'm in way over my head."

She paused. "They warned me that the goblin who impersonated Edellina might try to harm me again. Goblins can really hold a grudge."

Aron grimaced and crossed his arms. "At least Greymore and Marlow will be with you," he said, and desperately wished he could protect Elly. But he wasn't a protector, and he wasn't really cut out as the warrior type . . . unlike Kaelan.

Marlow had refused to be parted from Elly again. Papa was planning to appeal to the High Council to let Marlow join her in the human realm. "Animals can adapt to foreign environments a lot better than elves, and they don't need manna," Papa had said. "Marlow will be able to survive in Gaya."

Elly grinned at Aron. "Obviously, Marlow needs to be in disguise when he's in Gaya around humans. So he's going to be transformed into a small creature that I can take around with me." She giggled. "A hamster!"

Aron's eyes widened with disbelief. "No way!" he sputtered, laughing.

Marlow felt utterly insulted; how could he, a noble griffin, be diminished in that way? A hamster! But Grandpapa patted his neck fondly. "Do not underestimate little creatures, Marlow. Even the smallest creature can change the course of the future. You'll see." Marlow responded with an indignant squawk.

When Aron caught his breath back, he looked at Elly seriously. "So when will you be leaving?"

Elly stood up and stretched. It felt so good to breathe such pure fragrant air again. "The High Council will set the date." She smiled sheepishly. "I need to undergo some intense, gruelling training to prepare for whatever's in store for me. For one, I have to build up my stamina for inter-realm teleporting. I can't afford to black out or turn to mush after every teleportation. It would be terribly impractical." She sighed. "So it might take a while to be groomed for the task."

Aron smiled as he stood up, glad that Elly would be home for a while longer. For a moment, they gazed out at the Shevanie River, deep in their own thoughts. Behind them their long shadows stretched into empty darkness.

From afar, a pair of cold gleaming eyes watched the two friends in silence.

EPILOGUE

ON A DARK HILL NEAR the Ancient Wells, two figures were silhouetted against the crescent moon. They were both quiet as they looked down at the Shevanie River, gleaming like a silver ribbon in the moonlight.

The Vierran spoke first. "You knew about her immunity. You knew she would not succumb to contamination in Gaya."

Galdor Celendis did not reply. He suddenly looked very old, his face creased with quiet worry as he gripped his silver staff. In his other hand he held a small silver ball. If there had been daylight, one would have seen the entwined letters *TJ* engraved on it.

The Vierran persisted. "You did not tell her everything."

Galdor shook his head slowly. "It is too great a burden for someone so young. She needs more time." He gripped the silver ball tighter.

"But she should learn the truth about her parentage, sooner or later." The Vierran looked up at the moon. "Since their coming of age, the bond between Ellanor and her twin sister has been getting stronger. You know of this. She has been seeing her sister in her dreams, has she not?" He paused. "In fact, I believe the sisters have been dreaming of *each other*."

Galdor leaned on his staff heavily. "Yes. I am aware of this. She will one day discover the truth. She will find out about her twin sister, Marigold, who lives in the human realm." His blue eyes shone with regret in the moonlight. "One day, Elly will discover that she is part human."

ABOUT THE AUTHOR

KATHRYN TSE-DURHAM GREW UP IN Australia and now lives in Hong Kong with her husband and family. Her honours thesis was published in a European academic journal, and she has written articles for educational magazines. She completed a creative writing course through the University of Oxford, which further fuelled her love for writing fiction. Kathryn strongly believes, just as Roald Dahl imparted, that those who don't believe in magic will never find it. She hopes that through her stories readers young at heart will connect with that magic.

Lightning Source UK Ltd.
Milton Keynes UK
UKOW04f0009040615

252840UK00001B/6/P